Almost Everything Very Fast

D1167007

A NOVEL

Almost Everything
Very Fast

Christopher Kloeble

*Translated from the German
by Aaron Kerner*

GRAYWOLF PRESS

This publication is made possible, in part, by the voters of Minnesota through a Minnesota State Arts Board Operating Support grant, thanks to a legislative appropriation from the arts and cultural heritage fund, and through grants from the National Endowment for the Arts and the Wells Fargo Foundation Minnesota. Significant support has also been provided by Target, the McKnight Foundation, the Amazon Literary Partnership, and other generous contributions from foundations, corporations, and individuals. To these organizations and individuals we offer our heartfelt thanks.

A Lannan Translation Selection

Funding the translation and publication of exceptional literary works

The translation of this work was supported by a grant from the Goethe-Institut, which is funded by the German Ministry of Foreign Affairs

Published by Graywolf Press
250 Third Avenue North, Suite 600
Minneapolis, Minnesota 55401

All rights reserved.

www.graywolfpress.org

Published in the United States of America

ISBN 978-1-55597-729-0

2 4 6 8 9 7 5 3 1
First Graywolf Printing, 2016

Library of Congress Control Number: 2015953589

Cover design: Kyle G. Hunter

320145731

FOR Saskya

Almost Everything Very Fast

Prologue

I haven't forgotten a thing. I remember the beginning and the end, and all that lies between. I've seen a story become history and the other way around.

But nobody's interested in that, not here. My senile neighbors can barely concentrate for a couple of minutes at a stretch, without having to put themselves down for a nap. And most of the young nurses have better things to do than listen to an eighty-year-old's tales. They think they're supposed to feel sorry for me. And yet I feel sorry for them. If only they knew what lies ahead of them! The poor things believe that their lives will spool out just the way they've imagined. Eventually, they'll figure out that you can't set a course for things. And I don't mean that just figuratively: blood must flow. I try to explain it to them, I want to warn them. And what do they do? Pat me on the hand, and tell me I shouldn't exaggerate.

My memory is better company. It grants me the scent of an incomparable bridal gown; grants me the love of women, many women; grants me the heat of a devastating conflagration; grants me the hope that my children are still alive out there, somewhere; grants me the glitter of gold, and the fear in the eyes of dead soldiers.

Nor is it frugal with pain.

Only, sometimes, I wish it would send me peace. Even when I'm asleep it won't leave me alone and sends dreams after me. It's always there. It won't let me forget.

✳

PART I

A Hero and a Son

Five Fingers

Up in the sky, the last two clouds were drifting slowly toward each other. A lightbulb with blurry edges, and a white, puffy shape that defied comparison.

Down below, Albert stood flanked by his suitcases in the patchy front yard of a house in Königsdorf, eyeing the doorbell, lost in thought. Anyone acquainted with Albert—admittedly something only few could claim—would know that he couldn't help it. When he was younger the other kids had called him bookworm, or four-eyes, though he didn't wear glasses and was anything but studious. Whenever some assignment was handed to him, he attempted to tackle it, whatever it might be, by thoroughly thinking it through. That was all. And it didn't mean he always got good grades, either. For Albert, there was no sentence so surreal as *I would never have thought of that.* How could you *not think* of something? (He often thought.)

But the toughest assignment Albert had ever been given—the solution to which he'd been seeking for nineteen years now—was waiting for him behind the door whose bell he was touching, but hadn't yet pressed.

On this particular afternoon Albert had a journey of more than seventeen hours behind him—on the night train, the commuter train, and finally bus 479, whose driver had made every single stop in the Bavarian uplands, from Pföderl via Wolfsöd through Höfen, though no one at all had gotten on or off—and now that he had only a tiny scrap farther to go, he wasn't so sure he even wanted to arrive.

This is what Albert always thought when he came to Königsdorf: that he'd been coming to visit Fred since he was three years old, initially accompanied by a nun from the orphanage at Saint Helena, and later alone. That he and Fred had never grown particularly close. That when he was five (and, as far as Albert knew, Fred forty-six) he'd made sure that Fred had donned his water wings when, hand in hand, they'd leapt into the Baggersee. That only a few years later he'd started paying for Fred whenever they found themselves facing a cash register, because Albert could count up the change without having to use his fingers. That at the age of twelve, he'd tried to dissuade Fred from his dream of becoming an actor. (The latter had fully rejected this plan only later, on the grounds that he didn't want, as he put it, people watching him while he worked.) That the following year, he'd still been vigilant about Fred's water wings. That at fifteen he'd tried to explain the facts of life to Fred, who hadn't wanted to hear, and had simply responded with a sheepish laugh. That Fred had never called him anything but Albert, and Albert had never called him anything but Fred. That he had never called him *Father*.

Fred was just Fred—this was the first rule in Albert's life. It had been that way since he was born, and it would be that way this year as well.

For a few more months, in any case.

In his office the cardiologist had waved the fingers of one manicured hand, and Albert had asked himself if the doctor always did it like that, if he generally told his patients the number of months remaining to them with his fingers, to spare himself the search for sympathetic words. Five fingers. Albert had barely paid attention to them, had taken Fred by the hand and left the hospital with him, ignoring the doctor's shouts, as later he would his phone calls.

Because he couldn't talk about it with Fred, he prattled on about other things as they made their way home, especially about the foehn, how strong it was for this time of year, really unusually strong.

Fred had interrupted him: "Five fingers are bad."

Albert had stopped in his tracks, searching for something to say.

"Five fingers are very bad, Albert."

"Five fingers aren't all *that* bad," Albert had eventually answered.

"Really? How many do you have, Albert? How many fingers do you have until you have to go dead?"

"I don't know."

"Is five a lot?"

"Five is a pretty good number," said Albert, as encouragingly as he could.

"I *have* five fingers!" A relieved laugh. "And you, Albert, I bet you have plenty of fingers, too."

That same evening Albert had left town again, to take his high school exit exams. An obligation that, in light of the news, seemed to him as ridiculous as his decision to fulfill it.

Though in fact, all he really wanted was to get away.

Two months later, after the exams, most of his friends had vanished beyond the horizon. Australia and Cambodia were destinations especially popular with orphans; when they returned from a trip to Angkor or the outback, not only had they "found themselves," also they had an idea of where they belonged in the world, and what they wanted to start doing with their lives. Supposedly. Albert, on the other hand—who'd never been able to understand why so many people assumed that answers unobtainable in the immediate neighborhood were awaiting them in far-off lands—had decided to move in with Fred. He hadn't known what to expect, and still didn't this afternoon, standing before Fred's house—he knew only that, whatever it was, there wasn't much time.

Three more fingers, thought Albert; he rang the bell, lowered his head, grabbed the handles of his suitcases, and stood there, motionless. The heat bored down into his skull. People would remember this summer for a long time. Contrary to all predictions, there had not been a storm for weeks now. The grass in Fred's garden was rust-brown, even the chirping of the crickets sounded feeble, and the shimmering heat on the stretch of the main street that ran in front of the property was playing tricks on Albert's eyes.

Ambrosial!

Now the door opened and on the top step there appeared a gangling, six-and-a-half-foot-tall giant, sheepishly dipping his head.

They stared at each other.

"Albert!" shouted Fred in his silvery voice, and before Albert knew what was happening to him, he'd been plucked off his feet and pressed hard against Fred's bony chest.

"Hello, Fred."

"You're fat, Albert!"

"Thanks," said Albert, looking him over—unsure, as he so often was, whether or not Fred was aware of what he was saying. Albert knew him well enough to sense that he didn't really know him at all. In that respect, at least, he seemed like any other father.

Still, Albert had to admit to himself that Fred had a point. After a shower, Albert usually wound the towel around his body so that he wouldn't have to look at his belly when he stepped in front of the mirror. Where all that auxiliary lard had sprung from he couldn't quite explain. He didn't think he ate and drank any more than other people. Presumably he didn't move around enough: regular jogging, power walking, or even strolling would, as they say, "do him good." But the notion of movement merely for movement's sake didn't especially appeal to him.

"Is it the holidays again?" asked Fred.

"No, not this time. This time I'm staying longer."

Fred looked at him hopefully. "Till when?"

"Until . . ." Albert dodged his glance. "As long as possible."

"As long as possible could be a long time!" shouted Fred merrily, clapping his hands. "That's ambrosial!"

"Right. It's great."

"It's *ambrosial!*" Fred lifted a forefinger in rebuke. "You need to read the encyclopedia more, Albert."

With Fred, *reading* bore no necessary relation to *understanding;* he seldom saw beyond the sounds of the words that he scanned with the aid of his forefinger, to take note of their meanings. And even when he did, most of them slipped from his memory in short order, bursting like soap bubbles.

Fred tore the suitcases from Albert's hands and marched into the house. Albert followed. He paused in the vestibule. Though the sugary odor of Fred's home had been there to meet him whenever he'd arrived, year in, year out, it still managed to take him by surprise.

"Albert?" Fred turned back to him. "Are you feeling faint?"

"No." Albert drew a deep breath. "It's fine."

Albert draped his jacket on a coat hook beside Fred's royal blue poncho, within whose collar a childish script warned: *This belongs to Frederick Arkadiusz Driajes!* A plaque by the doorbell bore the selfsame name. Nobody addressed him by his full moniker. Quite possibly because nobody knew how to pronounce it. Naturally, there were a couple of oafs in Königsdorf—permanent fixtures at Hofherr's beer garden, where they sat nursing their glasses—who maintained he was slow in the head, and called him *Freddie-are-you-stupid?* But for most people, he was simply Fred, the hero of the bus accident of '77, who spent half the day at Königsdorf's only bus stop in order to tally the green cars that passed along the town's main street and wave to their drivers.

As Fred set down the suitcases by the stairs and proceeded into the living room, Albert felt a fit of déjà-vu coming over him; or, to be more precise, a déjà-vu of many previous déjà-vus.

He thought: First, they'd sit themselves down on a worn-out, cherry-red chaise longue, precisely where they always sat, and no matter what he touched, thousands of crumbs would adhere to Albert's hands, reminding him that, now, he rather than the nurse would have to provide Fred with at least one warm meal per day, tie his shoelaces, make sure his teeth were kept spruce and the house spick-and-span.

His eyes would fall on the world map fixed to the wall, where a ring drawn with a green felt-tip marker, which was supposed to indicate Königsdorf, actually encircled all of Bavaria. He would ask Fred how things were going, to which, of course, the answer would be "Ambrosial," and the next moment Albert would be asked to read aloud from Fred's favorite book, the silver encyclopedia, as he so often had in the past, before bedtime or afternoon naps. Fred would snuggle up to him, lay his head, pleasantly warm, in spite of the heat outside, in Albert's lap, and close his eyes, and Albert would hardly dare to move. Still, he'd open the encyclopedia and begin reading somewhere, say at *Billiards*, and wouldn't get any farther than *Binary star*. Fred would snore, looking much younger in his sleep, midforties at the most. Albert would flip the book shut, then slip a pillow under Fred's head and lay a short fleece blanket over his long, long legs. In the kitchen, Albert would have something to eat, soothing his stomach with thick slabs of brown bread while running his eyes across the crack-shot window above the sink, whose lower-left corner was adorned with two taunting letters, *HA*. He didn't know who had left them behind, nor when, but since they'd been scratched into the pane from the outside (six tiny scratches, Zorro style), he could only assume that they were the initials of his grandmother, Anni Habom. Albert would lean forward, his left hand braced on the sink, and breathe on the window, and on the clouded pane he would trace his own initials beside those of his grandmother— *AD*—thick as his finger. And watch them fade. Later, in his bedroom on the second floor, he'd make sure that there was enough of Fred's medication left in the little nightstand by the bed. Only then would he allow himself to be wooed by the sagging mattress, and feel the exhaustion creeping over him, though he wouldn't be able to fall asleep.

And that's just what happened.

Though the whole time Albert was telling himself that he ought to be feeling something special—not *déjà-vu*, but *dernier-vu*. After all, he'd come home for the very last time.

Most Beloved Possessions

Albert had lain on his bed for barely ten minutes, leaden, empty, and with a towel over his eyes—the sun was still blazing in through the curtains, as though this day would never end—when Fred burst in: "Are you sleeping?"

Albert waved him over—what else could he do?—and Fred plopped himself down on the mattress.

"Tell me," said Albert, observing Fred's chin, "when was the last time you shaved?"

Fred blinked. "Yesterday."

"You're sure?"

Fred blinked again: "Totally sure."

"You may have missed a few spots."

More blinking.

"Frederick . . ."

"Mama says I look handsome!"

Fred was particularly fond of bringing Anni into play, in order to stress that this, that, or another notion hadn't sprung from his own head, but from that of a significantly higher authority. An authority who had last said anything to Fred sixteen years earlier, when Albert had been three years old. Albert's memories of her barely deserved the name; it sometimes occurred to him that he might simply be imagining them, since he'd spent so much time examining the innumerable photographs of her in Fred's house, comparing her features with his own, searching for resemblances. She had lived to age seventy, an apparently hard life, saddled with chronically high blood pressure (as revealed by the cardiologist's postmortem diagnosis). In the end, her condition had led to systolic heart failure; that is, her heart had succumbed to its own imposing bulk, and Albert's grandmother, his last real link to the past, had died. That much he knew. In a handful of file folders, whose primary function had been to support the bottommost shelf of a rickety bookcase, he'd discovered a scrappy collection of documents revealing mainly that she hadn't been insured. Evidently she'd never set foot in a hospital or doctor's office. No one had ever told her how many fingers she had left.

Albert sat up, mimicking a pair of scissors with his index and middle fingers.

Fred clapped his hands over his prickly cheeks: "But my dad had a blond beard!"

Fred claimed that his father—Albert's grandfather Arkadiusz—had been a diver. A man with extraordinary lungs who had reconditioned subterranean canal systems, who had once dived to the floor of the Baltic Sea without aid of equipment, and who, back when Fred was barely larger than the belly in which he'd spent nine months, had been snatched away by a sudden rush of water and disappeared forever into the rambling network of sewer pipes beneath the town. It may have been true, or just a fantasy, but in any case it meant that someone always had to flush the toilet on Fred's behalf, something he balked at even more than he did shaving: "My dad is traveling forever through the pipes—sometimes he's in America, and sometimes he's in Poland, and sometimes he's here, too."

Albert stood up, stepped into the bathroom, and plugged in the electric shaver, but when he turned around, Fred was gone. After hunting through the whole house, he finally found him out in the backyard, in the BMW 321. It was a vintage model from the late thirties that belonged to Fred, even though he didn't have a driver's license. He called it the Speedster. Its mint-green paint looked as if it had suffered a high-temperature pressure washing. Its tire treads hung in tatters. The sound of the horn was best described as whiny. The leather upholstery smelled—in Fred's opinion—deliciously musty, just like it did between his toes. An empty flowerpot kept the passenger-side door from falling off its hinges.

Albert climbed in beside Fred, who was sitting at the wheel. His stubble gleamed in the late sunlight, and the encyclopedia lay in his lap. He had it open to *D. D* as in *Death*. With his index finger he pointed to the illustration of a tombstone in Carrara marble. "What color is that?"

"Dove-white?"

"Do they have swan-white, too?"

"Definitely."

"Can I have one like that?"

"A swan-white tombstone?"

Fred nodded. "It has to be a very beautiful stone, Albert."

"Done," said Albert. "A swan-white tombstone for you."

They sat silent for a moment while, outside, the noise of cars passing along the main street subsided, and they were blinded one final time by the sun before it plunged behind the moor. Fred looked dreamily at the picture of the tombstone.

"Everyone always says going dead is bad. I don't believe it. I'm sure it's completely different. I bet it's great. Like a huge surprise. Actually, I'm looking forward to it. It would be even better if the two of us could go dead together, Albert. Only, I think that would be hard. Because I'm faster than you."

"I'll hurry," Albert promised him, and immediately Fred beamed at him like a child—a child who had gotten on in years, with bags under his eyes, gray temples, and little creases around his mouth.

Then the smile slipped from Fred's face: "Mama says all your Most Beloved Possessions go dead, someday." The tone of his voice had changed, as if he'd just that moment remembered what dying actually meant.

"And what would that be, a Most Beloved Possession?" asked Albert.

Fred laughed, as if Albert had asked an unbelievably stupid question: "A Most Beloved Possession can be anything at all!"

"A father, for instance?"

"Sure! Or a car."

"And what's your Most Beloved Possession?"

Fred snorted and rolled his eyes. He stretched out one arm, opened the glove compartment, and drew out a dented tin box in which something rolled and rattled. While opening the scratched lid, Fred bent over the box, obstructing Albert's view, as if he wanted to make sure that what he expected to find was still there. Then he held a chestnut-sized stone, which gleamed metallically in the evening light, under Albert's nose. "Take it!"

To call the look on Fred's face one of pride would have been an enormous understatement.

Albert weighed the Most Beloved Possession in his palm—it was astonishingly heavy, and resembled a wadded-up, petrified sheet of rich yellow paper. An absurd thought came to him, which Fred promptly uttered: "Gold."

"Really?"

Fred whispered, "My Most Beloved Possession."

Even though Albert nodded appreciatively and stuck out his lower lip, he was skeptical. The stone in his hand corresponded precisely to his idea of a gold nugget, and that immediately aroused his suspicion.

"Who did you get this from?" asked Albert, and handed the gold back to Fred.

Satisfied, Fred stowed the stone back in the tin box.

"I said, who did you get it from?"

Fred said, "It's mine."

"Did you steal it from somebody?"

"I never steal."

"Was it always here? Why haven't you shown it to me before?"

"When I'm dead, you can have it," said Fred, and looked at him excitedly; the green of his eyes shimmered like the surface of a lake, one whose depth it's impossible to gauge. "Then you'll be rich."

Albert returned his look, wishing once again that it was possible to ask Fred a simple question and receive a simple answer. A completely normal conversation, that's what he wanted, one in which Fred didn't sidle away from his questions. Most of all, he wished he could believe Fred, that he didn't find himself doubting every last one of his statements.

"Hmm," said Albert.

"Hmm," said Fred.

At that precise moment, the neighbor's rooster unleashed a wild cry. Fred grimaced and rolled up the driver's-side window. "He never knows when to be quiet!"

Albert tapped on the stopped dashboard clock beside the speedometer. "It's late," he said. "The Sandman is making his rounds."

Papaaa

That evening Albert couldn't sleep. He lay there with his eyes fixed on a luminous, fingernail-sized, star-shaped sticker on the beam above the bed. When he was younger he'd looked at it every evening until his eyes shut; he'd found it comforting that this tiny light had shone for him, shone defiantly against the blackness of the country night.

From a drawer in the nightstand he drew a yellowing newspaper article. The second April edition of the *Oberland Messenger* from 1977. Right on the first page there was a report by one Frederick A. Driajes, a story that as a child Albert had read over and over again before falling asleep. It bore the title:

On the day the bus attacked the bus stop, the rain was stronger than ever before. Every drop was separate! I never wait in the wooden house they built so that people don't get wet. Inside there's a big picture of a clown from the circus, whose name is Rusch. His eyes are black and shiny and you can see all of his teeth. I'd rather wait in the rain. That's why I've got my poncho! The Königsdorf bus stop is right on the main street. Everyone who drives through Königsdorf drives past it. The cars are all different colors. But I only count the ones that are green, like my eyes. Once I counted almost fifty green cars—that's almost more than fifty green cars! There's also a sign there. Which says 479. Farther off, there's the church's bell tower. When it strikes twelve times, it's twelve o'clock, and I go home for lunch. The 479, which arrives at 6:30, was the bus that attacked the bus stop. But that day it arrived at 6:15! The 479 certainly was driving two hundred miles per hour. Because I wait every day at the bus stop, I can calculate that easily. Even if I've never ridden on a bus before. I will never ride on a bus. After all, a bus can make you go dead.

Apart from me, Herr Strigl was there, too. Herr Strigl is a little man with a mustache. He used to work as a driving instructor. But he worked too fast, and now he has to take the bus. Frau Winkler was also waiting for the bus with her little baby. Mama says that Frau Winkler is ambrosial. When you see an ambrosial person, then it's like you don't see anything else. You can't see anything else. And if you *do* see something else, it looks like nothing at all. And then, there was a man in an overcoat waiting for the bus, too. Mama doesn't know him. I've always thought funny things about him. That he was like the spider in my room. I always imagine that it walks across my face while I'm asleep. It was like that with the man in the overcoat. I didn't think he walked across my face while I was asleep, only that he was the kind of man who did things I didn't like. He never smiled. He was always next to the picture of the clown, and he never talked.

I'd like to hold on to the point before the bus attacked the bus stop. So that it never moves on, and the bus never comes. But time is not something real. Time isn't like the Speedster, or my encyclopedia. You can't touch time. You can't hear time. You can't smell it, either. Or taste it. Or see it. Not really. A clock is a clock, it isn't really time. So a person can't hold on to time. But I can take it apart into little pieces. And that's what I did, too, when the bus attacked the bus stop. And if I close my eyes, I can do it again. Then I see everything, I see all the little pieces of time. I see the bus coming toward me very slowly, even though it was really going very fast, its wheels spinning and its windows gleaming with rainwater and its headlights much brighter than normal. I see the picture where the clown's mouth laughs as if it's swallowing air. I see how the bus wobbles so strangely left and right. I see Frau Winkler clutching her stroller, but she can't push it out of the way because the man in the overcoat slams into it as he tries to run off. I see Herr Strigl shouting at the man in the overcoat as loud as he can. I see many black birds in the sky. I see Frau Winkler's little baby in the stroller, making his hands into little fists. I see the bell tower.

It's only at the beginning that I think I might have to make someone go dead. That's a feeling that's very far from ambrosial. There really isn't a word for that at all. The man in the overcoat shoves Frau Winkler so he can run off. Herr Strigl grabs Frau Winkler and pulls her away. The bus is already twice as big as a normal bus, and its headlights as bright as a sun and another sun. The man in the overcoat runs away from the bus. Behind the bus's window sits Ludwig, who I used to play with when I was little. The clown on the poster looks so real, like a nasty man, and laughs, and says nothing but words that you mustn't ever use. The hands on the

bell tower haven't moved yet. There's a terrible taste in my mouth, and my belly hurts. Herr Strigl makes a face that doesn't look like him, because Frau Winkler doesn't want him to pull her away, because she's trying to get to the stroller. The man in the overcoat runs into the wooden house. The bus makes a noise that's almost so high that only dogs can hear it, but I can still hear it. The words that the clown is saying are very bad, they give me a hard feeling in my belly, one like I've never had before, and his eyes are gleaming completely black. Frau Winkler's baby no longer has fists, it's fidgeting like usual. The birds in the sky are still flying. Herr Strigl won't quit pulling at Frau Winkler. Where it comes from I don't know, but I hear *Mari* or *Marine* or *Mina*. I feel sick. Frau Winkler's eyes are red and wet from the rain, but maybe she's crying, and she punches Herr Strigl because he won't let her go.

Now I want to do something, like my dad would, I don't want to be nothing, I want to tell Frau Winkler and her baby and Herr Strigl that they have to run away, and tear down the poster with the clown, and I even want to help the man in the overcoat, but I know I can only do very little, because the bus is much too fast, and everything is already much too late.

But I notice that I'm not wearing my poncho anymore, it's lying beside me, and then I think that maybe without the poncho I can be faster, and then I start running. With the hand he isn't using to hold Frau Winkler, Herr Strigl tries to grab my shirt, and I really believe he's just trying to be nice. The clown goes *Harr-harr-harr,* he goes *Harr-harr-harr,* and he sounds like Peg-Leg Pete. The black birds are acting as if the bus isn't attacking the bus stop, they're circling like they always do because, Mama says, they're waiting for more birds. I punch Herr Strigl in the face, so that he lets Frau Winkler go, and I feel all my fingers, and feel very briefly ambrosial, even though I know that you're supposed to feel very bad when you do something like that. Frau Winkler is free now, and falls to the ground. The bus's window breaks and Ludwig flies through it, as if he could fly, and all the tiny shards of glass glitter beautifully. Herr Strigl's eyes are huge. The bus is much slower now, and little pieces of fire spray from where its wheels are, but the bus is still much too fast for a baby and for me and for Herr Strigl and for the man in the overcoat. I think I see the big hand on the bell tower move a little. The man in the overcoat hides himself in the wooden house. I take Frau Winkler's baby out of the stroller and it screams so hard my ears hurt, and it feels like a little dog, and I wish, I wish my dad was here to help me, to carry us away. It's so hard not to be nothing. Ludwig flies into the pipe on the wooden house where the water from the roof flows through, and all the little shards of glass from the bus's broken window that no longer exists look like hail. Herr Strigl just stands there staring at the bus and he looks like a tree that doesn't know what is going to happen when the bus will hit it. *Harr-harr-harr,* goes the clown. I scream to Herr Strigl that he should run away, but he just stands there as if someone has done something to him, like that thing men with turbans do to snakes. Frau Winkler, lying on the ground, stretches her arm out to me. The man in the overcoat is in one corner of the wooden house, and I shout to him that he should run away. *Man in the overcoat,* I shout, *go away,* I shout, *the bus is coming,* but the man in the overcoat doesn't move. The big hand on the bell tower moves a little. Ludwig falls to the ground beside the wooden house, and his throat looks as red as real blood, but there's a big smile on his face. I feel like I don't have any strength left, and I imagine that it's not me who's inside me, no, my dad is inside me, and with all of his muscles he has plenty of strength, so much that he can save everyone, before the big hand on the bell tower stops moving. And then I *am* my dad, and that's a very terrible feeling, because I realize how little my dad is here, and then I jump, and the bus blows thick air, which pushes me to the side. The bus comes and falls crookedly and takes Herr Strigl with it, and the stroller, and hides the man in the overcoat. A squealing bashes me in the ears, and now the bus attacks the bus stop, and the clown, and that *Harr-harr-harr* finally stops, and the bus breaks the wooden house and gets stuck there, and it stinks like at the gas station, and the wood makes a noise like it's not doing too well, and then it collapses onto the bus, because it's completely kaput, and then there's still a kind of snake-noise, and then it gets softer, and I hear Frau Winkler, she's crying, and I give her her little baby, and I look at the bus and the wooden house that isn't there anymore, and Ludwig and Herr Strigl and the man in the overcoat aren't there anymore either, and I'm sorry for that, I'm sorry, I'm not like my dad at all, I'm nothing, that's very true, I'm nothing and that's the whole story, that's all, that's all I saw, and I'm sorry about it, I'm sorry, and I never want to say any of these things ever again, and also not tell them to anyone, no.

When Albert read the report today, as a nineteen-year-old, he recognized in it some of what bothered him about Fred: most of all, the way he exaggerated, describing things so that you could never be quite sure if his mental disability was responsible, or his character, or some combination of the two.

But as a child he remembered he had loved Fred for this more than anything—that people called him a hero. Back then he'd seen Fred as an even greater hero than He-Man or Raphael, the turtle with the red bandanna, named for some other Raphael that Sister Simone was all gaga over. At Saint Helena, Albert bragged about Fred, thereby drawing the envy and hostility of all the other orphans who not only didn't have heroes for fathers; they had no fathers at all. Why did he live in Saint Helena if Fred was so great, they asked him, and shook their heads maliciously. Albert ignored that. Sister Alfonsa had prepared him for such situations; he followed her advice, didn't stick his tongue out at the other kids, and told himself that because they didn't have anyone, they wanted to be like him, they were just being jealous, petty. And that helped Albert, who was the only one of the younger kids in the orphanage who knew what *petty* meant. At Saint Helena, Albert favored the lower mattress in the bunk bed, on the one hand because he was no lover of heights, and on the other because he could decorate the underside of the bed above him with what he wanted to be the last thing he'd see before falling asleep: Fred's newspaper report. Even back then he had never called Fred *Father.* As a one-year-old he'd called him *Ped,* then *Fed* at two, and a few months later he was proudly gurgling *Fred.* Anni had told him to. And after Anni's death, Sister Alfonsa wanted it to stay that way. Which confused Albert. Often he wanted to call him *Papa,* with an elongated second *a* that opened the throat and cleared the mind. Whereas *Fred* curled his tongue and sounded like an out-of-tune doorbell. Yet he trusted the nun, for in spite of his precocious mind, he was still small enough to believe that adults, among whom he counted Fred, knew everything, and always did what was right.

It wasn't until age five that he realized how wrong he had been.

During a visit to Königsdorf he and Fred lay, as usual, on the chaise longue in the living room, in front of the television set. Albert couldn't recall anymore which program had been playing at the time. He'd never cared much about that, for him the important thing was snuggling up against Fred and feeling his inextinguishable warmth. And that's how it had been that evening when Albert, needing to go to the bathroom, had worked himself loose from Fred, whose gaze never slid from the TV even for a moment. After Albert had pressed the flush on the toilet, he stood there waiting, for Fred's sake, until the sound of the rushing water had subsided, before opening the door again. When he bounced back into the living room, feeling almost perfectly happy, he saw it.

Even before Albert first beat Sister Alfonsa at chess, even before he wowed his teachers with essays cobbled together out of quotes cribbed from German writers (never getting caught), even before he began learning the English version of his favorite book, *The Hobbit,* by heart, even before he baptized a stray dog "Maxmoritz" and trained it to pilfer sausages from the convent kitchen, even before, bored by the inflationary use of kindergarten curse words like *dummy* or *poopy butt,* he started to call his envious peers "cretins," even before he explained to said cretins, who, when exam time came around, scored worse than he did across the board, that his namesake, Einstein, had never been a poor student, merely Swiss—even before all of this happened, Albert understood for the first time just how little his father understood.

Fred was lying in exactly the same position on the chaise longue, but his gaze didn't reach what was happening on the screen. He was staring in its direction with the concentrated yet unambiguously desperate expression of someone marooned on an island, scanning the horizon for ships.

The first words Albert addressed to Sister Alfonsa after that visit were "Is he crazy?"

Alfonsa greeted him with a bear hug and one of her standard tooth-concealing smirks—back when she was a child, people had put little stock in either tenderness or orthodontics. She was famous far beyond the walls of Saint Helena for her inscrutable facial expressions. Albert himself had once witnessed how an adventurous orphan—Rupert—had mistaken her smirk for a suppressed smile, as he clambered up onto the unstable roof of a garden shed accompanied by her shouts that he should *definitely* go on scrambling, there would be *absolutely no* consequences, she thought it was an *excellent* idea, if only *all* the boys were daring enough to try to break their necks. A penance of fifty Our Fathers had brought Rupert considerably closer to an understanding of the concept of irony. Some people thought everything Sister Alfonsa uttered was devoid of emotion. But even as a child, Albert had felt this was only half the story. It sometimes seemed to him as if she'd found her way to Saint Helena by mistake. Something about her just didn't fit there. What exactly it was, he couldn't say. But he had a suspicion it was connected with how seldom she left the building, and how often she listened to Frank Sinatra.

"Is Fred crazy?"

This time Albert pronounced the question as if he was expecting a yes. Sister Alfonsa shut the door to her office, and led him over to a little table on which a chessboard of stained boxwood was waiting. To the left and right of it stood wooden stools. Lately she'd been teaching him to play chess—an honor she bestowed only every few years on an orphan who, in her opinion, had great potential, or, as she phrased it, seemed "bright enough." In Alfonsa's lessons, chess pieces were dispensed with. In her opinion, a clever-enough mind could make do with checkers—memory would take care of the rest.

Albert hesitated, he had little desire to play, but he also sensed that he had no other option, if he wanted to hear her thoughts. Faint daylight fell through a tiny window—it was another of those murky autumn afternoons. Albert took his seat. His feet didn't reach the floor. For a moment his hand hovered above his bone-white troops, before opening the game in classic fashion (pawn to e4). The nun mirrored his move (pawn to e5), and then sat down.

"You think your father is crazy?"

"Yes."

"Maybe we are, too."

"No way."

"How do you know?"

Albert made his next move (knight to f3), which she again mimicked (knight to f6).

"Okay," she said, "let's assume that we're not crazy, and Fred is. Isn't that merely our thesis, then?"

Albert wrinkled his forehead (knight takes pawn), Alfonsa didn't (likewise).

"What's a thesis?"

"A beginning." She smirked. "In our society the stronger rule over the weaker. A clever little fellow like you declares: 'Fred is crazy.' And because Fred is hardly capable of refuting you, everyone concludes that you're right."

"I *am* right" (pawn to d3).

"So: guilty until proven innocent" (pawn to d6). "And what if we're wrong?"

"..."

(Pawn takes knight, and likewise.)

"What if *we're* crazy? What if the whole world is controlled by madmen, who lock away all the sane people like Fred, so that nobody gets wise to them?"

"That's not possible."

"Says who?"

"Me."

"All children are mad," said Alfonsa.

"Why?"

"As the stronger of the two of us, I've just decided it."

"I'm not crazy!"

"You are now."

Albert slammed down a game piece beside the board. "I don't want to play anymore!"

"It was just an illustration." She tousled his hair. "Do you really want to know what I think?"

He nodded, and looked at her obliquely from below, to express that he wanted to be taken in her arms.

"You are both perfectly insane."

No ambiguity intended. Albert might have understood less than half of what she was saying—even his brightness had limits—but he could feel that this time she was speaking with admiration.

"That's good," he said and, just to be safe, added, "right?"

"That's special," she said, "and the very reason why you can only ever call him Fred. He'll never be a proper father."

"I can explain it to him!"

Sister Alfonsa smirked. "Nobody can do that. Not even you."

A week later Albert ran away from the orphanage for the first time. Over the following month, he absconded on four separate occasions. Thereafter he repeated his escape attempts with reliable regularity. On average he made around twenty per year. At first he failed because of the bus drivers, who wouldn't let some squirt, especially a smart-alecky squirt, ride unaccompanied by a grown-up. Often enough, the other orphans ratted him out. But even when an attempt succeeded, the nuns were barely ruffled; they knew where he was going every time. And why.

"I'm your son," said Albert to Fred.

"You're Albert," said Fred to Albert.

"And I'm your son," said Albert. "And you're my father."

"I'm Fred."

"And my father."

Fred blinked.

"Do you understand me?" asked Albert.

"I always understand everything," said Fred.

"What did I say?"

"You said, *Do you understand me?* I understand you, Albert."

"And before?"

"You said, *And my father.*"

"Do you understand that?"

"Yes," said Fred, "and I'm hungry."

"I come from you," said Albert. "Without you, I wouldn't exist."

And Fred said, "Thank you. That's nice. Can we make pancakes with raspberry jam? Pancakes with raspberry jam are ambrosial."

Later, at Saint Helena—there was always a later-at-Saint-Helena—Albert would fight his disappointment by reading Fred's newspaper report each night before falling asleep, and imagining that the child

Fred had saved was him, not some girl called Andrea, who, after the bus accident, had left Königsdorf, along with her mother, forever.

He always hoped, and sometimes believed, and occasionally *knew*, that someday Fred would come and rescue him—that in the middle of the night Fred would storm into the dormitory, flip on the lights, run to his bunk, and take Albert with him. Where to was negligible— all that mattered was that it be away.

But the passing years withered his hope. Even his boundless long- ing couldn't shield him from that. Again and again he ran to Fred, counter to Sister Alfonsa's claim; it will work this time, he told him- self, incorrigible; this time Fred will get it—and then Fred got noth- ing at all. It was all the same as ever. And Fred was simply Fred.

Albert put Fred's report away again and pulled on a bathrobe. Out in the garden, he lit a cigarette. He could risk smoking only late at night. Fred had admonished him, "Smoking makes you sick!" and Albert didn't want to provoke him needlessly. The smoke vanished into the night. As his gaze fell on the BMW, he flicked the butt over the garden fence; it flew in a high arc into the main street, like a crashing glow- worm. Albert kicked at the car's fender, expecting that it would hurt, but he barely felt a thing. It seemed as if this fender had been designed for him to kick, so he gave it another go, and slammed the hood for good measure, clobbered it with both fists. He hoped someone would happen along and try to stop him—then he'd be able to pummel or be pummeled. But nobody came.

Out of breath, he let himself fall into the BMW's passenger seat, and flipped open the glove compartment. He took out the tin box and placed it on the dashboard. The streetlamp's flattering orange light concealed some of its dents, and gave it a coppery sheen. Albert would have preferred that the box held no gleaming stone, but rather some piece of solid evidence: mementos, some kind of a clue, say, a diary by Anni, or a sheaf of family photographs, or at least some documents—he knew nothing about his ancestry, his family, he knew nothing about his mother. Albert had an infinite number of questions, and his only hope for an answer was Fred.

Albert looked at the fingers of his left hand. A tiny, faint, dwindling hope.

Out of some indeterminate need, he opened the tin box and took the gold in his hand. Beneath it, at the bottom of the box, was an audiocassette; on its yellowed label was written: *My Most Beloved Possession.* The ornate, schoolgirlish handwriting didn't at all resemble Fred's chicken-scratch script. Albert retrieved Fred's Walkman from the living room, went back to the car, slipped the tape in, pushed the button from "off" to "on," and saw the little red light by the time display come on.

He pressed "play." A crackling, at first. Then a persistent, slowly swelling white noise, which seemed vaguely familiar, and demanding. A sort of audible silence. He searched through the tape, rewinding and fast-forwarding, laying his ear against the speaker, examining side A and side B.

Nothing.

He climbed over the center console and sat behind the wheel, pulled one of Fred's diaries out of the pocket in the door, and flipped through it. He ran his hand across one page covered in magenta scribbling, whose odor echoed the sweetish atmosphere of the house, and felt the slight unevenness of Fred's notes, pressed into the paper. *Monday, 5/24/2002: 76 green cars, 8 green trucks, no green motorcycle. Tuesday, 5/25/2002: 55 green cars, 10 green trucks, 2 beautiful green motorcycles, 1 green tractor. Wednesday, 5/26/2002...*

Albert tossed the diary onto the backseat, switched off the Walkman, and felt the weight of Fred's gold in his hand.

Hansel and Gretel Crumbs

Stumbling across clues that led him nowhere was nothing new to Albert. For years now he'd been trying to ferret out something about his origins, and especially about his mother. That he was a half orphan, or rather, as he privately thought—and which, given Fred's mental state, seemed like a justifiable term—a two-thirds orphan, didn't discourage him at all, but spurred him on. Earlier, no visit to Fred's house had gone by without at least one trip to the attic. Whenever he clambered up the ladder to the loft, he was overcome by a tremendous excitement, though he'd soon rummaged through all the crates, all the bags and chests, all the boxes and duffels and bins and binders, many times over. Maybe, just maybe, he'd overlooked something. Even the word *attic* seemed to promise so much truth. Somewhere up there in the house's memory there must be tucked away the critical clue that would point Albert toward his mother's whereabouts.

Albert hadn't been able to coax much from it, though: merely a photograph and two hairs.

He'd turned up the picture two days before his fourteenth birthday; it had been tucked in a battered wallet among Canadian banknotes showing the image of the Queen, who gazed serenely into the future. In the photograph, Fred had the posture of a schoolboy caught cutting class. Slouching, head lowered, he squinted in the direction of the camera. His right hand was stuck in his hip pocket, his left arm bent strangely sideways, as if someone had ordered him to do so, and he was holding hands with a freckled young woman whose chin-length, curly red hair sat on her head like some sort of outlandish hat, and who was nowhere to be seen in any of the other pictures Fred possessed. Her expression was a blend of pride and giddiness. She looked like she might step out of the photo at any moment.

Albert studied the picture with a magnifying glass and narrowed eyes for hours at a time. A stamp on the back confirmed: it had been taken in 1983, the year of Albert's birth.

He showed it to Fred.

"Who's that?"

"Who?" asked Fred.

"The woman next to you, what's her name?"

"She's pretty. The Red Lady."

"Does she have a name?"

"Yes."

"Well?"

"*Well?*"

"Fred, who is she?"

"She's the Red Lady."

"Do you know her real name?"

"No." Fred rolled his eyes. "But maybe it's in the encyclopedia?"

"Were you in love?"

"With the encyclopedia?"

"With the woman, Fred, the woman."

"She's pretty . . ."

"Did you . . . kiss her?"

"Mama says you shouldn't kiss girls."

"But she was a woman, right? And pretty. And if you really love someone, then you definitely kiss them. You even give me a kiss, sometimes."

"Sure, but you aren't the Red Lady. You're Albert."

"Did you kiss her, or not?"

"She kissed me."

"Did you do anything else with her?"

Fred wrinkled his brow.

"Did she touch you?"

"Sometimes."

"Down below?"

"Below where?"

"Down there."

"No!"

"Fred?"

"M-hmm?"

"Can you tell me where the Red Lady went?"

"Yes."

"Really?"

"Of course, really!"

"Where?"

Fred pointed to the front door.

When Albert was brought back to Saint Helena after an escape attempt and for punishment was forced by Sister Alfonsa to tie his shoes two hundred times under strict supervision—knots, bows, double knots, unpick them, and start again from the beginning—the thought of the Red Lady gave him the strength he needed to keep going. At fifty knots, you hit that prickly border, the sound barrier of penitential shoelace tying, after which your fingertips go numb, skin begins to tear, laces dig into the sore places. With the image of the Red Lady in his head, Albert was able to continue with inflamed hands, never breaking off before the stipulated number. He held the record for the orphanage. If you added up all his offenses, by the age of fourteen he'd reached over four thousand knots—not including the regular ones he had to tie so as not to trip. What with the innumerable little scars that covered them, his hands looked like those of a craftsman. That he'd managed to survive this time, as he believed today, because the Red Lady in the photograph had filled him with strength—that was for him the decisive evidence that she must be his mother.

Not to mention the fact that Albert's hair was as red as hers.

But even more precious to him than the photograph was a bottle-green barrette in which a pair of auburn hairs had snagged. He had lost one of them at Saint Helena, when he fell asleep holding it one evening, and on waking couldn't distinguish it from the numberless others, his own, lying curled on the mattress. The second hair he kept in a homely makeup compact he'd bought at a flea market, and which he carried always on his person, like an asthmatic does his inhaler. At lonely moments, especially during his trips to visit Fred and back to the orphanage, he ran his hands across it, and it made him itch—like when a wound is healing.

That spring, when Albert discovered the photograph, he wiped it clean with a damp sponge and slipped it into a transparent plastic folder, which he carefully sealed with several layers of clear tape before stowing it away, wrapped in two shock-absorbing editions of the *Süddeutsche Zeitung,* in an attaché case covered with fake alligator skin that he'd taken from the attic, and which zipped shut with a comforting *weeep.* And with that he walked—optimistically smacking his gum, as only a teenager can—over to Fred's next-door neighbor. She was a potter named Klondi, who lived rent-free in a huge old farmhouse, badly in need of repairs, on the main street. In return for her housing, she kept the space "in good order"—nobody but Klondi was allowed to set foot on the second floor of the place, because only she knew which boards you could step on without falling through to the first floor. But Klondi—whose passport displayed a less silly, more mundane name—much preferred—when she wasn't working late into the night, shaping vases and coffee mugs and ashtrays with her hands—to groom the garden behind the farmhouse. During the daytime, even in spring storms and November snow, you'd find her there, transplanting a rhododendron or trimming the hedges.

"Hello?"

Albert stood before a gate some ten feet high, all overgrown with roses. The smell was as overpowering as the incense at Sunday Mass at Saint Helena.

"Anyone there?"

He preferred not to have her name in his mouth. There were words that left behind a stale aftertaste. *Klondi* was one of them, *Father* another.

"Yes, someone's there," answered a hedge to his left.

Albert spat his gum into an empty terra-cotta pot and, as he followed the voice, pondered how many cigarettes Klondi must have smoked in the course of her life to earn herself such a sepulchral basso. She was down on her knees in a flower bed, cutting up slugs with a pair of gardening shears. Pale slime welled from the severed halves. A cigarette was stuck in Klondi's ferocious smile, her hair lay bundled over her shoulders in a pair of schoolgirl pigtails, which hardly concealed the fact that Klondi the onetime flower child had long since become a flower woman.

"Do you know why I spare the ones who carry around their own little houses?"

Albert glanced at the dying slugs seeping out on the pavement. "Because they're nicer looking?"

"I'd prefer to put it thus: survival of the sexiest." Klondi laughed— or coughed, it was difficult to distinguish. "Want one?" She offered him a half-empty packet of Gauloises.

Albert shook his head.

"Good boy. But you'll still have to take the gum with you."

"Huh?"

"That chewing-gum crap. In the terra-cotta pot." She stood with a flounce, as if she were sixteen, and knocked the dirt from her knees. "I've got enough butts lying around already."

"Okay," mumbled Albert.

"Is that for me?"

He tightened his grip on the attaché case, which he was carrying under his arm. "No. Yes."

"Which is it?"

"Can I show you something?"

She waved him forward, and he followed her to a granite table in the middle of the garden, which she slapped with the flat of her hand. He unzipped the case and handed her the photo. She tilted it into the light.

"Well, so?"

"Do you know the woman?"

"No."

"Sure?"

"Of course I'm sure." She blew smoke from her nostrils. "Why?"

"Nothing important."

He wanted to take the picture back, but she wouldn't let it go. "Albert, in the eleven years you've been visiting your father, you've never once set foot on my property. Nothing important? I believe that right now there's nothing *more* important to you than this photo."

"Maybe."

Glancing down, Albert noticed he'd stepped on one of the dead slugs. He wiped his sneakers on the grass.

"She . . . could be your mother."

"Do you know her?"

"Nope. We never met. When you were born, at the beginning of the eighties, it wasn't a good time for me. I preferred to steer clear of people."

"Why?"

She cleared her throat and tapped with an earth-smeared index finger at the gap between Fred and the Red Lady. "You would fit into this picture. Right there."

Albert peered at the photo more carefully. She was right.

"Do you know . . . ," he began, but wasn't sure how to end the sentence without it hurting. *Where she went? Why she abandoned us? Why she didn't care about us? What she was thinking?*

"I don't know anything," said Klondi and drew thoughtfully on her cigarette, as if she might be able to suck information from the butt. "Mothers are overrated, Albert. If you ask me, you can count yourself lucky that you grew up without one." She handed the picture back to him, and he immediately stowed it in the attaché.

"I wouldn't keep searching," she said. "I'm afraid nobody in this village will have anything to tell you. As far as they're concerned, your father is a Virgin Mary. You'll find nothing."

At this early stage, *nobody* and *nothing* were words far too glib to make Albert call off his search. For three long years he behaved like a young detective during the holidays, roaming through Hofherr's beer garden, accosting the diners just after they'd gulped down the last scraps of their meals—since, according to a radio crime series he'd been listening to late at night with a couple of other orphans, that was the ideal moment to take a potential informant by surprise—until at last a dirndl-clad barmaid chased him off with noises like *ksss* and *psh,* as if he were a stray dog begging for treats. For three long years Albert knocked at wickets, at garden gates, at front doors with frosted-glass panes, at open doors, at doors upon which, during Epiphany, trios of children in royal garb had scrawled the initials of the Three Kings, $C + M + B,$ in chalk, and at doors that were locked and bolted. For three long years he schlepped his attaché case around with him, eagerly presenting his mug shot to every pair of eyes he encountered. For three long years he made photocopies of the picture, on which he spelled out with letters cut from the newspaper: HAvE yOu SeEn THis wOMaN? RePORt it TO dRIaJES! and tacked them up on the bulletin board in front of the town hall, in the little shelter at the bus stop, on telephone poles and electrical boxes and over the logo of an American fast-food chain on the only advertising poster in Königsdorf, across from the only supermarket, until the community of Königsdorf, in the person of a man in a beige-green uniform, whom everyone referred to simply as the Village Fuzz, forbade him to paste them up on public property, on pain of a "hot ear." For three long years, while staying with Fred, he answered every knock at the front door and ring of the telephone with hard-to-quash hopes for a female voice, a euphoric hug, and, naturally, red hair. And for three long years, people came forward—people who, in Albert's opinion, must be suffering from dyslexia or attention deficit disorder, because they would solemnly proclaim to him that they certainly knew the man in the photograph: he was the invalid from the '77 bus accident.

And so, over time, *nobody* and *nothing* became things to be taken seriously.

One late-summer morning, the morning on which, a few months after his seventeenth birthday, he'd shaved for the first time, after another fruitless six-and-a-half-week summer holiday, Albert sat in the second row of pews for morning Mass, his head lowered, his chin against his chest, his hands folded, and as the prayers dropped from his mouth, wished for the first time that he'd never found the photo. What was it, anyway? A two-dimensional, possibly factitious, and in any case ambiguous reproduction of reality, the mere assertion of a time that Albert understood only hazily. He remembered what Klondi had told him three years before—that he would find nothing. She'd called him a fourteen-year-old simpleton, and advised him to let the picture be, to let the case drop. That's just what life was, she'd meant: a heap of puzzle pieces that never added up to one great whole, but merely filled you with false hope, because they let you believe that something like an answer—the truth!—existed out there, somewhere. Her last words rang in his head: "Those damned puzzle pieces," she'd said, "are nothing but Hansel and Gretel crumbs."

Where the Gold Comes From

Albert mulled over all of this, that night he spent sleepless in the BMW, and it left him, when morning came, with a feeling of helplessness. The fact that *capitulation* was part of *recapitulation,* he thought, seemed entirely appropriate.

On the other side of the windshield a dark blue was already mixing with the black, and the first birdsong heralded dawn. Albert pressed "eject," and with a whirring sound the tape struggled from the slot. In the past, the two of them had sat here listening to the adventures of Benjamin Blümchen, the only talking elephant in the world. For a while, Fred had been entirely intent on the episode in which the elephant believed that acting meant you were lying. He'd replayed it again and again, ten times a day. Until Albert simply couldn't help himself any longer, and threw the thing away. He could do precisely the same with Fred's lump of gold and the cassette, he thought—then he wouldn't have to waste any more thought on these Hansel and Gretel crumbs. He plunked the tape back into the box and reached for Fred's nugget, marveling again at the weight of that little stone.

"All right, then," he said.

Early that afternoon, Albert called Fred for lunch in the kitchen.

Within seconds the door sprang open. Fred was wearing his diving goggles, though outside the sun was shining. Usually Fred put them on when he stood by the bus stop in the rain. They'd belonged to his father. Sometimes Albert filled the bathtub with cold water, poured a packet of salt into it, and declared: "Voilà! The Pacific!" Upon which Fred would leap with his goggles into the water, slosh around like an inebriated frog, and complain if the brine went up his nose.

Albert had cooked up some scrambled eggs with tomato. Fred pushed the tomatoes to the edge of the plate because "they didn't taste good at all," and Albert said, "Eat your tomatoes," and Fred devoured all of the egg, but not the tomatoes, and Albert repeated, "Eat your tomatoes," and Fred quickly rinsed off his plate, and Albert warned, "You aren't getting any bread and honey," but Fred swore that next time he'd eat "the healthy tomatoes," at which point Albert did, in fact, smear some honey on the bread for him, while attempting to ignore Fred's whispered self-praise: "That was a good trick."

Albert's best trick was mixing Fred's medication into his food, without Fred noticing.

After the meal, Albert set the gold on the kitchen table. "Today I went to a jeweler in Wolfratshausen, who said we have almost enough here to buy a small house."

"I already have a house."

"Frederick, you're going to tell me where you got this right now."

"I found it," grumbled Fred, fumbling with the clasp on the goggles.

"Where?"

A mulish stare.

"Sometimes I feel like a schoolmaster," Albert said, sighing.

Fred shook his head. "But you're Albert."

"Nothing else?"

"That's plenty!"

Plenty was rarely so little, thought Albert, pouring himself a glass of milk and drinking it down.

"Albert!" Fred drew the cassette from the tin box, which Albert had set beside the sink. "You have a cassette, too!" His grin twitched. "A totally similar cassette."

Albert emptied his glass so hastily that milk ran over his chin. "That's *your* cassette."

Fred held his breath. Silence. Then his grin returned: "You couldn't sleep, Albert?"

"How did you know?"

"That tape makes an ambrosial noise, like water. And Mama said you always sleep best by the water."

"Where did you get the tape?"

Fred bit his lips.

"Did somebody give it to you?"

"No."

"Let me guess: you found it."

"Yes."

Albert rolled his eyes. "Where did you find it?"

This time Fred licked his lips like a contestant on a quiz show, confident of his answer, and even before he replied, Albert knew what that answer would be.

"The same place the gold came from!"

"Oh, *there*," said Albert, and set the glass down so heavily that the sound of it shocked even him. "Listen, Frederick, this is very important to me. I absolutely *have* to know."

"It's dangerous."

"*What's* dangerous?"

"Everything!"

Albert thought for a moment. "And what if we keep an eye out for each other? I take care of you, and you take care of me. Wouldn't that be better? Wouldn't that be less dangerous?"

Fred looked thoughtfully at the gold.

"The two of us on a quest for gold," said Albert, sensing that this was his chance. "That would certainly be something."

"It's dangerous," Fred softly repeated.

"Would it be a long trip?" asked Albert.

Fred wobbled his head. "It's deep."

"What does *that* mean?"

"It's a long way below us."

"Well, that much I understood."

"Then why did you ask?"

"Because . . . forget it," said Albert. His gaze fell on the *HA* scratched into the kitchen window, and he fought down the urgent desire to hurl something through it. Trying to hold a conversation with Fred, one that actually amounted to anything, was the most terrible, Sisyphean labor he knew.

He was about to flee the kitchen, in order to smoke a cigarette somewhere in secret, when Fred said, "You'll have to dress yourself really well, though."

Albert stood still. "Does that mean you're actually going to show me?"

"It's going to be soaking wet," warned Fred. "From below *and* above!"

Albert nearly embraced Fred in relief, but held himself back, examining him. As always, Fred's face wore an expression of childishly self-important seriousness, yet if Albert wasn't mistaken, he could detect behind it an air of genuine worry, one so perturbing that he quickly looked away, and said, "Let's go."

＊

PART II

Siblings
1912–1924

The Sacrificial Festival

On a hot August night at the height of the summer of 1912, the village of Segendorf celebrated its three-hundred eighty-sixth Sacrificial Festival.

Three hundred and eighty-seven years earlier, a wandering monk, expelled from his monastery, had paused for a rest at the highest point of the very same hill. He'd dozed off in the shade of a little grove of spruce trees. God had appeared to the monk in his dream, demanding he prove his devotion to his creator by sacrificing his Most Beloved Possession. A princely reward awaited him. So it happened that, after awakening, the desperate monk, banished to this thinly populated region of the alpine foothills, approached the rocky bluff on the south side of the hill, drew out a bronze chalice (which he'd purloined from his former monastery as compensation, so to speak, for his exile), and, after a brief hesitation, allowed it to tumble down into the abyss. He waited. For a sign. Waited. And doubted. Then, at last, a delicate, tinny pling came echoing up over the lip of the cliff. There should have been a plong, bronze against stone, a plong, absolutely— but instead, there followed a pling-pling. It was mocking him, that pling-pling, calling: Come look for me! Come on down! Come to me! And the monk heeded its call.

Down below, gleaming metal ran like a jagged scar through the stone. The monk caressed every inch of it, as if he were kissing the Holy Father's Piscatory Ring. The newly uncovered vein of gold considerably eased his ascent from destitute drifter to bishop. He consecrated the spot, calling it Segenhügel, the Blessed Hill; and soon, thanks to the exploitation of its gold deposits, the village of Segendorf sprang up nearby. Before it had time to develop into a thriving community, however, Segendorf began to wither. On the one hand, the mine petered out within months; on the other, the landscape itself significantly contributed to the settlement's ruin. Hereabouts there was little but fields scattered with scarlet corn poppies; the Moorbach, a piddling tributary that wound its way around the Segenhügel; lean game; and hostile grasses that sliced at your hands if you tried to pluck them. When the villagers decamped, the old, the sick, and the idiotic were left behind. Along with the tradition. At first the remaining Segendorfers celebrated the discovery of the gold mine each summer by flinging their Most Beloved Possessions over the edge of the cliff. But as too many animal cadavers had begun to pile up at the foot of the hill, contaminating the drinking water, they decided instead to kindle a sacrificial bonfire each year on the market square, so as to celebrate the ritual in a more civilized fashion.

Back then the population of Segendorf numbered no more than three hundred souls. Of course, there were barns and cowsheds and cesspits, the cobbler right next to the general store, the butcher just behind, and the smithy not much farther off; of course, Segendorf had a moor to the east and the west, and the sheer rock walls of the Alps to the south, and to the north, the sole road that led into the village (and ended there as well); and, of course, just beyond the town limits there was Wolf Hill, atop which an oak tree spread its limbs, and beneath which local women were knocked up every year when spring rolled around. But for anyone who took the map as gospel, Segendorf didn't exist at all. The place had barely changed since its founding. Light was still generated with sulfur matchsticks, candles, or torches, the people still scrubbed their clothes in the Moorbach, and the next parish was a ten-day march away. The residents first heard about World War I only after it had been lost.

In 1912 all the villagers gathered in the market square, as they did every year, formed a spiraling line, and, one by one, hurled something dear to their hearts onto the flaming pyre of high-piled brushwood. The flames swallowed them noisily, rewarding those assembled with warmth and light.

That same night, in the granary—Segendorf's largest structure, after the church—a secret was conceived. Among sacks bursting with oats, wheat, poppy seeds, and barley, sacks that in the gloom resembled limbless torsos, fourteen-year-old Josfer Habom explored the body of his sister, Jasfe, with his lips; and although both felt unbearably hot, they trembled as if there were a killing frost.

44

It was said that no Segendorfer could compete with my parents' beauty. So tantalizing was Jasfe's glance, so striking Josfer's dimpled chin, that the pair were never invited to weddings, lest the bride or groom begin to have second thoughts about the business at hand.

Anne-Marie Habom, my grandmother, had died giving birth to the twins, and my grandfather Nick Habom, one of Segendorf's numerous hunters, and a considerably unattractive man, concerned himself only with putting enough food on the table and making sure that the two had a warm bed to sleep in. He never said more than was absolutely necessary. He was respected for that. In spite of his dwarfish stature, Nick was a man who loomed large in people's memories. Many maintained that the vertical crease between his eyebrows divided not merely his forehead but also the compartments into which he sorted mankind: those whom he liked—and the rest, among whom he numbered his children. Just recently, he'd broken Josfer's nose because the latter's hand had slid between his sister's thighs while they were bathing—"Don't put your hands on each other!" he'd bellowed. Since then, Josfer's beauty had been marred. But Nick's harshness drove the two children even closer together. Though they didn't dare oppose him openly, and kept their hands to themselves, as he had ordered them to do, they nevertheless took advantage of every minute they were alone to secretly rub their pale bodies against each other. Until they were crimson.

On the night of the three-hundred eighty-sixth Sacrificial Festival, the pair stole away and raced to the granary. Sneezing, they undressed themselves in the dusty air, tied their hands together behind their backs, and fondled each other with their feet, caressed each other with their noses, kindled each other with their tongues. They smelled sweetly of elderberries, and holy water, and down pillows aired in the west wind.

The next morning Jasfe was seized with elation. While outside a warm wind scattered the ashes of the Most Beloved Possessions that lay charred in the market square, spinning gray-black dust devils through vegetable gardens, inflaming eyes and coating windowpanes with sooty muck, she *felt a pleasurable tingling beneath her belly button that grew stronger and refused to fade, as if Josfer were still kissing that spot, and would be forever.*

In the months that followed, Jasfe concealed her swelling belly from curious eyes. Her dread of her father was surpassed only by the fear that she might give birth to a Klöble.

When it came to begetting children, Segendorfers weren't always choosy. It frequently happened that somebody's brother was also his cousin, or somebody's daughter also her sister. Quite a few local families had produced a "Klöble"—a "clumsy, stupid fellow." Mothers of such children were spat upon. They were accused of having no pride, of having seduced their own fathers, sons, brothers, because—hideous, impudent, and slothful as they were—no other man would take them. Klöbles were known for chewing sorrel all day long, fiddling with themselves shamelessly in public, and playing patty-cake with cow dung. They also argued passionately among themselves about whether God existed, somebody none of them had ever seen; and about why nobody believed in them, the Klöbles, although they were easily visible. And whether, perhaps, they wouldn't be visible any longer, once people started believing in them. The incest had another side effect, though—it helped Segendorf remain hidden behind a wall that had never been built: anyone who wanted to could have seen and entered the town. But nobody from elsewhere wanted to see it. Much less enter it.

In spite of her fear of having a Klöble, Jasfe would, of course, still love such a child; that's what she told herself, and what Josfer told her—but a perfectly healthy child would be easier to love.

For five long months she wore a shawl wrapped tightly as a corset around her belly, and endured the pain. Only then did she decide to confess the pregnancy to their father. She searched carefully for the appropriate words, weighing one sentence after another for days, until she saw that the right moment had come.

While Josfer checked the toad traps in the swamp, Jasfe sat down beside Nick on the wooden bench in front of their house. In the evening light her father picked filth from beneath his nails with a hunting knife, and whistled a melancholy tune. Jasfe gathered her courage and spoke her first sentence. She spoke her second sentence. She spoke her third and fourth and fifth sentences. And after she'd spoken her last sentence, she waited. Calmly, Nick laid the knife down beside him, pressed his lips together, drew a deep breath, and grabbed her by the neck. Only then could she see the minuscule tears slipping down his face. Silently he increased the pressure. Black spots flecked her vision, multiplied, melted together, and she tumbled into a lightless void.

When she came to, she was lying alone in the mud by the wooden bench. And later that evening, she was unable to hide from her brother the pale purple bruises on her throat.

From the next hunting trip with his father, only Josfer returned.

Nick was never found, and the twins never spoke about what had happened out on the moor. It was said in the village that Nick had been smothered by quicksand, and because he'd been unpopular in Segendorf, nobody asked any questions.

From then on, my parents shared a bed every night. Soon they couldn't sleep unless they were lying naked beside one another, each with a hand resting on the other's sex. Their hands were comforting shields—intimate, impermeable.

Klöble

I came into the world on a rainy day in May 1913. For a long time my parents couldn't agree on a name, so they finally chose one that reminded them of their own: Julius. At my birth I emitted only a single scream, prolonged and furious. Then I piped down, struggling for a while in silence, waving my arms. The midwife worried I might suffocate—she didn't understand that I was merely underwhelmed by the world into which I'd been hatched.

Three years later, at the birth of my sister, Anni, who was christened with the name of her grandmother, the screaming was shrill and continued for hours on end, until Anni, alongside our equally exhausted parents, at last fell asleep.

Even as a child my high forehead was flat, and my eyes lay too deep in their sockets for my taste, but my mother said they had a tantalizing glitter that made people want to grab them; my mouth was a little too small, my nose a little too wide, and my ears stood out just enough for people to smile but not laugh at them.

The fact that I was Anni's brother would have escaped even a careful observer; our differences were more conspicuous than our similarities. Anni's skin was as pale as mine was only on those spots that the light never touched. The curls of her hair, which reached all the way to her elbows, seemed wholly unmanageable, and the crown of her head rose no farther than my chin. Her mouth was bracketed, halfway to her earlobes, by a pair of dimples, which stubbornly persisted even when she wasn't grinning or laughing, and the sight of her lips often reminded me of the words of Cobbler Gaiger, who in addition to footwear also produced remarkably sturdy fishing rods: "They're as round as a fish's."

Everyone in Segendorf, apart from the Klöbles, had a clear idea of who'd fathered Anni and me, but our parents didn't care that they were always the last ones served at the tavern, or given the leanest sausage at the butcher's. And for two good reasons: neither Anni nor I was a Klöble.

So we grew up surrounded by the suspicion and malice of our peers, whose parents had filled them with grotesque, but essentially true, stories about Jasfe and Josfer. While we were in the crib, they'd pinch our bellies when our parents weren't looking; as we took our first steps, they'd trip us, or push us into the mud; as we learned to lace our dirndls or button our shirts, the scornful, mistrustful looks of other mothers, mimicked by their children, nipped in the bud any hope of playing a single round of Fangamandl; and once we'd reached the age when we blushed if anyone saw us bathing in the Moorbach, people would steal our underwear. It didn't take long for us to resign ourselves to our fate, the two of us exploring the cliff on our own to look for gold, running races together on a bet to the oak on Wolf Hill, or playing who-can-fill-the-cup-with-spit-first?

Yet sometimes I was, in fact, alone.

One summer evening I was gathering brushwood in a forest clearing when a pine- or sprucecone (I couldn't tell them apart) struck me on the head. Above me the sky glowed an ominous pink. Five snickering boys came toward me through the bushes, their pockets bulging with pine- (or spruce-) cones.

"Heya, we just want to play," shouted the smallest of them; his name was Markus, and his father ran a pig farm.

"I have to go home," I said.

"You never want to play with us!" cried Markus.

The last time they'd played with me, they had stuffed my pants with stinging nettles. I said I was going now, and even as I did, I felt angry that my words sounded like an apology.

Markus was juggling a pair of cones. "We're going to play 'hunting' now. We're the hunters, get it? And you, you're a wild boar."

I clutched the brushwood to my chest, lowered my head, and ran. Three cones missed me by a hairbreadth, a fourth hit me on the neck. I dropped the wood. From behind me: jeering, screaming, clattering. As long as I kept up my pace, I could outdistance them, I thought, simply keep running, leaping, sidestepping. Trees sprang up in my path, branches threw themselves at my feet, sunbeams blinded me—but I didn't stumble. The voices and noises remained behind me. I threw a glance back over my shoulder, and couldn't make out any movement. My throat burned, snot ran from my nose. I listened to the forest: only the cries of ravens and the sighing wind. I took a step back, tripped on a root, and toppled over. A bed of moss cushioned my fall. Once I'd wiped the mud from my pants, I looked up. Markus was standing over me, offering his hand. "Heya. Need help?"

They shoved and dragged me to a deer stand where I sometimes climbed with my father when he was hunting. While the others held me down, Markus tied a rope around my ankles. They threw the line over one of the deer stand's beams, and hauled on it together until I was suspended upside down. Only then did I notice the bowl they'd set on the ground beneath me, from which there arose a revolting stink. Sewage sloshed against the rim.

"Dinnertime, Klöble!" shouted Markus.

Then they let go of the rope.

Z as in Zwiebel

Weeks later, as Anni and I were collecting dust in a beer stein, out of which, with the help of a little wind and water, we intended to whip up a raincloud, we discovered a cookbook hidden in a fruit crate. It had once belonged to a cook's apprentice from Franconia, who'd ventured into the swamp in search of escargots. He clearly hadn't known that it was considered the sacred right of every Segendorfer to relieve any vagrant who set foot on their property of all—and particularly the most beloved—of his possessions.

Anni and I carried the cookbook into the kitchen and flipped carefully through it, handling each page as if it were a butterfly's wing. Anni wanted Jasfe to read it to her, but our mother couldn't tell an A from a B any more than Josfer could. In Segendorf, no one but Pastor Meier could read or write. I tucked the book away till later in the evening, then studied it by moonlight. I considered myself cleverer than others my age. And I was, too. All day long I struggled to teach myself the alphabet. The pictures revealed to me most of the sounds—B as in Bread, P as in Potato, and S as in Salt. It turned out that only a few of the ingredients were unknown to me, yet Pastor

Meier explained what I couldn't puzzle out for myself, and when I finally arrived at Z as in Zwiebel—onion—I laid the cookbook in Anni's lap.

"Flip it open and pick a word," I said.

"This one," she said, tapping a little cluster of letters surrounded by an overwhelming throng of words.

"M-e-a-t-l-o-a-f," I spelled out, and then pronounced: "Meeetloooooooaf."

"You can read! You can read!" screamed Anni, leaping up and running to our parents. "He can read! He can read!" she cried again, and dragged Jasfe and Josfer back to me. Deep into the night I read them one word after another: "Veeeeeeeeniiiiisooon" and "Eeemmeeentaaaleeer" and "Caaaaaroooots" and "Tiiiiimm, no, thhyyyyymmme." It became a game, the favorite game in the Habom household. After every evening meal I would sit on one side of the table, Anni, Jasfe, and Josfer on the other, and teach them the alphabet. Anni learned to read the recipes markedly faster than our parents, and Jasfe faster than Josfer. But I learned faster than all of them. As time passed I succeeded in reproducing whole sentences without a single error: "Mix ingredients into a loose dough, let rise, then knead." Or: "Prop the oven door open slightly with the help of a wooden spoon, to allow the humidity to escape." And my favorite of all, because of the fascination produced by the list of ingredients I couldn't understand: "Stir in the finely diced candied orange and lemon zest."

As soon as Anni had any difficulty spelling out a word, she'd fix her impatient eyes on me. That look! Even back then I wasn't good at refusing her anything, and whispered the answer to her every time.

Ridiculous Twaddle

On the afternoon of my ninth birthday, I stood immersed to my knees in the Moorbach, soaping myself up, scrubbing myself down. My body was cold, but since my thoughts were back at home, I didn't feel it. Jasfe had baked a poppy-seed cake for me, and Josfer had been working for days in his workshop. (I had my fingers crossed for a hunting bow.)

I closed my eyes to wash my face, and when I opened them again Markus was sitting on the bank before me. He was alone, and greeted me with a friendly nod; beside him lay a wooden crate, which suddenly began to shake. Markus pushed the lid aside. Amid a litter of straw and rotten vegetables, two rats were mating. "Heya," he said. "Know what they're doing?"

I rolled my eyes. "Making babies?"

"Good! You aren't so dumb after all." Markus slapped me on the back. "But I'll bet you didn't know that they're brother and sister, did you?"

I slipped into my pants. "They're just rats."

Markus closed the crate and shook it hard. "Yep. Rats." Then he threw it into the river. Bubbles streamed from between the slats. "I call them Jasfe and Josfer."

"You idiot."

"Why? They're definitely brother and sister."

The bubbles from the crate grew smaller and smaller; I wanted to pull it from the water. "My parents aren't."

Markus put a foot on the crate. "Everyone knows they are."

"Liar."

Now Markus stood on the crate. "I couldn't care less if you believe it, Klöble."

"I'm completely normal!" I shouted, louder than I'd intended, scooped up the rest of my clothes, and made off.

I didn't see the final bubbles rising from the crate.

Jasfe and Josfer and Anni started singing a birthday song when I opened the front door of our house—and broke off as soon as they saw a half-naked boy with wet cheeks and reddened eyes. I was wrapped up in a blanket, stroked and kissed, and asked what had happened. All by itself, my voice grew higher and higher, faster and faster, as I told them about Markus, the rats and the bubbles and the Klöbles—the Klöbles above all.

My parents exchanged a troubled look, shook their heads, and said, as if with a single voice, "Children are cruel."

"Markus told me you're brother and sister."

"Twaddle," said Josfer.

And Jasfe: "Ridiculous twaddle."

After that, the poppy-seed cake tasted so sweet, the hunting bow felt so smooth and strong in my hands, the songs so merrily sung gave my heart such a lift, that I fell into bed late that evening at peace and exhausted, and drifted off to sleep with nary a thought of Klöbles.

So as to have some time to themselves, Josfer and Jasfe occasionally sent us off to fetch fresh milk, or to hunt for mushrooms. One time they told us to go to church and say ten Hail Marys. I begged Anni to say my Hail Marys in my stead because, as I explained to her, I'd rather go and read. The truth was, I always felt like I was being watched in church—even a whisper would swell to a telltale murmur if you weren't careful, and anyway, I couldn't see why a prayer had to be repeated so many times. Certainly even God must get bored with it. Back at home, I slipped unnoticed through the parlor, overheard my parents' heavy gasps, followed them, rounded the green-tiled oven, and, just as Jasfe and Josfer cried out, saw them.

It wasn't the first time I'd witnessed it. Before they noticed me, I slipped back to the front door, opened it, and slammed it loudly shut again.

When I walked back into the parlor they'd pulled their clothes on again, and everything was where it belonged.

Jasfe cleared her throat. "Hungry?"

I nodded, as though nothing were the matter.

After Anni had returned from church and everyone had sat down at the table, Josfer and I gulped down our food. Jasfe took barely a bite. She eyed the blade of her knife, lost in thought. Anni entertained the table with a description of the beautiful stained-glass window in the church, and mentioned, by the way, that for her birthday she wanted one just like it for her bedroom.

After the last mouthful, Jasfe asked everyone to follow her outside. It was dark, and candle flames flickered like will-o'-the-wisps behind the windows of neighboring houses. Anni sat herself down between Josfer and me on the wooden bench. Jasfe remained standing. She kissed Anni and me, and folded her hands. Gently, she spoke one word after another. Carefully set one sentence after the other. With brief pauses between them. So that we'd be able follow her little speech. So that we'd have time to understand. So that we wouldn't think anything bad. She wanted to formulate sentences better than those she'd set before her father. Perfect sentences. Accurate. And true.

"Really?" cried Anni. "You, too?"

I stood up. "Brother and sister?" I said. "Ridiculous twaddle!"

Jasfe nodded. "I know." Her chin shook. "My two beautiful, healthy children." She wanted to hug me. I pushed her away and she fell. Josfer grabbed me by the arm. I tore myself away, and slammed into the back of the bench, splitting the skin of my elbow, and I ran to my room, shutting the door.

Later that night, when quiet had fallen on the house, I stole out to the kitchen and took the last piece of poppy-seed cake. On the way back, I pressed my ear to the door of my parents' bedroom. The rustling of their sheets, amused chuckles, whispers, hurried stop-start breaths—the sounds penetrated the wood and filled my imagination with pictures. I wanted to let the cake fall to the floor, wanted to fling the door open and scream, "Do you know that they call you? Rats! Filthy rats!"

But I didn't move. I stared at the closed door, polished off the cake. And with every bite, I swallowed my rage.

From then on, for all my parents' soft-spoken confessions, for all their sincere but irritating devotion, for all their exaggerated indulgence of my malicious commentary or loafing, I had only one answer: "Leave me alone."

Apart from that, I didn't speak a word.

I Love You

When we sat together at the table eating dinner, when the fire crackled in the oven, the soup burbled in the pot, the beams creaked, when the smell of fried potatoes and ham and apple cider and wild garlic filled the room, when Jasfe admitted to some foolishness or other and everyone laughed— even me, almost—when I felt so comfortable, and thought that Jasfe was just my mama and Josfer just my papa and Anni just my sister and I just her brother, on those evenings when I felt so much love for them all that I wanted to scream, I would scratch at the wound on my elbow beneath the table, tear the scab away, and dig with my fingernails into the skin, until at last the arm went numb, numb and dead.

When at age ten I threw my Most Beloved Possession, a pillow, full of holes and stinking of onions, into the sacrificial bonfire, I observed how Josfer took a wooden comb from Jasfe, and in spite of her tears, hurled it onto the heap of brushwood, together with his best hunting knife. As always, a good many Segendorfers wept on the way home, but Jasfe more than any of them.

"Where's Herr Kastanie?" Anni asked, whining like any six-and-a-half-year-old who didn't want to admit what had happened to her favorite toy, a little man cobbled together from twigs and chestnuts.

"Jasfe," said Josfer, "you never used that comb."

She shook her head. "It belonged to our mother!"

The sight of her pain triggered something in me. Over the next few days various articles vanished from the kitchen and the hunting shack, including a cooking spoon, shoelaces, an apron, a leather strap, a clay bowl with salt in it, a piece of chalk, a bucket, and last but not least, a rabbit's foot. Neither Josfer nor Jasfe blamed me. Which only encouraged me to steal more, hacking the stolen items into pieces when necessary and scattering them under the firewood in the hearth. Only Anni's things I left in peace.

It was as if a door in my head, previously hidden, had suddenly sprung open, a door through which a hot wind blew. I burned a bouquet of wild-flowers picked by Jasfe, and I burned Josfer's hammer. (The hammer's head I buried in the swamp.) I spared neither Josfer's dagger nor Jasfe's doily, which covered the table between mealtimes. Once I even stretched my arm into the fire, and let the fuzz of bright blond hairs coating it singe. I wanted to see my parents weep, I wanted to make them unhappy, as unhappy as I'd been, struggling for air in that bowl of sewage.

Yet nobody took me to task for it. In the summer of 1924, Josfer sat on a sawed-off tree trunk during meals because he hadn't had time to build a new chair, my parents' bed was missing all four of its legs, and Jasfe was constantly having to sew herself new knickers.

On the day of the Sacrificial Festival, I was uncertain which Most Beloved Possession I should single out—my one-year-old pillow (which stank just as powerfully of onions as the one from the year before) or a box of matches—when they called me into the parlor.

"Have you decided?" asked Josfer.

"Leave me alone," I said.

Jasfe brought me to the door. Anni was waiting outside, absentmind-edly rocking Frau Puppe, the first doll she'd sewn together herself.

Jasfe pressed a torch into my hand. "You know what you have to do." She stepped back into the house and locked the door behind her.

"We know who burned all of our things!" called Josfer through the door.

"Leave me alone!" I shouted back.

"Today is the Sacrificial Festival. Today you're allowed to burn what-ever you want. So go ahead! Burn the house!"

"But . . . but you're still inside."

"Someone remembers how to speak!"

"Leave me alone," I said.

"Don't you love us, Julius?"

"That's our house!"

"I'll burn it, I love you!" cried Anni, to whom no one was listening.

"Julius, those were our things that you threw in the fire."

"But that was different!"

"Aren't you brave enough?"

"I don't want to do it!"

"I love you. I'll do it," said Anni softly, as I screamed, "I'm not going to do it! I hate you!"

My vision was so blurry with crying that I couldn't tell Jasfe from Josfer when they stood beside me again, lifted me up and embraced me, kissed me.

"We love you," they whispered. "We love you."

"Me, too," said Anni. "Me, too."

After the Sacrificial Festival everyone went to bed early. I couldn't sleep, I thought about how I should have answered my parents, how I wished I'd answered them, and how good it would have felt to say those words. I slipped from the house, walked to the Moorbach, and hung my feet in the water. I plucked marsh marigolds, threw them into the current, and asked myself where their journey would take them. I cleared my throat, and said, "I love you."

Maybe that didn't sound perfect—but then, what did sound perfect? On the way home I imagined how my parents' faces would look when they heard me speak—first sleepy, then befuddled, and a moment later, happy—and had to smile. As I looked up at the night sky above the village, it seemed to me that this year the sacrificial bonfire was sending up a brighter glow than usual. But it wasn't the festival. A house was burning. Our house was burning. Josfer and Jasfe's house, and Anni's, and mine. I ran toward it. The heat struck me in the face, and I flinched back. The fire had reached the second floor. There were no screams, I listened closely, I knew that in Segendorf people screamed at the slightest opportunity, but in my ears there was only a rumbling like that of a gigantic cooking pot on the boil, the fire whispering and hissing in a particularly hateful language. And I saw and I saw and I saw the flames dance through the rooms.

Somebody tugged at my sleeve. Anni. She looked at me anxiously, clutching a torch in both hands.

"I love them," she said.

✳

PART III

You Are My Mother

Good at These Things

They set out right after lunch. Albert had trouble keeping up with Fred, who settled immediately into a brisk stride. As always when he left the house, Fred was wrapped in his royal blue poncho, which fluttered behind him like a cape as he walked and intensified his already imposing appearance. His tufted Tyrolean hat sat askew on his head. His bulky, sagging backpack, which suggested a cargo of junk, the encyclopedia doubtless among it, didn't appear to be hindering him. Albert, on the other hand, had allowed himself to be persuaded into wearing a plastic raincoat, and was now sweating freely beneath a flawless blue sky.

In a decidedly unsporty tote bag Albert was carrying a few slices of buttered bread, a Tupperware container filled with bananas, a few peeled carrots, a bottle of apple spritzer, Fred's medication, and a pack of cigarettes. And in his hip pocket, the makeup compact.

After they'd followed the main street a ways, they curved to the right down Ludwigstrasse, a narrow side street littered with dried cow patties, where at the age of eight Albert had taught Fred to ride his bicycle without training wheels. Albert had run back and forth beside him, pushing him along, encouraging him, nursing his skinned knees after each tumble, and wiping away his tears, until finally, during the May school holidays, Fred had rolled his first few feet sans training wheels, the wind blowing into his proud, radiant face.

Fred paused beside a garden fence, stretched his arm over the wire, and waited. A white-and-brown-mottled foal broke from the shadow of an arborvitae hedge, trotted closer, and lifted its head so that Fred could stroke it between the ears. Albert watched as Fred tickled it, said hello, and asked how its day was going. He got the impression it enjoyed Fred's company—it whinnied, as if at any moment it might break out into unceremonious chatter.

Fred waved him closer. "Gertrude? This is Albert."

"Gertrude?" Albert took a step toward them, and the horse flinched.

"It's okay," Fred said to the foal, which was holding itself just out of reach. Albert wasn't surprised; he tended to have this sort of effect on animals. Presumably they were able to sense that he still couldn't grasp why most people had more pity for a stray cat than for a vagrant on the subway.

Albert cleared his throat. "Let's get going."

"Can't we stay for a minute?"

"No."

"But Gertrude—"

"No!" said Albert, louder than he'd intended. He really wasn't in the mood for a petting zoo.

Fred pulled him aside. "When I'm dead, you have to come see Gertrude every day," he whispered.

Albert hadn't expected that; wiping the sweat from his forehead, he said, "I'm not good at these things."

Fred clapped him on the shoulder. "It won't take you long to learn."

Then he said his good-byes to the foal. Fred had never mentioned Gertrude after returning from his rambles through Königsdorf, thought Albert; and if Fred didn't mention something, it usually meant he'd been up to no good.

Fred interrupted Albert's train of thought when he came to a halt in the middle of the street. "We're there."

Albert glanced around. Farm plots stretched away on either side. The sun stung them. Flies traced rectangles above dried cow dung.

Fred drew a crowbar from his backpack, kneeled, and began struggling to slip its end under the manhole cover.

"What are you doing? Stop it!" shouted Albert.

Fred turned to look at him, and with an aggrieved bass note the cover slid back into its recess. "We have to go down there."

"What if someone sees us? What if a car comes along?"

Fred glanced at both ends of the street. "There's no car coming."

"Look, that's not the point. We can't just climb down into the sewer."

"Why?"

"Because . . ." Albert thought for a moment. "Because it isn't allowed." He took the crowbar from Fred. "And you should ask me before you play around with something like that. You could hurt yourself."

"But you told me I have to show you where the gold comes from!"

"From down there?"

Frenzied nodding of the head. "Can I have the crowbar?"

Albert pointed to the manhole cover. "Seriously—down *there?*"

"I need the crowbar now," said Fred.

"Isn't there any other way?"

With a single motion Fred was up on his feet, towering over Albert, grabbing the hand in which he held the bar. At first, Albert didn't feel anything, he tried to pull his hand away, but it was held fast, and he struggled in vain to loosen Fred's grip with the other. *"Let. Go."* The pressure increased, it felt as if Fred were driving Albert's fingers right into the crowbar's iron. Fred's hat had slid forward, hiding his eyes, his lips silently opened and closed. The pain fused with a numbness that wandered up along Albert's arm. Just before it reached his elbow, he pushed himself backward with all his strength. "Fred, stop it!" he shouted, and Fred finally let go. Albert stumbled backward. The crowbar landed next to his feet.

Albert picked up his tote bag and walked away.

Beside Gertrude's fence he examined his now dark-red hand, wiggling one finger after another. They didn't seem to be broken. "The joke of it," he shouted to the foal, "is that *I* worry about *his* health."

Gertrude actually neighed.

At age six, Albert had once called Fred a retard because he'd broken his He-Man figure while attempting to turn him back into Prince Adam. In response, Fred had aimed a kick at Albert and broken two of the latter's toes. While pretending to box, Fred had inadvertently given him plenty of shiners. Albert's body was long accustomed to little wounds and bruises.

Gertrude snuffled in the direction of his hand, which he was extending over the fence.

"What now?"

A glider was circling in the sky above them, making the usual glider noises, sounding like summer. Albert glanced around to see if Fred was following him. With his undamaged hand he lit a cigarette. Gertrude cropped with her teeth at a tuft of grass. Albert was hot—he pulled off the raincoat, tangling himself up in the process. The plastic didn't want to let him go. He tossed it away into one of the plots. For a while he stood doubtful in the street, trembling. He knew that, left on his own, Fred wouldn't budge from the spot. Once he'd spent two whole days sitting in the BMW without any food because of some fight that Albert could no longer remember the reason for, and who knows how long he would have kept waiting if Albert hadn't eventually given in. Fred was at least as stubborn as Albert, and precisely because he knew he had to go back and get him, he didn't want to. He flicked his cigarette to the curb.

Now Fred had managed to make Albert feel like a child.

The asphalt's heat drilled up through the soles of his shoes.

Albert sat down in the shadow of Gertrude's fence, closed his eyes, and imagined that Fred would come for him, just this once, that Fred would come and apologize, that they'd talk everything out, and laugh about it, and clap each other on the shoulders.

He was nineteen years old now, but as far as his wishes were concerned he still felt just like the three-year-old who'd stood on the steps of Saint Helena, arms defiantly crossed, refusing to set foot in his new home. Who'd countered all of Sister Alfonsa's rigorous pleading with "Bert won't." Whose granny—fully half of his known family—had just died. A stubborn child who'd spent his first night at the orphanage *in front* of the orphanage, curled up on a doormat stamped with the word

AMEN. Who'd been woken early in the morning by the tolling of the bells, and had immediately realized that Sister Alfonsa had spent the whole night there with him, just behind the door in the entrance hall. Who'd suddenly felt a tremendous hunger, and followed this new ersatz family member into the kitchen, where he'd been allowed to dunk a few rock-hard dinner rolls from the previous day into honeyed milk. A child who stopped calling himself Bert only when Sister Alfonsa threatened him with five hundred shoe tyings. A child whose mental capacities had not only earned him chess lessons but also allowed him to write, at age four and a half, in one of Fred's encyclopedias, when the latter, during a picnic, was weeping over Anni's death: *Downt be saad.* Who, while playing cops-and-robbers in the woods, for which purpose the orphans armed themselves with darts that they'd fling every which way with no restraint whatsoever, had incurred a scar the length of a matchstick at the left-hand corner of his mouth, a scar that could transform itself in the blink of an eye into a laugh line. And the only child in Saint Helena with a father who *couldn't* be a father, in contrast to the many parents who didn't want to be.

Thumper

When Albert came back, Fred was standing in exactly the same spot where he'd left him. Beside him was Tobi, a man of Albert's age, who was seldom seen standing still. One couldn't call what he did *moving,* exactly—it was more of a wriggling mated with a shuffling. The reeling of a land rat who suddenly finds himself shipboard.

Albert hid himself by the curb behind a Dumpster, which reeked sourly of discarded wine bottles.

Tobi was a well-known figure in the village, huge and vigorous, with an arrogant peasant haughtiness; he gave a quick, wheezy laugh, yet all he said was "Freddie." He said it eagerly, as if sure it would fluster its target. But Fred didn't move. Tobi's disappointment showed itself in a shuffling of the feet; they wanted to move on, no rest for them, that's what they were famous for. Whenever he was on the road in his milk truck, making his rounds from farm to farm in order to suck up the fresh milk with a hose like an elephant's trunk and deliver it to the creameries in the uplands, his feet jammed the pedal all the way to the floor. These impatient feet of his had made him the quickest, most cost-effective driver in eleven towns; their distaste for the brake pedal meant that the milk didn't slosh around, keeping it from going bad on the way. Today, however, Tobi's truck was nowhere to be seen.

His second "Freddie" had the same effect as the first, which is to say, none whatsoever. Tobi circled Fred, ran his hand across his freckled face, scratched his neck. The heat was getting to him. His feet writhed in their loafers as he stepped closer to Fred, clapped one hand to his pursed lips, and let out an ululation—"U-U-U!"—waited a moment, then repeated the whole operation: "U-U-U!"

Albert knew it was time for him to step in, he ought to go over and send Tobi home, clearly, directly, no two ways about it. "Go sleep it off, fella," something like that, and then, once Tobi had absented himself, Albert would take Fred by the hand, no, in his arms, and say he was sorry for leaving him alone so long and, most important, offer him some sort of reward for all the strain he'd suffered—for example, pancakes with raspberry jam.

And just at that moment, Fred raised his hand to his mouth, and went, "U-U-U!" Tobi nodded, his feet formed themselves into an arrow aimed in Fred's direction, and he replied, "U-U-U!" Now they took turns, and Albert closed his eyes and clutched the makeup compact in his pocket. To Albert, Fred's voice sounded euphoric, like that of a child who's unexpectedly come across a playmate.

But Tobi's strained laughter made Albert uneasy; he thought better of his impulse to rush over, for the time being. He was no match for Tobi.

Tobi slapped Fred in the face. Which didn't immediately stop the U-U-Us. They merely slowed for a moment, then took up their previous tempo again, a few halftones higher, clearly in hopes that this new friend had intended something other than the obvious by the gesture—a nice pat on the cheek, maybe. "U-U-U," went Fred, and Tobi's feet pointed at him again, and then came the second slap, right to the middle of Fred's face, and he fell silent. The Tyrolean hat sailed off his head. Fred's lips trembled, he mumbled something Albert couldn't make out, but which he supposed was an apology, because this last one had been, unmistakably, a slap, and anyone who gets hit in the face has clearly done something wrong, has been bad. Fred let his hands, his head, his shoulders sink, his whole body melt, and Tobi, whose feet were now merrily dancing, moving closer to each other with every step, slapped him again, this time with his left hand— pasted him so powerfully that Fred lurched sideways.

Ludwigstrasse was an unfrequented strip of tar in an isolated backwater. Where were the cars when you needed them? Albert was hoping Fred would resist, but he was also a little frightened of what would happen if he did. More than a little. Again he peeped around the corner of the Dumpster, and this time saw that Tobi, who had just swung for the fourth time, was waving his arm in the air like a schoolboy keen to give an answer. Tobi was looking straight at Albert. Just then Fred took a step toward Tobi, and stopped. The tip of Fred's nose was nearly grazing the truck driver's cheek, there was something almost conspiratorial about the way the two were standing. Fred whispered something that caused Tobi to lower his hand again. His feet had stopped moving. Relieved, Albert drew a deep breath, forced himself to let go of the makeup compact, and hoped Tobi would finally retreat.

"That's your dad," said Tobi to Albert, soberly.

To Albert, that *dad* sounded like *dead.*

"That's your dad," Tobi repeated, "isn't he?" Fred was half-hidden behind Tobi, whose loafers were pointing at Albert now.

Fred glanced back and forth at the two men, as if following the ball at a tennis match.

Though he didn't need to clear his throat, Albert did so anyway. "Get lost," he said. His injured hand throbbed in his pocket.

"It doesn't hurt at all," Fred said, and clutched his nose, which was dripping blood. He rubbed the red between his thumb and index finger, then displayed the hand, saying, "Look!"

Albert wanted to go to him.

Tobi stood in the way. "How long have you been squatting there?"

Albert could feel Fred's gaze on him, and turned to Tobi: "Can we talk?"

Tobi's feet were perking up again. "So why didn't you do any-thing? I mean, he's your dad. Hey, Freddie, this wonderful Albert of yours didn't do a thing." One of Tobi's feet was pointed at Albert, the other at Fred. "He must not care, Freddie. Guess you don't mat-ter to him."

"Of course I matter to Albert," said Fred sorely, and that disturbed Albert, because he should have said so himself.

"You think so?"

"Come on." Albert extended his hand to Fred. "Let's go."

Fred, whose blood was now running freely over his upper lip, didn't move.

Albert didn't know what to say.

"Albert?" Fred's nose was gushing.

But now a midnight-blue tractor had appeared on the road, and was bearing down on the trio at a good clip. Its approach shook Albert from his stupor. At once he was wide awake. As they stepped aside to let the tractor pass, he moved closer to Tobi, waited for the cover of the engine's noise, and then, once they were completely enveloped by it, spoke quickly but clearly and unmistakably, because he had only a couple of seconds. Fred, he said, was terminally ill, had no more than three months left, and if he, Tobias Gruber, the milk truck driver, wanted to be answerable for the premature death of Albert's severely disabled father, then he should simply carry on as before.

As he pronounced his last syllables, the tractor passed with a boy hugging the steering wheel, dragging behind it a wind as hot as the foehn, and the roar of the engine and crunching of gravel subsided.

At a mute command, Tobi's feet turned, and he walked away with the double-time pace of someone less than eager to display how much he wants to run.

"There's a lot of blood," said Fred, making a cup of his hand and holding it beneath his chin, without managing to catch even one drop.

"Lie down. On the grass." Albert gave him a handkerchief. "Hold it under your nose."

"Thank you, Albert."

"No. Thank *you*."

"Why?"

"Don't you know why he ran away?"

"Because he was afraid of you."

Albert moistened his shirtsleeve with saliva and began to wipe Fred's face. The fabric went pale pink. "No, of you."

"Of me?"

Albert nodded.

Fred smiled. "I am a hero after all." He coughed, flinching a bit, spitting blood. Fred's right eye was slightly swollen, his skin waxy.

"You have to lie down," said Albert.

"I'm already lying down."

"At home."

Fred sat up again. "We have to go down into the pipes, Albert!" Fred was looking at him seriously. "I want to do it today!"

Albert knew it was a dumb idea, but how could he turn down a request from someone who had only three months to live? "All right. But you have to tell me if you aren't feeling well. And if I want us to turn around, then we're turning around."

"Okay," groaned Fred.

Albert set Fred's Tyrolean hat back in place. "What did you say to him?"

"What did I say to him?"

"When Tobi hit you, you said something to him."

They stood up, gathered the tote bag and backpack.

Fred buttoned his poncho up to his chin. "I told him that he had feet like Thumper."

"Who?"

"Thumper, from *Bambi*."

"You mean the rabbit? Who does this the whole time?" Albert stamped his foot a few times as fast as he could.

"Just like that!"

Albert laughed.

"Was that wrong?" Fred asked.

"No, Fred, it was right on the mark." Albert adjusted his hat. "I'm sorry, I shouldn't have left you alone."

"That's right," said Fred, without making any effort not to sound reproachful.

"Frederick Arkadiusz Driajes," said Albert, reaching for the crowbar, "sometimes I ask myself who you really are."

Fred shrugged in an entirely Fredish way. "Me."

"You don't say," said Albert, slipping the bar beneath the manhole cover, and wrenching it out of its slot.

A minute later, they were both beneath the street.

Damn It All

They stood at the foot of the metal ladder, and Fred looked bewildered. Albert knew this was no cause for alarm. This expression, mouth hanging open as if in disbelief beneath reddened eyes, simply meant that Fred was thinking. And thinking, as Albert very much hoped, about which direction they should take. Thin columns of light fell through the holes in the manhole cover above them. To Albert's surprise, the sewer pipe had a rectangular shape. The humid air down there was difficult to breathe, a sort of oxygen porridge, and the story its stink told was highly unappetizing. Gleaming, glutinous water dripped and rippled down the walls, whose slick surfaces called to mind a reptilian skin. It emerged, this water, in a thin trickle out of the darkness behind them, vanishing again into the darkness before them.

"Well?" The reverb repeated Albert's question, imitating the acoustics of the rambling corridors at Saint Helena.

Fred pulled a flashlight from his backpack and flipped it on. "There."

They proceeded at a slog, because Fred was forever shining the flashlight up and down, back and forth, but scarcely ever in front of their feet.

"I think Tobi and his wife need to have a child," said Fred.

"Sure. He'd be a model father," Albert said.

"Klondi told me Tobi and his wife can't make a child."

"Since when do you talk with Klondi?"

"I talk with Gertrude, too."

"Klondi told you the guy can't have children?"

Fred paused. "Albert, do you think I can have children someday?"

"*You* want to have children?"

"Yes."

"Real children?"

All of a sudden, from out of the blackness ahead of them, a menacing roar was approaching, shaking droplets of water from the ceiling, making the sewer pipe quake. Albert pushed Fred aside, grabbed the flashlight, and aimed its beam into the dark. Then the noise was upon them. And then, just as quickly, behind them.

"A car," said Fred. "Sounded green."

Albert tugged at his ear. "Let's keep going." He held on to the flashlight, and for a while they proceeded at a steady splish-splash pace, whose echoes swelled and redoubled, like the massed footfalls of a tour group. Albert tried to breathe only through his mouth, and followed Fred without complaint.

He hoped in vain for a "Here!" or a "Finally!" from Fred whenever they hit a fork or junction. Why the hell did a little town in the alpine uplands have such an extensive network of sewer tunnels, anyway? He couldn't get used to that unsettling rumble of cars above them, any more than the irregular gurgling in the distance, the sound of fresh deliveries of that substance the word *sewer* always immediately calls to mind.

"Do you come down here often?" asked Albert.

"Yes."

"And what do you do?"

Fred snatched the flashlight away, and shot Albert a look as if he'd already explained it thousands of times: "I look for my dad."

"You know, he might not be down here," Albert ventured.

Fred blinded him with the light. "He *is* here."

Above them something ponderous set itself in motion, slowed down, then rolled on again. Albert thought, for some reason, of a wheel from the Stone Age.

"How do you know?"

Fred let the flashlight sink, and looked him in the eye. "Because the gold is his."

"Why didn't you tell me?"

"You didn't ask."

"So we're going to see him? Right now?"

"Almost exactly."

"What does that mean? Yes or no?"

"I'll show you."

"Damn it all—"

Albert's foot hit something slick, and slid: the sewer tunnel spun counterclockwise, and he crashed down on his back. When he opened his eyes again, his gaze fell first on a bundle of tightly bound cables on the tunnel's ceiling. Königsdorf's veins, he thought. Fred sat beside him, supporting his head.

"Are you weak?"

"No."

Fred raised his eyebrows, and Albert had to smile: "Okay, maybe a little."

The sweat stains beneath the arms of his shirt had merged with those on his back and at his throat. The dull ache in his shoulders heralded soreness, though the tote bag weighed only a fraction of what Fred's backpack weighed. Only a single drop of sweat pearled on Fred's cheek, then vanished into his beard. He'd managed to last for sixty years; now there were only three months left, and he was still overbearingly fit.

"Rest a minute," he said, almost fatherly. "I'll look for the way."

"Wait!"

"Don't worry, Albert." Fred smiled confidently. "I'm a hero after all."

Before Albert could contradict him, Fred was off.

Righter

A banana peel lay beside Albert in a pool of stagnant water, to one side of the sewer pipe. Albert sat on Fred's backpack, smoking while he waited. This was par for the course. Whether it was the next trip to

Königsdorf, some sign of life from his mother, his graduation exams, Fred, or death, Albert was always waiting for something.

Sister Alfonsa called it "living in the future tense." Fred, for his part, put it like this: "Albert, you always want something to start, and once something has started, you always want it to end." And Violet, the only girl Albert had ever dated, had once claimed he was waiting because it was the "right thing." Albert found this implausible. The underlying message of the numerous films that Violet recommended to him, and that he downloaded on the sly in the computer lab at Saint Helena, was simply: do something because it's the "right thing" to do. Which Albert didn't get. Naturally, nobody would do something because it was "wrong." And even if you came to terms with the fact that many things were righter than others, what was the point? What was the point in searching for his past yet again? To bring Fred back home, or simply to remain squatting here, to throw away Fred's medication, or mix it into the salad—what difference did it make? Ultimately, thought Albert, knocking his ash into the sluggish stream of water and watching it drift away into the darkness, ultimately, it all came to the same thing: Fred would die, and it didn't matter if he ever grasped who Albert was, and what Albert himself might be to Fred, Fred would die whether or not Albert called him *Papaaa,* three more months and it would all be over, and it would be foolish to give any credence to the feel-good justification that Albert had done the "right thing" just because he'd set out with Fred on this wannabe odyssey.

It was hardly the "right thing" to expose one's father to such serious health risks.

He would have been glad to hear Sister Alfonsa's opinion of this business. Whenever he thought of her, it was with a mixture of incredulity, exasperation, and melancholy. When dealing with orphans she was magnificent, in her way, though she had the irritating habit of doling out bits of wisdom that generally trailed behind them that most annoying of all promises: "You'll understand that someday. When you're grown."

Albert was grown now, in fact was somewhat on the heavy side, and a smoker, and he had squired his father—who had no idea that he *was* a father—down the rectangular sewer pipe of a small Bavarian town on far too hot a summer day, in order to discover where his gold came from. And he had only five cigarettes left. And he wasn't sure how much time had passed since Fred set off on his own. Thus far he hadn't responded to Albert's shouts. What if Fred needed him?

Hoping to distract himself, he opened Fred's backpack and rooted through it. The first thing he found was the silver encyclopedia. He'd figured it would be there. And the tin box with the gold didn't surprise him either. The condolence card, however, brought him up short. There was a picture of an outspread hand on it—five fingers. It was a reproduction of a charcoal drawing. Strong contrast of light and shadow, dirty-gray foggy background framed with heavily drawn lines. But something wasn't right; the hand seemed imprisoned in the picture, as if it hadn't been laid down on the paper from above, but rather was pressing up against its plane from the opposite side. Upon closer inspection, Albert realized that the drawing wasn't a reproduction at all, but an original, and he asked himself how such a work could have wound up in Fred's possession. On the other side of it, in spidery handwriting, he read: *Mama says getting older still always means being younger but I don't know if that's good or not. .*

Albert was familiar with the aphorism; it belonged to Fred's standard repertoire. What irritated him was the two periods. They stared up at him like a pair of button eyes, neither ending the sentence nor indicating something further. They sat beside each other, stubborn, disturbingly wrong. Albert licked his thumb and attempted to rub one of them away, but merely blurred them, endowing them each with a sort of tail.

What if Fred needed him now? Albert called out to him again, listened, heard no answer. He put the card back. Every child knew that when you got lost, you shouldn't go wandering off, but should stay in the same spot, *waiting*, thought Albert—and set off into the dark.

That struck him as righter.

Berlin-Tempelhof

Albert ran and paused, ran and paused. The diffuse light falling at intervals through storm drains and manhole covers only ever illuminated a couple of feet, then quickly dwindled again into darkness, leaving Albert to grope on with outstretched arms toward the next source of brightness. The sewer pipe's walls were as greasy to the touch as they looked. To begin with, Albert kept to the right at every bifurcation of the tunnel, but soon gave up on this tactic, realizing he was going in circles.

Each of his calls was answered by an echo of *E-ed.*

At the end of a narrow duct, he saw light. He moved toward it and discovered an exit covered with a metal grate, in which some sort of vegetable matter, looking and smelling like kelp, had gotten tangled. Beyond it, forest. Albert inhaled, savoring the fresh, cool air. For a long while now, he hadn't heard a car above. It was possible he'd made his way out to the moor. All roads out of Königsdorf led to the moor. He shook the grate; it gave just a little, its mounting didn't seem particularly stable. Maybe he could get it open. Albert wasn't too keen on risking his life by ascending a shaft that emerged who knew where, maybe in the middle of some street where the locals went tear-assing around curves at eighty miles per hour. He took a step back, then kicked as hard as he could at the grate. It gave a little more. As he wound up for another kick, something stirred at the edge of the forest. A fox separated itself from the shade beneath a birch, and stood there staring at him. It hardly moved, only curling its tail a bit. Albert had never seen a fox in the wild before. The animal lifted its snout, never taking its eyes off of him.

"Albert!" came a shout from behind him. Fred arrived at a run, lugging both his backpack and Albert's tote bag. "You shouldn't run away!" he said, exasperated.

Albert glanced back over his shoulder. The fox had vanished. "Where've you been?"

"I was sleeping," Fred said as if stating the obvious.

"Why?"

Fred passed him the tote bag. "Because I was tired. It's very hot."

Albert almost didn't dare to ask, "Are we moving on now?"

After a brief pause, Fred nodded. "It's very far."

"I've noticed."

Fred's eyes fell on the grate. He pulled the plant matter from it. "My papa wants this to stay clean."

"Now that that's taken care of," said Albert, "where to?"

Fred looked at him, surprised. "You aren't very strict."

"Oh yes I am strict!"

"No, Albert," he said, grinning, "you're ambrosial."

"Maybe. A little," said Albert, and smiled. "Because you're doing okay. That's important, understand?"

Fred nodded. "I always understand everything."

They went back up the little duct. Fred was in the lead with his flashlight. Albert wasn't feeling annoyed anymore, but optimistic. Soon they'd reach their goal, and then he'd be able to wash away this endless summer afternoon with a cold shower. How long could it possibly take before they'd threaded their way through the whole sewer system? It was only Königsdorf.

They made two more turns, and Fred shouted, "Ah!" They retraced their steps, made yet another turn, and ran up against a cul-de-sac.

The treasure chest sitting there at the end of it did, in fact, look just like you'd expect a treasure chest to look: dark, moldy wood, battered edges, rusty lock. Fred indicated it with a sort of may-I-introduce-you gesture, and said, "My Most Beloved Possession."

"I didn't know you could have more than one of those," said Albert.

"Only a couple."

"And the gold was in there?"

"All Most Beloved Possessions come from there!"

Albert set down his tote bag, knelt before the chest, and opened it. There was a sticker pasted to the inner surface of the lid: a cartoon bear wearing red-and-white pants, sailing with outspread arms over the legend *Berlin-Tempelhof.*

On the floor of the chest, precisely in the middle, parallel to the side walls, lay a snow-white lily. Albert lifted it and sniffed. Bittersweet odor of compost. The blossom was barely wilted. It couldn't have been in the chest for more than a few hours.

"Why did you put it in there?"

"It wasn't me," said Fred.

Albert lifted an eyebrow.

"It really wasn't!"

Albert smelled the lily again, though the odor made him uneasy, then passed it to Fred, who promptly buried his nose in the blossom. "What kind of flower is it?"

Albert told him.

"Then it's for me. Lilies are specially for dead people."

Albert shut the chest and sat down on it. Fred stroked the lily's petals with his finger as if the flower were the head of a parakeet. "When I go dead, you'll have to come down here and open the chest. Because when I go dead, I won't be able to open the chest anymore."

"Do me a favor and stop saying *dead.*"

Fred took off his Tyrolean hat, stuck the lily into the band beside the tuft, and put it on again. "Am I chic?"

"Extremely."

Fred's grin was lily-white.

"Frederick, I'd like you to tell me who put the flower in there."

"My papa."

"Have you spoken to him?"

"No." Fred's head sank, then sprang up again. "But I wished for a dead person's flower from my papa, and now there's a dead person's flower there!"

Albert quietly repeated the words "Now there's a dead person's flower there," which from Fred's mouth sounded so plausible, so unquestionably true. From Albert's they seemed so insubstantial—he felt stupid just having them in his head, let alone on his lips.

"Okay then." Albert rose to his feet, clapped his hands, and spoke loudly into the darkness, "I wish for an ice-cold lemonade!" He flung open the lid of the chest.

Fred stared at him.

"Oh. Didn't work. Oh well. These things happen. Try again." He flipped the lid closed with a bang.

Fred winced.

"Maybe that wish didn't come from the heart," said Albert, feeling his rage swell. "How about this: I wish for some sign . . . No, why be so modest when you've got a chest of wonders? . . . Dear spirit of the chest, I wish for my mother." Lid up. "There you go. It's obviously busy at the moment. Ah well. Good things come to those who . . ." He gave the chest a kick. "How about we ask for your papa, hmm? Or our family tree? Or a smaller heart for you?"

Albert wasn't bothering to check the chest anymore.

"Are you angry?" asked Fred.

"What makes you think that?"

Fred opened the chest. "Albert! Look!" He reached in and pulled out the bear sticker.

"A miracle," said Albert. And then he saw that on the underside of the lid, at the spot the sticker had covered, four words were written: *My Most Beloved Possession.* Again, that ornate schoolgirl's hand.

Fred put the sticker in his backpack. "My papa likes giving me things."

"Have you ever seen him?"

"No." Fred leaned forward. "Have *you* ever seen him?"

"No, Fred. No, I haven't."

Before they began the trek homeward, Fred asked for refreshments. They sat back-to-back on the chest, sharing the bread they'd brought along, the peeled carrots, the bananas, and washed it all down with the apple spritzer. Fred ate with tremendous appetite, and though Albert was just as hungry, he held back so that Fred would have his fill.

They'd barely been under way for five minutes when Albert's thoughts started off again. It was his own fault: he couldn't fool himself. Whenever he tried it, a second voice immediately piped up in his head, contradicting him; and when the argument of these voices ran into a cul-de-sac, a third voice intervened, summing things up; and that summation was then pronounced aloud in a fourth voice, Albert's own. In this case it said, "Are you sure, Fred, that nobody but you knows about the chest?"

Fred said, "No."

"I mean, apart from you and your papa."

"Besides my papa and me, only one person knows the chest is there."

"Who?"

"You."

Albert's fingers fidgeted, they yearned to be holding a cigarette. To calm them he shoved his hands into his pockets and gripped the makeup compact.

Fred scratched at his nose. "You shouldn't be sad because you don't have a lily. Everyone will get a dead person's flower eventually. Even you."

"You think so."

Emphatic nodding. "Definitely!"

Albert let go of the mirror and set down the tote bag. He stood on his tiptoes, took the hat from Fred's head, and looked again at the lily. He ran his thumb along the stem. It had been cut smoothly. With a knife. Or a pair of garden shears.

A Surprise

Though his heart had been more or less calm ever since they'd left the sewers, the moment Albert stepped onto the property of Fred's neighbor and read the name beside the door—*Klondi,* written out in a lovely schoolgirlish script—it immediately lost its cool, and he had trouble concealing the fact from Fred, who was waiting behind him while, for the second time in two days, he stood with lifted finger at a front door, and hesitated before ringing the bell.

"Albert?"

"Yes?"

"You have to ring."

The gentle summer air was certainly more pleasant to breathe than that oxygen paste in the sewers, but now that he was outside again, at approximately three in the afternoon, Albert felt exposed. Too much space to think. Clearly delineated boundaries, like those at a Catholic orphanage, for instance, were more his speed. Only, how could you build a wall inside your head? How did you keep yourself from thinking: Klondi. It can't be Klondi. Can it be Klondi?

Fred rang.

"Thanks," said Albert.

"You're welcome," said Fred.

"Over here," called a husky female voice from the garden. Fred and Albert stepped around the house, whose balcony slanted down and to the right like a lopsided smile. Klondi was sitting on a little patch of turf by the frog pond. Five years had gone by since Albert had come to ask her about his mother. The years hadn't changed her, except that she now wore her silver-gray hair down and at shoulder-length. As they approached she plucked one greenish noodle after another from the saucepan lying in her lap, stuck their ends into her mouth, and sucked them in through her lips.

"Want a taste?" she asked. Albert declined. Fred dropped his eyes to the ground and flared his nostrils, semaphoring *Yes*. Klondi passed him a handful of noodles, which dangled from her fist like earthworms, and, taking them, he imitated her suction technique.

"It's just like *Lady and the Tramp*, without dogs," he said.

"I plucked the wild garlic myself. Sure you won't partake?" asked Klondi, and offered the pot to Albert, who could feel his hunger waxing.

"No appetite."

Fred and Klondi went on slurping happily. Which Albert endured for another minute and a half. Then he said, "We've found a Hansel and Gretel crumb," and Klondi stopped eating and looked at him. Albert pointed to the lily in Fred's Tyrolean hat.

"This isn't the right time," she said.

Albert was glad she wasn't trying to lie. "I don't think there *is* a right time for this."

"But there's a better one," she said through gritted teeth, from which green shreds of wild garlic hung, and nodded at Fred, who was fishing in the frog pond with a long noodle.

"Can you wait here for a minute, Fred?" said Albert. "Klondi wants to show me something in the house."

Fred dropped his noodle into the pond. "She should show me, too!"

Klondi laid her hand on Fred's back. "I could do that. But then it wouldn't be a surprise anymore."

"A surprise for me?"

"Among others," said Klondi.

Fred opened his backpack and retrieved the encyclopedia, then rolled onto his belly, and started reading at page one. Albert wanted to say something nice to him, but all that came to mind was "We won't be long."

No Harry Potter

The chill inside Klondi's house, which had succeeded in holding fast against the surrounding summer, made Albert wish he had, in fact, accepted some of the spaghetti. A little inner warmth against the shivers. He followed Klondi into the kitchen, a replica of one of those cozy Alpine rooms you find pictured in German furniture-store brochures. A little seating area with wooden chairs whose backrests had heart-shaped holes sawed into them, white-and-blue-checked clay beer steins on the windowsill, a tiled stove, and a low ceiling supported by old, petrified beams, which even Albert, in spite of his undistinguished size, had to duck his head to clear.

"Cigarette?"

Klondi extended a packet of Gauloises, just as she had five years before.

"I don't smoke," he said coolly.

"Fibber. Want one or not?"

Klondi plucked two cigarettes from the pack, lit them both, stuck one between Albert's lips, and drew deeply on the other, as if it were providing her with air. "God, finally! Were you the one who told Fred about lung cancer and smoker's leg?"

Silently Albert shook his head; as always, Klondi had an overwhelming effect on him: in her presence he felt so young and inexperienced.

"Anyway, you can't smoke anywhere near him without him going completely nuts." Her cigarette bobbed up and down as she spoke. "I always have to find some excuse for the smell."

"What color was your hair when you were younger?"

"At least sit down first."

"No thanks." Albert ground his cigarette out in an overflowing ashtray. "Look, are you my mother, or what?"

From somewhere in the depths of the house came a creak, eerily extended, like the parody of an opening door in a horror movie—though to Albert it also sounded a bit like indigestion—and as silence fell again, Klondi said, "Ah, well."

Albert wasn't surprised. Hundreds of times, thousands of times, he'd imagined this moment, fearing he might faint, hoping he'd be able to react without reproach, wondering whether they'd embrace, or smile, or weep, or all three at once, expecting to feel in every fiber of his body, and perhaps even beyond it, relief, confidence, joy.

But there was nothing.

He sat down on one of the chairs and looked at Klondi, who just stood there, tapping ash from her cigarette and letting it fall to the floor like snow.

"I expected the thought would occur to you someday." She turned one of the chairs back to front and straddled it, shaking her head. "But my hair used to be blond, not dark blond, not platinum blond, and definitely not strawberry blond. Sorry."

Albert glanced through the four-paned window. Outside, Fred lay stretched flat on his belly, his head resting on the encyclopedia, like somebody who'd been shot from behind.

"What were you looking for in the sewers?" Klondi asked.

"The truth."

"But let's be honest here, do you actually *want* to find it? Or just your own version of it?"

"There's only ever one truth. That's what makes it truth."

"I've heard," said Klondi, without responding to his commentary, "that Dickens and Rowling are both strangely beloved by orphans."

"What does that have to do with anything?"

"Those kinds of stories can arouse false expectations," she said, poking around in the ashtray with her fingers. "Who, after all, turns out to be a Harry Potter or an Oliver Twist? Who actually discovers something special about themselves, or develops some magical power? Most orphans aren't princes or students of magic; they're just kids who've gotten less love than the rest."

Of course Albert knew that, and yet it hurt to have it said so baldly, right to his face. What was Klondi up to? He asked himself whether it wasn't time to go.

Klondi ground out her cigarette. "Maybe I can tell you who your mother is."

Albert coughed.

"I said maybe." She smiled at him sympathetically. "I don't want you to get your hopes up."

"Don't bother yourself too much about me," he said as calmly as possible, avoiding her eyes. When somebody asked him not to get his hopes up, he could do nothing but get his hopes up.

A husky laugh. "You'd be a miserable poker player." She bent forward, so that her chair stood shakily on two legs, grabbed his head with both hands, and pressed a kiss onto the cheek with the cops-and-robbers scar. "But not such a bad son."

Albert pushed her back onto all four chair legs, and she let rip with her truth. The sunshine falling through the window lacked warmth, and there wasn't much to spare in Albert, either. His body felt stiff, he shivered, but he was too exhausted to do anything about it. So he listened.

Klondi's Story

It all began with Klondi bringing a little girl into the world in 1971. She'd been pleased about the prospect, actually—she could hardly wait to hold the child in her arms. Just before the delivery she'd switched hospitals because, as she'd discovered very late, in the clinic where it was supposed to happen, all the babies were washed after birth, before being passed to their parents, and Klondi wanted no part of that, she wanted to hold her daughter in her arms while the baby was slick and bloody—in for a penny, in for a pound—and so she and her husband, Ludwig, hailed another taxi and shouted to the driver, "Next hospital!" And he answered, "But there's one right here!" And they tossed all the cash they had onto the passenger seat. And the driver put his car into gear.

And so, at that next hospital, Klondi gave birth to a girl, her name was Marina because Ludwig had wanted it that way, Marina, it sounded almost like Mina, which had been Ludwig's mother's name. Marina fidgeted and squalled just like Klondi had imagined she would, and Klondi smiled, because she felt like she'd made up for the two abortions she'd had earlier in her life, or at least one of them, and she pressed Marina to her breast and cupped a hand over her head like a helmet, and sniffed her. They say that babies don't smell, but this baby, Klondi's baby, *did* smell—though not good, somehow. That's what she got for absolutely having to hold her daughter in her arms right away, thought Klondi, nobody had told her about the smell, they all talked about the miracle of having a living being slide out of you, the miracle of creating—with a little masculine help— a brand-new life, but nobody warned you how badly said life could stink. Klondi didn't want to do any violence to her nose, her body had already been through enough, and she passed Marina to the nurse, so that she could get started with the washing. "Make sure she's really clean," Klondi said, and added, because the nurse had shot her a confused look, "Give her a mirror finish!" and when she was alone, she gave her hands a sniff and made a face. Klondi slept for a few hours, waking just when she started to dream she was going into labor. Marina was brought back to her, this time spotlessly clean, wrapped in white blankets, what a sight, and Klondi took her, full of joy, she wanted to hold her daughter, this creature who had never been separated from her for so long, she raised the little bundle to her face, wanting to kiss it, and pursed her lips and pushed her head forward, and just couldn't do it. That simply didn't smell good. Maybe it had something to do with hormones, maybe it was an allergic reaction, the doctor couldn't explain it. Marina smelled fantastic, he assured her, and Ludwig seconded him, and Klondi didn't like that at all, they were making it sound as if it were her fault, yet her nose was just fine, as later investigations confirmed. Possibly it was the hospital's fault, the doctor interjected, whereupon Klondi decided to go home immediately.

Half an hour later Ludwig was steering their car toward the house in Königsdorf, and Marina lay in a little basket on the backseat beside Klondi, who wasn't sad or frightened in the least, only confused, because she couldn't say where her happiness had gone. For nine months she'd waited, for nine months she'd restrained herself, hadn't gone out dancing until dawn or gotten drunk, hadn't gone swimming in the frigid Isar or smoked any grass, had followed through with the whole maternity program, heavy breathing and listening to music and letting them run tests on her and the whole nine yards, everything that was meant to do you good, in order to stay the course at least once in her life, and now she wanted her reward, she wanted the happiness.

The car pulled to a stop in front of their semidetached house, for which they'd recently made the down payment, in Osterhofen, a neighborhood of Königsdorf that borders the moor, and Klondi got out and carried Marina in her little basket through the garden, taking no notice of the pink banner above the front door that read *CONGRATULATIONS!!!*, waited for Ludwig to let her in, then brought Marina into her room with its green walls. There Klondi unwrapped Marina, tossed the basket and everything else that had been in contact with her out onto the porch, and washed Marina again with her own hands. Maybe they hadn't done it thoroughly in the hospital. Gently she ran the sponge across Marina's skin and through every fold, speaking to her, explaining to the little whiner that she was sorry, it had to be like this, but not to worry, it would all be over soon. Then she dried Marina off and wrapped her up in towels that had been washed with their own usual detergent, line-dried in their garden, stored in their linen closet, and she carried Marina into the living room, where Ludwig was waiting, the sweetheart, though at the moment she couldn't spare a thought for him, he could look as confused as he liked, there were other things to worry about, and she sat down on her chair in the solarium, which she'd arranged there because during her pregnancy she'd thought how nice it would be to sit in this chair with its view of the garden and a couple of houses and the expanse of moor, and suckle her daughter, and Klondi opened her blouse and lifted her breast from the bra and smelled Marina and clutched her breasts and smelled her again and stood up and passed her daughter to her husband.

The marriage held out for another seven months.

In 1976, Marina, five years old, discovered a slightly bitter-smelling bridal gown in a box of rags in the basement of the house where Ludwig was now living alone. Later on, Ludwig told Klondi that their daughter had insisted on wearing the dress, even though he, Ludwig, had explained that it was much too big and old for her. Marina merely stamped her feet and said that Mama would certainly have let her do it, and moreover, at Mama's house she could stay up as late and eat as much chocolate as she wanted. Ludwig, whom this hurt more than he could show, did not reply that Mama took care of her only on the weekends, Mama had left her behind, Mama loved her from the depths of her heart, but not enough to actually be a mother to her. Instead, Ludwig said, "That's just Mama." And Marina said, "Mama is much nicer." And Ludwig said nothing.

A couple of days later Marina wore the dress out. When she showed it to Klondi, Marina proclaimed that it was moon-white, Ludwig had taught her that, *moon-white,* and Klondi, who wanted to make an effort to do her part as a parent, said, "White is the brightest achromatic color." "Moon-white," said Marina, "sounds much prettier, though." The dress's shoulders were covered with ruffles that Ludwig had had a seamstress work up from cuttings of its fine old material. For that, Marina had given Ludwig an extra kiss, she told Klondi, even though it scratched a bit because he didn't shave regularly.

Klondi saw her limited skills as a mother confirmed by the fact that it had never occurred to her that when she sent her daughter "home," Marina might not, in fact, go home. Even today, she explained to Albert, she often imagined what had happened next. Klondi knew that her daughter had wandered through the village, showing her dress to everyone she was acquainted with, and even to those she didn't know at all, telling everyone her father had given her this dress because he loved her so terribly much, even though it was actually much too old and big.

It had been midsummer, and because the shadow thrown by the church was particularly cool, Marina had presumably decided to go there. She knew the way well enough, Ludwig always took her with him to Mass. The people there always became very serious very quickly, and Marina found this funny. Marina skipped past the church entrance and pressed herself against the cool walls, maybe she even licked the salty stone with her tongue, the way Klondi had shown her, and that must have been the moment when she caught sight of the old oak tree on Wolf Hill. Marina knew that, for Klondi, it was the loveliest tree there was, because it was just as big as a tree ought to be, with leaves just as green as leaves ought to be. Before Marina was born, Klondi and Ludwig had walked there together all the time. But after the separation, Klondi preferred to walk alone. Anyway, she had more than enough trees in her garden.

Marina ran to the oak, excited, yet there was a certain oppressive feeling in her belly, too, because she knew that her parents, especially Ludwig, wouldn't want her to climb a tree in a dress, definitely not one this new, and moon-white to boot. But Marina was five years old, she believed that from up there you'd be able to wave to climbers on the mountains, and sailors out at sea, all she had to do was be careful and nothing would happen. And now she was climbing the old oak, she knew precisely which branches would bear her weight, and which were the quickest pathway to the canopy. Marina was a talented climber. In no time at all she'd reached the thin upper branches and looked around and was so entranced by the radiant colors of the church's rose window opposite her on the Segenhügel that she didn't notice the pastor leaving that same church with a battered briefcase under his arm. On this sort of hot day he tended to walk with a stoop, as Klondi had noticed, but on this particular afternoon he actually stumbled, as he later explained, when he stepped on one of his own shoelaces, and as he was standing again after having retied them, he glanced up and saw Marina in the crown of the oak, much too high, and in his terror he let his briefcase fall, took off at a run, and shouted as loudly as he could for her to come down.

At first, Marina didn't hear him. But then, when one of the cries of the pastor, who had meanwhile reached the dip between the Segenhügel and Wolf Hill, finally reached her ear, she turned with a jerk. At which point a pair of branches broke: the one she'd been gripping with her hand and the one on which she'd been standing. The pastor made it to the base of the oak. Marina fell with a short, high shriek. And stopped short, suspended. The frills on the shoulders of her dress had been skewered by a branch, and Marina dangled like a ripe fruit among the oak boughs. That seamstress who'd altered the old bridal gown into Marina's moon-white dress would curse herself later—the old-fashioned ruffles had smelled so pleasantly of dried flowers that she hadn't had the heart to replace the almost antique material with new fabric.

When the ruffles tore, Marina didn't scream a second time. Maybe because she thought she'd gotten off with a simple scare. She hit the ground a few feet in front of the pastor.

When it was time for the burial, the whole community gathered at Königsdorf's cemetery, which had never been so lively. Klondi didn't know how to act, she wanted to take Ludwig's hand, but he wouldn't let her. No one gave her a friendly glance, they all thought it was her fault, and all of them sympathized with Ludwig, who had lost a daughter. Why would they feel anything for Klondi? Everybody in this one-horse town knew she'd withdrawn from her role as mother, that she'd wanted little to do with Marina. They thought: she's probably glad. Klondi couldn't reveal to anyone that there was, actually, something to that. Naturally she would have done anything to save Marina's life, naturally she would have traded her own life for her daughter's, naturally she cried herself to sleep every night, naturally she'd started smoking weed again—yet for the first time she felt that strange happiness she'd been waiting for since Marina's birth. She'd loved her daughter, she could see it only now that she was standing by her grave, she was grateful for every day she'd spent with Marina, and if someday she should succeed in showing this happiness to Ludwig, then maybe he'd forgive her and take her hand.

And Ludwig, the bus driver on line 479, who now lived alone in the semidetached house where he'd originally moved with his family, and who never answered Klondi's phone calls, burned the bridal gown on his compost heap, using a bit too much ethanol, so that he nearly went up with it, and the neighbors had to call the fire department. That was all the same to Ludwig, as long as the white scrap of bad luck was destroyed. He bawled drunkenly while they extinguished the bonfire in his garden. The next morning he resolved that he'd let himself grow a full beard, since his unshaven cheeks would not bother anyone ever again. After the divorce, he'd allowed himself to drink only after Marina had gone to sleep and it was dark outside. After Marina's death he started drinking even before the sun was up. That's how it was in October, November, and nothing had changed in December. In January he frequently found himself wondering whether it had just gotten dark, or whether it was going to be light soon. In February he went raging, blind drunk, through Klondi's garden, nearly drowning himself in the frog pond, at which point she had him committed to a rehab clinic. And in March, after a long talk with Klondi, he finally grew sick and tired of his self-pitying existence, shaved himself, had a successful interview with his former employer, and for the first time after a six-month hiatus, sat sober again behind the wheel of a bus.

For three days, everything went smoothly. On the fourth day, a doddery old one-legged man asked him whether that sweet little Marina of his was already in school. Ludwig asked him to get off the bus. On the fifth day he saw Marina in his rearview mirror, dancing in the bus's central aisle in her moon-white dress. On the sixth day she sat in his lap while he made his rounds, and criticized his driving. On the seventh day he drank a thimbleful of vodka for breakfast, and she disappeared, and that was a tremendous relief. On the eighth day he filled a 1.5-liter mineral-water bottle with vodka, and took a swig from it at every stop. From the ninth to the twenty-first day he emptied half a bottle daily, despite which he was the most punctual and friendliest driver in the whole district. On the twenty-second day, the boss choked on a cough drop during their weekly meeting, and

Ludwig offered him a drink of water. On the evening of the twenty-second day, Ludwig was dismissed. For a week after that, things were dark, black.

Then, on April 4, 1977, Ludwig ironed his bus driver's uniform, took a long time in dressing, secured his necktie with a Windsor knot, put on his official cap, called Klondi up and told her about the month that had just gone by, saying he was sorry for all of it, and hung up before she could reply, then slipped into the garage of his former employer, illuminated the line 479 indicator on one of the buses, took a swig from a mineral-water bottle, which contained nothing but mineral water, and turned on the engine. Outside it was raining. Three-quarters of an hour later, at 6:15, fifteen minutes early, Ludwig arrived in Königsdorf.

Klondi didn't dare show up at the burial of her ex-husband. She didn't even want to think about everyone who would be there, his family, friends, *her* family—she preferred to roll herself a joint, using the page of the newspaper containing a photograph of a certain Frederick A. Driajes, the hero of the bus accident, the son of her neighbor. Klondi smoked on the balcony of her crumbling farmhouse, because she suspected the rotting old balcony wouldn't be able to bear her weight much longer, and as she stood there waiting, she remembered how often Ludwig had thrown her weed away, and how she'd hated him for it, and how she'd loved him for it. She didn't know much about his family or his childhood in Königsdorf, Ludwig had never wanted to talk about it; in all those years, the only thing she'd succeeded in getting from him was that his mother had died when he was ten, after which his father had taken off—and it was in spite of that, or maybe because of it, that Ludwig had become so strong, always knowing what he wanted, and what he didn't. He wanted children, a wife, a house, and a job. And he'd been happy with them. Klondi envied him that, what she wanted was to think less, not always to be turning every decision over and over in her mind until she had absolutely no idea what to do. Ludwig had helped her, he'd been the arrow pointing the way for her, for him she'd given up smoking pot and moved from Bremen to Osterhofen in Upper Bavaria, and she'd slept with him, seduced him, like in a soft-core video, in an abandoned barn during a hike on Herzogstand Mountain, staring him straight in the eyes the whole time, and finally, finally she felt certain of something, of this, because he was only the third man she'd ever been with, and were she to have her way, he'd be the last, too. The balcony, however, didn't support this plan. Even bouncing and shaking wouldn't make it collapse. So Klondi started tending to her garden again. Plants didn't contradict you, plants didn't look at you awry, plants didn't pretend they knew how it felt when your daughter died and your ex-husband dragged two people with him into the grave. Plants didn't say, *None of this is your fault,* which immediately made you think, all of this is my fault. Plants were simply there. As fertilizer Klondi used an algae-ish biomass that she collected at least two times a week from a runoff pipe of the Königsdorf sewer system. She lingered there, wandering the tunnels for hours, enjoying the echoes of her footsteps, feeling safe. Up above, life was sheer torment, but down here, it couldn't find her.

After a couple of years, though, it did find her. During one of her subterranean expeditions she saw Fred climbing into the sewer in his diving goggles, and at first she felt like fleeing and getting stoned on her balcony, but then she wound up following him, as softly as she could, maybe out of curiosity, maybe because it didn't seem quite right that an invalid like him—heroism notwithstanding—should be tramping around in the sewers alone. Fred led her to a wooden chest, which he carefully opened and spent a long time looking into, motionless, like someone deeply disappointed.

Which made her think of the porcelain box. It had always sat on the highest shelf in her parents' kitchen, filled to the brim with pink peppermint candies that Klondi's father would give her for good grades or when she mowed the lawn, according to how good the grades were or whether she'd done the mowing without his having to remind her. Actually, he didn't *give* them to her, he *awarded* them to her. Helping herself to one was strictly forbidden. Klondi's father called these bits of apportioned affection *Gold Medals,* and accordingly awarded them rarely. Otherwise he allowed no sweets in the house, so that Klondi continued to rejoice in the reward of a sweet long after puberty had set in. She was fifteen when, after a long spell without a Gold Medal, she decided to open the porcelain box with her own hands. She clambered up onto a chair, stretched, grabbed the box, set its lid aside, pulled out one of the candies, licked the sugary peppermint coating, laid it on her tongue, sucked it, and quickly replaced the lid before she could stuff any more of them into her mouth. She was just climbing down from the stool when her father stepped into the kitchen. All he said was "We had an agreement."

With that, the age of the Gold Medals was over. Klondi never dared ask if she could have one, and her parents behaved as if they'd never existed. The porcelain box remained where it had always been, and sometimes Klondi felt the desire to look inside, to see whether there were still any sweets in there, but she was afraid she might find the box empty, washed clean and odorless. Her relationship with her parents, never characterized by any great warmth, gradually devolved into a sort of vague familiarity, lacking any common ideas or interests. The thought that these two, of all people, had brought her into the world seemed as strange to her as the notion that she was therefore duty-bound to love them. By the time Klondi moved to Bremen in the mid-sixties to study landscape architecture and discovered the finer points of toking up (while rolling a joint she liked to mix dried peppermint with the tobacco), she considered her parents mere pitiful slaves to the capitalist system. Even the unemployed bus driver in her communal house couldn't sway her from this conviction. Sure, he had a beautiful smile. But what could some kid who'd grown up in his grandmother's bakery in a backwater town in Upper Bavaria, and was called Ludwig to boot, possibly know about the class struggle?

Klondi didn't dwell on Fred's excursion through the sewers. At first, anyway. Everyone's looking for something he'll never find, she told herself, a painful experience, but one that was part of life. As far as she could judge, Fred had survived his mother's heart failure, and it would eventually occur to him that *his* porcelain box, the chest—whatever he was waiting to find in it—would remain empty. Besides, it didn't concern her at all, maybe she'd completely misinterpreted the whole thing. It wouldn't have been the first time, her head never gave her any peace unless it was weighing every option, and in this case it had come to the 100 percent correct conclusion that she ought to mind her own business, avoid the sewers for a while, keep out of Fred's way, fire up the bong again, that was it.

But the very next day, while shopping at the supermarket, she found herself standing in front of the candy rack, and a few hours later she was secretly observing Fred as he opened the chest, reached in, and pulled out a bag of peppermints. He munched the whole lot of them then and there, and Klondi had to cover her mouth to stifle her giggling, a strange, delighted, girlish giggling that bubbled out of her as if someone were tickling her most sensitive places. Soon enough, Klondi was following her walks in the sewers with excursions aboveground, in the course of which she'd not-quite-accidentally run into Fred at the bus stop and start chatting with him. Fred would show her what he'd found in the chest; his papa, he'd brag, would never let a mere accident stop him from bringing Most Beloved Possessions.

Another time, Klondi made herself comfortable on a deck chair in the garden, squinted up into the sun, and pressed the button with the red dot on a tape recorder. She wanted to tell Fred a story about a woman who had stumbled across a new source of courage in the sewers. She wanted to thank him. But Klondi wasn't quite sure how to begin, and brooded about it so long that she fell asleep. Later, after she'd treated her sunburn with a cheese poultice and slices of aloe, she discovered that the wordless sighing of the tape was probably better than anything she would have been able to say. The peaceful breathing of a woman who could finally sleep again—she couldn't have expressed herself better with words.

During that time, Klondi traded one old habit for three new ones:

She didn't go out on her balcony anymore.

Instead, she put Fred's wishes into the chest, turning them into Most Beloved Possessions.

And she laughed, almost always alone, whether in her garden, by the frog pond, or in the sewers, simply laughed, delighted by the sound.

And she began taking pottery lessons, which she frequently interrupted and finally broke off, because the only pottery instructor for miles around had an unusually keen nose for cannabis. Which didn't, of course, prevent her from carrying on by herself. Her teacups and ashtrays sold well enough to support her, even if only to day-trippers from Munich, stopping over on their way to the Alps. Königsdorfers took care not to get involved with her.

Except once, she said to Albert, who had been listening to her silently this whole time. Except once. No more than these two words, and Klondi's face, pregnant with significance, were necessary to tell Albert that she was talking about him, the visit he'd made to her at fourteen, searching for Hansel and Gretel crumbs, searching for his mother. His eyes had shone greedily, said Klondi, and she'd only wanted to help him, and so she'd told him to abandon all hope, and it had almost broken her heart when he'd shaken his head and his red hair had flopped about. She'd felt sorry for him, because he didn't understand how good he had it without a mother. It had been the right decision not to help him further, she said, more to herself than to him. She regretted nothing. He'd had a decent life at Saint Helena. Of course she could have told him about the nurse, the woman next to Fred in the photograph, but back then she hadn't thought it was a good idea. Albert had wanted a mother so badly that nobody would've been able to fulfill his expectations, and if she was telling him the truth today, it was only because she could see that he'd never find peace otherwise.

At that she fell silent, and Albert immediately asked her the question he needed to ask.

Klondi answered:

Britta Grolmann

Albert and Fred walked home as night fell. When they got there, Albert fixed them both some bread and butter, and nodded at everything Fred said without really listening. All he could think about was Britta Grolmann. A nurse who'd looked after Fred at the beginning of the 1980s, and afterward had gone to work at a nursing home near Hamburg, at the other end of Germany. Now Albert knew that much. Or rather: that little. Klondi hadn't been able to give him answers to further questions. Did Britta Grolmann still work at the nursing home? Did she also live there? Alone? Did she think about him sometimes? Did she fear he might show up at her door unannounced? Would she recognize him? Maybe they'd take each other's hands. Maybe they'd embrace. Maybe she'd smile. And invite him in. And want to see him again. Maybe every few days he'd take the overnight train to Hamburg. Maybe he'd move in with her. Maybe she'd kiss Fred. On the mouth. Maybe they'd all live together. Maybe she'd read to Fred daily from the encyclopedia. Maybe she'd congratulate Albert for passing his exams. And be proud of him. And talk with him about his future. And tell him about what it was like when she'd been pregnant with him. And about Fred. And about Anni. Maybe she'd tell Albert that she'd been waiting for him.

After they'd eaten the bread and butter, Albert and Fred dozed on the chaise longue, in front of the TV. Albert couldn't help himself, and kept looking at the telephone; he knew that after everything they'd been through and learned today, it was best to sleep on it. He shouldn't rush into making this kind of call, but do it with a clear head. He had to keep calm. At this point a few more hours wouldn't make any difference.

Ten minutes later he locked himself in the bathroom with the telephone and dialed the number he'd gotten from information. It rang only once before someone picked up. "Hello, Golden Years Senior Living Facility."

"Hi, I'd like to speak to one of your employees."

"If you'd like to register a complaint, you should—"

"No complaints. Just questions."

"Who are you trying to reach?"

"Britta Grolmann, please."

"Speaking."

"You're Britta Grolmann?"

"I just said so."

". . ."

"Are you still there?"

"Yes."

"What is this about?"

"I'm Albert Driajes."

"Fine—and?"

"From Königsdorf."

"And why are you calling, Albert Driajes from Königsdorf?"

"You don't remember?"

"What don't I remember? Is this a joke? I haven't got time for this kind of thing."

"Please, don't hang up—I think you're my mother."

She hung up.

The telephone rang five times before someone picked up.

"Golden Years Senior Living Facility."

"I'm going to keep calling until you hear me out."

"You're on the wrong track." Her voice was shaking. Albert hadn't expected that. And even less, the satisfaction it gave him. This woman knew who was on the other end of the line, and even if he couldn't see Britta Grolmann, he was sure that, unlike the expression in the photograph that had been taken over nineteen years ago now, neither pride nor giddiness was on her face today.

"Have you ever worked in Königsdorf?"

"I've never even heard of the place."

"I'm Fred's son."

"Fred who?"

"Frederick Arkadiusz Driajes."

"Don't know him."

"You were his nurse, nineteen years ago. He calls you *the Red Lady*."

"Must be a mistake."

"I have a photo that shows you holding his hand."

"You have no idea what I look like."

"Maybe it'll jog your memory when we come to see you."

It was a bluff. Fred flatly refused to climb into a bus, and Albert had no driver's license.

A short pause. "*Fred* take a bus?"

A little sigh. "Okay. Call back in half an hour. Then we can talk."

The telephone rang eight times before she answered.

"Just so we understand each other: I'll tell you what I know, but after that, you have to promise to leave me in peace. And don't come up here. No calls, no letters."

"Fred's going to die soon."

"Okay," she breathed into the receiver, "that sucks. What am I supposed to say? That I'm sorry? I'm sorry."

"Why did you go away?"

"That sounds pretty damned reproachful. Let's get one thing straight right away: I'm not your mother. Even if I'm sure that you aren't going to believe me so easily."

"No kidding."

"Fine, you want more details. So you can convince yourself you know the whole truth. But I don't believe I'm going to be much help to you. *In your memory, the past is always a story,* Anni used to say to me. *In your memory, the past is always true.* She churned out that kind of patter nonstop. You should be glad you missed most of her. There was a rage in her—she woke up with it first thing every morning, flailed it around her all day long, until she nodded off in the evening, so as to let it build again. Fred couldn't take two breaths without her finding fault with him. Even when her voice gave out and she couldn't manage more than this husky squawking, she never gave it a rest. On the contrary! Then she ramped it up even more. Spitting bile was her raison d'être. Most of it landed on Fred. He completely knuckled under to her, indulged her every whim. Brought her tons of flowers, and quoted her at every opportunity. *Mama says* this and *Mama says* that. As if she'd rewritten the Bible. I felt sorry for him. I'd just finished my nursing exams and still hadn't caught on to the fact that you can't have sympathy for your patients. Sympathy only causes problems. But that's exactly what Anni used to lure me in. She wanted me as a helper, because she couldn't deal with Fred *and* you on her own."

"Did she ever tell you who my mother was?"

"No."

"People must have asked."

"Of course. But that's precisely why she picked me for the job. My red hair, not my references, were what decided it. She announced on the spot, during the interview, that she'd hire me. On the condition that, if anyone asked, I'd pass myself off as your mother. I should have simply walked out right then, but instead I explained to her that I had a bad feeling about the whole business. I figured she'd tell me to leave. Instead she listened to me, without interrupting once, and when I'd finished she gave me a hug, as if we'd come to some agreement. I was just the one she was looking for. Next thing I knew, she was ushering Fred and me outside so she could take a picture of us, demanding that we hold hands, which was awkward for both of us since we didn't know each other at all, but I figured it would make the old lady's day. Her excitement made me think seriously about the job.

"From then on she wouldn't leave me alone. Day in, day out, she called me up, begging me to take the position.

"One day she actually posted herself in front of my door and implored me. I wouldn't have to feel like a mother to you, just worry about Fred. She'd take care of you herself. No responsibility on my part. No burden. No stress. Though of course I'd always be welcome to change your diapers, if I felt like it. She assured me you'd be such a lovely son, a gorgeous son. And she said something else, which I still remember today: that you weren't a Klöble. When I asked her what that was, a Klöble, she just shook her head—she had a tremendously persuasive way of shaking her head—and said, *Some other time.*

"The next day, I decided to start. In the end, I believe it wasn't so much a decision in favor of your family—on the contrary, it was a decision against not helping you."

Albert didn't want to believe a word of it. Britta Grolmann had ample reason to lie to him. But as hard as he searched for signs of it, this time her voice wasn't shaking at all. An empty, anticlimactic sensation pervaded him. "How long did you stay in Königsdorf?"

"Not even three weeks."

"What happened?"

"At the beginning I tried to keep Fred from going out to the bus stop. I mean, sometimes it was just coming down cats and dogs. It didn't make sense to me, him standing around pointlessly out there, waving at cars and catching cold. Also, most of the folks in the village didn't take kindly to it. They saw him as not right in the head, unpredictable. Hero or not. Parents didn't let their children wait for the bus alone anymore. Naturally, nobody *said* anything. They all just stood around, more people than were actually planning on going anywhere, watching Fred from the corners of their eyes. Fred was pleased as punch. *Almost twice as many people are waiting for the bus, and if something happens again, I can be twice as much of a hero!* I didn't have the heart to tell him the truth.

"Instead, I tried to distract him. Invited him to help me make breakfast, or polish shoes, or weed the garden. For a while, it worked perfectly. He isn't as clumsy as people think. Thanks to him, everything went faster. But after nearly a week without any excursions to the bus stop, Fred wouldn't get up in the morning. I didn't know what to do. I tempted him with his favorite food, pancakes with raspberry jam. I promised him he could clean the dust out of the corners of the living room—he liked the sound the vacuum made sucking up dirt. I even offered to read to him from the encyclopedia. No dice. He burrowed down in the bed and didn't shower anymore and couldn't even be persuaded to eat anything. If I didn't know any better, I'd say he was depressed.

"It was only when Anni kicked him, literally, out of bed, and forced him to get dressed and tramped out to the bus stop with him, it was only then that things got better. She pointed her finger at me, said I shouldn't meddle with him anymore. I tried to explain to her that I'd only meant well. To which she replied, only she knew what was good for Fred. Conceited old witch. But she wasn't so wrong about that.

"After two or three days Fred was back in his old rhythm, counting green cars, and had found his smile again. It was the worst thing that could have happened. If Fred hadn't been happy again, then we wouldn't have had so much fun together, and if we hadn't had so much fun together, then . . .

"In the handful of days that I was with them, the two of us spent a lot of time together. Fred took me with him on walks and counted green cars, which I noted in his diary. Or he'd lift me up so I could clean the top panes of the windows, so easily, as if I weighed nothing at all. And he introduced me to a horse that he visited all the time, and fed her fresh weeds.

"And one Thursday, I still remember perfectly, he showed me his Most Beloved Possession. It was dark, and we sat in his BMW, the Speedster, as he called it, which was already more or less in ruins. I don't even want to imagine what it looks like now—if it even exists anymore. Fred showed me a tin box where he kept a lump of gold. An enormous thing. He held it up to the light, gently, as if it were a premature baby, and he seemed so happy that he was able to share this secret with me. I liked that, that closeness. Fred made me feel like I was the only other person on the planet. I didn't care whether or not the gold was real. It seemed real to me. I could have asked Anni, of course, but after that night I barely had an opportunity.

"I shouldn't have settled in so well, I shouldn't have let myself believe that Anni's house could somehow be my house, too. I shouldn't have taken it on myself to tidy up the attic, and I certainly shouldn't have opened that leather-bound portfolio. Anni said, *It's just his imagination, pure imagination.* But Fred, who'd overheard us, tore the drawing out of my hands: *I made it, it's all true imagination!* At first glance, the drawing simply showed a hand. But somehow it made me so afraid—it was like I was four years old again and lying alone in the dark, listening to noises outside my window, I couldn't look at it for long, I felt queasy. I asked, *What's with this hand, what does this picture mean?*, and he said: *It's my Most Beloved Possession!* Anni, who was holding you in her arms, stepped between us. *He's confused,* she said, as she set you down in your crib, and tried to take the drawing away from him. And he hit her in the face, he hit her in the face, full strength, and she fell. She hit the floor. And Fred just stood there, saying nothing, breathing as loudly as if he wanted to suck all the air out of the room. And I didn't move, I didn't dare look at him, I just listened to his breathing and closed my eyes. I don't know how much time passed before I opened them again. Fred was gone. His drawing lay on the floor. Anni lifted herself up, blood dripping from her nose onto the paper. *All well,* she said. I wrapped a package of frozen vegetables in a dish towel, handed it to her, and called an ambulance. When the medic arrived, she claimed she'd tripped. Our eyes met. She smiled. And I looked away. At that moment it became clear to me that I wanted nothing, nothing more to do with those people. I stroked your head one last time, and left. You must have sensed that something wasn't right, you screamed like you'd never screamed before. I can still hear it today. Sometimes, when I'm not feeling well, it's suddenly right there again, and I almost can't stand it. I've been to every possible doctor, and nobody can explain it to me. The only thing that helps is counting. Fred taught me that if I can't sleep, I should simply imagine I'm at a bus stop and count the green cars. And that's just what I do, when the screaming rings through my head. I count and count and count."

Oxymoron

Albert dozed in wine-red light. The red beech casting its shade over him was the only remaining tree in Königsdorf's cemetery. The town had felled the rest, for lack of room.

Sweat ran down his forehead. The makeup compact lying on Albert's chest stirred a bit with his every inhalation—he would have liked to open it, to run the red hair within over the scars on his hands. But that would be too risky. One gust of wind and the hair would be gone. Instead, he tugged at his earlobe.

Even though the Red Lady had proved a dead end, he didn't want to give the compact up. Who knew, the hair might still belong to his real mother.

To his left and right stood gravestones of black marble, which gleamed as immaculately as if they were polished daily. Franz Stöger and Herbert Älig, both of whom had died this year. Stöger's grave was snowed under with bouquets and wreaths; on one of the mourning ribbons, black against pale blue, stood the word *Why?* An idiotic question, since it was so easy to answer, thought Albert. Industrial accident, cholesterol buildup, car accident, testicular cancer—*that's why.* Or might *Why?* really mean *Why now, of all times? Why just two days after his retirement? Why during our golden anniversary cruise? Why while we were arguing? Why not later? Why so late?*

There was a simple answer for that, too: *because.* This whole search for meaning had already been getting on Albert's nerves, even before he'd left the church—as early as possible, and much to Sister Alfonsa's disappointment—on turning fifteen. There was no meaning, no reason, there was merely sooner-or-later. What was really repulsive about the question *Why?* was that it articulated a reproach to the dead on the part of those still living. *How dare you die before me? How dare you leave me alone here? Do you have even the slightest idea how badly I'm doing? You can't just scoot off and leave me behind! What am I supposed to do now?* Mourning, thought Albert, is nothing but a word. People contrived it to make things simpler. But what you actually feel for the dead isn't sorrow, isn't pity either—what hurts so fucking bad when someone disappears forever is nothing more than the realization that you've been alone from your very first day in this world, and that you'll stay that way till the end.

"This is a good spot!" shouted Fred, who lay on his back on an empty plot in the row of gravestones in front of Albert, flapping his arms and legs, making a grass angel. "You should give it a try!"

Albert walked over to Fred and stretched out beside him.

"You can see plenty from here," said Fred. "You can see the clock tower of the church. That way I'll always know how late it is. And you can see the moor. And you can see the whole sky."

"And you can see me, when I come to visit you."

"That's ambrosial! Will you come a lot?"

"Every day. Maybe I'll even bring someone with me now and then."

"Klondi?"

"For instance."

"Gertrude?"

"I doubt that horses are allowed in the cemetery."

"Mama?"

Albert fingered his makeup compact, searching for the right words. But Fred gave him one of his big claps on the shoulder, and pointed at the wall at the edge of the cemetery, in which the funerary urns were kept: "That's funny! Of course you can't bring Mama with you. Because she's already here."

Albert smiled, acted amused.

For a few minutes they lay silently beside each other. Fred closed his eyes and ran his fingers through the grass. Before long it was too hot for Albert—he sat up, sniffed at Fred, nudged him, and looked him in the eyes.

"But I really *did* shower!"

"Go tell it to Gertrude."

"Why?"

"It's a figure of speech."

"*Tell it to Gertrude* is a figure of speech?"

"Don't change the subject. *Have* you showered?"

Fred blinked.

While Fred steeped in the bath, a lit candle in his hand—dripping wax into the water to tell the future—Albert stood on the stairs in front of a framed photograph showing Anni spraying the driveway with a garden hose. She was wearing a dress—she wore dresses in all of her photographs—and the expression on her face was sober, thoughtful.

Albert said to the photo: "I've spoken with Britta Grolmann."

He heard splashing, and glanced up at the bathroom door, which was standing ajar.

"What was it you wanted to hide?"

Albert turned away, descended three steps, then paused. Out of the corner of his eye he'd spotted a photo in which Anni was pushing a wheelbarrow full of leaves.

"Does the gold have anything to do with it? Klondi mentioned that the cassette, the lilies, and a couple of other things were from her. But not the gold."

A step farther down, Anni was mending a pair of blue jeans. She wasn't even looking at the camera in that one.

"Ah, shit."

"You shouldn't say that."

Fred stood on the upper landing, wrapped in a bathrobe that barely reached his knees.

"Did you pour something pretty?"

Fred held up a little clump of candle wax. "A real skull!"

Albert looked straight at him. "It looks more like a piece of cheese to me."

"It looks more like a real skull to me," said Fred seriously. Lather hung in his beard.

"Let's go wash that off," said Albert.

Fred tugged at his sleeve and said softly, "It's okay that you're talking with Mama, you know. Mama said we should never forget her."

Before Albert could say, *There's not much about her for me to forget,* Fred added, shrugging his shoulders, "We're all Most Beloved Possessions."

"Are we?"

Fred sighed, as if Albert once again didn't understand anything. "Mama says everyone is somebody's Most Beloved Possession."

Then he went back to the bathroom, to blow-dry his beard.

Albert thought, maybe you can only love someone or something if you possess him, her, or it—partially, at least; and for the first time since he'd left Saint Helena, he missed Alfonsa. She would have liked this theory.

Later, after Albert had gotten Fred into bed with the help of a few freely quoted passages from the *A–F* volume of the encyclopedia, he took a piece of paper, corralled all the thoughts that had been whirring around in his head, and wrote them out. In the past, that had always helped him: capturing all of his questions, doubts, dilemmas on paper. Letting everything out.

The next morning, Albert's bed was surrounded by crumpled pages, scrawled over with sentences difficult to decipher. He tossed them one by one into the trash can. On one of them, he found: *Most Beloved Possession? Oxymoron!!!* On another: *My mother can stuff it.* And: *Things are going downhill. Downhill? Cliché! Better say* (and then nothing). And: *Life is a Hansel and Gretel crumb. Ha ha.* And, on the only one that he folded up and stuck in his breast pocket:

Really, we ought to act as if there were no unanswered questions. (Cue curtain)

And for the next four weeks, that's exactly what they did.

Fred and Albert swam in the Baggersee, where Fred demonstrated how well he could do the dead man's float.

Fred and Albert counted all the green cars that passed the bus stop, with Albert keeping the tally, and Fred making sure that no "half greens," like police cars, were accidentally counted.

Fred and Albert found a rosebush on their doorstep, with an attached card reading *I'm sorry,* and Fred asked who it was from, and Albert lied, saying he didn't know.

Fred and Albert descended into the sewers together up to three times per week (Albert always twice as often on his own), and found Most Beloved Possessions in the treasure chest—among them a miniature pocket encyclopedia, green crayons, and a brand-new electric shaver.

Fred and Klondi pulled weeds in her garden, and Albert watched them from afar.

Fred and Albert fed weeds to Gertrude.

Fred and Albert cooked spaetzle according to a recipe they found on the Internet, and an hour later ordered pizza, from which Fred scraped the "pukey tomatoes" with a spoon.

Fred and Albert listened to Klondi's cassette, and Albert admitted that the sound was like the distant noise of the ocean.

Fred and Albert repainted Fred's room in olive green, May green, turquoise, and reed green.

Fred and Albert sat firmly belted in the BMW, and Albert cheered for Fred, who raced almost as fast as Michael Schumacher.

Fred and Albert went to see Klondi, because this time Fred insisted that Albert come with him, and the three of them fired up the potter's wheel, and Klondi made an ashtray, which she gave to Albert with a wink, whereupon Albert made a candy dish, which he gave to her also with a wink, while Fred made a "cobble-paving-stone," which he kept for himself.

Fred and Albert argued because in Fred's opinion Albert smelled "smoky"—which Albert blamed on Klondi.

Fred and Albert played chess, and Fred won almost every time because he was playing white, and all the white pieces could move like queens.

Fred and Albert left a rosebush on Klondi's doorstep, with a card that read, *It's okay,* and Fred asked what was okay, and Albert said, "Everything."

Fred and Albert traced the outlines of their hands with green marker on the kitchen window, beside the initials *HA,* and inside the hands wrote *Fred* and *Albert.*

The Biggest Bird in the World

"What are you going to do when I go dead?"

Albert, slowly revolving in an office chair, looked up from a note-book in a plastic cover—one that Alfonsa had given him once upon a time, so that he could record what he'd learned during his chess lessons. The notes Albert took, however, concerned other things en-tirely. The battered pages were filled with the various death scenar-ios that Albert had imagined for Anni and jotted down—like Fred his green cars—and in which a certain sealed kitchen window, shot through with a crack, invariably played a central role. In the past he'd found himself smiling after each entry, because with every new idea his hope had grown that he'd finally found the truth.

Wind blows the window wide open and it shatters and Anni climbs up on a rickety chair to see if she can shut it for the night with glue, but then the chair starts to tip underneath her and she tries to stay up on it, but she's pretty old and so she falls and that's it for her heart.

Or: Anni doesn't want to be in Königsdorf anymore. She wants to take Fred and me and move in with our family, with my mother, and she has to hire moving men to help her because I can't carry anything, I'm too small, and because she can't carry anything, she's too old. And Fred certainly can't carry anything, because he's Fred. But one of the moving men is like Fred, too, a little slow, and smacks the window with a long, golden pole that looks like a wizard's staff, and that gives Anni such a shock that she gets hopping mad, and that's it for her heart.

Or: A couple of cretins like the ones here in the convent are throwing stones, and one of them flies through Anni's window, but she's not the kind just to put up with that, that's for sure, and she scoops up the stone and goes to throw it back into the street. But she can't. She hasn't turned chicken, it's not that—she feels a stab in her heart. She can't do anything anymore. She sinks slowly to the floor, as if falling asleep.

Or: Anni takes pills, because everything's difficult with Fred, plenty of people do it, they even tell the priest about it in the confessional, people take an amazing number of pills, even people like Anni, so many that they feel tipsy, like someone who's been sneaking the sacramental wine. She wants to get the window open. She smashes the window with something, so that she can grab the sky and pull it into the room. For real! She wraps herself up in the clouds and falls asleep and never wakes up again.

Or: Anni goes on a trip with Fred and me. But she wants to take something with her, so that she can remember Königsdorf whenever she likes. So she takes the window, because the view from it was the most important view of all in the dark farmhouse. She packs the shards of glass in a couple of kitchen towels, but she doesn't do it especially nimbly, she cuts herself and bleeds, bleeds a whole lot, and the whole pane goes pink, and Anni goes white, and all of her color, her whole heart, is in the window now.

"You aren't dead by a long shot," said Albert.

"I only have two fingers left." Fred slouched on the red chaise longue, plucking lint from his hat. "That's less than a lot."

"I don't think so." Albert snapped the chess notebook shut. "You know, that's more than one thousand four hundred hours!"

Fred let his hat fall from his hands.

"Around ninety thousand minutes."

"That's a lot," said Fred, savoring the number: "ninety thousand." He bent to pick up his hat. Albert opened his notebook again.

"Are there *still* ninety thousand?"

"Yes," said Albert, without looking up.

"How about now?"

"Still the same."

A thud came from the kitchen. Fred and Albert looked up at each other.

Fred ran to the kitchen. Albert laid aside his notebook and followed. After they'd spent several minutes searching in vain for the source of the noise, Albert's eyes fell on the kitchen window; he rushed outside, around the house, and found a robin lying in the grass below the pane; it was jerking its legs and wings, and its beak opened and shut soundlessly. Fred shoved Albert aside. In both hands he held a shovel, which he let fall with a crash. The bird's last sound was high and shrill.

"How about now? Is it still ninety thousand?" asked Fred, as if nothing had happened.

"Why did you do that?"

"What?"

"Why did you kill the bird?"

"It made him happy."

"Maybe he wasn't so bad, maybe he could have managed."

"Mama says birds that don't fly can't fly. Mama says I'm the biggest bird in the world."

"Come again?"

Fred said louder: *"I'm the biggest bird in the world!"*

"Next time we're going to wait a bit before we kill any animals."

"Okay, Albert," said Fred, and lowered his head. "Are you . . ."

"No," said Albert, "I'm not mad."

Fred proposed burying the robin in the garden, next to a rowan bush, because it'd have plenty of visits from its friends there. An ambrosial thing.

"I'm sorry, bird," said Fred, and crossed himself before the grave. Albert shut his eyes.

> *I let the light wind lift me up,*
> *I love to glide with outspread wings*
> *Leaving every bird behind.*
> *Reason? That's a rotten thing—*
> *Reason and speech bring all to naught.*
> *Flying freshens me with strength*
> *And teaches me lovelier lessons still.*

Fred smiled. "You can talk the way people sing."

"That's by Nietzsche."

"Is he one of your friends?"

"Sometimes."

Albert thought about the time Alfonsa had first read to him from *Beyond Good and Evil*. It was the day the dart had pierced his cheek. Albert had lain in the Saint Helena infirmary, the left half of his face swaddled in bandages, the taste of iodine in his mouth. The slightest blink or movement of his lips had sent stabbing pains through his head. When Alfonsa stepped into his room, he'd assumed she was planning to punish him with the shoelaces again. But she passed over the episode without a word, and instead sat down beside the bed, opened the volume of Nietzsche, and started to read. Albert's six-year-old mind had glided over every third word, but Alfonsa's emotionless voice had soothed him and given him the feeling that his wound was just an insignificant injury, something that would soon be healed.

Now, standing with Fred beside the tiny grave, this memory sparked such a need for comfort in him that he immediately walked into the house and called Alfonsa. It was only when she answered with a cool "Yes?" that it occurred to him that he hadn't spoken to her since leaving for Königsdorf.

"It's me."

"Albert." Was he wrong, or was there a faint trace of pleasure in her voice?

They were silent.

"I wanted to call you," he said finally.

"I figured that much."

Somehow, he'd imagined this differently. How was he supposed to tell someone who'd never been all that good at hugging that he wanted to wrap his arms around her? And what's more, to tell her over the telephone?

"We buried a robin today," said Albert.

"An exciting day, then," said Alfonsa. "Anything else?"

"Fred only has ninety thousand minutes left."

"You know what I think about that." That he and Fred would be in better hands at Saint Helena. Before Albert had left, she'd taken every possible opportunity to make that clear to him. Which had only strengthened his conviction that he and Fred had to spend their remaining time in Königsdorf. At Saint Helena he would be forced to share Fred with nuns and orphans, at Saint Helena Fred wouldn't be able to go through his usual daily routine, at Saint Helena Albert would never have learned about the gold, about the chest in the sewers, and about Britta Grolmann.

"You're calling because it isn't working out," she said. "Think it over."

"I have," he said. "We'll manage."

At that moment, Fred stepped into the living room and looked at him, puzzled. Albert almost never used the telephone (his conversation with Britta Grolmann had been an exception, one he'd kept secret from Fred), and people rarely called them, mostly telemarketers, whom Fred jabbered at so interminably that they were glad to hang up. Fred asked him whom he was talking to, so loudly that Albert couldn't understand what Alfonsa said to him next, and he would have entirely missed those words that he'd never be able to forget, if Alfonsa hadn't cleared her throat and repeated, "I could show you who your mother is."

✷

PART IV

Three Loves
1924–1930

A Pair of Boots

Between 1525 and 1924, seventeen houses in Segendorf burned to the ground. But most of them not in the sacrificial bonfire. My parents' house was number eighteen. All the hamlet's inhabitants formed a chain from the Moorbach to the village center, passing buckets of water along as fast as they could, though, admittedly, they concentrated their collective effort on the neighboring houses, to prevent the conflagration from spreading.

Everyone agreed that a flying spark must have been responsible for the blaze.

No one had seen how, before I'd fled, I'd torn the torch away from Anni and hurled it into the burning house, how I'd taken her face in my hands and looked her in the eyes and said, "I love you."

Up on Wolf Hill, I curled up against the side of the oak that faced away from Segendorf and wept. I drew in my legs, pressed my knees against my chest, wrapped my arms around them, and buried my face there. I wanted to make myself as small as possible, so that nobody would be able to find me, and I thought, if I make an effort, then maybe I can crawl inside myself, and reach someplace better. I stayed there till late in the night, scratching at my wound and spelling out one word after another: H-o-t, b-l-a-z-e, f-i-r-e, d-e-v-o-u-r, s-m-o-k-e, J-o-s-f-e-r, J-a-s-f-e, J-o-s-f-e-r . . .

It didn't help much.

The west wind carried smoke and ash my way. I fell asleep with my index fingers plugging my nostrils.

During the night, I found myself wandering through a burning house. I knew I was dreaming, there was no noise at all, the ceiling fell in, the chimney exploded—yet none of this disturbed the silence. I strode calmly from room to room, and finally reached my own. Heading for bed, I laid myself down between my parents, and drew up the covers.

"I love you," I said to them, surprised that they were alive, and what's more, that they didn't answer.

"I love you," I repeated.

My parents snored.

"ILOVEYOUILOVEYOUILOVEYOU!"

Someone or other prodded me. I shot up, grabbing at something smooth, sleek, and redolent of leather, and saw a girl whose polished boots rose past her knees.

"You're Julius Habom," she said. "That's you, isn't it?"

Mina Reindl was my age, but at least a head taller than me. Her hair shimmered, now gray, now blond, her tanned skin made you think of lacquered wood, and as she stood there inspecting me, she didn't blink once. Typical Klöble. A few months before, her father had fallen victim to a rabid fox. Since then, the rumor had gone around that her mother, the master baker, had developed a weakness for an undertaker from out of town—certain nocturnal screams supposedly proved it.

Mina stamped her foot—I still had hold of her leg.

"I like it when you grab my leg," she said. "You can grab my head, too. If you want."

I let go.

"I hold my own legs, too, sometimes. But you hold them much better. You have beautiful eyes. Did you sleep up here? There are rabid bears out here, and wolves, and . . ."

"Foxes."

"Yes, exactly!" She gave me an amiable smile, and that made me relax a bit. My stomach growled.

"Why are you making that noise?"

I shrugged. "You smell like bread."

A short time later, I was munching on rolls with bacon in them. Mina had smuggled them out of the bakery.

"Come with me. We'll look for your sister," said Mina.

"No, I'm never going back there."

"But I'm not bringing you rolls every day. That's bad for business."

"I don't need you."

"But you mustn't starve. You have beautiful eyes. Take another roll. And then we'll look for your sister. She has wavy hair."

"I'm staying here."

Mina fiddled a toothpick between her rotten black teeth. Thanks to all the poppy-seed pastries in Segendorf, Carpenter Huber did a brisk trade in toothpicks of all sizes.

"I have to go home. Or else my mother will get mad. She's the master baker. And a widow!"

"I know."

"Did you know that she likes the Wickenhäuser?"

"Wickenhäuser?"

"A Wickenhäuser is a mortician." Mina pricked herself in the gums. "Agh! I'm not allowed to tell about that. Now you're not allowed to tell about it either, okay?"

"That depends."

"Depends on what? I'm not bringing any more rolls. That's bad for business."

"Do you think you could bring your mother up here?"

"Only if you hold my leg again."

Mina stretched out her left leg, and I wrapped both arms around it.

"Do you like my boots? The pretty leather came from Hunter Josfer."

I didn't let go. I didn't let go, but clung tighter, closed my eyes, nestled my cheek against the leather, and inhaled deeply.

"You do that really well," said Mina. Then she went back to the village.

As the hours went by, the oak's shadow moved on Wolf Hill like the hand of a clock. I peered at the village over the top of the hill, afraid that Mina's mother might have betrayed my hiding place to the mayor, or, much worse, to Pastor Meier.

Nobody came. In the evening the sun was swallowed by the moor, and

thinking Mina had forgotten me, I curled myself up again and was at-
tempting to recall what my father had told me about the edibility of moss,
when someone called: "Habom! We're coming!"

Mina ran toward me. A wheezing figure, tall for a woman but svelte for
a master baker, followed, leaning for a moment on the oak's trunk to gasp
for air and throwing Mina a reproachful look. "I told you: quietly!"

"But Mama, he has to know that we're coming."

Master Baker Reindl was out of breath, but her appearance was even
more impressive now that she was out from behind her counter. "I know
someone," she said, "who has work for you."

"I learn fast," I said, truthfully.

"How old are you?"

"Eleven."

"You'd have to leave this place."

"Good."

"And your sister?"

I hadn't thought about that. "Can't she come, too?"

The master baker shook her head. "She wouldn't make it."

"I can help her."

"You're going to have to help yourself. So: you're sure you want to go
away?"

Dead certain, I wanted to say, but only nodded my head.

"A friend will pick you up tomorrow."

Maybe, I thought, I could convince this friend to take Anni and me
together.

"The Wickenhäuser is visiting," whispered Mina.

"Shh," went her mother. "He still owes me a favor."

Mina giggled. "She's always helping him explode."

"Keep quiet! What have I told you?"

Mina rolled her eyes, and said: "The bedroom is taboo. You sleep in the
bedroom, you hear what's happening in the bedroom, but you neeeever
talk about the bedroom."

"Do you know how Anni's doing?" I asked.

"Someone will take care of her." Mina's mother stroked her gray-blond hair. "Come on, let's get going."

"And Habom?" Mina said.

"What?"

"The foxes. The wolves! And the bears."

"There aren't any wolves or bears here."

"But foxes."

"Mina!" said her mother.

"It's fine," I explained to Mina. "I like being alone." And though I'd told her the truth, that evening it was a lie. As they were leaving I hugged Mina's leg one last time, and when they'd already walked off a ways, I called after them: "Why?"

The master baker lifted her arms, palms upward.

"Why are you helping me?"

She pointed at Segendorf behind her with her thumb. "I know a certain master baker who, when she was young, always wanted to get away from this muckhole."

"You can come, too."

"No," she pressed her daughter against her with her long, brawny arms, "Mina likes it here. Someone like Mina wouldn't like it anywhere else." Then they tramped down Wolf Hill together. With every step they took away from me, the sound of Mina's prattle grew softer and softer. "WhatsamuckholeWhatsamuckholeWhatsamuckhole?"

I ran a hand through my hair, and ashes fluttered from my head. I ran to the Moorbach, slipped out of my clothes, leapt into the ice-cold water, and dunked myself again and again, scrubbing my skin with a piece of slate until it turned bright red. Jasfe and Josfer were in the air now, their dust pollinated the poppies, danced in the highest treetops, it was captured by spiderwebs, seeped into the earth, flew through the airways of the Segendorfers, penetrated their very lungs.

Auf Wiedersehen, *Muckhole*

I woke before sunrise, stirred by sparrows quarreling over a worm in the boughs of the oak. I felt good, lighter. Fog swirled around Wolf Hill like a milky broth, lapping shyly just short of my feet, but out on the horizon the sun was coming up, dawn light shining in shades of forget-me-not blue, lilac purple, and dandelion yellow. And the wound on my elbow was itching. So the healing process has begun, I told myself.

A chubby man with a fat, crab-red face walked up to me, wearing wrinkled, wine-colored velvet pants and a coat of the same shade stretched across his belly. I hadn't imagined a mortician looking like that. There was a gravedigger in Segendorf, but he was gaunt and pale, and wore a mud-splattered cloak from which his hands and head protruded as if from a tortoise's shell, and even when he was younger his facial features had been slack, supposedly as a result of the sulfurous fumes from the Segendorf graveyard.

"Let's go," he said to me.

"Wait! My sister has to come with us."

"How old is she? Seven?"

"Eight."

He shook his head. "Either you come now or both of you stay here."

I thought about Anni, how I couldn't just leave her alone, she was naive and much too good-natured, she needed her brother. But I couldn't stay. I couldn't.

"Do you have a knife?" I asked.

Wickenhäuser hesitated, reached into his breast pocket, and handed me a penknife with a sandalwood grip. I thanked him, bent down over a thin, conspicuously snake-like oak root, and carved three words, the best three words I could think of, into its bark. As deep as I could. Maybe Anni would find them someday. And maybe then she'd think of her brother.

"Let's go, boy, the carriage is waiting."

Wickenhäuser grabbed me by the collar and hauled me along behind him. The "carriage" was a rickety two-wheeled cart drawn by a mule named Hoss, and barely large enough to accommodate a driver and a coffin.

"Where are we driving?" I asked the undertaker.

"To your new home."

"And where's that?"

But no answer was forthcoming.

During the ride I had no choice but to sit on the coffin.

For six days and seven nights I juddered on Wickenhäuser's cart across the deserted moorland's broken roads. We hardly ever spoke to each other. My longing for Anni left me wordless. Occasionally, with no warning whatsoever, Wickenhäuser would belt out one of his own poems at full volume, his shrill voice scaring whole flocks of birds skyward.

It gnaws at the heart,
To attempt it is hard,
The ocean of feelings tears it apart,
While a ragged voice from a vanishing cart
Whispers, What are you missing?

So take hold of your heart,
Kill the pain,
Stab it a thousand times and don't complain,
Even if doing so drives you insane,
You're determined, so it won't be in vain,

Proceed with the task, however cruel,
However much it makes you feel like a fool,
Complete it and victory is yours
Ignore the despair, ignore the remorse.

Then you'll have finally achieved checkmate,
And tragedy continues to twist your fate.

Eventually I grew accustomed to this awkward form of locomotion, and was able to doze as we rode along, when I wasn't softly repeating the verses to myself. The farther I traveled from Segendorf, the better I felt. I missed Anni fiercely, but with each new morning a strange intensity was growing in my breast. I was going to discover the world now. Explore strange places. Never eat poppy seeds again.

As the seventh night fell, Wickenhäuser stopped the cart and pulled me down from the coffin. I shook the feeling back into my limbs. Wickenhäuser pointed to a log cabin in a clearing in the middle of the forest: tree trunks stacked and wedged together, with a shingle roof on which yellowish lichen sprouted.

"What's that?" I asked.

"Your new home," said Wickenhäuser.

"You live here*?"*

"Good Lord, no!" He slapped me on the shoulder. "This is where my mother lives."

First Love

The old woman concentrated the light. Her white dress sucked every last atom of brightness into itself. Even after two days I still narrowed my eyes instinctively whenever I looked at her. The circumscribed space of the cabin offered no possibility for retreat. A misted window in the rear wall was the sole connection to the outside world, and in front of it there hulked an armchair in which I had passed the first two nights, just to the left of the stove and the fireplace, just to the right of a door that led to the bedroom I wasn't allowed to enter, catty-corner from another door that walled off the stink of the latrine, and which was almost hidden behind an enormous wardrobe, from which there seeped the same ancient odor that had settled in Wickenhäuser's mother's white dress. It smelled like grease and dried flowers, and emitted a strangely bitter scent.

Since Wickenhäuser had introduced me to his mother, leaving that same evening to continue his journey toward a city called Schweretsried, where he worked as an undertaker, I hadn't stepped outside at all, out of fear that the old woman would shut the door behind me and refuse to open it again, in which case I'd be forced to survive alone in the forest. Wickenhäuser's mother always noticed when I meddled with the deadbolt, and then she'd scream hysterically. It was unlike anything I'd ever heard before—her tongue was barely bigger than a uvula. A congenital defect. Each morning she wandered from the bedroom to the armchair, shooed me away, spitting, then sat herself down and closed her eyes. Sometime around noon, she'd moan:

"Uhh-iii!" (Hungry)

and I'd cook her some lentil soup, as the undertaker had instructed me. Two sacks of lentils by the chimney, filled to bursting, ensured that we were sufficiently provisioned. While eating, the old lady took elaborate care not to spill on her dress. She didn't slurp, either. I'd never met anyone before who didn't slurp. After the second bowl she'd be full, and caw:

"Uhhhn!" (Done)

at which point I'd take her dish away. Then she cried:

"Iii-uhh!" (Pillow)

and I'd prop up her head with a down cushion. Before long, she'd have dozed off. In the evening she'd abruptly open her eyes, beat the pillow, and march to the latrine. Finally, she'd disappear into the bedroom again.

Wickenhäuser had asked me to look after his mother for "a little while." After a few days I asked myself how long that little while might last— a week? A month? Two months? Even if I slipped barefoot to the door in the dead of night and slid the bolt aside so slowly I could barely see it moving, the old lady would notice and start her panicked shrieking. For four days

I tried to leave the house on the sly, without her hearing. While she was eating, while she slept, while she was answering the call of nature. I tried it before dinner, after dinner, early in the morning, late in the evening, and at high noon, tried it by way of the window, tried it while I was spelling out one of the newly memorized poems, and I even tried it through a little gap in the outer wall of the latrine.

No luck.

Either the old lady groaned:

"Uhh-iii!"

Or she cawed:

"Uhhhn!"

Or she called:

"Iii-uhh!"

When she woke me again on the fifth day, shoving me from the warm lap of the armchair, I ran furious to the door, flung it wide open in spite of the screaming, and stepped outside. My feet had barely touched the soil when everything went quiet. I stepped back inside, thinking all the screaming had finally finished her off. But she wasn't gasping for breath on the floor. And she wasn't clawing at her chest. She stood upright beside the armchair, stroking the cushion as if it were a dog's neck, and smiling dreamily.

"Uhh-ehh?" she asked.

I cleared my throat, bewildered.

At which point she rushed over to me and slipped her arm through mine. "Uhh-ehh!"

What was I supposed to do? I liked her smile. Together we stepped out into the daylight. The sun dazzled me; I blinked.

"Uhh-ehh!" urged the old lady, and licked her lips. Her white dress glittered like new-fallen snow. "Uhh-ehh!"

She showed me the way. Our stroll took us once around the cabin, then the old lady began to wheeze so alarmingly that I moved her toward a dirty gray chair on the porch. Only she didn't want to let go of my arm. As she sat gulping air, I knelt beside her. Before long her head tipped to one side, and softly she began to snore. As soon as I dared to move, she tightened her grip and snuggled her head into my shoulder. This close to her, that ancient odor was especially strong. Even as she slept, the smile didn't slip from her face. And something peculiar was happening to my lips and eyes, to my cheeks. I wished I had a mirror, a window, or just a puddle of water, but even without them I knew what this was.

I was smiling.

The next day we went out for a walk before lunch. The old lady gathered the hem of her dress so that its skirt wouldn't drag in the dust. This time we rounded the house twice: a porch with a chair, a blunt ax, piled cordwood, the opaque window, rusty saw blades and nails, a big rock, flat and level like a table, and beside it a slew of daisies, a worm-eaten wooden chest with a padlock, spiderwebs, a metal bucket filled with slate, a tattered snakeskin nailed to the wall, the porch with the chair . . .

Now and then, the old lady cheerfully said:

"Uhh-ehh!"

and tugged at my arm. Later on, she ate three bowls of lentil soup.

"Uhhhn!"

"Iii-uhh!"

Within a week we'd increased our daily workout to six circuits of the cabin. Sometimes we even went counterclockwise. The old lady was breathing more smoothly now, and it was rare that I had to support her. Three times a day she spooned her soup, and three times a day she disappeared into the latrine. At night she left the door to her bedroom open a crack. While eating, she muttered:

"Uhh-ehh."

While walking she panted:

"Uhh-ehh!"

After getting up, and before going to bed, she'd greet or take leave of me with "Uhh-ehh."

Strangely, only I grew sunburned from our walks. The skin of my face was peeling. Delicately the old lady pulled shreds of it from my forehead; I put up with it.

"How come you live here?"

The old lady shrugged her shoulders.

"My name's Julius. How about you?"

She dangled an especially long strip of skin in front of my nose.

"Eh."

"What?"

"Eh."

"Can you write? Yes?"

The old lady nodded.

"I can read," I said.

She clapped her hands.

"Do you have any chalk?"

She shook her head.

"Coal, we can use coal."

Again she shook her head, and when I made to stand up, she pushed me back into the armchair, took a plate from the kitchen, shoveled a dishful of lentils onto it, and laid it in my lap.

"Hungry?"

She sighed, bent over, and shaped four letters from the lentils.

"Else? Your name is Else?"

"Eh!" *She nodded, erased her name, and wrote:*

"Du"—*the informal "you."*

"My name's Julius."

She shook her head, and tapped her hand against her chest.

I understood, and repeated, addressing her informally as Du: "Your name is Else."

"Uhh-ehh!" she shouted.

"What does that mean? What is it? Write it, write it out!"

Else pressed her lips together, crossed her arms behind her back, and stepped from one foot to the other like a little girl caught red-handed. What I read in the lentils was this: For more than sixty years Else had lived in this cabin, she'd been born here, married here, gotten pregnant here, and one day, like her ancestors, she'd be buried in the forest. Her parents had chosen her husband for her, and over forty-five years she'd first gotten to know and then to love him. When at the end of World War I (this was the first time I'd heard of it) she learned that her husband had fallen at Verdun in France, she'd thrown open the wardrobe and pulled on the most expensive fabric she owned: her wedding dress. Bedecked in that whitest of white embroidery, she'd managed to suppress the fear of being as alone as she now was. Since then that whiteness had shrouded her in comforting memories—of her husband's desperate groping for the dress's buttons on their wedding night, of the napkin with which her mother had so frequently patted her mouth, of her grandfather's pale hair, of the first time she'd seen her baby boy, of the wreath of daisies she'd worn on her head at her wedding.

By now, the dress wasn't blinding to me anymore. Instead, it shone. I polished off each spoonful of lentils with gusto, and the tastiest were the ones that Else had used for writing. At night, I peeped through the cracked bedroom door, trying in vain to see more than I could smell: grease, dried flowers, and bitterness. Every day I plucked a daisy and adorned the edge of Else's plate with it. On the velvet nap of the pillowcase I wrote I love you, *wiping the letters away before Else could read them. I conversed with her with the help of the lentils, observing carefully how she bent her fingers, clenched her hands, swung her arms.*

This change did not go unnoticed. One evening, the bedroom door was cracked wider than usual. I hesitated not one moment, only took a deep breath, and went in to her. I lay down beside her. Maybe, I thought, on that next-to-last night in Segendorf I'd actually crawled deep enough into myself, and now I'd emerged in that other, that wondrous place? She touched me only once, stroking my face before she fell asleep, with a motherly "Uhh-ehh," giving me a warm moment in which I felt so at home, suspended in that letterless silence, that for the first time I was able to drift off without missing Anni.

My first love was, at the same time, my shortest. The next morning, a faint autumn morning, she lay stiff and cold beside me. I noticed it immediately on waking, but clenched my eyes shut and clung to her. Until the afternoon, I barely moved. The fall of her hair shimmered silver, her pale skin, generously strewn with age spots and birthmarks, made me think of porcelain. She smelled bitter, rancid, with a fading undertone of sweetness. Her eyes were open, and gleamed with every color from hazel to mossy green. I shut them, passing my hand across her face, feeling furrows and crow's-feet, and dimples like Anni's, and couldn't look away, nor bring myself to give her a farewell kiss on the cheek.

The feeling of having to do something finally drove me from the bed. Anything would work, as long as it distracted me. I decided to cook. I went to fetch firewood. I hacked up five logs. And another ten for later. I lit a bundle of dry grass and stuffed it among the wood. I went to fetch water. A little brook snaked its way through the forest, five minutes distant. That day, I made it there in only three. By the time I got back, the fire was already blazing. I put the pot on, poured in some water, threw in a handful of lentils. And another. And another. Waited for it to boil. Softly, I said "Else" to myself, and felt scared by how unearthly it sounded—I tossed even more lentils into the water. And then it was finally boiling, and I scooped lentils from the pot with my bare hand, scalded myself and screamed, and sampled them anyway, and they were hard and grainy and tasted like nothing.

I forgot the pot, the fire, the lentils, slipped in beside Else again, and pressed my face into the pillow. I wouldn't weep—I'd wept for my parents, I wouldn't weep for Else, too. As long as I wasn't crying, it couldn't all be so bad. Only, my eyes didn't know that. I drove my face deeper and deeper into the down pillow, until it was just a damp piece of fabric. Water on the pillow, nothing more. And Else was only resting, sure: just taking a little nap. I plucked every daisy I could find, and slipped them one after another into Else's hair, until it looked as if they were sprouting from her head.

Toward evening I began to feel that Else's smell had changed. The odor of grease had grown more dominant.

"Uhh-ehh," I said to her. "Can you say that? Just once. Say Uhh-ehh one more time."

I put my ear to her lips, and listened.

"Tell me. Uhh-ehh."

I pressed closer.

"Uhh?"

As close as I could.

"Ehh?"

The next morning I stuck into my nostrils two scraps of fabric I'd torn from a rag, and cooked the morning bowl of lentils for Else; around noon I brought her a second helping, that evening the last, and once night fell I dumped all the cold lentils down the latrine. I began to tidy up the cabin, washing the window, eliminating the cobwebs, scrubbing the pots and bowls, polishing the flatware, and airing out the wardrobe. My new home should be shipshape, clean. Since Else had fallen into a deep sleep, I spent the night in the armchair again, ate barely anything, and looked forward to her awakening. Patience, it was all just a question of patience, of time, until she'd call me to her side. Soon.

How much time passed before footsteps approached and the door was opened? The leaves of the lindens and beeches had flushed to a fiery red. Cold seeped into the cabin through knotholes and cracks in the wood. I shivered in spite of the moth-eaten sheepskin I'd thrown around myself, having decided that an old woman like Else was in greater need of the blanket.

Wickenhäuser paid me no mind as he stepped into the cabin, hurled open the bedroom door, and froze. I stumbled over to him. As far as I could see, Wickenhäuser wasn't breathing, wasn't even blinking. For a couple of seconds he looked like a gravedigger. Then his face bloomed crab-red again and the piggy little eyes fixed themselves on me, a pale, emaciated boy who stood swaying beside him.

"Is she awake?" I asked.

Wickenhäuser grabbed me, threw his thick arms around me, and pulled me so powerfully against his round, firm gut that it drove all the air from my lungs.

Second Love

White light stabbed at my eyes. I woke in a bright room. Attempting to free myself from the two blankets lying heavily on my chest, I tumbled from the bed and crawled, since I could barely feel my legs, to the window. Grabbing the curtain, I hauled myself up, and looked outside.

It was pitch-dark. Turning back to the room, I noticed a candle flame imprisoned in a glass ball. I'd never seen a lightbulb before. To me, it was fire that lived without oxygen. Holding myself upright with the help of a chair, I teetered over to the door, lost my balance, made a grab for the knob, slipped sideways, and slumped to the floor again. It cost me a good deal of strength to pull myself back onto the chair. Panting, I rested a minute. Now, with my back to the room, I looked up at the wall and the golden switch protruding from it. I bent forward, pressed it, and the sun went out. I screamed in terror, groped for the switch, shoved my thumb against it—it grew bright. I stared at the candle flame in the glass ball and pressed the switch again. The light was extinguished. I pressed. The light flared up. Pressed—on. Pressed—off.

Distracted by my discovery, I didn't notice the door being pushed open. The sight of Wickenhäuser's fat, crab-red face surprised me, I fell from the chair, and shadows sprang at me from all directions, blocking my ears, shutting my eyes. Before I hit the ground, my shoulder struck the switch: night. Dark. Out.

When I opened my eyes again, I lay in bed. Sunbeams slipped in through the window. Real sunbeams. Wickenhäuser sat on a chair watching me.

"You look like one of my clients," he said.

I pointed to the lamp above him. "What's that?"

"Electric light."

"Electric . . ."

"How are you feeling?"

"Are you rich?"

"Don't answer a question with another question. That's impolite."

"You are rich."

"How would you know?"

"The innkeeper in Segendorf is rich. When you ask him if he's rich, he always dodges the question, too."

"Better go back to sleep, you little rascal."

"What's a rascal?"

"Sleep!"

Thanks to his business with the dead, Nathaniel Wickenhäuser was one of the few who had profited from the world war. Not just soldiers, but many of those left behind, whose hearts and thoughts had accompanied their sons, husbands, fathers to the front, had died as well. The inflation hadn't harmed him either, since death didn't take a break, even in the midst of an economic crisis—on the contrary, he put in overtime. In spite of the lucrative business, however, Wickenhäuser owned only Hoss, his mule, and a carriage on which there was just room enough for a single coffin. Wickenhäuser didn't hold with automobiles. They were unreliable. He preferred to obtain his coffins from the countryside, where they were cheapest. He particularly esteemed the specimens from Segendorf, because of the quality of their wood, for which reason (as well as the waiting bed of Master Baker Reindl) he undertook these tedious trips. Behind their hands, people called him the Jew of Schweretsried. Wickenhäuser knew it; stepping into a pub, he sensed instinctively who among those present thought that about him, but Wickenhäuser didn't mind, the role appealed to him. Wickenhäuser liked the Jews. And their suits. Secretly he dreamed of traveling to Paris one day, and there, in a shop on the Champs-Elysées, having an elegant frock coat cut for himself. Although he could easily have afforded a more favorable location, his own shop was all the way at the far end of the Marktstrasse. He appreciated the symbolism. His apartment, in which he spent two weeks nursing me back to health, was directly above the establishment. Three times a day he'd knock at the door of the guest room, three times a day I'd tell him to come in—he'd bring me oatmeal, semolina, or a steaming bowl of soup—and three times a day I expected him to ask me to leave the house. With the exception of lentil soup, which I strictly refused even to taste, I ate voraciously, and didn't leave a scrap behind. Meanwhile my face was filling out, and whenever I sat on the toilet—flushing fascinated me nearly as much as the light switch—the water beneath me splashed as if I were discharging stones. During the day I yearned to go out into the fresh air, but Wickenhäuser ordered me to stay in bed. "You rascal," he said. "I'll decide when you go out."

"What does rascal mean?"

"It means Julius, more or less."

"And what, more or less, does Wickenhäuser mean?"

He laughed. "Certainly not rascal. I'm not pretty enough for that. But you, you have the potential to become one."

"But I don't want that at all."

"Go back to sleep!"

The first time Wickenhäuser let me out on my own was to go to Else's funeral, and I didn't have to be asked twice. For the occasion the undertaker laid out a black suit on the bed for me.

"It might not fit me," I said.

"Trust me, my little rascal. I have a good eye for bodily dimensions."

I was amazed: the sleeves weren't overlong, nor did the suit pinch; there wasn't even any need for provisional pinning or bunching. Nothing at all like my best and worst—since seldom worn and thus terrifically uncomfortable—lederhosen back in Segendorf, which had been pulled from the closet exclusively for Sunday Masses. I used to have to stuff hay into my formal leather shoes. I'd never before been able to break in my clothes before they'd started to reveal their defects, but this new funeral attire felt like sheer layers of colored air, not like cloth at all. And yet it protected me, this new outfit, disguised me, and allowed me to walk the road to the church without being noticed. So fascinated was I by my brand-new exterior that I ran after Wickenhäuser thoughtlessly, like a child following his father, and the town of Schweretsried flowed past me unnoticed, as if I'd traversed it already a thousand times.

Then, by Wickenhäuser's side, I stepped into the parish church, and saw the casket. On its side a brass plate was mounted, upon which ELSE was etched in curving characters. So different from those lines of lentils, arranged with a shaking hand. In the cool air of the church hung the odors of wood polish, candle wax, and, above all, incense. There was no trace of grease, dried flowers, or bitterness.

I swallowed my tears. No one, especially not Wickenhäuser, was to know what I felt—I cried inside, didn't squeeze the tears out of my eyes, but rather pulled them into my head, down my throat, and stowed them away in my belly.

On the way home after the funeral, Wickenhäuser said, "Let's celebrate!" and we turned in at the Iron Pine Tavern; Wickenhäuser ordered for himself an ale and for me a sweet dumpling.

"Don't make such a face, rascal."

"I'm not sad," I lied.

"Good," he said, "neither am I," not much better at lying.

"But she was your mother!"

"That's what she always claimed, anyway."

"If she wasn't, why did you take care of her?"

"Me? It was you who took care of her!"

The ale and the dumpling arrived. For the first time in my life I tasted custard, it was almost like fresh honey, only much better, and while I delightedly shoved spoonful after spoonful into my mouth, Wickenhäuser described to me how for years on end his parents had prevented him from leaving the house: with stories about monsters that lived in the cities, with a crushing daily round of chores, and panicked screams if he ever so much as touched the latch without permission. After his father had died in the war, his mother had sat silent all day long, wrapped in her bridal gown, staring through the walls, and through Wickenhäuser. In the end, it wasn't that he'd been fleeing *into* the great wide world, but fleeing *from* her.

"She hated me," said Wickenhäuser.

"Why do you think that?"

"She made me feel as if I'd killed my father."

"But he died in the war."

Wickenhäuser heaved a that's-just-how-she-was sigh.

"I don't believe that a mother can actually hate her children," I said.

"If that's the case, how come you aren't with yours?"

I didn't say anything.

"My little rascal." Wickenhäuser wiped a bit of vanilla custard from my chin with his napkin. "We're all better off without our parents."

That same night I shunted my memories of Else from the living to the dead side of things. It didn't show much sense, letting thoughts of people who didn't exist anymore make you sad.

December arrived, and with it the first frost, and the recognition that between Wickenhäuser and me there existed a sort of unspoken agreement. As long as I didn't make a nuisance of myself, Wickenhäuser wouldn't send me away. The undertaker was single, and appreciated the company.

Every once in a while he invited over men who wore makeup like women, or a woman and a man who both wore makeup like women, or, rarely, just women without makeup. Such visits were as much of a passion for Wickenhäuser as a support for the bereaved. On many a Friday, but most often on Saturdays, before sunrise and from out of the foggy gray, they would step into the house, wrapped in long cloaks. On such occasions the fire leapt merrily in the hearth, and Wickenhäuser would recite new poems for his guests in his shrill voice, which I could hear all the way from where I lay up on the second floor:

> If you hear this
> then I don't not love you anymore,
> no,
> I love you more.

Later, when the night was well advanced and smelled of schnapps and to-bacco, Wickenhäuser would conduct one or another of these guests to his bedroom. The morning after, I noticed, the undertaker always changed his sheets.

I ate with him, accompanied him on shopping trips, helped him buff the coffins to a high shine. I didn't earn a single reichsmark for any of this, but was allowed to sleep in a bed as soft as one million mullein flowers, dine on beef tongue, foie gras, and wild strawberries with cream, and dress myself in clothes cut to measure, without which I could barely fall asleep anymore, so cozy was the costly cloth against my skin. Between the spelling lessons I gave to the illiterate mason so that he wouldn't blunder when carving the headstones, and arranging bunches of flowers (I added a couple of daises to every one), I had plenty of time to explore Schweretsried. Whenever I stepped out the door with Wickenhäuser, it was as if I were his Most Beloved Possession—I was introduced to everyone the undertaker knew, however slightly. I felt especially awkward when Wickenhäuser proudly alluded to my "lovely, lofty brow" or my "lovely pitch-black hair" or my "lovely figure," and called me Adonis, instead of rascal. Thus I preferred to take my walks alone. Having arrived in the big wide world, I soaked up every trifle: the cough-inducing fumes of the automobiles; the discomfort in the faces of former customers, for whom I was Death's emissary; the brawling at the Iron Pine, democrats versus reactionaries; the hue and cry of the Yugoslavian book peddler, representative of a dying breed of conscientious salesmen, who struggled to read every book he had in stock, for which reason this Yugoslav was probably the only resident of Schweretsried who actually registered the appearance of Mein Kampf; all the varieties of seasonings, from oregano to turmeric (and their spellings!); the soft glow of the gas lanterns.

However, my fascination often gave way to anger at the pedestrians who crossed my path or bumped into me. I couldn't stand walking behind someone, the streets seemed overcrowded, saturated with noisy, foul-smelling men, which is why I made a point of breezing past all those walkers, until I reached the city limits or some deserted area whose quiet reminded me of home, and of Anni. The longing for Anni was like an invisible thread coiled around my chest. Now and then it was as if she tugged on it, so that my heart throbbed and I was afraid I might forget her. Then I'd ask myself why I hadn't tried to make contact with her by now, and I answered that it was impossible: there was no mail delivery to Segendorf, Wickenhäuser's next excursion south was beyond the horizon, and I was much too young to travel on my own.

Looking back, I think these were only excuses to salve a guilty conscience. The real reason was that I preferred Schweretsried to Segendorf. Even if I had to sacrifice the proximity of my sister.

One morning Wickenhäuser and I were polishing a coffin that a local glass blower had chosen for his daughter. Burglars had slit her throat with shards of glass from one of her father's vases.

"What's your opinion, rascal?"

"About what?"

"About this girl's death."

"The thieves are murderers. They ought to be executed."

"A fine opinion. But now: imagine a different truth."

"Maybe the thieves broke into the wrong house at the wrong time? Maybe the girl . . . killed herself?"

"Clever as always, my little rascal. You see, it isn't so hard. You can make sense of anything, if you want to, as long as you're willing to exert your brain a bit. Everything can be true. What you decide to believe is always the truth. Remember that. Rascal, would you be happy as an undertaker?"

"No."

"Why not?"

"It would be lonely."

"Maybe. And now . . ."

"The opposite?"

Wickenhäuser nodded.

"If I were an undertaker, I could earn a lot of money."

"Good."

"I could keep you company."

"Very good."

"I could eat orange marmalade every day. I could own a flush toilet. And electric lights."

"Right, keep going!"

"I could collect money from the church, which has deep pockets. I could console people. I could always wear nice suits. I could keep the best plot in the graveyard for myself. I could do something respectable."

Wickenhäuser slapped the coffin lid with a loud bang. "And you could have any woman you want."

That same evening he introduced me to a girl my own age whom he'd brought to the house.

"Her name is Stephanie," he said, at which the girl briefly wrinkled her brow. As we introduced ourselves, I was surprised by her strong handshake. Wickenhäuser slapped me on the shoulder and winked at us. He hurriedly wrapped himself in his coat, and opened the front door. An urgent appointment, he said, he might be gone a long time.

Then we were alone.

The girl, who presumably wasn't called Stephanie, was neither pretty nor ugly. You wouldn't have turned to look at her in the street, at any rate. Without a word, she began to unbutton her dress. I didn't move, just watched, as she peeled away one layer of clothes after another and took off her jewelry. Her body was petite, her skin pale and firm. Next, she started to undress me. It all seemed so strange, but nevertheless, I let it happen. Her touch wasn't unpleasant. She knew how to fill a young man with self-confidence, when to groan, when not to snicker. I stopped her only once—when she went to kiss the scar on my elbow. While I was sleeping with her, I thought, fascinated: I'm sleeping with a woman. And I asked myself why I'd waited so long to try something that felt so good. I was hardly irritated by the fact that in the hours we spent together she barely looked me in the eye; that was just part of her profession, I told myself.

Sometime around midnight she dressed again, nodded a good-bye, and left the house.

I never saw her again.

At breakfast the next morning I felt Wickenhäuser watching me. I let him fidget for a while, and picked the salt from my pretzel as always, as if there were nothing to discuss. Only after washing the dishes did I say, "Okay then."

"What do you mean?" asked Wickenhäuser, though I think he knew immediately what I was talking about.

"I'll stay."

In Schweretsried I saw the world, and that was exactly what I wanted. Wickenhäuser showed me the business of death, and, since I learned quickly, *the undertaker never had to repeat an instruction. At first I served as assistant; later on,* rascal *came to mean* partner.

Back then, the pastor of Schweretsried marveled at how strikingly often baptisms followed hard on funerals in the same family. So many husbands, it seemed, had sired children shortly before their demise. The preacher ascribed this to the righteous equity of the Lord. The Grace of Heaven, so to speak. At the regulars' table in the Iron Pine he told Wickenhäuser about this joyous miracle; the latter smiled and shook his head. "What a rascal!"

"Who?" asked the pastor. "God?"

"Sure," said Wickenhäuser. "Who else?"

Wickenhäuser explained to me things no woman would have been willing to explain herself. After each burial ceremony, I'd ask the widows in a whisper to follow me into the office for some final paperwork. They never refused; their eyes were puffy with weeping, and their thoughts weren't running as smoothly as usual. In the newly furnished guest room—my office—I offered them a seat on my bed. None of them suspected anything. Patiently I asked the widows if they were satisfied with my services. They always said yes. Slowly I scooted my chair closer, and proposed a slight discount. They always welcomed it. I sat beside them on the bed, and warily slipped an arm around them. At which point they'd always cuddle up to me. Finally I admitted what exceedingly intense feelings I cherished for them. (The truth is always what one decides to believe.) Most of them tensed up, leapt from the bed, and excused themselves, polite, aloof; but some, more than a few, gratefully kissed my face. They smelled of makeup applied too thick, and sweetish sweat. In bed they were quiet, almost noiseless, as if they didn't want to wake their departed husbands.

Wickenhäuser assured me that I could have my fun with the widows, as much and as often as I liked, none of them would ever dare to confess such a misstep. But he warned me that I should never, at no point whatsoever, look one of those women in the eye. That's why he'd taken care that my first time hadn't been anything special. As far as Wickenhäuser was concerned, making love didn't mean sleeping with someone; in his opinion *making love meant that you created love, you actually* made *love. "It happens quicker than you'd think," Wickenhäuser pointed out, and added with a significant smile: "And then suddenly all you'll want is to be with that one person."*

On weekends, guests were no longer invited over. Instead, the two of us celebrated alone, and it would be wrong to say we didn't have a good time, playing our rhyming games. If one of us recited badly, that is, without rhyming, we'd have to take a hearty swig of brandy.

    This happened fairly frequently.

> I love to play: whenever I've a chance
> I cry aloud and dance a wild dance.
> My cheeks flush ruddy as a crimson star
> And now and then, I'll shout: You've gone too far!

> Many men have met their jolly doom, my dove,
> By hiking up my skirt beneath the moon above.
> You call me pert: I like that well enough,
> But not as much as I love making . . . merry.

These evenings usually ended—more often than I liked—with the under-taker, emboldened by alcohol, begging me to share his bed. To make a little love.

    I turned him down. To me, Wickenhäuser was a teacher and a busi-ness partner, nothing more. Hidden in my affection for him I sensed the possibility of a love that I didn't want to permit. To love someone again the way I'd loved Else was too great a risk for me. Because one morning the undertaker, too, would fail to wake up.

    I sometimes capitulated to Wickenhäuser's pleas purely out of pity, and slept beside him, under separate blankets. Even when he wept and wist-fully described that moment in the log cabin when, for the first and only time, we'd embraced, I refused to take him in my arms, and corrected him, saying that on that particular occasion, he'd been the only one doing the hugging. This melancholy, which by day withdrew behind the sparkle in Wickenhäuser's eyes, broke out again at night. It was only following his visits to Segendorf that Wickenhäuser was able to suppress it for a few days—or, at best, weeks—at a time, and I asked myself what Master Baker Reindl was able to give the undertaker that he couldn't find among such a rich assortment of men and women here in Schweretsried.

For me, Segendorf lay far in the distance, as if the first eleven years of my life had been merely a dream, one that was fading with every day. Anni helped me with that. My sister answered none of the letters I sent with Wickenhäuser, never returned a single greeting. Which is why I never went with him to Segendorf. I took it to mean she didn't want any contact with me. And whenever I tried to understand why, Wickenhäuser consoled me, saying I shouldn't stew over it, and instead enjoy the freedom I had here in Schweretsried. He told me that of all God's cruelties, the greatest was saddling a man with family.

In the cool summer of 1930, when I was a handsome seventeen-year-old, the undertaker returned from another excursion to Segendorf. "Have a look, rascal," he said, pulling the tarp from a hazel coffin. "We've picked up another bargain."

"How much?" I asked, excited.

Wickenhäuser whispered it in my ear.

"In that case, you're buying me dinner tonight," I said solemnly, hesitated, and pushed two more words over my lips: "Did Anni . . ."

"I'm sorry."

"Is she doing okay?"

"She looks gorgeous. But not as gorgeous as you."

"Did you ask if she wants to come see me?"

"She's a village kid, rascal."

"Did you ask her?"

"The girl runs away as soon as I drop your name."

"Maybe next time."

"There won't be a next time. I've finally decided not to go back. It's too far away."

"What about Reindl?"

"She understands. Besides, she isn't getting any younger."

That evening I tossed and turned in bed, and kept examining my elbow; the scar was pale; unless someone was looking for it, they wouldn't notice. When Wickenhäuser had spoken about my sister, she had tugged hard on that thread around my chest. I didn't understand how a lack of news from Segendorf could so preoccupy me—as if it were bad news.

I threw off the covers and walked in the dark to the door of Wickenhäuser's bedroom, paused, and while I was debating whether or not to knock, heard a conspicuously unshrill voice: "Come on in."

Wickenhäuser was sitting upright in bed. His eyes were bloodshot.

"I knew you'd see through it, rascal."

"What?"

"But I was hoping that if I didn't tell you, you wouldn't go."

"Tell me, already."

"Your sister's getting married."

"To whom?"

"Fellow called Driajes."

"When?"

"In the fall."

"Fall? Why not spring?"

"They're in a hurry."

Wickenhäuser patted the mattress beside him. "Please."

I sat down. "Do you think I should go see her?"

"I think that if you don't go now, you never will. But I also think that if you go to her, you won't come back."

"Nonsense. What's your opinion?"

"Rascal..."

"What's your opinion?"

"I want you to stay."

"Fine," I said. "Now imagine another truth."

"I...want...you...to..."

"Yes?" I prompted.

"...go."

"Good. Go on."

"You should set out tomorrow."

"Very good."

"Rascal? Stay here. Just for tonight."

"But not for long."

"Will you hold my hand?"

"No."

I left the next morning. After a long back-and-forth I'd decided against taking Hoss; I could cover the bulk of the distance faster by bus, and the remainder on foot. I didn't pack any of my suits; as long as I took little with me, I'd have enough of a reason to come back soon. Along with sufficient food for the trip, Wickenhäuser gave me a map whose southernmost marking was a ring in red ink, above which someone had scribbled Segendorf. Furthermore, as we were saying good-bye, the undertaker passed me a parcel that felt like it contained a pillow.

"Don't open it until you're sitting on the bus," he cautioned me, and swallowed hard; he looked as dismal as a Segendorf gravedigger. He glanced mistrustfully at the bus. "You'll come back?"

"Of course I will."

"My lovely rascal," Wickenhäuser said, laughing through his tears, "and what if I told you that I never delivered any of your letters to her?"

I dug my fingernails deep into the skin of my scarred elbow. "Anni doesn't know anything?"

"Suppose she doesn't?"

"Then," I said, "then that would change everything."

I gave Wickenhäuser a short, cold handshake, nodded, and took a seat at the back of the bus. The engine banged like a rifle shot. We lurched off down the road.

Third Love

On a windy Indian summer evening in September, I walked past the triple-horned cow skull (the result of a highly questionable breeding experiment) that marked the northernmost border of the village. The first barnyards I passed seemed much smaller than I remembered. In my memories, the houses were massive skyscraping structures, but now my impression was that Segendorf consisted largely of flat, skewed buildings that you could watch sinking gradually into the swampy ground. Even the church, which had instilled such respect in me as a child, now seemed to resemble nothing so much as a poorly maintained mausoleum. I felt amazed that anyone could spend his whole life here. It wasn't melancholy I was feeling, but surprise that I'd actually grown up in such a place.

To remain incognito, I steered clear of people on the street and made straight for the tavern, where I took a seat at a shaky wooden table. The air was full of rancid odors, the taproom empty, apart from the busty innkeeper.

"You from around here?" she bleated.

"Bring me something," I bleated back.

"A pint?"

I nodded. With a filthy rag, the innkeeper spread a puddle of beer around on my table. I sat there till late at night, bolting down reams of red cabbage, dumplings, and leathery cuts of roast pork. After a trip as long as mine, anything tasted good. And the more often I bent deep over my beer stein, the more often the innkeeper looked across at me, asking whether I wanted anything else, making little detours past my table. After she'd put up the last of the chairs, she planted herself before me.

"You're not from around here."

"No."

"Then you won't know my barn."

"No."

"It's out on the moor."

I looked up at her.

"I'll show it to you, it's very comfortable."

She showed me a couple of other things, too, before returning, in the gray dawn, across the labyrinth of rotting wooden planks that crisscrossed the moor, to her husband, who hadn't kissed her with that kind of abandon in years. Like a kitten lapping up milk for the first time, she'd said.

I spent those first days after my arrival out on the moor. It was still too soon, I needed some time to figure out how I could meet my sister, from whom I'd been separated for six years. Almost every day the innkeeper came looking for me, bringing me horse knockwurst, freshly baked poppy-seed rolls, cracklings, Moosinger—a variety of cheese produced exclusively in Segendorf, which ripened only after an exceedingly long and damp storage—tepid milk, poppy-seed cakes, pickled frogs' legs, poppy-seed buns, mushrooms, and eggs. In return, I deployed such knowledge as I'd acquired from the widows of Schweretsried, and hoped that her screams wouldn't disturb anyone but blindworms, storks, and toads. It seemed to me as though, with every thrust that sent flabby waves rolling across the innkeeper's backside, I was plunging deeper and deeper into my native town. I thrust, and she screamed. Soon, I was airing my own first screams as well. On those nights that the innkeeper couldn't manage to slip from her husband's bed, I explored the village. Behind every window I peeped through, someone was screaming. Screaming was part and parcel of Segendorf, like the Sacrificial Festival. Children in the dark screamed for light, husbands screamed for their wives, and the wives screamed because of their violent husbands. But nobody screamed as untiringly as the innkeeper.

"Can you go a third time?" she asked me, drizzling rose-hip marmalade on her heavy, pale upper thigh.

The better I got at imitating her screams, the louder and more piercing the innkeeper became.

One night, when I believed that I'd become familiar with every possible variety of scream, the sound of singing drew me to a greenish glowing window. The house lay at the edge of the village, not far from Wolf Hill, precisely where my parents' house had once stood. Someone was carelessly (and tunelessly) singing a song. Unfortunately, bilious green vines behind the window and rank ivy in front of it obscured my view; I could make out only tessellated pieces of a plump female shape dancing in the room. There was a pink elbow, there beige ruffles, there a snatch of white skin, there the rounded tip of a nose, there a lock of hair. This girl, the third love in my life, of which I knew nothing at that moment, accompanied her swaying dance with a breathy voice, and in spite of its unpolished tone it was so serene and artless that I felt an urge to shatter the window and study her décolletage and throat and lips as they shaped a kind of music so beautiful it made you feel as if there were no such thing as right or wrong.

I fell to my knees and pressed my hot face into the dewy grass. A moment later I was running toward the cliff and standing at the edge of the abyss, where the monk had sacrificed his Most Beloved Possession 405 years before. In contrast to the monk, however, it wasn't an object I hurled away from me. My own scream, which told of polished leather boots and a gleaming bridal gown, of lentils and walks around a log cabin, of homemade verses, lonely widows, tailored suits, and an undertaker's melancholy, pierced through the whole village, tore Blacksmith Schwaiger from his uneasy sleep, drove the residual ashes of the Sacrificial Festival before it, burrowed into the soil, plucked at the leaves of the oak on Wolf Hill, and brought a brief pause to the dancing of a girl named Anni Habom. And as I turned my back to the abyss, the latter returned an echo—soft and delicate, but so unambiguously clear that there could be no doubt whatsoever that this place was my home.

It went: pling.

✳

PART V

Objects in Mirror

Violet

Albert crossed the main street. By the town hall he hung a left, following a narrow, tarred footpath downhill, past a playground and a meadow where he and Fred had often gone sledding. Before long he'd leave the last farmhouse behind and reach the glider airfield. The thought of it made him nervous. During their conversation three days ago, Sister Alfonsa had refused to tell him over the telephone what she knew about his mother. So he'd just have to come to Saint Helena—those were her last words before Albert hung up, immediately regretting it. Since then, every attempt he'd made to reach her had failed. Fearful of missing her call, he hadn't left the phone for a moment. Under normal circumstances he would have been well on the road to Saint Helena by now; to ferret out something about his mother, he would gladly have undertaken a much longer journey. There was one thing holding him back: panic gripped Fred whenever he had to board a bus. Albert traced it back to the traumatic experience of the bus accident. And Albert himself had neither car nor driver's license. So he'd dialed Violet's number, the only number that could help get the two of them swiftly to Saint Helena.

Their breakup was already half a year behind them. Albert hadn't expected that the mere thought of seeing her would stir up the desire for something that was officially in the past. It made him think of the warning you saw printed on the side-view mirrors of American-made cars: *Objects in mirror are closer than they appear.*

The same thing applied to the past.

A year before, in the autumn of 2001, Albert had been sitting on the bus, reading the backs of heads. On a good, that is, a busy day, the selection would surely have been larger. But given the slim offering on hand, he began much as he did when watching TV: by flipping around. The asymmetrically shaved nape of the teen to his left simply bored him—it wasn't evidence of a cheap hairdresser, an underprivileged family, rather the opposite: the homemade shave on either side of her lime-green hair was an expression of rebellion; she was probably on her way back from hanging around the provincial train station, frightening elderly people, flinging beer cans, and kissing the new Alsatian pup her daddy had bought her for Christmas.

And that woman whose little chignon resembled a puffy sandwich roll? How completely tickled she'd be if somebody plopped down in the seat beside her. To loosen her bun and let the long hair tumble free, how divine that would make her feel! She certainly didn't have it easy, what with two kids and the house to look after, and her husband, whom she called "the old man" while talking on the phone with her girlfriends, just as her mother had done with her father. I certainly don't have a smooth time of it, the tilt of her head declared, but what can I do, the world's hard on me, I give it my all, but nobody's interested, except maybe you—yes, you. Won't you sit next to me and loosen my bun?

Albert yawned and pressed himself into his window seat in the last row so that he wouldn't appear in the rearview mirror of the bus driver. Sheer habit. On this October 7, 2001, his last escape from Saint Helena was months behind him. There was no reason to run away any longer: he was of legal age, nobody could force him to stay there. But, as it is with things you've done for a long time, whether willingly or not, it was difficult to break a habit. To let himself appear in rearview mirrors, to deny himself chess duels with Sister Alfonsa, to forgo Sister Simone's goulash or Fred's newspaper report fixed to the upper slats of his stealthily squeaking bunk bed, would have been a violation of the rules of the past fifteen years of Albert's life. The orphanage was his home—where else was he supposed to live? With Fred?

The bus pulled to a stop and Albert glanced away from the aisle, so as not to ruin his game if someone new should get on. Outside, a line had formed in front of a dry cleaner's. Three of the waiting housewives carried IKEA bags filled to bursting. Nobody was chatting, they consulted their watches, they rolled their eyes: they weren't happy. The bus drove on, and only then did Albert notice the small female head in the row before him. Dark-blond hair screened her neck and hid her ears. It was unusual for someone to sit directly in front of him. In his experience, people generally took the seat that would allow them to be as far as possible from their fellow riders. Someone should write a dissertation on that, he thought. The young woman was wearing a washed-out gray shirt with a soberly cut collar. She was doing something to her face with one hand. Gnawing her fingernails, applying lipstick, scratching her nose? No. She had a cell phone. Albert couldn't tell what she was looking at on the tiny screen. Not texting, that was for sure, her thumbs weren't moving. In 2001 not everyone in the Bavarian uplands had a cell phone. Her clothing suggested she could hardly have afforded a cell plan. It was more likely a gift from her not-especially-imaginative boyfriend for their one-year anniversary. If she were from the city she would have long since found herself a new man, but since the selection out in the country was humbler, she had to content herself with the kind of guy who compensates for lack of imagination with kindness. The only question was, how much longer? As soon as graduation was in the bag, and she'd enrolled at some Bavarian university, various fellow students would become keenly aware of her sassy way of tucking her naturally blond hair behind her ears. And said enticing fellow students would be in direct competition with her carpenter boyfriend, who expected nothing more from life than a solid mortgage and healthy offspring.

The bus hadn't stopped, but the young woman stood up, and the way she was clutching the support strap scared Albert, since it meant she was going to twist her body to the left, that is, away from the exit, and toward him. Her gaze struck him like Sister Alfonsa's when she caught him attempting to escape. Her face was shockingly beautiful. She came over and sat down beside him, blocking his escape route.

How she managed to keep a straight face was a riddle to Albert. Seconds passed without her saying a word. Albert understood none of this, and therefore he didn't like it.

"I'm going to Königsdorf, too," she said.

Albert acknowledged this information in what was to him a reasonable fashion: he nodded. Under no circumstances would he show that she'd ruffled him, he'd play it cool, as if young women he'd never so much as set eyes on before sat next to him daily to make some disturbing communication or other. Albert was the observer, the head reader, he never lost his perspective.

"This is the part where you ask me how I know that *you're* going to Königsdorf," she said.

Albert turned to face her (making his appearance in the rearview mirror): "Or the part where I ask you to find another seat."

"That would be unfriendly."

"Frankness is like that, sometimes."

"And what if I refused to go?"

"That would be even unfriendlier," he said.

"But frank," she said.

Albert tugged at his ear. He hadn't counted on having to conduct an aimless, meandering Fred-dialogue before even reaching Königsdorf.

"My name is Violet." She offered him her left hand, he reached out his right, and she took it in hers. "And you're Albert."

Albert often thought that he and Violet would never have gotten together if he'd known in the beginning all he found out about her in the course of time. The more she divulged about her life, so different from his own, the greater his fear grew that a relationship with her would never work out.

Once, when Violet was five years old, she'd been asked by her parents to use her fork when eating spaghetti, and she had replied: "Children, if you love your life, shun scissors, candle, fork, and knife." At six she captured the attention of the grown-ups' table with jokes about Honecker and Franz Josef Strauss. One year later she wrote a letter to George H. W. Bush, counseling him not to invade Iraq. Ever since childhood, Violet had been surrounded by an aura of self-confidence—it was as if she knew something no one else knew. Her first boyfriend put it like this: "What do you think, that the sun only rises for you?" He was immediately demoted to her first ex. Violet was the girl who asked questions that no other kid in the class would have dared to ask. She was the girl who never did anything just because she *could*, only because she thought it was right. She was the girl whom all the boys were intimidated by, and of whom they dreamed. She was the girl who played hooky to protest the Gulf War. She was the girl whose life, portioned out in videocassettes, filled a whole wall of shelves.

Her father, a television producer, had owned a video camera as early as 1980—the kind you had to lug around on your shoulder, unwieldy as a sack of potatoes, connected with a tube-like cable to a backpack that held a hundredweight battery. Everything was documented. Especially first times: Violet sleeps on her back. Violet gets swaddled. Violet takes a bath. Violet screams. Violet eats solid food. Violet laughs. Violet spits up. Violet sleeps on her belly. Violet says something. Violet crawls. Violet trips. Violet walks. Violet speaks. Violet sings. Violet swears. Violet sleeps on her side. Violet swims. Violet rides a bicycle. Violet goes skiing. Violet goes to kindergarten. Violet goes to elementary school. Violet sleeps on her other side. Violet wins the spelling bee. Violet rides a horse. Violet is in love. Violet reads. Violet gets a piercing. Violet has a skin infection. Violet has a boyfriend. Violet has a driver's license. Violet films. Violet sleeps sitting up.

Every second of her life, the camera told her, was valuable: you are precious—her father's declaration of love. The camera—the Cyclops Eye, as he called it—was a part of him. No way for Violet to think it away. In the evenings, after work, when he returned home from his stressful back-and-forths with unimaginative TV editors (on the door to his office hung a little plastic sign with his favorite saying: *I always wanted to be an etidor—and now I are one!*), Violet would sit down on the couch between her parents, and together they'd fly into the archived past. Even more often she'd watch the films alone, letting them run in the background while she dispatched her homework or drafted an article for the school newspaper, in which she exposed one of her teachers' racist remarks. All the pictures. All the direct quotes. Violet was her own role model. She expected nothing less of herself than to act as Violet would have acted. She didn't know how life would have been if she hadn't had herself to aspire toward. Sometimes it struck her that maybe she wasn't the way she would have been if no one had been recording her. Then again: who was ever the way they might have been?

Once, when she and Albert were talking about their first meeting, she sidestepped the question of whether she'd liked him right from the beginning. Violet explained that she didn't believe in love at first sight. "How can you love someone you don't even know?" Actually, she wasn't convinced by the concept of love. Love—what was it, anyway? She wasn't going to let herself be led down the garden path on a search for definitions. The countless aperçus on love dropped by various minds, more or less clever, sounded good, no question, Violet said—they spiced up every discussion of the subject and lent depth to Valentine's cards. "But what," she said, "if love's most significant quality is that it eludes definition?" A definition that, in the end, Violet found as superfluous as any other.

What had awakened her interest in Albert, the red-haired boy in the last row of seats on the bus from Wolfratshausen to Königsdorf, was that Violet had never before met anyone who went to such trouble not to be seen. And what had astonished her even more: when she'd boarded the bus, he hadn't looked at her, but rather out the window. She'd learned his name and destination from the driver. After she'd sat down in the seat in front of him and the bus had pulled out, she'd felt his gaze on her. With her cell phone she'd taken photos of his reflection in the window: he'd been looking at her like a book whose genre one isn't too keen on, and so merely skims—and yet, for some reason, one doesn't just set it aside. It hadn't been any great struggle for Violet to sit down beside him. His facial expression, when she'd said his name, had been priceless.

"And the kiss?" interrupted Albert.

That had crept up on her, she hadn't planned it, and looking back, she found it, to be perfectly frank, neither tender nor intense, rather tight-lipped, poorly aimed, almost pathetic, she would have apologized for it if he hadn't preempted her with his own "I'm sorry." As if *he'd* kissed *her!* Or as if he'd been so irresistible. And that had spurred her on, she couldn't let herself stand for that, and so she laid her hand on his neck and kissed him again, kissed *him,* so that there'd be no mistake about it, and this time, yes, this time there had been some kind of feeling, nothing especially intense, her knees wouldn't have been weak if she'd stood up—though it was good enough, she stressed, to ensure that they saw each other again the very next day—but it had made her close her eyes and for a moment forget that she was riding bus 479 down Highway 11 on an overcast afternoon.

The distance that Violet and Albert had overcome at their first meeting they built up again during the course of their second. Sitting across from each other by a window hung with toast-brown curtains at the Hofherr Tavern in Königsdorf, neither of them said what they most wanted to say. Albert kept silent about his life at Saint Helena, about being a two-thirds orphan, and about Fred. Violet, for her part, kept up with him. She didn't have much of a talent for lying, but pretended to be a college student (even though she was, like Albert, in her last year of high school), making an argument for communal living (though she still lived with her parents in a four-thousand-square-foot villa on Lake Starnberg with a private dock and a sailboat) and demonizing Germany, particularly its publicly subsidized TV (which had—indirectly—funded her entire life, as well as having paid for the coffee that, in their nervousness, they both drank so quickly that they burned their tongues).

It probably would have been their last meeting if, as they were leaving the restaurant, they hadn't run into Fred, who was on his way to the bus stop.

"Hello, Albert!" chirped Fred.

"Hello, Fred," said Albert, tugging at his earlobe.

Violet looked at him, but he made no move to introduce her. So she stepped up to Fred, extended her hand, and said, "I'm Violet."

Fred considered the hand. "Who are you?"

The question struck her—the valedictorian, the star of family videos, the editor of the school newspaper, the only child—with unexpected force: her second *Violet* had an interrogative lilt to it.

Albert shook himself out of his stupor. "This is Violet, Fred. A friend."

Fred looked at her for a moment, as if trying to reconcile Albert's information with what he saw in front of him. His sudden grin was spectacular. "Friends are ambrosial!" He embraced her, and Albert wanted to intervene, but she shook her head: *It's okay.*

"I'm Frederick Arkadiusz Driajes," said Fred, letting her go.

Violet smiled. "An *ambrosial* name."

Fred gave a start and looked at Albert.

"Did I say something wrong?" she asked.

Albert shook his head. "On the contrary."

Fred whispered something into his ear.

"Don't do that, it's rude," said Albert. "Anyway, you can ask her yourself."

Fred struggled visibly to lift his gaze from the ground. "Will you come with us?"

Violet asked, "Where to?"—though she'd already decided.

Albert nodded in the direction of the bus stop. "To count green cars."

They counted over fifty of them that day, not because traffic was heavy, but because they stayed so long. While Fred noted the individual vehicles in his journal, Violet questioned Albert about his life with Fred. Albert noticed that Violet's hands were shaking, and she stuck them into her pockets as she confessed that she liked him—which clearly sounded, to her, once spoken, much too moderate, so she added that she was sure she'd always remember the time they'd spent here today, and Albert sat stiffly beside her, because he wasn't sure what she expected from him. Violet asked if she could spend the night with them (he presumed she hadn't said "with him" in order to sound less obvious), and he was so delighted to hear it that he forgot to work in a cool, strategically placed hesitation before nodding yes.

Albert moved up his next visit to Königsdorf, returning later in October and inviting Violet over for lunch. When he went to dish up his homemade chili con carne, he found little shreds of paper in it, and confronted Fred. "Why is there paper in the food?" he asked, and Fred widened his eyes: "It wasn't me!" and Albert raised his voice: "Don't lie, Fred," and Fred screamed, "I never lie!" and Albert said, louder, "You can't mess around with the food!" and Fred declared, "I didn't *want* to mess around!"

Violet's more understanding approach elicited from Fred the confession that there was a question he hadn't dared to ask, so instead he'd written it on a piece of paper, torn it up, and mixed it into the chili.

"You can ask me anything," said Albert.

Fred ran a hand across his face. "Why do you two make such funny noises when Violet is here?"

Albert gulped. Violet laughed, and said, "We're making whoopee."

"And when do people make whoopee?"

She glanced at Albert, who, drinking a glass of water, avoided her eyes. "When they feel very, very good."

"Ambrosial?"

"Completely ambrosial."

That night, Albert was woken by odd noises. Violet was already awake, sitting upright in bed. "Making whoopee," she said, pointing toward Fred's room and chuckling, and after they'd made love a second time that night, Albert admitted that had he been alone he'd have found Fred's imitation annoying, but with her everything was different, with her *he* was different, as if, since he'd known her, he could see Fred better, or was able to make more of an effort. Now he traveled to Königsdorf because he wanted to, not because he was obliged to, and for that he was grateful to Violet, he whispered to her, very grateful, and Violet replied that nobody had ever given her such a beautiful compliment, and she kissed him, and they made love a third time, and Albert felt so happy that for the first time in his life he wasn't yearning for a different life. Everything could stay just as it was.

The following evening she introduced him to the Cyclops Eye.

The Cyclops Eye

October 27, 2001

Blurriness slowly gives way to focus. Rumpled bedding. Light of sunrise or sunset. Albert blinks. He has bags under his eyes. The scar on his cheek is shimmering. He asks, "And what am I supposed to do now?"

Violet's giggling from offscreen. "Be yourself."

"How can I not be myself?"

"Plenty of people are only rarely themselves."

"Well, at the moment I feel very much like myself."

"Do you find it uncomfortable, being filmed?"

"A little. But exciting, somehow, too."

"You've really never been on camera before?"

"At Helena, they only take pictures on birthdays, and at Christmas."

"I wish I could see you as a kid, I'd love to know how you crawled, how you walked. How you talked."

". . ."

"I'm sorry."

"I wish I had a shelf full of tapes, like you. It wouldn't matter so much to me whether it was a good past or a bad one. As long as there was one."

"The last thing you want are bad memories."

"How do you know? Not only can you look at most of your life whenever you want, but it's mostly good, too. It says, Look here, Violet, you have a pretty good life."

"We could go looking for your history."

"I've done that, more than once."

"Somewhere in this house there must be . . ."

"A heap of Hansel and Gretel crumbs."

"A heap of what?"

"Hansel and Gretel crumbs. You follow them because you think they're going to help you get out of the forest. And all they do is lead you deeper and deeper in. Till you can't tell the day from the night anymore. Then, all of a sudden, the trail ends."

"You don't get lost so quickly if you're traveling with someone else."

"Or else much quicker."

"You're living in your own head again."

"It would do most people good to live in their heads a little more. They'd cause less harm."

"We'd make it through the woods."

Albert's hand obscures the picture.

"What's wrong?"

"That's enough."

"Why?"

"Please, turn it off now."

November 16, 2001

Violet's slim legs disappear into dark water. Feet invisible. Swarms of insects. Splashing. Whip pan: Albert sits on the bank, wrapped in a coat. Pines. Underbrush. Naked roots.

Violet's voice from off camera: "Come in!"

"It's fucking cold."

"I'll help you warm up."

"Water's not my thing."

"You go swimming with Fred."

"Water's *his* thing."

"I love the feeling of not knowing what's around me. What's under me."

"That's just the feeling I can't stand."

"Then let me help you. Let me ask Fred a couple of questions."

"About the past?"

"He must know who your mother is."

"I already told you, I've mucked through all of that."

"Maybe I'll see something you missed."

"Promise me you won't ask him."

"Albert."

"Violet."

"I promise."

"Can we go now? I'm cold."

December 7, 2001

Zoom in on a leather sofa with a metal frame. Albert's naked back. Pale and freckled. Before him, a stereo from Bang & Olufsen. Not a speck of dust on its mirrored surface.

Violet's voice from offscreen: "Hey!"

Albert flinches, spins around. "I thought it was your parents."

"Sorry."

"Do you have to do that?"

"I could film you for hours."

"You *could?* You do. Sometimes it's hard for me to picture you without that thing in front of your face."

"You don't need to be afraid of it just because you're not used to it."

"It doesn't have anything to do with that. It's just that I'd like to look you in the eye now and then."

"Someday you'll thank me."

"I don't need recordings to remember how things were."

"So, what—you think I'm one of those people who videotape the paintings in a museum, and only realize what they've seen when they get home?"

"Please, switch it off."

December 23, 2001

Grainy grayness. Moaning. Heavy breathing. Violet's voice from off camera: "Wait." Something bumps the microphone. A streak. A pan across pale thighs. Albert's hairless chest.

His cold stare. "You can't be serious."

"It could be—"

"Turn it off."

"But it's the kind of video I want for Christmas."

"Very funny. Not the kind *I* want."

"Just pretend it isn't here."

"Violet!"

January 21, 2002

Fred's profile. Hazy outlines of brownish-green clouds behind him—a map of the world.

Violet's voice: "Okay. Let's go. What's your name?"

"You *know* what my name is, Violet."

"Of course. But when other people see this, they'll certainly want to know what you're called."

"Most other people know that I'm Frederick Arkadiusz Driajes."

"And who gave you that name?"

"Mama."

"Can you remember her well?"

"I can remember everything."

"Good, then . . . what did she say, when Albert was still a baby?"

"Mama said, *Albert is a Most Beloved Possession.*"

"I already know that."

"Then why did you ask?"

"Never mind. Fred, do you know a woman who has red hair, like Albert?"

"Mama says, *Nature says that red means danger.*"

"How so?"

"What?"

"Why is red dangerous?"

"Because red is the littlest color, of course. You mustn't touch red, or eat it, or drink it."

"Fred, did you touch red once?"

"I never, ever touch red! Green is much more ambrosial. I have green eyes."

"But everyone needs a little bit of red sometimes. Strawberries, for instance, who doesn't like strawberries?"

"Mama says strawberries make my skin red and steal my breath."

"Well, she's right. But you like Albert. And he's pretty red."

"Yes."

"Well . . . ?"

". . ."

"Do you understand what I'm getting at?"

"I always understand everything."

"Fred, there are times when it's just fine to touch red. Everyone does it."

"Mama says everyone who touches red says that touching red is okay."

Door slam. Footsteps.

"Albert!"

Violet's voice from off camera: "I thought you were going shopping."

"They'd already closed . . . is that thing on?!"

"Violet's doing an interview!"

"I asked you not to."

"We've only been chatting a bit."

"I have to talk a lot. Violet doesn't know that red is dangerous."

"Fred, can you please go to your room?"

"But we aren't done yet!"

"Yes, I think you are."

"It's okay, Fred. We're done."

For the first time Fred looks into the camera, as if he's seeing something that he hadn't noticed before. Then he goes. Shadows flit across the green-brown clouds.

"I don't think this is working out."

"Albert, you're overreacting."

"We're just too different."

"That could be to our advantage."

"It doesn't feel right."

"I love you."

"I thought that's a concept you aren't convinced by."

"At least take a little time before you make a decision. Don't do it for me. Do it for us."

March 4, 2002

"Is the camera running?"

"Of course not."

"The red light's on."

"It's off. Don't you believe me?"

Albert in a coat and hat on a park bench. A torn-open envelope in his left hand.

"Violet, what is this?"

"Tickets."

"I can see that."

Violet's reddened hand moves toward Albert. He flinches. The sound of crows cawing.

"I want to apologize."

"With first-class tickets?"

"You don't return my calls. Fred says you were in Königsdorf the other day. You could have told me."

"You told me to take some time." He slips the tickets back into the envelope. "This isn't a good idea."

"Why not? One of my father's friends is putting his house in Newfoundland at our disposal, right on the east coast, you know, there should be tons of blueberries, we can hike the East Coast Trail and look for whales. And we'd be far away from here."

"And what about the camera?"

"I could leave the camera here."

"You *could*."

"Really!"

"And Fred?"

"You could tell him you're at Helena." Her hand reaches for his. "So, what do you think?"

March 7, 2002

A curtain covers the only window in the room. A knock on the door. An older man's voice from off camera: "Are you okay?"

Violet: "Yes."

"Why don't you come on out for a while?"

"Go away!"

Footsteps fading. Violet's hand, with gnawed fingernails, reaches for the camera. Her pale face appears.

"I eat rice pudding with too much sugar. I cocoon myself in the bedsheets. I don't go to the bathroom for so long that my belly hurts. The cell phone has grown into my hand. The 'redial' button is sticking. I press it every few minutes. Even though you never answer, I think every time that you're going to, you're going to explain that you were out, that you're sorry you canceled the trip, that now it's clear to you how wrong it was, and you want to make up for it, and that you're already on your way to me, with two new tickets."

She weeps.

Two Fingers

Violet had sent Albert these seven recordings after their breakup. And he'd made the mistake of watching them. It was with difficulty that he prevented himself from calling Violet and apologizing. That would only have unnecessarily extended the separation phase, thought Albert again, as he finally approached the airfield. He waited beside the only barn in sight and watched a prop plane with a glider in tow take off. The hill on which the church with its onion dome rose from among the farmhouses of Königsdorf was surrounded by a flat plane of moorland, where the glider airfield had been built back in the fifties.

The street he'd come down, still damp with dew, ran past the barn into town. From the opposite direction, a new Beetle, solar yellow, was approaching—it slowed, and finally drew to a stop a few steps away from him. The engine cut off, but the driver's-side door didn't open. It made Albert think of a scene from some sort of Upper Bavarian mafia flick. Violet clearly wanted him to come to her. He obliged. She had her head turned away, he had to knock on the window, and then she took her time rolling it down, and turned her face only halfway toward him, as if she hadn't come out of her way to Königsdorf just to see him, as if she got up early every Saturday morning and drove out across the foggy moor to the airstrip, as if she hadn't lain awake all night wondering what could be so important that he couldn't tell her about it over the phone.

"Hello, Albert," she said, looking at him and then away again.

Albert couldn't explain it, but now, seeing her again after so long, he doubted whether he'd made the right decision back then, not answering her calls anymore. To his own surprise he realized he wasn't just glad but happy to see her; he wanted to give her a hug.

"Hello," he greeted her, uncertain whether he ought even to ask her to get out of the car, because he didn't believe she'd do it. From where he was standing, all he could see of her was her smooth, white left cheek.

"Albert," she said, clutching the wheel, "why am I here?"

He laid his hand on the side panel of the Beetle. Maybe this was a beginning: "It's nice that you're here."

"You think it's *nice* here?" She pointed at the airstrip. "It reminds me that I gave you two tickets once. Tickets we never used."

"Shit. I hadn't thought of that." Albert withdrew his hand. "How've you been?"

Violet looked at him again, but didn't turn away this time: "Totally great!"

He read the real answer in her red-rimmed eyes.

The previous day, fifteen minutes before his call had reached her, Violet had been on her way to the office. Stuck in traffic in the firm's car, a Jeep Cherokee, still umpteen one-way streets distant from the production company's parking lot, on a Friday evening. It was one of those lonely situations in which thoughts of Albert resurfaced, thoughts she did her best to chase off by saying "Violet!" loudly to herself. But it didn't help, and so she edged the Jeep to the right of the Munich ring road, turned off without using her blinker, and stopped at a gas station. She didn't get out; the tank was two-thirds full. Her right hand gripped the engaged emergency brake. The cinnamon bubblegum scent from the car's last cleaning filled her nose, and she rolled down the window to replace it with the odor of gas. For the hundredth time, she read, on a label affixed to the visor, *K&P Commercial*—a commercial advertising agency her father had a good relationship with, and which had allowed her to snag, without even having to go through an interview, one of those internships that every other media and communication studies student yearned for. Though she couldn't understand why they did. She spent most of her time ferrying actors, camera operators, directors, and friends of the producers, or rattling stacks of film cans across Munich. This was supposed to help her make "contacts," so-called. Since she'd had her license for only half a year, she had her hands full simultaneously studying the Google driving directions, shifting gears, steering, and obeying traffic signs and one-way streets, which had a way of funneling inexperienced drivers to the most remote corners of the city in no time at all. Violet had already had to call the office two times, with a lump in her throat, begging for help. And alongside all that, she was supposed to make "contacts"?

When she'd started the internship, only a month after graduation, she'd assumed that the people at K&P Commercial were smarter, more interesting, more open-minded—in every sense above and beyond the product they produced. An overoptimistic judgment, as she'd since found. When Violet came into the office in the morning and was asked how she was doing and answered, "Not so good," she always received the same response from her colleagues: "Great! Me, too!" Violet wished it was meant to be sarcastic. Of course she missed the old Violet, the one who'd rebelled against everything, left, right, and center, but she also observed how much easier it was to protest and do the right thing when one's parents paid for the train ticket to the demonstration. After knocking off for the evening, a group of her coworkers, 80 percent of them interns, gathered regularly around a Mac to applaud a few of the recent commercials—except for Violet, who was easily able to contain her enthusiasm for cappuccino advertisements featuring cowboys and sea monsters. Accordingly, she'd been pulled aside by the producer and encouraged to show a little more spirit. So that now, in the mornings, when the inevitable question came, she always answered, "Totally great!"

Now, behind her, a Mercedes honked. She stepped on the brake, and wanted to shift to "drive," but her hands were shaking. That happened once in a while. She couldn't drive on like that. She got out and topped off the tank, to buy time. In the snack shop she wandered aimlessly along the aisles, without buying anything. She paid for the gas with her credit card, and bent low over the receipt as she was signing, so that the cashier wouldn't notice her shaking. She couldn't read her own signature. She went back to the car, saying "Violet!" again to herself, then took a deep breath and slipped behind the wheel, started the engine, and steered back into traffic. By the next stoplight, the Jeep began to judder and buck. She had to floor the gas pedal to get the thing moving. Midway through the intersection the engine flooded, and the Jeep stopped short. She turned the key, the indicator lights flared, the engine coughed. A terrible suspicion crept over her that she should have refilled with diesel rather than unleaded. Pairs of headlights rushed toward her and flashed. A concert of horns. She didn't dare get out of the car. A soft melody tickled her ear. She dumped her handbag out on the passenger seat and managed to get hold of her cell phone. The screen read: *Albert.*

"I'm really sorry about the airstrip." Albert swallowed and crouched, so as to be at about eye level with Violet. "Listen, I need your help. I have to get to Helena."

"And?"

Albert took a breath. "I wanted to ask if you'll drive us."

"Us?"

"Fred and me."

Violet looked him in the eye, and he took a step back. "Take a bus!"

"You know he won't do that."

"Then leave him here!"

"I can't."

"Why not? I mean . . ." She leaned out the window and her hair fell in her face and she flicked it aside. "Why not? How far away can this Helena of yours be? Four hours by car? Five? What's the problem with leaving Fred alone for that long?"

With a stuttering squeal of rubber brakes, a glider touched down behind them, and at the same moment, Albert, holding up a pair of fingers, began to explain.

You Don't Go Dead Every Day

The sky seemed to be mulling the pros and cons of rain and sunshine, as the Beetle followed a country road through thick pine woods. Violet cut a good number of curves, not altogether unintentionally. And in particular, whenever Klondi gave a histrionic groan from the backseat, or asked exactly how long it was that Violet had had her license. And Violet, almost without moving her lips, would answer, "You don't go dead every day." The argument came from Fred, who had refused to accompany them to Saint Helena if Klondi didn't come as well: "You don't go dead every day. But when I go dead, Klondi has to be there, too."

That was a moment that hadn't been at all to Albert's liking; the four of them standing across from each other in Fred's garden, nobody saying what everyone (aside from Fred) was thinking: *Do I really have to lock myself in a car with them?* Albert had clutched the makeup compact tighter as Klondi stepped over to Violet and the two of them shook hands. A natural, reciprocal aversion had been detectable between them ever since, and this was concentrated now in the enclosed space of the Beetle. There was no obvious reason for them to dislike each other, thought Albert; after all, they barely knew anything at all about each other. On the other hand, there was no particular reason for affection. Albert wasn't about to interfere; he'd be happy as long as Violet didn't steer them into every pothole on the road, wedged as he was between Fred's passenger seat, which was pushed as far back as possible, and the car's awkwardly slanting roof. Crammed into this sardine can of a car, it was hard for him to ignore the fact that they were all on the road because of him. All for one, and one for himself. It made him uncomfortable. In spite of this, he had to get to Sister Alfonsa, he had to find out who his mother was. He wanted an answer to the great WHY. And if it was someone banal, fine, he'd be satisfied, actually, he'd even prefer that, then there wouldn't be any doubt that he hadn't lost anything much in the first nineteen years of his life, that growing up in Sister Alfonsa's care had been, in the truest sense of the word, a blessing.

Fred bent his upper body over the digital clock in the center of the dashboard. "There certainly aren't ninety thousand minutes left anymore, are there?"

Klondi leaned forward. "What do you mean, sweetie?"

"Albert says, 'In ninety thousand minutes I'll be dead.'"

Klondi glanced over at Albert. "Is that what he says?" She laid a hand on Fred's shoulder. "You'll live much longer than that."

Violet downshifted and stepped on the gas. "I'm not so sure you should say that."

Albert, who didn't want to get caught in the crossfire, lifted up his chess notebook, in which he'd recorded a few *becauses* over the past years, in front of his face.

Because this woman is perilously stupid, she believes nothing can happen the first time you do it. And then, of course, it happens. As I enter the world, I want to tell her: Do something clever for the first time in your life and keep me, I'm pretty smart, I can give a little of that to you. I'm trying my damndest to make her hear me, I'm screaming. But she's too dumb. She thinks screaming is nothing but noise. And dumber still: she believes that if she runs away, she won't hear that screaming anymore.

Or: *This woman thinks a mother's role is overrated because she didn't have one of her own, and after all, in the end she made something of herself, didn't she?*

Or: *According to this woman, "pregnancy denial" is nonsense, how could there be such a thing, every woman knows when she has a bun in the oven! No, in her opinion it's just indigestion. Until, suddenly, there I am. And what does she do then? She says thanks a lot, washes herself off, gets dressed, and marches out of the hospital without me, glad that the indigestion has finally faded.*

Or: *For this woman, getting pregnant is simply part of life, like brushing her teeth. She can't explain why it keeps happening to her of all people, miscounting now and then while taking the pill isn't such a big deal, and it isn't as if she's entirely renounced condoms simply because it feels better for women, too, without them, she makes a genuine effort, hand on heart, in her opinion none of her girlfriends are as careful as she is, but then, none of them are so fertile. If she'd been around in the early forties, they would have awarded her the golden Mother's Cross, at the very least. Can anyone really hold it against her that sometimes she loses sight of the big picture and forgets where exactly she's scattered her genes?*

Or: *Somehow this woman understood it differently, when her man told her he wanted only the best for her. Many big, expensive things were what occurred to her, not a wizened parcel of flesh that shrieks reproachfully at you when you give it away.*

Or: This woman thinks it's a shame when pregnant women don't take responsibility for themselves, but I'm not, strictly speaking, her child yet. In her opinion, a child isn't automatically your child just because you've been pregnant with him, no, it takes much more than that, a child only becomes your child when the mother and the baby have properly bonded, that is, established a rapport, and if that doesn't occur—which, regrettable as it may be, can happen—then the child is indeed related to you, it has a place on the family tree, but really, what does that mean, and anyhow, you can't love everybody, our social behavior is selective, and if that holds for friendships and life partners, it would be backward to claim that it's heartless for the same principle to apply to children. Mothers should finally buck the idea that they have to accept supinely everything that life sets before them!

"So there aren't ninety thousand minutes left?" asked Fred.

"Maybe a few less," Albert added now, trying to keep the peace.

Violet smiled into the rearview mirror.

Klondi rolled her eyes, then said, "Fred's told me about the two of you. How long have you been together?"

For a fraction of a second, the Beetle crossed the road's center line.

Albert looked Klondi in the eye, and shook his head.

She raised both eyebrows. "Oh. What happened?"

Albert didn't answer that, and to his great relief, Violet kept silent as well.

Fred said, "My nose is tickling."

Albert was grateful to him for the distraction.

Klondi and Violet answered at the same time: "Then scratch it."

Albert looked straight ahead, and was reminded once again that Fred was one of those very few people the back of whose skull he could make neither head nor tail of. A pair of hair whorls twisting in opposing directions lent it an aristocratic note, which otherwise never came to the fore.

Violet shifted to a higher gear. "Have you ever been to Saint Helena?"

"Me?" asked Klondi.

"You," said Violet.

"Never so far," answered Klondi, and presented her teeth to the rearview mirror, which Violet quickly twisted to the right without looking, removing Klondi from the reflection.

"Do you have children?" Violet asked.

The way Klondi's chin trembled for a moment before she answered in the negative didn't escape Albert, and it made him think of her ex-husband, the bus driver Ludwig, and her daughter in the moon-white dress.

Violet glanced over her shoulder: "Something wrong?"

"No," said Klondi. "No, no."

"How's your internship going?" Albert interjected.

Violet nudged the rearview mirror back into position, and cleared her throat. "Totally great."

"Glad to hear it."

"Yeah, me, too. I've gotten to know so many exciting people. It's cool."

"My nose tickles," said Fred.

Albert: "Then scratch it."

The car left the woods, and Violet didn't slow down when they passed a highway sign, so Albert could make out only the second half of the name of the town they were going through. He'd always made the trip to Saint Helena by train, plus a couple of miles on the bus. He felt as though they weren't traveling toward Saint Helena at all, but some other, unfamiliar place. Reason urged him to remain calm; two or three hours more, then they'd arrive. He'd find Sister Alfonsa, and she'd share what she had to share, and after that they'd head home. That was all.

"My nose . . . ," said Fred, and his head fell sideways.

A Stranger

Violet slammed on the brakes in the middle of the street. Albert, like Klondi, was thrown back in his seat; they had both leaned forward to look at Fred, whose taut seat belt had held him upright. Violet went to open her door without checking the oncoming lane, and Klondi screamed to stop her from stepping out into the path of a minivan that blew past them, honking. Albert had trouble unfastening his seat belt, and Klondi had to help him. One after another they leapt from the driver's-side door. The last one out, Albert ran around the Beetle, shoved Violet aside, tore the door open, and saw the blood streaming from Fred's nose, flowing over his lip, his chin, down his throat, staining his shirt rust-red.

"Fred?" said Albert, and louder: "Frederick?"

No reaction.

Albert bent over him and undid his seat belt. Someone laid a hand on his back, and he heard whispering—but it was all far away. Here in his head his pulse was thudding, and the sweetish-metallic smell of blood filled his nose, and he knew that the time had come. Fred was dying.

Small, rough hands grabbed his shoulders and pulled him away, and he inhaled the fresh air. Klondi slapped him and spat a torrent of words into his face: "PullyourselftogetherAlbertpullyourselftogetherthisgod damnminute!" Then she turned away and, with Violet's help, wrestled Fred from the car. Together they dragged him over to the curb, then laid him down on the sidewalk. Albert clutched his makeup compact, knelt beside Fred, and checked his pulse: weak. Klondi grabbed Albert by the collar and told him not to move, before hurrying off toward the next house on the street. Violet wiped tears from her face, ran back to the Beetle, and started the motor. Albert yelled, "Hey!"

"What is it?" asked Fred. His voice was muted, as if he were speaking from the far side of some thin membrane.

"Quiet." Albert laid a hand on his chest, which felt warm and damp. "You shouldn't talk."

"Am I going dead?"

"No."

"I still have to say good-bye."

"You don't, you certainly don't," he said, and saw that Violet was turning the car's wheels to the right. There was a bump as she went up onto the curb. The car was left aslant on the sidewalk.

Warmth pressed into Albert's side: Klondi was back, and nodding in the direction of a terraced house, whose front door stood open. She gripped Fred beneath the arms: "Let's go!"

Panting and taking many tiny steps, they carried Fred to the house's entryway. Albert had slung Fred's right arm over his shoulders, his thigh muscles were shaking. Klondi's breath rattled. Violet tried to help her but couldn't get a firm grip on Fred.

Fred said that he was dirty.

Just before they reached the threshold, a man stepped out of the house to meet them. He wore jeans and a plain white T-shirt that contrasted sharply with a salon tan. Klondi and Albert wanted to carry Fred farther, but he struggled and slipped loose, and hit the ground. More blood ran from his nose; he wiped it with the sleeve of his shirt. "Not in there!"

"Why not?" asked Klondi.

"That's a stranger!"

Klondi, who was leaning against the wall of the house with one arm and struggling for breath, shot Albert a questioning look.

"What's your problem?" said the man, and planted himself in front of Fred, who repeated: "That's a stranger!"

Violet laughed the way one laughs to defuse a situation; she stepped over to the man and whispered something in his ear. He looked at Fred, Violet, back at Fred, and his furrowed brow smoothed itself, and he squatted and extended his hand. A yellow-toothed smile: "My name is Clemens."

Fred shook his head in slow motion.

"Give him your hand," ordered Albert. "Now."

To Albert's amazement, Fred complied. "I am Frederick Arkadiusz Driajes!"

"What are you so afraid of?"

Fred snorted. "I'm never afraid!"

With a welcoming gesture, Clemens pointed to the doorway: "Well, come on, then."

Everything's Okay

Clemens, Klondi, Violet, and Albert drank lemon tea at an oval plastic table. The kitchen reminded Albert of illustrations from a furniture catalog—it was too coherent, too tidy. No coffee stains, no personal snapshots of weddings or office parties pinned to the walls, no chipped edges or notepads lying around or, for that matter, windows with Zorro-esque initials. Even Albert, with his impoverished past, would have been able to breathe more warmth into a kitchen than this one had.

"Do you live alone?" asked Albert.

Clemens slurped at his tea louder than necessary. "Is it so obvious?"

Behind the door to the living room—a sofa-, book-, and plant-free zone, remarkably bare, even for a bachelor's house—Fred was sleeping on two air mattresses set end-to-end, since Clemens's bed had turned out to be too short for him. The recommendation of the local doctor—a man in his early fifties whose beard, and the heavy bags beneath his eyes, made him look like a man in his late sixties—had sounded to Albert like the result of a self-diagnosis: rest. Shouldn't they at least take Fred to the hospital? Shouldn't they hook him up to an IV and inject him with vitamins? Monitor his pulse? The doctor's answer: "You could do that." Albert had never heard anyone put such an emphasis on the word *but* without actually pronouncing it. His memory supplied scraps of dialogue from the prime-time hospital TV shows that Violet's father had produced: *But don't get your hopes up.— But enjoy the time you have left with him.—But just look at him.—But try to keep calm.—But make arrangements.—But tell him the things you've always wanted to say.—But accept that things are going to run their course.*

Clemens gestured toward the living room: "If you don't mind my asking: what do you call what he has?"

Albert answered the way he always answered this sort of question: "Fred is simply Fred."

"Has he always been like this?"

"Yes," said Albert, annoyed, "yes," and, setting his cup down, splashed some tea on the table.

"It was only a question," mumbled Clemens.

Klondi suggested stepping out for a smoke, and Albert, who'd been longing for a cigarette, declined, while Violet, the nonsmoker, eagerly accompanied her.

Clemens slipped both hands around his teacup. "Please don't imagine I haven't noticed how completely stressed out you all are. Are you related to him?"

"He's my father." Even in his irritation Albert registered how uncommonly easily the words passed through his lips.

"I'm sorry," said Clemens.

"Why?"

"Why what?"

"Why are you sorry? Why does everyone always say that?"

Clemens leaned back, holding the teacup defensively in front of his chest. "Because it certainly can't be easy."

"And why should anyone be sorry about that? It isn't your fault, right? You have nothing to do with it, you have no sense of what it's like—easy or hard or whatever. You don't have the faintest idea."

Albert was thinking—and not for the first time—that people said that they were sorry only because they were glad. They were expressing how goddamn happy they were not to be dealing with the same shit. People like Clemens, who lived all alone in their awful terraced houses and wanted only to fit in, to dress their little girls in pink and their little boys in sky-blue, and sort screws on the weekends in their very own garages, just like everybody else; Clemens, all of them, were so goddamn glad that they'd finally found someone whose life was even shittier than their own, and that's what they were celebrating with their stupid *I'm sorries.*

"My father's sick, too," said Clemens. "Parkinson's."

Albert shut his eyes and let his head droop. "Now you must really think I'm an idiot."

Clemens set his cup down and turned it slightly counterclockwise. "Right. But I understand. Someone you love is dying."

And with that Clemens left the kitchen. There was something shockingly clear in his bluntness. Because Fred was dying, Albert was feeling bad. It was as simple as that.

It wasn't long before Violet came back in.

"Hey," she said.

"Hey," he replied.

"Everything okay?"

Albert nodded, and, feeling tears in his eyes, looked quickly into his teacup. "Yes."

A soft hand touched his neck, and Albert slowly turned to her.

They hugged. Albert held her tight, he'd never held anyone so tight before, and he couldn't remember the last time something had felt so good, and he wept and made noises he couldn't recognize, they were flowing out of him, frightening him, and he held Violet even tighter.

Where To?

In the twilight even the Beetle's solar yellow was merely bright gray. Fred sat huddled in the backseat, wrapped up in wool blankets that Clemens had given them, his head propped on Klondi's shoulder, while she hummed him a lullaby. Violet stood by the open driver's-side door, looking over the top of the car as Albert gave Clemens a good-bye handshake. "Thanks for everything."

"Take good care of him."

Albert cast around for a decently worded valediction, but couldn't come up with anything better than "Sure."

Clemens pointed to Fred. "Your mother must be proud of the way you look after him."

Again Albert rummaged his head for a suitable answer—and again had to settle for "Sure." From the corner of his eye he saw Violet signaling him to break it off: snipping her middle and index fingers like a pair of scissors.

After a few more insubstantial good-byes, Clemens went back into the house, and Albert slipped into the passenger seat.

"Kids," said Klondi, "we need to decide where we're going."

Albert ran both hands across his face. "Maybe we ought to turn around."

"No!" shouted Fred. "No, we have to go to the church!"

Albert turned to him. "You aren't doing so good. And I don't want anything to happen because we pressed on."

Fred gave a booming laugh, as if someone were tickling him. "But a church is a totally great place to go dead!"

Violet looked sidewise at Albert, as if to say, "When he's right, he's right."

Klondi nodded.

Albert laid a hand on Fred's shoulder. "All right: on to Helena."

To the Moon

The less-than-attractive smile (asymmetrical teeth) with which Alfonsa greeted Albert corresponded almost exactly to the sort she'd marshaled for him whenever he returned to the convent after one of his escape attempts: a combination of the motherly and the know-it-all. Without uttering a word, she was saying, "Lovely to see you!" as well as "I knew you'd come back."

Albert disliked it when he felt that someone, especially the nun, was predicting his actions. And Alfonsa had a particular talent for doing just that. He stood at the entrance to her room. The space between the crown of his head and the top of the doorframe seemed vast.

"I'm here," he said.

"I can see that," said Alfonsa. She rose from her writing desk, came over to him, and patted his upper arms with both hands, as if measuring just how wide he was.

Her smile contracted to an equivocal smirk. "You smoke?"

"Occasionally."

"Often, it smells like. Not very healthy, they say."

"No kidding." Albert tried to imitate her smirk.

"We've missed you terribly, smart aleck."

Albert couldn't help himself: though it sounded like irony, it didn't come across that way at all.

Alfonsa nodded toward the chessboard. "How about a game?" Even in the floor lamp's meager light, he could tell that she'd polished the checkers she still made him use.

"That isn't why I'm here."

"You're here because of your mother." No question, and nevertheless her words affected Albert. He reached for the makeup compact in his pocket, but didn't find it. He'd left it behind in the car. Alfonsa bent over the laptop on her desk, and cued up Frank Sinatra with the mouse. Albert knew what was coming next. In a dreamy sort of tone, she'd say, sighing: *What a stunner of a voice.*

Alfonsa settled herself on one of the wooden stools: "What a stunner of a voice."

Fly me to the moon
Let me play among the stars

Albert didn't stir from his place by the door. "Really, I don't want to play right now."

"But of course you do." She pointed to the empty stool across from her. "And afterward, we'll talk."

Let me see what spring is like
On a-Jupiter and Mars

Was it just him, or would nobody give him what he wanted? Where was it written that things couldn't just run smoothly? Sister Alfonsa, for example, could've just told him—no drama at all: "This is your mother." Or at least: "That was your mother." It wouldn't even have to be true, just as long as he could believe it.

In other words, hold my hand

Children, thought Albert, not for the first time, should be allowed to choose their parents. Parents were far too careless in producing offspring. What had his own parents, no, what had his mother, been thinking? He would have been spared a good deal. He would have been spared worrying about Fred, whom he'd left back in the Saint Helena infirmary. He would have been spared holding Fred's pale hand, promising him that he'd be back before Fred "went dead." He would have been spared the five-minute walk from the infirmary to Alfonsa's room, which had ballooned to half an hour because on the way he'd paused again and again to ask himself whether he ought to go back and say his good-byes to Fred—which course he finally rejected, preferring the risk of never getting the chance to say good-bye over the prospect of having to do it twice. And he would have been spared— along with all of the irritating, stressful, painful things that had filled the last nineteen years—sitting down across from Alfonsa, now, just after midnight, not even an hour after their arrival at Saint Helena, behind his army of white checkers, and for his first move sending one of his pawns to certain death.

In other words, baby, kiss me

Albert wanted to get this game over with. So he had to lose. A quick win against Alfonsa was a contradiction in terms. But to lose deliberately without her noticing would be almost as hard as bringing her to checkmate. Albert would have to go at it shrewdly. For a while he went on the attack, guns blazing, and so let her take three pawns, a knight, and a bishop. (Alfonsa, teasing, said he was rusty.) Then he re-grouped, played cautiously, and even took one of her rooks. (Alfonsa purred a respectful *Hmm* or two.) Secretly, though, he was working to wall in his king, using his own retinue to cut off all escape routes, so that finally the black queen was able to set up the deathblow. (Which

Alfonsa punctuated with a satisfied *Ha!*) Albert glanced at the clock. They'd been playing for barely forty minutes.

"Let's talk," he said.

Alfonsa took one of the white checkers and looked at it carefully. "Were you actually making an effort?"

"Yes."

"Rematch?"

Albert just looked at her.

"I understand."

"I want you to tell me what you know," he said. "Now."

Ever since they'd left for Saint Helena, there'd been an unpleasant feeling squatting in Albert's chest. At first he'd thought it was simply the fear of finding himself stuck in some new impasse. But that hadn't been it. It was the fear of finding no new impasse at all. Fear of the truth. What do you do with the truth, once you've finally found it?

"We have to go to the Zwirglstein," said Alfonsa.

"Zwirglstein?"

"It's a mountain. There's an old-folks home there."

"And that's where my mother is?"

"She'll be there."

Albert leapt up. "Just tell me her name."

"I'm not going to do that."

"Why!"

"It's complicated."

"What's so complicated about a name?"

"You'll understand when we get there."

"And if I go there alone?"

"Then you'll never find her."

Albert stepped over to the window, stared out at the night. His whole life he'd been waiting, for nineteen years he'd searched and hoped and waited, and Alfonsa, who'd raised him and whom he'd trusted, this woman could have helped him, could've put an end to his waiting long ago; she couldn't just sit there now, refusing to cough up the truth, sit calmly, as if everything were fine, he wasn't a five-year-old chess student anymore, he had a right to be told his mother's name, who she was, and why she'd abandoned him.

But when he turned back to Alfonsa to make that clear to her, she was already sitting at her desk, flipping through her papers, and wishing him, without glancing up, a good night.

He left her room without a word, walked quickly down the corridor, away from her, starting to run now, across the yard, toward the chapel, where it was even chillier than outside, and hid himself, the way he used to, in one of the confessionals.

✳

PART VI

Head-Shaking
1924–1930

Anni and the Somebodies

Later, my sister told me that she'd stared at the plumes of smoke and sweated in the heat of the fire that was devouring our house, until somebody covered her eyes and threw her over a shoulder and carried her away.

The next morning she was woken by a gentle voice; she opened her eyes to tell Papa or Mama or me about her nightmare—but the light falling through the window was unusually bright, and the air smelled different, like cow dung, and someone, somebody, passed her a cup of milk. Later a different somebody gave her a violet dress. Yet another somebody ran hot water for her to bathe in, water boiled especially for her. The same somebody who'd given her the violet dress suggested they milk the cows together, bake a cake, play with the cat. But Anni shook her head. The somebody with the gentle voice explained that she couldn't go back home, that from now on she'd live here, with her new family. But Anni didn't see any family. There was only a somebody, another somebody, and yet another somebody. She shook her head again and shouted for Julius. Somebody said, "Your brother's in heaven now." And then Anni shook her head so long that she got dizzy, and nobody said anything more.

Anni and Mina

Anni didn't realize she'd set our house on fire. Her eight-year-old's mind screened her from the knowledge. It rejected the truth for her own protection, as Anni herself rejected so many things. As the months went by, she practiced shaking her head, training herself, whenever other children called on her to play with them, or at lunch, when somebody suggested eating a little more. Or after her First Communion, when Farmer Egler asked her in a whisper whether she was interested in the closely guarded secret he kept inside his pants. And one day, when she discovered my I love you *carved into the winding root on Wolf Hill and asked herself who'd writ-ten it and when, she shook it as if she never wanted to stop again, left and right and left, with raised chin, staring eyes, and white lips pressed firmly together, locks of hair whipping against her cheeks, wiping the world away.*

When winter came, our burned-out house, surrounded by snow, looked like a black-and-white photograph. She went there looking for something, without knowing what. Something pretty, small, familiar, something to press against her breast and cherish. She poked a stick through the mound of ashes, whipped it at rats, wrote Mama *and* Papa *and* Julius *with it in the soot. On each of these forays she pocketed something. A collection of Most Beloved Possessions accumulated in a basket under her bed, which she guarded like treasure: hairpins melted into one another, a stove tile broken in fifths, the spine from the cookbook, two smooth, gleaming candlesticks, a dagger, a handful of nails, arrowheads, teeth, and much more. A dirty black film covered everything, which Anni couldn't get rid of, no matter how much she scrubbed each object in the cold water of the Moorbach. And whenever a somebody suggested she choose one of them for the Sacrificial Festival, she just shook her head and said, "It's already been burned."*

One of her chores was to go and fetch rolls from the bakery every Sunday. If Reindl's daughter was at the shop, the two of them would swap Most Beloved Possessions. Sometimes Mina would roam through the burned house as well, hunting rats and stuffing her pockets with whatever junk was lying around. In her company it was rare for Anni to shake her head, because, like many Klöbles, Mina treated her no differently than she had before the fire.

All the other people of Segendorf had changed. No matter whom she met, even people she didn't actually know, they would greet her, ask her how she was doing, praise her new home, invite her for a slice of poppy-seed cake, or slip her an apple.

One day, while trading Most Beloved Possessions, Mina's polished boots caught her eye, and she couldn't resist the temptation to touch them.

"Do you like them?" asked Mina. "You can hug my leg, too, if you want. The leather came from Hunter Josfer."

"Where did you find them?"

"They're mine."

"What will you trade for them?" Anni spread some of her Most Beloved Possessions before them. "You can take whatever you want."

"Whatever I want?" Mina's eyes glittered, she bent down, biting her lip and reaching for the dagger—then drew back, folded her arms. "No. These are my favorite boots."

"Please, let's trade."

"No."

"I'll tell you something."

"What?"

"My secret."

"Like Farmer Egler's?" said Mina. "Then I don't want to know it."

"No. A real secret."

"Maybe I already know it. You have to tell me first." A moment ago Mina's hair had been gray, but now it shimmered blond, as if the sun shone on it.

"But you can't tell anyone else," whispered Anni, glancing back at the door to make sure they were alone. "Nobody!"

Mina nodded eagerly.

Anni held one hand in front of her lips and leaned forward: "Sometimes I wake up. Late at night. And then I have this feeling, as if . . ."

"What?"

"As if Julius is thinking about me."

"Julius Habom!" gasped Mina.

"'That's impossible,' I say out loud to myself, 'he's—'"

"Anni!" Master Baker Reindl interrupted them, shoving her long, lean body between Anni and her daughter. "Your rolls are getting cold."

Anni nodded, silently gathered her things, and set off. Back at the some-bodies' house she put the rolls in the breadbasket, covered them with a kitchen towel, went to her room, pressed her face deep into the pillow, and screamed: "He's burned, he's burned, he's burned!" Afterward she felt a bit better, washed herself, and went to milk the cows, shaking her head. She tried a few more times to get her hands on the leather boots her father had made, but had to concede that it was as good as impossible to separate a Klöble from something she liked. And Mina loved her boots.

Anni and Markus

As the years wore on, the attention people paid to Anni didn't dwindle half as much as Anni did herself. She ate now only when her stomach ached or her fainting spells increased—a swig of milk fresh from the udder for breakfast, and half an apple at lunch. When evening came she was often too tired to chew.

Her cheekbones stood out, throwing shadows across her face, and her curls hung slack from her scalp as if exhausted. She could assist with the milking for only an hour or so before black filled her vision, and her arms were so thin one of the somebodies would have to help her lug the milk pail. On her excursions to our former house she was seized with fits of convul-sive coughing, so she could seldom enlarge her collection of Most Beloved Possessions. Women beckoned to her, called her over to them, invited her inside; Master Baker Reindl gave her bacon rolls with cheese crusts, the innkeeper foisted jars of sweet rose-hip marmalade on her, and Farmer Obermüller's widow let her sample her viscous cake batter. Not even the most persistent head-shaking could repel them. It was scarcely more effec-tive at repelling people's looks.

Sometimes, washing herself in the Moorbach, she found herself break-ing out in goose bumps, even though she wasn't cold, and then she'd glance *around and notice half a dozen boys stretched out in the riverside pasture, chewing grass stems and staring at her. Mina explained that it was Anni's own fault, she'd reached the age when one started to bleed. Shrugged shoulders greeted every question Anni asked: Where, why, when—and who was* one?

It was only after months passed without a single drop of blood that her worries evaporated. After all, Anni told herself, Mina's just a Klöble.

One rainy autumn evening Anni sat atop Wolf Hill beneath the shelter of the oak, running a comb carved from a stag antler through her hair. The moor steamed in the distance. Now and then she ran her fingertips across the I love you *carved into the tree's meandering root overgrown with moss. She liked touching it, this root; she was proud that, apart from Pastor Meier, she was the only person in the whole village who could decipher the letters.*

"Aren't you cold?" came a husky voice. A boy leapt down from the oak's branches and landed beside her with a somersault. Right away Anni's heart was beating harder, she did her best not to increase the pace of her combing, and she said, "How long have you been hiding?"

"I could smell your hair. Even from up there."

At first glance Markus looked slight for his age, he was barely bigger than Anni, yet he'd herded many a fat swine for his father to Butcher Scherfeil; there was plenty of strength in his arms and legs.

"I have to go," said Anni.

"Just talk with me a little."

Anni shook her head. She noticed that Markus was handling his words differently than he used to.

"You never play with anyone. Why not? Are you scared?"

"I have to work."

"You don't have to work now."

Anni stood without looking at him, tied back her hair, and moved calmly away from him, which wasn't so easy. Her legs wanted to run.

"I love you," called Markus.

Anni stopped short.

"I love you," he repeated. "That's what it says there, right?"

She turned back to him.

"Did you carve it?" he asked.

"No!" she shouted. And then softer: "You?"

"Me!" He laughed. "You Haboms, you've always had books."

Anni stepped from one foot to the other. "Then how do you know what's carved there?"

"You aren't the only ones who can learn to read."

"Who helped you? The pastor?"

"You'd like to know that, wouldn't you?"

"Tell me already, who?"

Markus gnawed at one of his black fingernails. "Let me smell your hair. Then I'll tell you."

Anni balled her hands into fists, the comb's teeth bit into her flesh. "But only for a moment."

Markus came over and stuck his nose into her mop of hair. Goose bumps broke out across Anni's back.

"That's enough."

"Why?" His husky voice was now very close to her ear, almost inside her head, he tugged at her violet dress, his breath grazed her throat. One of her hands was shut tight around the comb, with the other she clutched Markus's shirt. "You smell good," he said, and shoved a hand under her skirt.

A tingling ran through her skin and wandered into her belly. "Don't do that," she said. Markus pulled her to the ground. The grass was damp, it prickled and stroked her as if it were alive. Raindrops slipped across her brow, she opened her eyes—when had she shut them?—saw her hand on Markus's face, her fingers in his mouth, felt the soft, warm wetness of his tongue and lips, the way his fingernails brushed her leg. Lightning split the sky, and she tore herself loose, slashing with her comb at his many hands and words, ran away, slipped, tumbled over, went rolling down the hill, got to her feet again, ran stumbling on, and reached our old home. She threw herself down on a heap of soot in a dry corner, wanting to disappear.

She swore to herself she'd never touch another piece of soap, that she'd shun water from then on, be it rain, the Moorbach, or the weekly hot bath. She wanted to be more than merely dirty, since everybody in Segendorf was dirty already—to be precise, in Segendorf dirty was considered relatively clean. Anni wanted to look filthier than Butcher Scherfeil after a day at the slaughterhouse, wanted her mouth to stink even more than Blacksmith Schwaiger's. Then nobody would stare at her anymore. Or try to feed her goodies. Or smell her hair and grope around under her skirt.

After four days without washing, the stink of her lap was coming through her clothes. The day after that, one of the somebodies laid fresh underwear on her bed. Another two days and she bit a tiny piece of skin, which tasted like chicken, from the upper arm of a somebody who'd attempted to wrestle her into the bathtub. Three more days of house arrest, and she could smell herself even when she leaned over the hole in the latrine. Early on the morning of the eleventh day, Anni was allowed to leave the house to fetch water from the Moorbach. While filling the bucket she took care not to dampen her hands. On the way home Markus approached her, a sledgehammer over his shoulder. When he saw her he stopped short, just in front of the shadow thrown by her body across the meadow (and the sun was still very low in the sky). Anni smiled, satisfied, and took a step in his direction. Would he shrink away from her? Her shadow head swallowed his foot. Markus didn't stir, but still, Anni could see how his chest rose and fell. He turned around, as if about to leave. Anni's smile expanded into a grin, at which point Markus let the sledgehammer fall, leapt at her, and threw her to the ground. His hot face pressed against hers.

"Whatareyoudoingwhatisthiswhathaveyoudone?" Markus's hands plunged into her hair, his nose buried itself in her armpit. She beat at him, searched with both hands for anything within reach, anything she could use to hurt him, tore up grass, reached again, more grass, then felt something

similar, but thinner, denser, more firmly rooted, which she pulled with
all her strength, because she knew her life depended on it, and if only she
pulled hard enough she'd be able to make everything that had gone wrong,
everything bad, false, evil, make all of it right again, with a single jerk.

Markus tumbled away from her, clutching his head. His crying sounded
like breathy, voiceless coughing. In her right hand Anni held a thick clump
of his hair. She dropped it, and wiped her hand on her skirt. His howling
was mixed with incomprehensible words and grunts. Anni stood, knocking
the grass from her no-longer-so-violet dress. Markus was rolling back and
forth, she couldn't look away, there was no trace at all of the Markus she'd
been afraid of. It was only a little boy who lay crumpled there in her long
shadow's belly, a little boy over whose cheeks ran an endless stream of tears.
She might have yelled, "You deserved that!" and "Never touch me again!"
and "Repent!"—but not a word passed her lips.

Anni positioned herself in front of Markus, prodded him with her foot
to be sure he saw her, and shook her head; then she picked up her bucket
and, the sun at her back, followed her shadow homeward.

From then on, Anni washed herself three times a day, with water and
soap, thoroughly, including the place that little girls—as one of the some-
bodies had drummed into her—should never touch. As soon as the curly
hair that proliferated wildly on her body, and in which a strangely power-
ful but not unpleasant odor had taken root, grew long enough that the
pale skin beneath barely shimmered through, she trimmed it back. Smells,
she realized, were all the stronger in places where they could conceal
themselves: in hair, under the arms, between the legs, under finger- and
toenails, in folds and crevices of skin. Stubborn as they were, Anni tracked
them down and dislodged them with the aid of scissors, damp cloths, her
comb, and the first Q-tip in Segendorf: a toothpick on which she'd im-
paled a single catkin.

Still, there was a place deep inside herself that she couldn't reach. That
was where the rankest odors came from. A place, she told herself, where all

the bad memories and experiences sat fermenting, producing the sort of vapors that attracted bad men like Markus.

Eating helped. Apples strengthened bad smells, but a slice of bread, generously spread with butter, exorcised them for a couple of hours. Potatoes were especially efficacious, and likewise poppy-seed cakes. No somebody turned her away with a shake of the head if she brought her empty plate back to the kitchen for a second, a third, or a fourth helping. Rosy-cheeked and smacking her lips, Anni spooned up boiled pork belly, casseroles, sugared pancakes, Bavarian stew, she devoured liver dumplings and meatloaf. They tasted spicy and sweet, tender and tough, just right. They crackled, burst, gurgled as she chewed, swilled across her tongue, stuck between her teeth, and she gobbled, gulped, feeling them plunge down her throat, spread through her stomach, and fill her with warmth.

Anni and the Wishes

For every new morning, for every snipped hair, for every shake of the head, for every sunbeam on her skin and every crystal of frost on her window, a secret wish . . .

Mama, Papa, and Julius are alive

Not to smell bad smells

To eat without ever having to go to the latrine

Always sweet air, throughout the house, and in the cowshed, too

To be big without having to grow

A cookbook for Christmas, with pictures like in the one from before

Or a brick for the bed that stays warm all night long

To take away the eyes from the peeping boys

And the hands from the nosy men

And both from Farmer Egler

A surprise

To wake up in Mama and Papa's bed with Mama and Papa

Make it so that somebody could read my wishes, if I were to write them down (preferably a magician who likes me)

That Mina the Klöble gives me her leather boots

That snow is warm

And ice not slippery, but like snow

And that hair stops growing after trimming it

And that my eyes are as green as a cloverleaf

And that the Sacrificial Festival is a Gift Festival

And that Mama and Papa and Julius can hear me

And that I see them, Mama and Papa and Julius, really see them

Or else, that I am with Mama and Papa and Julius now, because I wasn't outside on the night of the Sacrificial Festival

To fly

Anni and the Shape-Shifter

White light stabbed at her eyes. Anni ran across a snow-covered field toward the Moorsee, sinking up to her knees in the snow with every step, a cold headwind whipping her cheeks and tearing at her cloak. When she reached the wooden pier from which, on hot summer days, the two of us had leapt into the water hand in hand, she closed her eyes and held her breath. Now she was alone with her heartbeat. Apart from my sister, nobody made the hour-long trek to the Moorsee during the winter. She came to the lake as often as possible. It was a nothing-place: no smells, no noises.

Cautiously, she lowered herself from the pier onto the frozen surface, dodging those spots where the ice was shot through with cracks, and rushed on all fours toward the center of the lake, where, wiping the snow and frost aside, she sat observing her reflection. Darkly gleaming curls spilled from under her knit cap, her thirteen-year-old face was full and round; since she'd started eating with gusto again, the number of dimples had doubled.

Something moved beneath the ice. Anni let out a shrill scream, shook her head, breathed on her reflection, polished it with her sleeve, and leaned so close that the tip of her nose touched the ice—nothing to see. The lake was as black as if night were hiding down there, waiting out the day.

During her last excursion a few days earlier, she'd stayed until her hands and feet had gone completely numb, and when she'd stood up to head for home, she'd noticed a little red dot, a tiny fleck of color in the snow, that marked where she'd been sitting. Immediately she'd examined her skirt and her stockings, following the trail back to her underwear. Am I freezing to death? had been her first thought, Will I go heaven? her second; the third, fourth, and fifth: to see Mama, Papa, and Julius? Apart from a slight feeling of dizziness, she'd made it back to Segendorf entirely unscathed, and washed herself and her clothes. And said nothing about it. But one of the somebodies had noticed the traces in her underwear. "Am I going to die?" Anni had asked curiously. This time it had been a somebody who'd given a shake of the head: "You're just getting a woman's flesh and blood."

Since then she'd devoted even more time to her bodily hygiene. Whenever she had an opportunity, while milking the cows, at night, or in the latrine, she'd check to see if it had happened again. That strange blood, how hesitantly it flowed, its rust-red color and piercing smell.

"I'm becoming a woman now," Anni proclaimed to her reflection in the ice.

"Dying," it answered, "you can do that some other time."

She skidded around on the ice for a while, and was about to say good-bye to her reflection, when she noticed an animal climbing from a hole in the ice near the opposite shore. It walked on two legs, had two arms, most of its hair on its head, and otherwise, as far as she could tell from that distance, it was naked. It had to be an animal. No man could endure this cold, not without clothing.

It vanished behind a curtain of dark-green fir boughs. As fast as she could, Anni slid back toward the dock, ignoring the soft crackling beneath her, and as soon as she'd reached the shore, ran back toward the village. Mina had lost her father to a rabid fox, and Carpenter Huber had been attacked by a wolf once in broad daylight. (Thus his odd posture while sitting—he had to balance himself on his remaining buttock, the left one.) Anni ran. But even that seemed much too slow to escape some beast that might catch her scent, come lunging after her, sink its teeth into her flesh— she ranranran. Her heart dictated the pace, her knees burned, her feet ached, the wind drew tears from her eyes and pumped frigid air through her body. When Anni reached the somebodies' house, she slammed the door behind her. Its creaking wasn't oppressive, as usual—it was the sweetest sound in the world. She sank to the floor and wept into her hands, without knowing why. I'll never go back there, she swore to herself. Never leave the village again.

The very next morning she set out again. She followed her own footprints. The night had frozen them into the snow. When she reached the Moorsee, Anni sat down at the end of the pier, letting her legs dangle, and waited. She kept her eyes on the hole in the far shore where the animal had appeared. Before long something stirred in the underbrush, and Anni hid herself beneath the pier—but it was only a deer that drank a bit out of the hole in the ice before vanishing back into the woods. Anni sighed. The sun was shining on her left cheek, it shone on her woolen cap, and then, for a little while, since she'd gotten a bit too warm, it shone on her bare hair, and finally it shone on her right cheek. Nothing moved. She'd long since devoured the little lunch that she'd brought along with her. She sucked on an icicle she'd broken off the pier. When the sun turned a pale lilac, she trudged off with slumped shoulders. Just before reaching the turn in the path, she spun back to the Moorsee and shouted, "You stupid muckhole!"

Under the somebodies' roof, such expressions were forbidden. Even though Master Baker Reindl thought it was the perfect description for

Segendorf. The pine trees on the opposite shore answered, *Ole-ole-ole!* At that very moment, the animal emerged from its hole and turned to look at her. Anni fell to her belly and peeped over the snowbanks: the creature was standing up to its chest in the water, scanning the opposite shore. Then it slipped back into the forest. Anni leapt up and ran along the lakeshore, dodging branches, leaping over roots, but never taking her eyes from the spot where the creature had disappeared among the trees. When she reached it, she heard a branch snapping, followed the sound as quietly as possible, pressing deeper into the woods, groping from trunk to trunk in the half-light, scraping her palms on the bark, creeping slowly along, then pausing to listen: the tentative groans of the trees, and beneath, her heartbeat. Anni panted for breath, coughed, stumbled, tripped over a pine sapling. Its needles fluttered. The last sunbeams hung in the treetops high above her, and down below the shadows were gathering. If our father had been there, she would simply have had to hold his callused hand to find herself home again: the forest had swallowed him up every morning, and every evening spat him out again, often with some sort of booty in tow. Anni stood up, and set her cap aright. "I know my way around here," she said to herself. "I KNOW MY WAY AROUND HERE JUST FINE."

Ine-ine-ine! mocked the pines.

The creature stepped out from behind a tree not five feet in front of her. It wasn't naked any longer, instead it wore pants and a shirt and a coat, like a man, and it nodded and even spoke to her like one: "Can you find your way home alone?"

In fact, the animal looked quite human, Anni thought, and shook her head, as if in a trance. She concluded he must be a shape-shifter. My sister had always been the more credulous of the two of us. Legend had it that shape-shifters were masters of metamorphosis. They could change their form at will, be it to fish, fir tree, or man.

"Have you hurt yourself?" he asked, pointing at her hands.

She bit her tongue to stop herself from shaking her head. On every side darkness blocked her way. In her head a chorus of children's voices shouted the moor rhyme:

> Child, dare to walk outside at night,
> Thinking yourself brave and strong,
> And our moor will take one bite,
> Silence, darkness, you'll be gone.

"Do you need a bandage?" The shape-shifter came closer. "Forgive me—I'm pestering you with questions." His bright voice sounded friendly, respectful, and he articulated every word with the utmost precision, which meant that he certainly wasn't from around there. "Probably best that you head for home." His posture was a trifle stooped, as if a bow were in the offing; had she met him under other circumstances, she might have taken him for some kind of servant. "It's getting dark." Before Anni knew what was happening, he was right in front of her; she could make out the tiny droplets of water hanging in his gray-brown beard. He said, "May I ask you something?" then slapped himself on the forehead with the palm of his hand, smiling. "Did it again!" A comely laugh.

Then he reached out to touch a lock of her hair. "You smell lovely." All of a sudden his voice was huskier and his nostrils flared and the muscles of his chest stood out.

He had transformed himself into Markus.

Anni flinched back, sucking in the damp air of the forest, her back colliding with a tree trunk. "What do you want?"

No answer.

There was a new, more acrid smell in her nostrils now. The shape-shifter blinked at her, his mouth opened and shut, opened and shut. Like a stupid puppet's. In her head there were so many words, and now all of them rushed out at once. Anni clawed with her hands into the tree bark, and it hurt her, that was a good feeling, she drove her fingers deeper and deeper into the wood, then a scream leapt out—and all of the words followed. The forest's echoes could barely keep up, the words leapt out from every direction and whirred through the air, one devouring the next devouring the next, and the night was as dark as it was crammed with Anni's words. "Do you want to kill me? Is that what you want? Then by all means, do it! It's not a bad thing, not to me! Then I'll go to heaven! Because I want to go soon anyway! Because, you see, Mama and Papa and Julius are there! They're waiting for me! They want me to come to them! Because they love me! They love me! They'll be happy when I'm dead! Then we'll be together again!"

The shape-shifter slapped her.

Anni lunged forward and slapped him back.

They stared at each other in silence. An owl screamed above them, shadows crawled below, somewhere snow slipped from a branch. His hand still lay against her cheek, her own still touched his beard, which didn't feel scratchy at all, but soft. She said, "I'm Anni," and the shape-shifter, more tenderly than anyone ever had before, muttered, "Anni." Then he introduced himself, and Anni's tongue leapt, rolled, arched itself as she repeated, "Arkadiusz Kamil Driajes."

Arkadiusz

Arkadiusz's father, Kamil Piotr Driajes, had fallen in 1914 at the Battle of Tannenberg, which hadn't occurred at Tannenberg at all, but rather at Allenstein. The poor man had been on a fishing trip in East Prussia, and no one had bothered to warn him that on that precise day, right on the plain where his favorite pond was located, the Russian and German armies were going to clash. His family never discovered which side was responsible for lobbing the fatal grenade. After his death, his wife, Aneta Natalia Driajes, found it impossible to support their nine children alone; so Arkadiusz, the oldest, who still lived at home at the age of eighteen—without a job, a wife, or children—promised her that he'd seek out remunerative work, that he'd conquer the proudest woman in all of Poland, and finally, that he'd provide her with so many grandchildren that they'd have to found a whole village called Driajes, at which point poor Aneta kissed his hand in thanks.

Then again, it might have been that after his father's death she'd simply kicked him out of the house—Arkadiusz expressed himself rather vaguely when he was describing all this to Anni. After he'd bidden his eight brothers and sisters farewell, he drew a deep breath, threw the leather pouch filled with his few belongings over his shoulder, and struck up a merry walking tune. Life couldn't be that difficult, could it?

Arkadiusz spent weeks looking for work, with no results, and more and more often he found himself slipping up shadowy side streets to avoid friends and acquaintances whom, once upon a time, he would have invited to share a bottle of vodka; he was ashamed of the tattered and desperate shape that stared back at him from mud puddles. The conquering of the proudest woman in Poland, whoever she was, had been deferred to some other day. After that cold, wet November, even half-moldy stew salvaged from the garbage cans looked delicious to him, and there were so many holes and tears in his clothes that they showed more skin than they hid. It wasn't that he hadn't tried, it was just that work wasn't generally associated with sleeping in, but rather with getting up at an hour when even roosters were still asleep. And rising early was not one of Arkadiusz's strong suits. No matter how often he promised himself to hop out of bed in the morning, as soon as his eyelids fell shut, he slept like the dead, arms folded behind his head, as if nothing and no one could do him any harm. Shaking, cold water, barked threats—none were of any help.

Every morning the risk grew that he might run into his mother on the open street. And what then?

He slunk from his native village, covered with dirt. And swore to himself he wouldn't return till he'd made his fortune.

With his last piece of silver he traveled to the Baltic Sea and signed on with a shrimp boat. Never once had any of his siblings managed to outfish him, and more often than not he'd even trumped his father. Arkadiusz possessed neither unusual baits nor a nose for propitious casting spots; he used common green flies that he found on the dunghills, and sat himself down by the water at whichever place happened to be closest. His success was just a question of time. It didn't matter how stormy the weather, how many other anglers were splashing around to his right and his left, how far the mercury sank below zero—Arkadiusz waited. Once he'd decided to fill his bucket with trout, perch, salmon, the fish didn't have a chance. They simply had less patience than he did. However, he had a difficult time conveying the value of this talent to the Prussian fishermen on the Baltic. When for the fourth successive time they found him still snoring in his bunk during working hours, the crew tossed him overboard.

As he was borne away by the waves, he watched the boat pulling off, and for the first time in his life felt hopelessly alone. There's no sense in living, he thought, I'll never amount to anything—and exhaling, he let all his muscles go slack and sank down into the frigid sea. His saturated clothing pulled him under, water smothered the moonlight, rushed into his ears, and he grew colder and colder, but the stream of bubbles spluttering upward from his nose and mouth simply didn't give out, no matter how much he blew and snorted. Just when he felt as though his head was about to burst, his feet brushed up against something yielding, uneven. He stretched his hand out into that utter darkness, digging his fingers into grainy sand and silt. He'd reached the seafloor. The air was still streaming out of him, wherever it was coming from. This could take quite a while yet, he thought—maybe it's a sign. Maybe it's not supposed to end today?

Arkadiusz waited a little longer, just to be sure, but even after he'd counted out another minute in his head, he didn't feel the need to draw breath, and so he pushed off from the bottom and swam back toward the surface, then into the harbor.

The Circus Rusch had erected its tents in the vicinity of the fishing village. Arkadiusz's sopping clothes still clung to his body as, shivering, he begged *for an audition with the circus director. A clown with hair as red as a rowan berry, bare chest, baggy pants, and a squeaky voice led him—turning somersault after somersault—to a miniature bathtub. Foam sloshed over its rim, its water steamed. Arkadiusz would've given anything to be able to plunge himself into it. When the clown left him alone, he looked quickly around, and dipped one hand into the hot water.*

"Pfui!" called a squashed sort of voice, and Arkadiusz whipped his hand from the water as if he'd been scalded. Behind the tub stood a dwarf, a towel wrapped around his waist, a bathing cap on his head.

"Who are you?" asked Arkadiusz.

"Who are you?" replied the dwarf, crossing his arms.

"My name is Arkadiusz, and I want to talk to the director."

"The boss, eh? Well, you're looking at him."

"You're making fun of me."

"Oh sure," said the dwarf, "just a bit of circus humor: me, a half-pint, the boss. Ha-ha."

"Well, can I see him, then?"

"Irony, kid. Where did you grow up?"

"Poland. On the East Prussian border."

"Big surprise." He straightened his bathing cap. "All right, what do you want?"

"I want to join the circus."

The director's bushy eyebrows drifted upward. "And why, pray tell, should your name be up on a marquee?"

Arkadiusz smiled; he'd thought this through carefully. "I never come back from a fishing trip empty-handed."

"My, my, remarkable. We can build you a big vat of water, set you on a pedestal beside it, and show the audience how you catch pike after pike."

"Really? You'll take me?"

"Tell me, kid, how have you managed to survive this long?" The circus director made a sweeping gesture, and suddenly held a coin in his pudgy little hand. "Here, for you. And now shove off. My bath's getting cold."

Arkadiusz fought back an impulse to snatch the gleaming coin. "Wait a minute! That isn't all!"

The director removed his towel. Arkadiusz glanced away.

"What? It's just my third leg." He laughed.

Arkadiusz met the director's gaze. "I can do something you've never seen before."

"I've seen everything."

"Not this. I can hold my breath."

At that the director's gaze, already narrow by nature, grew narrower yet. "Me, too. And I've already done it much too long today."

"I can hold my breath for a very long time. Very, very long!"

"How long?"

"Well . . . I'm not sure."

"So you'd like to be the Incredible Pole who doesn't know how long he can hold his breath?"

Arkadiusz drew a deep breath, leaned forward, and stuck his head into the tub. Underwater he counted the seconds, bubbles clinging to his face, the bitter taste of soap on his tongue, his eyes burning; and every time he reached the point when he thought he'd have to surface, to give up, he tensed his diaphragm and released a few more reserves of oxygen.

The director didn't interfere. He simply stood there with his mouth hanging open, watching bubble after bubble after bubble burst.

Four minutes and forty-three seconds later, Arkadiusz wasn't Arkadiusz Kamil Driajes anymore, but rather ARKADIUSZ THE FOUR-MINUTE-AND-FORTY-THREE-SECOND MAN. For years he toured with the Circus Rusch, first through the German Empire, and later the Weimar Republic, holding his breath in a huge glass bell jar constructed expressly for him, before anxious adults and astonished children. Since all performances took place in the afternoon and evening, he could usually sleep in. He saved the lion's share of his pay for his eventual homecoming. In letters to his mother and siblings—which, since he was illiterate, he *dictated to his boss, in exchange for a third of his wages—he described the Cologne cathedral, the Leipzig city hall, Munich's Frauenkirche; he recited hilarious and heartrending anecdotes from his wild nights out, which struck him as trite and banal as soon as they'd been written out on paper; he rhapsodized about his passionate love affair with THE INEFFABLY FLEXIBLE YING, a contortionist, who could balance herself on two fingers; he praised Bavarian wheat beer, lamented his breakup with THE INEFFABLY FLEXIBLE YING, and cited with disgust the various hateful slogans with which their circus wagons had been smeared in the course of their travels:* "Wer nicht zum deutschen Volk gehört, der bleibt nicht lange unversehrt"; *he didn't mention that, thanks to the inflation, people were paying millions for a sack of potatoes, briquettes, a jacket, a pair of decent shoes or pants, which meant that they didn't have money to treat themselves to an hour or so in a drafty patchwork tent that stank of sawdust and horse apples; instead, he claimed the circus was doing so well that he stoked his stove with twenty-thousand-mark notes that fluttered around in his wagon like confetti; moreover, he bragged about how he'd already mastered the German language, and told them how people salaciously misinterpreted his stage name, and how since the Treaty of Versailles no German walked the streets with his head held high.*

He never received any answering letters. "Circus people," *the boss asserted, once again having emptied a bottle of redcurrant schnapps all by himself,* "have no settled address. They drag around from place to place. From wallet to wallet."

All of this came to an end with the stock market crash in 1929. Coming in from the west, Black Thursday sloshed across Europe like a wave, and turned into Schwarzer Freitag. Numerous performances were canceled. The circus schlepped through the boondocks for a few more weeks, the audience numbers plummeted, and finally the boss put everyone on unpaid leave. At that point they were camped in Schweretsried. For a few days Arkadiusz had been tormentedly considering whether or not he should try his luck alone. He had finally received a letter from his mother; in it, she complained of how badly the family had been doing since the last, ill-fated harvest, and stressed how much she was relying on his support. During a conversation at the Iron Pine Tavern, he overheard rumors of a monk and a vein of gold and a village hidden far out on the moor. They told him the people out there weren't kindly disposed to strangers—which didn't disturb him at all, he wasn't looking for friends. His head held a single word, tolling as loud as a church bell: GOLD. And it boomed louder every day that passed without wages. Until, plagued by the thought that somewhere far away his family was starving, he made a decision.

It was hard for him to leave the circus troupe. The boss promised him he could come back anytime, THE INEFFABLY FLEXIBLE YING gave him a French kiss, and HANS THE TATTOOED SNAKE insisted that he wasn't crying, there was just something in his eye.

During those first days of his journey south, Arkadiusz spent more time crying than not; he was alone again, he'd left both his real and his adopted family behind. The only thing that kept his spirits up was that gold-golden vein of gold; it drove him onward, deeper onto the moor. At night by the campfire, he gnawed on the perch he'd caught, and dreamed of returning to his homeland as a savior.

A convoy of automobiles pulls to a halt before his parents' house, and his siblings flock around him, shouting for joy, as he leads his mother, nearly fainting with pride, from car to car, presenting her with wine from Champagne, beluga caviar from the Caspian Sea, lynx pelts from the Pyrenees, and gold bars, each stamped with his personal seal: a fisherman.

Two weeks later Arkadiusz arrived in Segendorf. He took that for a good omen. Cheerfully, he walked into the tavern, ordered a wheat beer, and told a walleyed barmaid about the gold. Her jaw dropped, she clapped her hands gleefully, and ran outside. A moment later, she returned with a gray-haired couple, likewise walleyed. Her parents said they'd be happy to assist him on his treasure hunt, very happy. When could they begin? Tomorrow? Today? Now?

Arkadiusz had never been one of the quickest, but he wasn't that slow, either. In the first pair of eyes he saw how they'd follow him to the gold and help him dig it up; in the second, how they'd hold the gleaming stones up to the sun and perform a dance of joy; and in the third, how they'd knock his head in with a shovel, and bury him out on the moor.

Arkadiusz excused himself, saying he had to use the latrine, and left Segendorf as quickly as he could.

He came across the Moorsee during his forays through the underbrush, and used it thereafter as both food source and landmark. Swimming in it reminded him of the moment when he'd nearly rendered his life to the Baltic. Since then he'd changed greatly—he wore a full beard, he had been initiated into love by female devotees of THE FOUR-MINUTE-AND-FORTY-THREE-SECOND MAN throughout the republic, and now—the gold, the goal, his triumph clearly visible—he was shortly to return to his homeland, a hero.

Each day that passed with no sign of the gold vein, without even a trace of the stone through which said vein might run, didn't dampen his spirits, but heightened his sense of euphoria. Indefatigable, he clambered up trees, dove to the bottom of the Moorsee, dug through the soil, and collected every suspicious pebble. Again and again he forgot to go fishing, since each night in his dreams he found himself feasting at tables heaped high with food.

His quest would have ended unhappily if one day he hadn't spotted a plump young woman on the snow-flocked surface of the frozen Moorsee. A little voice inside him, which sounded suspiciously like the boss's, began grousing, saying he shouldn't let some little provincial floozy throw him offtrack, the golden prize was close enough to touch! But Arkadiusz kept looking at the girl. Each of her gestures seemed perfection itself, and woke *in him the desire to touch her. The way she tapped her boots, and skidded across the ice, and smoothed back her hair—so beautiful, so simple!*

Later, he sought out the place where she'd been sitting, and found a red spot in the white. He carefully carved out the drop of blood, carried the snowball back to his camp, and regarded it thoughtfully. As dawn broke he punched a hole through a thin spot in the Moorsee's ice, undressed himself, and slipped into the water. He hadn't thought any of this through; as he glided with strong strokes through the frigid black, he hoped that some idea would come to him.

All that came was a desire to see the girl again.

It was fulfilled a few days later. She had followed him into the forest, and now she stood not five steps away from him. After that, everything went much too fast: he said something, she said something, he moved closer, smelled her, her scent, so real, and she spoke, and he spoke, and touched a lock of her hair, and then she said more and more and more, un-canny things that filled him with fear and in which she lost herself, which rose around her like a wall, an enclosure of evil that he had to tear down by slapping her, and once he'd done it he couldn't pull his hand from her cheek, her pink cheek, and when she slapped him in return she couldn't take her hand from his beard, even stroked it with her finger, her index finger, briefly, he felt it, while he looked into her eyes and she looked into his, and he recognized the bottom of the sea, felt it on his cheek and with his fingers, and pushed off, saying, "Anni," rushing toward the surface again, up, higher, breaking through the surface, filling his lungs with air and his heart with Anni's voice.

Anni and Arkadiusz

In 1930, on the night before their wedding, Anni and Arkadiusz stole away and rushed to their new home. There my sister sang and danced for

Arkadiusz in a dress with beige ruffles, which she'd put on for only one purpose: so that he could tear it off. The way the rough fabric scratched her skin made her feel as though she had sloughed off a redundant Yesterday and slipped into a fresh, form-fitting Now. Only once did she interrupt her swaying dance and stand listening, because she thought for a moment she'd heard a strange, yet familiar, voice. Mine. She breathed Arkadiusz's scent, which he renewed every time he immersed himself in the Moorsee, and his breath told her that deep inside him many good things were sleeping. Naked, she sang out his name, and there were as many ways to pronounce it as there were reasons to love Arkadiusz Kamil Driajes.

She'd brought him to Segendorf as a stranger, anticipating the usual: suspicious glances, shouts of "Klöble," and brandished pitchforks.

And rightly so. Not five minutes after they'd crossed the borders of the village, the innkeeper spat on the floor at Arkadiusz's feet, Blacksmith Schwaiger applauded, and a somebody with an angry scowl motioned Anni away from him. And what did Arkadiusz do? He let go of Anni's hand, made for the somebody, and before the latter knew what was happening, took his hand. Arkadiusz gave it a hearty shake, with his slightly inclined servant's posture, and congratulated the somebody on his divine farmhouse. Since Anni was well aware of how horribly brawls in Segendorf tended to end, she shut her eyes. As no savage fracas followed, she hazarded a second look: Blacksmith Schwaiger had stopped applauding, the somebody was still gripping Arkadiusz's hand, and the expression on his face was remarkably friendly, given that a Pole had stepped into Segendorf without warning, holding hands with the somebody's adopted daughter— a bit skeptical, yes, but with sympathy beginning to flash from the corners of his eyes.

That night he allowed Arkadiusz to sleep on a heap of straw in the barn, and the night after that, by the hearth in the parlor.

And that was by no means all. In December Markus and his gang tipped a bucket of pig's blood over Arkadiusz's head, and found the whole business rather comical; but as soon as January, they were helping him tear down the ruins of our old house—a demonstration of his breath-holding trick had made a deep impression on them. In March, though the thaw had barely set in, half the town was sawing, hammering, and drilling, putting up a new home for the couple-to-be.

For Arkadiusz, it was all just a matter of patience. Segendorfers were no different from fish in a frozen lake; to catch them, all you needed to do was stand watch long enough at the hole in the ice. He said hello and hello and hello, smiled and smiled and smiled, begged and begged and begged, asked and asked and asked. For days, sometimes weeks at a time, people would pay him no attention at all, and he simply held his breath. If he'd learned anything at the Circus Rusch, it was this: to carry on. Generally speaking, the supply of human patience was limited—but his own was infinite. Eventually he always reached the point where someone would return his greeting, his smile, do him a kindness, give him an answer. And then he'd seize the moment, and catch his fish.

For Anni, on the other hand, Arkadiusz was and remained a shape-shifter. As such, he could assume any form that would bring him some bene-fit: for Farmer Obermüller's widow, he was Farmer Obermüller, and for the somebodies, he was a well-bred lackey. For Anni herself, Arkadiusz was sometimes our mother or our father, when he held her close; sometimes me, when he romped around with her; sometimes a recalcitrant child, when she tried to teach him to read and write; and sometimes merely a mellow thirty-four-year-old man.

For those who were able to look a little deeper, Arkadiusz was sim-ply a foreigner. Someone whom Segendorf was willing to tolerate because they were happy finally to be getting rid of Anni—daughter of the Habom siblings, who'd murdered Nick Habom and been burned alive in their own house—a fourteen-year-old girl with a fanatical need to clean her body, who'd stripped Markus of half his scalp, who wandered through the *wilderness, who played with Mina the Klöble. A bad match for any man. What a relief that her love had struck someone from elsewhere!*

Whichever version was the case, the only certain thing is that every single one led to the night before their wedding, when Anni sang and danced for Arkadiusz in their freshly timbered parlor, and for the first time showed herself to him entirely unencumbered by clothing. Thanks to a generous distribution of Most Beloved Possessions from our former home, the room already seemed lived-in. A green radiance compensated for so much that had burned: flowerpots clustered everywhere, vines hung from beams or climbed up over them, leaves reached toward windows, exhaling sweet scents and trembling with Anni's dance, as she spun in place like a clumsy ballerina, and sang Arkadiusz's name. He didn't notice her awkward voice: as long as he could stare at her mouth, as round as a fish's, smell her hair, cast his shadow on her pale skin, nothing sounded wrong at all. And it also didn't feel wrong that he still hadn't rushed back to help his own family; staying here in Segendorf, he told himself, meant that he could continue his search for the gold. Even if he knew very well that the real reason was something completely different: Arkadiusz was happy with his life as never before, and in marrying Anni he'd be prolonging this state of things, making her dance eternal.

Now she stood before him, so close that her breath grazed his face. Stark naked, she loomed over him. She looked at him, looked at him with glittering, sparkling, glowing eyes, and as he stretched his hand toward her, there was a knock at the door, and Anni flinched away. She furrowed her brow, wrapped herself in a knitted blanket, and opened it. Arkadiusz certainly couldn't see me out there in the dark, but he observed something that he hadn't seen for months now:

Anni shaking her head.

✳

PART VII

Pushing the World

Saint Helena

For three days nobody knew whether Fred's heart would decide for or against a premature halt. Albert stayed at his bedside. Alfonsa had set up a bunk bed in the infirmary, where Albert and Klondi slept; Albert below, naturally. Which meant that, for Albert, sleep was out of the question; when his worries didn't keep him awake, Klondi did, with her tempestuous snoring. Every time they went to get something to eat, it felt wrong to Albert to sit at the nuns' table in the dining hall, but Alfonsa, with whom he hadn't exchanged a single word since their talk, insisted. Among the orphans, these interlopers constituted *the* subject of conversation. Most assumed they were a family. Some of them who knew Albert even believed he'd found his mother, and sat stewing with envy.

On the evening of the second day, Albert was sitting by Fred's bed. Someone had neatly parted Fred's hair with a comb. He slept with his mouth agape, and despite the state of his health still looked notably younger than he actually was. And yet, this man had at least sixty years behind him, probably even more; since no birth certificate existed, nobody could say for sure. Maybe, thought Albert, Fred really was a hero, one with superpowers: he aged slowly, was preternaturally strong, and, above all, was an imperturbable optimist.

Someone touched Albert's shoulder.

"Do you believe in God?" asked Klondi.

Albert wasn't in the mood to debate questions of faith. "No."

"Me neither. But wouldn't it be much simpler?"

"Wouldn't *what?*"

"Life. Wouldn't it be much simpler if you could count on the fact that someone had a plan for it all, that the whole mess wasn't in vain?" She didn't even wait for an answer. "I prayed for the first time yesterday. Felt good."

"I'm happy for you."

"Come off it, sweetie. You aren't the only one who cares about him." She tucked the blanket tighter around Fred. "So, are you coming?"

"Where?"

She nodded toward the exit. "To pray."

In the austere chapel of an orphanage in the Bavarian uplands, Albert sat down beside Klondi in the first row of pews, and folded his hands. Klondi was thinking—he was positive—of her dead daughter and her dead husband and a friend who didn't have much longer to live now. He was thinking of a woman who should have been his mother for nineteen years, and of a man who'd never been his father.

And as for Violet: after the first night, her Beetle had vanished from the parking lot. Albert assumed she'd gone on her way, and regretted that; he hadn't even been able to thank her for her help.

On the third day, however, they ran into each other in the kitchen while he was frying a couple of eggs under the critical eye of Sister Simone. Violet declined his invitation to breakfast.

That night, as Klondi once again struck up her snore solo, Albert stepped outside for a smoke and found the Beetle parked in the middle of a field where the orphans played soccer during the summer. The sunroof was open. Violet lay huddled on the backseat.

"Hello," he said, and sitting up suddenly, she hit her head.

"You scared me!"

"Sorry."

"What are you doing here?" she asked.

"I could ask you the same question."

"I'm here because you needed me. Until recently, anyway."

"Actually, what I meant was: what are you doing in this field?"

Violet sat up, and as she rubbed the back of her head, Albert remembered how much he'd liked kissing her there, once.

"Can I have one, too?"

"You smoke?"

"No."

Albert shrugged, lit a cigarette, and passed it to Violet, who propped herself in the open roof, sucked at it, and didn't cough once.

"You've smoked before, though, right?"

"Surprised?" Violet smiled, pleased. "It's my first time." Then she said, "I found a tin box in the trunk. There's a rock in it that looks almost like . . ."

"Gold."

"Fred's?"

"Yep."

"It looks real."

"It is real."

"Must be pretty valuable."

"No question."

"Where did he find it?"

"In the sewers."

"What?!"

"Don't ask me how it got there."

He liked the way she blew the smoke through her nose. "You've really never . . ."

She flicked the cigarette into the field. "I'm leaving tomorrow." She looked at him. "If you don't need me."

Of course he needed her, more than ever, but something in him shrank from saying it as long as she was waiting for him to say it.

"I was almost on my way yesterday. And then, halfway, I turned back. Stupid of me."

"You could stay for another day," he said, finally.

"And then?"

"I don't know."

"That hug the other day did me good," she said suddenly, putting into words precisely what he was thinking.

It wasn't that he couldn't understand her. They'd been on the road together for three days now. Without Violet they'd all still be sitting in Königsdorf. That Violet had questioned Fred against Albert's will, way back when, that had been a mistake—but she'd only wanted to help, wanted to see if she might be able to uncover something he'd missed. And wouldn't it have been wonderful to find his mother with her by his side? To accomplish something so big together? Sure, she'd touched a sore point, but had it really been fair to split up with her on that account? In any case, it hadn't been fair to call her up and beg her to drive Fred and Klondi and him to Saint Helena. For the sake of his mother. Whom Violet had been searching for. For which reason Albert had left her. And now they were here in a field, in the middle of the night, and everything that had happened between them lay months in the past, and he asked himself what, really, Violet had done wrong, and let his cigarette fall, and kissed her.

The next morning Fred opened his eyes, ignored the objections of the nurses, marched to the bus stop by the parking lot, and waved to Sister Simone, the cook, as she drove off to do her shopping in her leek-green VW.

Once Albert had managed to bring him back in, Violet served them breakfast.

Fred eagerly munched his food, as if making up for the meals he'd missed over the past few days. "Caramel pancakes!"

"You shouldn't talk with your mouth full," said Albert. "How are you feeling?"

Fred swallowed. "Ambrosial!"

"You look like it."

"Aren't you going to have some, too?" asked Violet, sitting down beside Albert and playing with his hair.

Albert glanced at the rolled-up pancakes. Fred stopped chewing.

Violet urged him on with a nod. So Albert took one of the rolls, and tasted it. They were magnificent.

"Caramel," said Albert.

"You shouldn't talk with your mouth full," Fred objected, and turned his attention back to his plate.

Albert said softly to Violet, "He's feeling ambrosial."

Her smirk was worthy of Sister Alfonsa. "He's not the only one."

Albert wasn't sure if, as Violet would have put it, it had been the *right thing* to kiss her. He worried he was longing to be close to her only because he was feeling afraid of what was yet to come. The kiss had allowed him to forget—for a moment, at least—that Fred was dying, that his mother was living in an old-folks home on the Zwirglstein, which he'd have to set out for, sooner or later. Albert didn't know what that would mean for him and Violet, and he didn't want to worry about it anymore either, so he more than welcomed Alfonsa wanting to meet him out in the orchard.

"I like it out here," she greeted him in the shadow of an apple tree. She acted as though two whole days hadn't passed since they'd last spoken.

"You used to have agoraphobia, right?"

Alfonsa stopped. "What makes you say that?"

"The other sisters always used to praise me for getting you outside so often. Once I looked the word up in Fred's encyclopedia."

"You were still very small. And you had too much imagination." Alfonsa went on. "Maybe that's why your girlfriend thinks so highly of you."

"Violet? She's not my girlfriend."

"Does she know that?"

Albert dodged her glance.

"It seems to me," she said, "that we haven't sufficiently prepared you here for the world of women."

From the very beginning he hadn't really thought of the sisters of Saint Helena as women. As teachers, tutors, yes, as parochial know-it-alls, oh certainly, but never as females—apart from a brief phase when, at the age of five, Albert had believed that the anatomical conspicuities specific to women were called "bad timing," because he'd surprised Alfonsa while she was undressing in her room, and asked her, pointing, what *that* was.

Albert picked an apple, inspected it for wormholes, polished it on his pant leg, and took a bite. It puckered his mouth.

"They need more time," said Alfonsa. "Another month at least."

"In a month we won't be here."

"You could stay. What are you looking for elsewhere that isn't here?"

Their eyes met for a moment.

"What in the world would keep me here?"

She smirked. "Shoelaces?"

"Sounds tempting."

"Albert," she said, stepped over to a crooked tree, plucked a rosy-cheeked apple, sniffed it briefly, and handed it to him. He took a cautious bite. You could taste the sun in it. "There were reasons not to tell you about her."

Albert dropped the apple.

"You were three years old when you came to us. Not old enough to hear such things. And when you were old enough, I waited for the right moment to tell you. But it never arrived. Eventually I thought maybe it was better that way. There are certain things it's better one never learns."

"Then why precisely *now?*"

"Because we've been worried about you." Typical of Alfonsa, not being able to say *I*. "When your call came, it confirmed our worries. We should never have let you go, especially not in this difficult situation with Fred. Only, you were so unbelievably stubborn. We didn't see any other way to bring you back."

"The ends justify the means," said Albert.

"You could put it like that." Alfonsa bent over, tasted Albert's apple, and showed her teeth in a pleased grimace. "I've always had a way with the precocious ones."

"I want to see her. For all I care, come along. But I want to get it over with."

Alfonsa brought the apple to her mouth, paused, then bit even deeper. "Fred feeling better?" she asked with her mouth full.

Albert hated her chomping. "Yes."

She looked at him. "Then what are we waiting for?"

As evening fell on the parking lot, Violet, Alfonsa, Fred, and Albert said good-bye to Klondi, who'd voluntarily given up her seat in the car. If they left right away, they could make it to the Zwirglstein by the next morning, including a rest stop during the night.

Klondi turned to Fred. "Take care of Albert, okay?"

"Albert is very young," said Fred, knowingly.

"Albert is present," said Albert, and mentioned yet again that it might be better if Fred stayed behind. They'd be gone for only twenty-four hours.

"But I want to come, too!"

"That's not an especially convincing argument, Fred."

"What isn't an especially convincing argument?"

"You don't have to come."

"I do have to come!"

"Why?"

"Because I want to meet your mom!"

Albert looked accusingly at Alfonsa.

She shrugged. "He has a right to know what's happening."

Albert felt a tingling at the back of his neck, he knew that any second now his thoughts would take off, and then he'd have to think about things he found deeply unpleasant to have running loose in his head. So he said, "Fine. Let's get going."

And so after three days they left Saint Helena with Alfonsa and a new destination, and without Klondi.

Love Story

This woman scratches at the back of her unwashed head, which must be my mother's head, no question about it, and asks: Who? And I repeat: Your son! And she repeats: Who? And I ask: Are you deaf? And she says: Very good! And I start again from the beginning: I'm your son. And she says: From where? And I say: That's what I wanted to ask you. And she says: Not today. And I say: It's me! And she says: Not that I remember. And I say: Can I come in? And she says: Sorry.

Or: This woman explains that the woman I've come to see was her sister, and that her sister is no longer with us.

Or: This woman grabs her shotgun as I introduce myself, and shoots me in the chest, and I think to myself: what the hell's happening here? And then she shoots me in the head.

Or: This woman scolds me, saying, It's about damned time, where've you been roving around all these years? She screams, Get inside this minute and wash your hands and go straight to your room, no supper for you, you're grounded!

Or: This woman throws her arms around me and says she's so sorry, she says it's all her fault, but she was young, and now she's older, she says, can't we start again from the beginning, and I tell her I'm sorry, but I'm much too old to start again from the beginning.

Or: *This woman has drool dripping from her mouth. She grins, finding just insanely ambrosial the fact that she's the one who made me.*

Albert sat in the passenger seat, reading his chess notebook. Violet steered with her left hand. Curve upon curve. Her right rested on Albert's upper thigh. Which didn't bother him. They weren't far from the goal now, and no matter what he'd hoped to get from it, hoped to achieve, getting it over with would be a basically good thing, he told himself. The same went for a woman's hand, like Violet's, on his upper thigh: basically good.

Her fingers stirred almost imperceptibly. "It's lovely to be with you," she said.

Albert glanced over his shoulder. Alfonsa's eyes were closed, but he didn't believe she was sleeping. Ever since they'd hit the road, she'd been conspicuously reserved.

Fred, on the other hand, sat staring out the window, his eyes flicking left to right, again and again, as if he were reading an encyclopedia. *Pushing the world,* that's what he called it. Fixing on something— a street sign, a tree, a license plate—holding it fast with his gaze, and shoving it aside with his eyes. Maybe he was right, thought Albert, maybe we all only believe we're moving, when in fact we never really move at all. We simply push life past us.

"Thanks," said Violet.

"For what?"

"You got me out of there. That internship at K&P was hell." She told him about her days at the production company, confirming what he'd read in her eyes at the airstrip. "I don't know what I want to do now, but there's no way I'm ever going back there."

"A few days ago you sounded completely different."

"You, too."

"What do you mean?"

Now she pinched his upper thigh. "You know exactly what I mean."

There was too much expectation in her grin for Albert's liking. On the other hand, a grin, too, was basically good. Why ask questions and risk breaking the mood?

The same thought occurred to him three and a half hours later, on the sagging mattress of a motel over whose front door the word *Gasthof* floated in black letters against a light-blue ground, as Violet sat on him, naked, rotating her hips. But there was one question he simply couldn't suppress: about the pill he hoped she hadn't forgotten to take. Violet just laughed, leaned over him, licked his upper lip. Which hardly reassured him. Forgotten pills were a by-no-means-insignificant part of their common past, as were small-hour journeys back and forth across the Bavarian uplands in search of the nearest twenty-four-hour pharmacy, and the patronizing commentaries of the smart-aleck pharmacists who'd clearly never made a single mistake in their whole lives, and finally, forty-eight hours in the company of an unbearable Violet, plagued by nausea and intestinal cramps, cursing, sweating, and smelling oddly of leeks.

Albert grabbed her shoulders. She stopped short and merely chuckled a single word: "Rough!" Then kept going, even more eagerly. Dark-blond hair tickled his chest. A basically less-good feeling crept over him. It wasn't so easy to separate himself from Violet, she took his efforts for play and clung tightly to him, giggling that they were "making *serious* whoopee," and pressing him into the mattress, until he finally tossed her away with a bounce and jumped from the bed.

"Did you take it or not?"

She was still grinning. "Albert, calm down."

"What?!"

"Let's stop with the little game."

Albert slipped into his boxers. "I have no idea what you're talking about."

Violet rolled her eyes. "Just come back to bed." Her voice took on a salacious tone. "Want to read the back of my head?"

"No."

"No?"

"No."

"All right, fine." She stretched herself. He knew that she knew how much he liked the way she looked. "What do you suggest?"

"Have you taken it, or not?"

"Would it be so terrible if I hadn't?"

"Are you nuts?!"

Now for the first time her grin flickered. "Okay, look, this is getting ridiculous. Truth is, you're afraid of losing me, and I'm afraid of losing you. Neither of us can imagine ourselves with anyone else. We need each other. We love each other."

And suddenly, as she was expressing it so unambiguously, it became clear to Albert: he didn't love her.

Violet took his silence for agreement. Her grin was bright white again. She leapt from the bed and threw her arms around him. Her cheerful breathing brushed his ear. "Of course I remembered to take it." He could feel her heartbeat clearly, and her skin was much too warm. "But maybe—in the future, I mean—I shouldn't take it anymore?"

He could have answered her honestly. He could have confessed that the mere idea of having children struck him as absurd, that he certainly wouldn't be producing any offspring, not in this life. He could have explained that he felt differently than she did, yes, that he asked himself whether what he felt for her wasn't simply the blind clinging of a two-thirds orphan to another human being. He could have explained how incomprehensible it was that she still wanted him. He could have ended this love story, which was more substantial in their heads than in reality, once and for all. But what did he do?

He returned her hug.

The problem, thought Albert, when someone loved you the way Violet loved him, was that you were always being pressured to ponder whether it was possible for you to love her, too. And when you arrived at the conclusion that you didn't love her, you started asking yourself whether you might not be able to, after all. If maybe all it would take was a little effort, a few relaxed days spent together, some heart-to-heart talks, a couple of tender interactions with each other.

By the time the sun came up they were on their way again. Violet had paid for both rooms, she'd rustled up a couple of poppy-seed rolls from a local bakery for breakfast, filled the car with gas, and on top of all that somehow managed to pick Albert a little bouquet of wild-flowers, which now, strapped tight in the Beetle's passenger seat, he held in one sweaty hand, amazed at how sure you could be that you didn't love someone, while in the backseat Fred snoozed in an impossible position, and Alfonsa listened to Frank Sinatra on her Walkman, and Violet chirped: "The road is all ours."

For a hundred miles, Albert pretended to be asleep. It was the only way to evade, somewhat, Violet's grip. Again and again she'd say his name and ask if he was awake in a tender tone of voice that left no room for any doubt that he would never be able to fulfill her expectations. Or she'd stroke his cheek. Which raised goose bumps on him. He told himself that a woman's love he couldn't return was better than no love at all. But he couldn't find any comfort in that. Not today.

Violet told Fred that before she'd met Albert on the bus, she hadn't believed in love at first sight, because she'd thought you couldn't love someone if you didn't know them. "Now I think otherwise," she said. "Maybe you can *only* really love people you don't know. Once you get to know them, it complicates everything." For a fraction of a second her voice quavered. "They become . . . different."

"I know," said Fred, decisively: a clear sign that he hadn't been able to follow her.

Albert's eyelids stirred. These kinds of conversations were pretty much the opposite of what you wanted to hear when you were about to meet your mother for the first time after nineteen years. His mother. What a word! It sucked all the other thoughts from his head. Albert attempted to calm himself by silently reciting *The Hobbit.* Till he got to the part with the dragon that lived in Mount Erebor. If only he could have fallen asleep! It was more exhausting than he'd thought to keep his eyes closed for two whole hours. His left leg was all pins and needles, but he thought it was smarter not to change his position, so as not to blow his cover. He was forcing himself not to clutch at the makeup compact. The wildflowers smelled too wild. The seat belt cut into his throat. And Violet warbled: "Albert, sweetie, are you awake?"

Mother. Mother. Mother.

Crunching gravel. Albert blinked: they'd arrived at the lower terminus of the mountain gondola, at last. They parked by the main entrance, where a few travelers bustled. In spite of the cloudless sky, the day was autumnally gloomy. Albert climbed out of the car and stretched his limbs; he showed Fred where the toilets were, and watched him trudge toward them, his rumpled poncho tossed over his shoulder, hat set crooked on his head.

Alfonsa said, "I'd better leave the two of you alone," and vanished into the station with a meaningful nod. Her black veil, which he'd never seen her without, prevented him yet again from reading the back of her head.

Violet set down Fred's backpack and Albert's bag. Slammed the trunk shut. Pulled out her purse, and passed him a fifty-euro note. "For the cable car."

"Aren't you coming?"

"Let's not make this harder than it already is."

"What are you talking about?"

"I thought you always catch on to everything."

She shoved the cash into his pants pocket.

"You . . . ?"

"Exactly."

"Why did you bring us here, then?"

"Should I have left you all on the side of the road?"

"You were only pretending?"

"Weren't we both?" She looked at him, sad, intent, and he realized what it was like to look at someone when you were looking at them for the last time. "I tried, I didn't want to just give up on us. But now I know—I don't love you, I love what we had, once. And I think that's how it is for you, too. When you hugged me last night I could feel how hard it was for you."

Albert wanted to say something, but she wasn't finished yet.

"I thought that maybe it was just a question of time for us, I thought that if I gave you some space and got rid of the camera, we might have a chance. And for a little while it was going pretty well, wasn't it? Only, people simply aren't made to live long and happy lives together. You get either the one or the other." She smiled wearily. "Anyway, don't worry. About me. It's not the end of everything. It's not."

It was ridiculous, but part of him wished she hadn't said all of this. He didn't want to say good-bye to her here and now, it was all happening too fast for him, he searched for some objection, some solution, there had to be something that could buy him time, and he rejected one word after another. *Fear. Mother. Expectation. Curiosity. Danger. Fred. Stress. Death. Bewilderment. Loneliness. Fear.* None of them passed muster, and no combination expressed what it was he wanted: that she stay, and that she go, and that he love her and she him, equally, and that they might have some kind of future together, and that they'd never met.

"Albert, one last thing—and one that has nothing to do with us: if you want, I'll drive you back. But only if we go right away."

"Before"—his voice was almost gone; he cleared his throat—"before I've talked to her?"

"If you ask me, you should forget her, take Fred and clear out, and go enjoy the time you have left with him. I realize how utopian that sounds, but believe me, I know what it's like to go chasing after something that doesn't exist anymore. I'm an expert at that. Don't make the same mistake. You don't mean anything to this woman. Otherwise you'd have heard from her long ago. She's not your problem. Forget about her, start worrying about your own life. And Fred's. You could still have a couple of good weeks together. All you have to do is open the passenger door and climb in."

Zwirglstein

Albert stood in the half-empty parking lot, a cigarette between his lips. The curb bent his shadow. Somebody tapped him on the shoulder. Fred.

"You're smoking!"

"You don't say."

Fred took the cigarette and tossed it away.

"Why'd you do that?"

"It makes your legs black! And then you go dead."

Albert lit up another. "That's just peachy. Didn't you say you'd rather die with me?"

"I said that."

"Great, so cheer up."

Fred snatched the second cigarette and stamped on it.

"Hey!"

"We can't all go dead!"

"Well, we'll see about that," said Albert, opening the cigarette pack. It was empty. "Shit."

"Albert!"

"Yeah yeah." He crumpled the pack, aimed, threw, and missed a trash can. "I guess you'll have to die alone."

Fred glanced around. "Where did Violet go?"

"Where the woodbine twineth."

Fred looked at Albert, smiled, and suddenly threw his arms around him. Albert inhaled his sweetish smell, feeling a heartbeat that might have been his own or Fred's—he couldn't tell.

"You'll find someone better," said Alfonsa. "Believe me."

Albert freed himself from the hug; he hadn't realized she'd come back. "Did you know that was going to happen?"

"The breakup? How was I supposed to know that?"

"I haven't even said that we've broken up."

Alfonsa smirked.

The gondola to the top of the Zwirglstein pulled away from the platform; they were taking the cable car because you needed permission to use the road up to the old-folks home—and a car, of course. The gondola moved with a metallic rattling and clanking. It amused Alfonsa to see Albert clutching the pole for dear life with both hands. Fred stood unsupported in the middle of the car, twisting his head excitedly in all directions as they began to climb. "Ambrosial!" He stepped toward the rear window. The tips of fir trees slid past them, tossing in the wind. The station shrank away. The panorama was like a model railway's plastic landscape.

"Please don't do that," said Albert.

Fred turned back to him. "What?"

"Move."

"You don't need to be afraid of heights yet, Albert." Fred pointed in the direction they were headed. "Up there it's much higher!"

"How comforting."

They reached the first support tower, and the gondola swayed. Albert slid down his pole to the floor. Even a five-foot bunk bed at Saint Helena had left him feeling uneasy. How many feet from the ground were they now? Too many, in any case. Albert pulled out the makeup compact and held the hair up against the light. A thin, sinuous rift in the white sky.

"You still have that with you," Alfonsa said, more to herself than to him.

As a kid he'd sometimes imagined that his mother, wherever she was, looked up at the sky just as much as he did, that they were both looking at the same thing, that a cloud hanging above her would soon be casting its shadow on him.

"Klondi says you're a good son," said Alfonsa.

"She's wrong about that," he said.

"He is a good son. Don't you think so, Fred?"

"Albert is a totally good son," said Fred.

Albert looked over at Fred. "Thanks."

"You're welcome."

Albert didn't want to ask Fred, but he had to. "To whom?"

"To whom what?"

"To whom am I a good son?"

"That's easy!"

"Oh really?"

"Yes! You're the son of your mom, and the son of your dad!"

Albert laughed. "So easy." He slipped the hair back into the makeup compact.

The gondola slowed, and slid jerkily into the rectangular maw of the mountaintop station. The doors were unlocked and opened. Fred jumped from the gondola, Albert climbed out cautiously behind him, and Alfonsa followed. They were greeted by a blast of damp cold, and by the cable car's operator, who shook his head and said: "You picked a fine day for it. There's nothing to see."

"Don't be so sure about that," replied Alfonsa.

They left the station and followed a well-trodden path. High fog hid the view of the valley. Which was fine by Albert. Bright-green letters on a dark-green sign: *Alp-View Senior Residence, 0.2 km*. Fred was taking smaller steps than usual, Alfonsa walked beside him, and Albert strayed off ahead. Only a measly three hundred steps to go! How many he'd already taken in quest of his mother. He thought of Fred's attic and the Hansel and Gretel crumbs, he thought of the gold in the tin box and the silent cassette tape and the lists of green cars, he thought of the streets of Königsdorf, of the flyers taped to every front door, he thought of Klondi's garden and the Hofherr and the rectangular sewer pipes, he thought of Saint Helena and the chessboard of stained boxwood and of darts and shoelaces and the backs of heads, he thought of Tobi's feet and Clemens's house and Gertrude's neighing, he thought about Klondi (*Mothers are overrated, Albert. If you ask me, you can count yourself lucky that you grew up without one*), he thought of Alfonsa (*What are you looking for elsewhere that isn't here?*), he thought of Violet (*You don't mean anything to this woman. Otherwise you'd have heard from her long ago. She's not your problem. Forget about her, start worrying about your own life*), he thought of Fred in the Speedster, with his encyclopedia, in the cemetery, with his diving goggles, in "The Day the Bus Attacked the Bus Stop," and he thought of a woman whose name he still didn't even know.

"I don't feel good," said Fred, as they reached the old-folks home: a modern building, reminiscent of a hotel, its front side of slanted glass in which the sky was reflected.

"Neither do I," said Albert, pointing to a wooden bench cut from a bisected tree trunk by the front door. "Should we rest for a minute?"

Alfonsa said she would go ahead and wait for them at the reception. Glass sliding doors closed behind her.

Fortunately, Fred followed Albert and lowered himself to the bench. He pulled his hat down onto his forehead and slumped over. Every part of him was pointing earthward, he seemed weaker than ever before. Albert helped him take off the backpack, slipped it under his head, and closed the collar of the poncho. Within seconds Fred seemed to be asleep. His chest rose and fell evenly. For a moment Albert let his hand rest on Fred's shoulder, feeling the comforting warmth of his body. At once Albert realized how quiet it was in his head. No thoughts.

When he let go of Fred, it felt as if he were saying farewell.

The air in the entry hall smelled of iodine. To Albert it felt brighter inside, as though the glass walls strengthened the daylight. His footsteps echoed. No one was staffing the reception desk. At a kiosk a pair of old folks in bright blue anoraks were examining a sodden trail map.

Alfonsa waited by a white column. She wasn't smirking now. Albert went over to her, and before he could say anything she lifted her arms and removed the black veil. He didn't move. Her hair was done up in a French braid; it was graying already at the temples, but otherwise the color was still strong. It glowed a fiery red.

＊

PART VIII

*Mina's and Anni's
and Arkadiusz's and
Markus's and Ludwig's
and Fred's and Alfonsa's
and Julius's Stories
1930–1983*

Grease, Dried Flowers, and Bitterness

Nathaniel Wickenhäuser, whose love for me was greater than my own for him, had folded up his mother's bridal gown for me—presumably with his eyes shut, so that its whiteness wouldn't blind him. It had smelled as Else would have, were she still alive: of grease, dried flowers, and bitterness. I can't burn you, he must have thought. I can't throw you out. But I can't keep you, either. So you're going to be a gift.

The next morning, in the bus, the bundle lay on the empty seat beside me. During the whole course of the trip, I didn't touch it, but stared out the window: the mountains grew bigger, the forests thicker, while the road dwindled. When the bus reached my stop, I left the bundle where it was. Gifts from liars I could do without.

"Wait!" a woman shouted, holding the package aloft. "You've forgotten something!"

I struggled to smile, and thanked her.

"Somebody sure is lucky today," she said.

"The question is, who?" I answered, stuffing the bundle into my travel bag.

That's where it stayed for the moment, sharing the space with my provisions. It first saw the dull light of Segendorf when the innkeeper emptied the bag onto the floor of the barn on the moor, pulled it over her head, and announced, "Now you can do what you like with me!"

Which is exactly what I did, though the innkeeper had presumably had something else in mind: I chased her out of the barn. "I want nothing more to do with you!" I shouted, bringing the wench to tears, something that no one had managed to do for a good long time.

The very same night I had secretly watched my sister dancing for Arkadiusz, I set out once more for their house. The innkeeper had confirmed that it was she who lived there. This time I had Wickenhäuser's present with me. Anni's wedding was set to take place the next day, the innkeeper had told me, and if the bundle contained what it smelled like, *then it was meant for her. I knocked, and Anni opened the door and shook her head, and I couldn't say a single word. All of a sudden I saw our old house looming before me. Behind a second-story window Jasfe and Josfer lay atop and within each other. Anni, little Anni, stood in front of the house with the torch in her hand. She stretched out her arm and painted a streak of fire across the front door. Flames leapt up across the wooden walls and wrapped the structure in a gleaming coat of burning colors. The wall of flame built higher and higher, till it reached the window behind which Josfer and Jasfe screamed. Our parents pressed themselves against the pane. Howling. Out of lust, or despair, or who knew what.*

"You're alive!" Anni threw her arms around me, tearing me from my thoughts. Else's scent rose into my nostrils, and Anni's warmth to my head, and both at once were almost too much.

"You're alive!" Anni repeated.

"Not for long, if you keep squeezing that hard."

Anni let go of me and looked into my eyes and said almost voicelessly, "You're alive."

I handed her the bundle. "For your wedding."

She smiled at me, moved, and tore it open.

"Do you like it?"

". . . yes."

"Are you going to wear it?"

"Julius, I already have a dress."

"It can't be as beautiful as this one."

"I believe it is."

"What you decide to believe is always the truth."

"Then I believe that my dress is more beautiful."

"At least try it on."

"No can do."

"Why not?"

"Because . . . it . . . it stinks."

"It has a bit of an odor!"

244 &

"Julius. It stinks. And I don't want to quarrel with you over a dress right now. You're here! You're alive!" Once again she clung to my throat, and she kissed my cheek and gave back Else's dress. "Today is truly the most beautiful day of my life," she whispered in my ear, and I kept to myself that I hoped life wouldn't go downhill for her from here.

"Is that Julius?" someone asked, in an accent I'd never heard before. A lanky man appeared beside Anni, slipped an arm around her waist, and offered me his hand. "I am Arkadiusz. It is a pleasure to meet you. Anni has told me about you so often. You must be a terribly special person."

I gave him a firm shake. That's right, I thought, and: so much friendliness can't possibly be genuine.

"You will stay with us, of course," said Arkadiusz.

I knew I should have refused, and let the two of them insist, and then act as if I were pondering the situation, and let the two of them insist even more, and then manifest a little interest with some polite formulation, à la "If it really isn't too much of a bother for you . . ." and then, hewing to the rule of third-time's-a-charm, allow them to insist once more, in order to give in at last with an ironic "Well, if that's the way it has to be."

Instead of which I flashed my teeth in a Segendorfish smile, and said, "Gladly."

Now my future brother-in-law threw an arm around me, too. "Welcome!"

That was too much of a good thing for my taste. I asked Anni if I could speak to her alone, and she turned to Arkadiusz and looked at him imploringly. He nodded immediately. And though that was just what I'd wanted, I would've preferred him to be a little less understanding. This man seemed flawless.

A little later, Anni and I were racing the way we used to, up to the top of Wolf Hill. I let her win. We stretched ourselves out in the shadow of the oak, and she told me about how she'd met Arkadiusz. Over the next few weeks we'd go back there again and again to talk about the past six years.

"You actually want to do it," I said.

"What do you mean?"

"Get married."

Her amused laugh robbed me of any hope that I might be able to foster some doubt in her. She could have left it at that, but she took my hand and said, "Arkadiusz is the most beautiful, the best man there is. I've never loved anyone the way I love him."

When Anni went off to finalize the preparations for the wedding, I went looking for distractions. I needed distractions. Right away. Unfortunately, the innkeeper was no longer an option. Still, I had an idea of where I might go.

Mina turned out to be sensational. A multiple widow couldn't have acquitted herself better. Out in the barn, we helped each other explode. The whole time, Mina wore the wedding dress. I'd made her a present of it. Over her tanned skin, the fragile white seemed somehow darker, nearly gray, and suited Mina's hair—which had become more gray than blond by now—perfectly.

"When are we getting married?" she asked, rolling herself on top of me and thereby ending our pause for breath.

"My sister's first," I said.

"But I already have a dress! We have to get married, too!"

"We will."

"Did you come back to Segendorf because you wanted to marry me?"

"Why else would I come back? You have to look after that dress. So that I can lead you to the altar in it."

"I'll look after it perfectly!"

"You promise?"

"I promise," she said—and exploded once again.

Mina took her promises very seriously. While all the women in Segendorf were dolling themselves up for Anni and Arkadiusz's wedding—pinking their cheeks with drops of blood, gracing their high-piled hair with wild-flowers—she folded her wedding dress up and laid it away in a box, in the safest place in the world: under her bed. She didn't let even a fleck of dust anywhere near it. Every morning after getting up, and again before her evening prayers, she wiped the lid clean with care. As the Sacrificial Festival approached, she told the dress, "From now on, you're no longer my Most Beloved Possession." And once the Sacrificial Festival was over: "From now on, you're once again my Most Beloved Possession." Sometimes, long after I'd moved in with Anni and Arkadiusz, she brought me the box, and lifted the lid to remind me of its brightness, and whenever she did I'd smile and lie, telling her how much I was looking forward to our wedding, I could barely wait, but she had to be patient just a little while longer. And Mina was patient. Simple enough, since she was up to her ears in work, helping her mother at the bakery (at seven seconds, she held the Segendorf record for pretzel preparation). But in the evenings, when she'd run through her daily ration of patience and had nothing to think about but her intended, the handsome Julius Habom, all she wanted was to be able to fall asleep, to recharge herself, and the more she wanted to fall asleep, the wider awake she felt. Then she had no alternative but to pull on the wedding dress. She slipped out into the Segendorf night, looking for all the world like the ghost of a bride. She stood before our house, not approaching the door, but rather moving from window to window until she'd found me and waved to me, and distracted me from watching Anni, who for her part had eyes only for Arkadiusz; she danced with him, tickled him with the ends of her hair, fed him raspberry marmalade, kissed him, sat on his lap, rubbed his neck, read to him from the Bible, held his hand. As though I weren't even there.

On one of those nights when Mina was once again circling the house, she noticed a shape crouching by the kitchen window. Pig Farmer Markus. In his eyes, she told me—and it disturbed me to hear this—she recognized the same look with which I observed Anni. His right hand gripped a hunting knife. Mina hid herself behind a wheelbarrow. Markus raised his arm—as he did, a bit of his hair shifted oddly—and scratched something into the kitchen window. When he was done, he looked at the result with *satisfaction. Then he slipped away. Mina glided over to the window and examined it. Markus had left a pair of similar-looking signs behind, of which the first came together at its tip; and though Mina couldn't read, she felt that these were more than just a couple of scratches.*

"It's just a couple of scratches," I said to her when we met in the barn the next evening and Mina told me about what she'd seen. "What are you doing at our house at night, anyway?"

"I don't have much patience."

"You can't just lurk around after dark. What will people think?"

"I don't know what people think."

"That's not quite what I meant."

"Julius, when will we get married?"

"We'll be married soon," I said, and plunged swiftly beneath the skirt of her dress. "Very soon."

A Human Anchor

Very soon *was still several months away, months in which the bridal gown began to stretch across her hips, and then wouldn't slip over her belly any longer, so that she brought it along to our meetings in the barn only to cover the two of us with it. One night, while Mina slept, I laid a hand on the spot just above her bulging belly button, and whispered:*

"Can you hear me? Do you recognize my voice? Do you like it? It must sound completely different from in there.

"Sometimes I wish I could crawl in there with you.

"You should take your time. You'll never again be as safe as you are right now. There aren't any safe places out here. That's why people say they feel safe—because they can never be safe. Maybe a little creature like you doesn't feel anything yet. But you are safe.

"Do you know that your aunt's belly is getting bigger, too? It frightens me. Anni isn't ready, not yet. Ever since I came back, I've been thinking about the fire. I'm not angry with her. She didn't know what she was doing. But . . . but she doesn't know what she did, either. Her memory is wrong. It wasn't an accident—it certainly wasn't a stray spark.

"Should I tell her the truth? Should I tell her how I found her with the torch in front of our burning house? Can you even tell someone something like that? And if so, how?

"Sometimes I wish I could crawl in there with you."

I made Mina promise me something else: to keep the name of her child's father a secret. Having no father, I thought, would still be better than having me as a father, an undertaker who loved nobody but his sister; who couldn't bring himself to tell her the truth about her past; who lived in her house and stuffed wax into his ears every night, because he was afraid he might overhear her and her Pole, and that would remind him of Jasfe and Josfer; who slaved away at the Segendorf cemetery, digging more graves than anyone needed, just to let off steam; who slept for the same reason with a Klöble who adored him and was convinced that any day now he'd make her a proposal of marriage; who, whenever he started awake from dreams of the house in flames, always immediately touched his elbow.

You could say that only my ears experienced the birth of my son. Mina's piercing shrieks kept all the customers far away from the bakery. In my room at Anni's house, which stood close by, I paced back and forth, pausing only when Mina's screams went silent and were replaced by those of our child. As night fell I crept to Mina's window: she opened it, grinning, and passed me the little boy. I asked Mina if I could take a little stroll with my son, at which she smiled and nodded eagerly, as if I'd finally proposed to her. I walked with my son counterclockwise around the bakery.

"You're right on time. Someday you'll grow into a very punctual man.

Unlike your cousin. No surprise there. Poles aren't known for their punctuality. Your aunt can't leave the house anymore. She just lies there waiting, breaking the world record for head-shaking. Your uncle has to wash her and rub her impressive belly, while muttering words that sound as if they're being said backward.

"You're so warm. The better to soften me, you're probably thinking. I'll tell you something: you wouldn't be the first to try. It's nothing personal, I just don't have much use for children. The only thing I really like about you is your discretion. You're an even better listener than the dead. A while back I was walking around a house with a woman who couldn't speak either. I miss her, sometimes. Else's image is clear in my mind. My parents, though—I can't even remember their faces. Whenever I try to picture them, everything goes fuzzy. Anni says it's the same for her. That's why I've decided against telling her about the fire. Why should I remind her of the deaths of two people whom we can barely remember?

"That's certainly no reason for crying!

"I'm going to tell your mother she should name you Ludwig. After our last king. What do you think? You're going to need that kind of name. With a mother like her. And a father like me."

Frederick Arkadiusz Driajes followed Ludwig Reindl into the world after a lag of five days. During the birth Anni gripped my hand with her right, and Arkadiusz's with her left—both of our faces were at least as painfully contorted as hers. Our worried creases smoothed only at the midwife's satisfied nod, and Fred's introductory scream was met with applause—which had nothing to do with him, but rather with the fact that at the same moment, not far away, the first cobblestone for the town's new main street had just been solemnly lowered into place.

Eight months later, by the time Ludwig mastered crawling (and Fred his own mode of locomotion, a sort of lateral roll), the cobbles already spanned the village from north to south, running right through the middle, as Mina put it, like a river of stones. Only two years after that, the main street, which Ludwig was allowed to cross (and Fred not at all) only after looking carefully left and right, had been extended even farther south, forming part of Reichsstrasse 11 toward Innsbruck. And in the spring of 1938, while its constant through-traffic and the rattling of one-cylinder engines brought happiness to Ludwig (and bad dreams to Fred), the construction of the most angular sewer system in the whole German Reich was brought to a conclusion.

Ludwig's (and Fred's) seventh birthday approached, and everyone in the village who had any interest in knowing had long ago learned who his father was. Mina had turned out to be more competent at keeping secrets than I was. On many days I simply couldn't resist the impulse to see my son. Together we wandered up and down the main street, adding up the number of cobbles, and then losing count. We tried to guess by the thunder of the approaching vehicles what kind they were, or else spat cherry pits over the river of stones. On mild summer nights Ludwig would steal out of the bakery, lay himself down in the grass not two steps away from the street, and sleep there better than in his own bed. Though I reminded him constantly how dangerous that was, showing him the squashed corpses of weasels, or giving him a slap, Ludwig wouldn't be dissuaded—and so I had no choice but to tie myself to him with a rope and sleep beside my son, not three steps from the street, a human anchor in the grass.

Though I didn't find much rest there, I took advantage of the little sleeper's open ear.

"I've never really seen myself as a father. And I still don't see myself as one.

"Maybe it's enough if you and your mother do. Her faith—and not just in our wedding—is stronger than Pastor Meier's.

"When you're older, think twice about whether or not you want to have kids. I'm telling you, you can't anticipate the consequences.

"You might wake up one day and realize that you love them!

"Or the opposite. Look at your aunt. The magnitude of her disappointment at having given life to a Klöble corresponds to the frequency and intensity of her head-shaking. Nobody understands that she doesn't do it because she's saying no, but rather because she's glancing left and right, on the lookout for a better life.

"The problem is, she's looking so desperately left and right that she doesn't see who's standing in front of her.

"She should never have gotten started with that Pole. She and I could have easily produced someone like Fred.

"I hope you don't play with him. What a useless lug! He stands in front of life as if it was a door—he knows you can open it, but not how.

"Have you seen his drawings? He has talented little hands, I'll give you that, but . . . who wants to look at dead birds? Who's interested in the eyes of pigs? Or the wings of dung flies?

"The pictures make it clear how sick he really is. Anni's right to destroy them. Like I've told her, Fred should learn to read. Reading breeds understanding. And understanding leads to more beautiful pictures."

Finding Something without Looking for It

On his seventh birthday, Segendorf's youngest parishioner opened the town's very first encyclopedia. The thicket of words on the page so frightened Fred that he immediately clapped it shut again, preferring to follow his father on his patrol of the sewer tunnels.

"Don't you at least want to learn your first word?" Anni shouted after them.

"It's his birthday," answered Arkadiusz.

"Tomorrow I'll learn two first words!" Fred promised.

Arkadiusz was responsible for the maintenance of the underground tunnels, casting around for leaks, patching fissures, dislodging clots of ash, *cleaning the outlet valves, exterminating rats, and, when the system flooded, submerging himself for as long as it took to trace the blockage to its source. Who better for the job than ARKADIUSZ, THE (FORMER) FOUR-MINUTE-AND-FORTY-THREE-SECOND MAN? Besides, down there the racket of motor-driven vehicles was pleasantly muffled, the trickling calm relaxed him like a warm bath. Anni told me how he often roamed the tunnels for hours at a stretch, doing the thing he'd always been so good at doing: waiting. For night, when the traffic would die down. For some message from his family, to whom after all this time and with Anni's help, he'd finally been able to write again—since Segendorf was now, thanks to the widening network of roads, within reach of the German Reichspost. For Fred's next drawing—brilliantly detailed sketches, in his opinion, which, despite their unusual subjects, filled him with pride, and at least one of which he always carried on his person. For a burst of inspiration that would reveal to him exactly which ingredient his homemade and less than entirely appetizing pierogi were lacking. For an end to the hateful diatribes that spewed from the Volksempfänger radio set, which Pig Farmer Markus liked to blare from his open window. For Anni's dancing. For Anni's song. For Anni's nod.*

"Mama says you used to be a diver," said Fred in a rather reedy voice, having stuffed his nose with catkins against the sewer's stink. "That's someone who stays underwater for a really long time."

"I was famous!"

"In oceans, too?"

"Once I dove all the way to the floor of the Baltic. Without any help!"

"Where's the Baltic?"

"Up north."

"Will you go diving with me, too?"

"Of course! We'll go to the bottom of all seven seas!"

Fred smiled. "That's a lot."

"But first," said Arkadiusz, pointing to a metal grate down at the end of the tunnel, all overgrown with scraps of vegetation, and pressing a scrub brush into Fred's hand, "first we have to make sure that Segendorf stays spick-and-span."

Arkadiusz waited long enough—or too long. On August 25, 1939, a week before the German invasion of his native land, he stumbled across a collapsed sewer tunnel. Instead of reporting the damage right away, he investigated it on his own. Possibly because his eye had been caught by a glitter among the stones. I imagine Arkadiusz climbing over the rubble, pushing clumps of dirt aside with both hands, picking up an unnaturally heavy stone, spitting on it, and wiping the filth away with his shirt—though he knew it would earn him a disapproving shake of the head from his wife. He smiled, thrilled, while a drop of water burst unnoticed on his shoulder. Arkadiusz was barely able to believe that now, without even looking, he'd managed to find it.

"Waiting always pays off!" he informed the sewer pipe, kissing the gold and laughing.

By the time he heard the rushing, it was already too late.

Days passed before they managed to retrieve his body, since only a handful of people took part in the search. These were tough times in which to mobilize help for a Pole. Via Markus's radio the news had reached Segendorf, delivered by an audibly outraged gentleman: "TONIGHT FOR THE FIRST TIME, REGULAR TROOPS FROM POLAND FIRED ON OUR TERRITORY. WE HAVE BEEN RETURNING FIRE SINCE FIVE FORTY-FIVE A.M. AND FROM NOW ON EVERY BOMB WILL BE ANSWERED WITH A BOMB."

I was the one who discovered Arkadiusz. At first I'd bristled at the idea of lifting so much as a finger for my brother-in-law's sake, but of course I couldn't have refused my sister anything. Without actually putting any effort into the subterranean search, I found him wrapped around an outflow pipe, sallow and bloated. But his face! I'd had plenty of experience with corpses, among them a whole crowd of indolently scowling

floaters—but Arkadiusz's face was in a league of its own. Even in death,
he seemed outrageously lovable.

Two Burials

I weighted Arkadiusz's body down with stones, and sank him in the Moorsee,
according to Anni's wishes. Out there where, years before, a girl from
Segendorf had first met a shape-shifter.

The same evening, I went to visit my sister in her room. She sat on her
bed, looking weary, too weary even to shake her head, and was surrounded
by her Most Beloved Possessions, all that she'd rescued from the ruins of
our parents' house . . . the spine of the cookbook . . . a stove tile broken in
five pieces . . . arrowheads . . . a clutch of hairpins all melted together . . .

"How are you doing?" I asked in a whisper.

"I don't know," she said.

I came closer. "I'm sorry." I sat down beside her on the bed and tenta-
tively slipped an arm around her.

Anni snuggled up against me.

"Back when I went away, I thought that I'd find someone out there,
someone who'd love me, and whom I could love. But my true love, I've real-
ized, my true love lives right here."

"You're going to marry Mina?"

"That's not what I meant."

"But you should! She's already waited so long! When two people love
each other, they should be together!"

"That's what I think, too."

"Then don't wait any longer! You never know how much time you have
left! Someday everyone you love will die."

"Not everyone."

"I'm an orphan. And a widow."

"You're a sister."

"That's different."

"Remember how we used to play who-can-fill-the-cup-with-spit-first?"

"Terrible."

"You usually won!"

"That was the past," she said. Leaping up, she hurled the Most Beloved Possessions into a box, and handed it to me. "Here. Do what you want with them."

"Are you sure?"

"I've kept them too long. They're burned. It's over. Go on, get rid of them."

That night I saw how patiently the bog swallowed the box of Most Beloved Possessions, and hoped that with this, the story of Jasfe and Josfer was finally at an end.

Afterward, I sat down on Wolf Hill by the tree's serpentine root, and read I love you. From now on, Arkadiusz would no longer stand between me and my sister.

From a pouch I pulled the gold I'd found on Arkadiusz. He must have stuffed it into his pocket just seconds before the surge of water had swept him away. I'd hold on to it for the time being; who knew what good it might do someday.

Then I saw Fred hurrying up the hill toward me, and tucked it away. Though he wasn't yet nine, my nephew's legs, thin as matchsticks, were known as the longest in all of Segendorf, and patches of downy beard were already sprouting on his cheeks. "Mama says she can't be a mama now!"

"And why are you telling me that?"

"I'm telling you because Mama says you can be my papa a little bit now."

"Me? No, Fred. Nonono. Only your papa can be your papa."

Fred shook first his right, then his left leg, looked up at the sky, cleared his throat. "Mama says you can be my papa a little bit now."

"You already mentioned that."

"What?"

"You said that already."

"I know."

"So you can go now."

"I can draw a picture of you!"

"I don't want any of your pictures. Go play with some kids, any kids!"

"Any kids are sleeping now."

"Then why don't you go to sleep, too?"

"I can't sleep."

"And why not?"

"Because my papa always sings a song so I can sleep. It has really funny words. Do you know that song?"

"No."

"I was in the pipes today," said Fred. "I looked for my papa. Mama says my papa is always traveling through the pipes. Sometimes he's in America, and sometimes he's in Poland, and sometimes he's here, too." He scraped at the ground with his feet, crossed his arms, stretched them out again, and sniffled. "Mama says you can be my papa a little bit, while my papa is traveling."

"Fred."

"Are you my papa a little bit now?"

"Listen."

"You have to be my papa a little bit now!"

"Listen, Fred, listen carefully: I'll never be your papa. Not today, not tomorrow. Never. Because I'm already a father. I have a son, a healthy son, who I like spending time with. His name's Ludwig. You aren't my son, and that's why I'll never be your father. I'm not going into the stinking sewers with you and I'm not singing for you and I'm definitely not going to be your papa. And thank God for that. Because I could never be anything for someone like you. You're nothing to me. You're nothing."

The Truth

A few minutes later my bad conscience sent me after Fred, who'd leapt up and run away. I told myself that I could at least try to be his papa a little bit. In the end, that would please Anni. And maybe then I'd be Fred's papa a little bit in her eyes, too.

I found Fred at the bus stop; he was crying. Before I could make my presence felt, Markus sat down beside him, and since I'd never had much sympathy for the pig farmer, I hid myself behind the maypole, where they wouldn't be able to see me.

"The next bus doesn't come for three days," said Markus to Fred.

"I'm not waiting for the bus," said Fred.

"For what, then?"

"For my papa."

"The Polack?" Markus passed Fred a handkerchief. "That could take a while."

Fred blew his nose. "I'm nothing."

"What do you mean?"

"Julius says I'm nothing."

"Ha. Julius Habom isn't so much himself." With a casual gesture that betrayed how often he did it, he flipped open a makeup compact and checked to make sure his toupee was perfectly seated on his scalp. Since the unfortunate encounter with Anni many years back, he'd used it to hide his bald patch.

Markus held the mirror up in front of Fred. "Who do you see there?"

"Frederick Arkadiusz Driajes."

"And is that nothing?"

"Yes?"

"The correct answer is: You can never be nothing. Otherwise, you wouldn't be there at all!"

"That's right."

Markus pointed to Fred's reflection. "Do you know what I see?"

"Frederick Arkadiusz Driajes?"

"To tell you the truth: no, not just that. I see a boy who could be something great someday, I see potential."

"You use a lot of words that nobody knows."

"I read plenty of books."

"As many as Julius Habom?"

"More, much more." Markus tapped his finger on Fred's reflection. "What color eyes do you have?"

"Green!"

"And what does green stand for? It's the color of hope, of nature—green stands for growth. Green grows!"

"I'm growing a lot, too!"

"Precisely! Most people never grow. They simply settle for their lives, and when they die, it's as if they'd never been. But the two of us, we're different. We grow, we change. Before, I was just the son of a pig farmer. But now, look!" Markus opened his coat and showed Fred a pistol. "My best friend. A Walther P38." He slipped it from the holster. "Want to feel?"

Fred hesitated.

Markus snatched Fred's hand and laid the butt of the pistol in his palm.

"It's heavy!" said Fred.

"It has to be. The weight reminds its owner of the power and responsibility that the possession of such a weapon brings." Markus held the mirror up before Fred once more. "Who do you see?"

"Frederick Arkadiusz Driajes."

"And what else?"

"Green."

"And what else?"

"A pistol."

"That's quite a lot, isn't it?"

Fred looked at the ground, and whispered: "Quite a lot."

"Why so shy? Say it louder: quite a lot!"

"Quite a lot."

"Even louder."

"Quite a lot!"

"Louder!"

"THAT'SALOTTHAT'SNOTNOTHINGATALLTHAT'SALOT
THAT'SQUITEALOT!"

I should have done something, I shouldn't have just surrendered Fred to
Markus. But then, I was glad someone was looking after him, sparing me
the task. During the next few days, Markus demonstrated to Fred how
you slipped the magazine into the gun, how you cocked the hammer and
stood with your legs spread and arms extended and supported your right
hand with your left and squinted your eyes and jerked the trigger. For tar-
gets they built scarecrows—which Markus called "blackamoors"—from
old clothes stuffed with muddy straw. Whenever Fred landed a bull's-eye
their heads burst like kernels of corn in a hot pan, and Markus applauded.
"Of course, killing is always the last resort," he said, "but one should never
forget: blackamoors steal children and eat them."

At home, Anni often forgot to cook anything for Fred, and when he asked
her for food she didn't even shake her head, but slipped out of the house
and ran to the Moorsee, where she spent most of her time nowadays. At
home Fred slunk around, always on guard, because he didn't want to run
into me. At home he sometimes awoke, thinking that the day had come
when his father would return, but the day never came. At home, it was
obvious, Fred didn't feel safe.

But he did with Markus, very much so. The man's mere proximity in-
fused him with a feeling of strength, just like the pistol in his hand. As long
as Fred walked along the main street by Markus's side, everyone said hello
to him. In the tavern, they were the first ones served. While listening to the
radio, Fred could sit right up in front of the set. Or he could stretch out on
the floor while Markus read to him from his books. Nobody called Fred

Klöble *anymore, they all addressed him as Frederick or Herr Driajes, and he liked the way that sounded: "Herr Driajes."*

In exchange for all that, Markus wanted merely a handful of drawings. At first, these showed Markus himself—with a full head of hair, blond hair, parted on the side. Later, his new friend began to take an interest in pictures of other Segendorfers, too. He made no secret of this, and allowed Fred to hand them over to him in public. He wanted everyone to be aware that he was aware of everyone. His monologues, seemingly directed at Fred, were in fact camouflaged addresses to the community at large. "Everything is mixed up with everything else," he said to Fred. "And that's why I need as many pictures as possible of as many people as possible. Pictures of whoever Blacksmith Schwaiger talks to in the tavern. Of wherever Farmer Obermüller's widow roams around at night. Of whoever Cobbler Gaiger sells his fishing rods to. Drawings help us understand life. Where it comes from, for example. And, in the best case, where it's going. And wouldn't it be marvelous if you could divine just how every life is going to unfurl? If you could hold the future in your hands, and step in at an early stage to shape it? No more subterranean drownings, no more blows of fate, no unpleasant surprises. You could prevent the bad, play midwife to the good, and never have to rely on God again. If you ask me, you, Fred, are the best draftsman there is. Most people see things the way they want to see them— for instance, when it's raining, everyone says it's rotten weather, and that the weather is good when the sun shines, but, as you've certainly found, we need rain for drinking and washing and irrigation, and thus rain is good weather, too—you, Fred, see things as they are. And draw them. You might not understand it all, you probably don't know many of the words I use, but I'm convinced that you have a grip on the deeper truth of things. You can't help but see the truth in things, that's why you're so valuable. You observe and you listen and you draw. Nobody can do that better than you. And it's no surprise that others have been struck by this remarkable ability as well. I know it's strange when people who used to talk with you are now always hurrying past. But you can chalk it up to envy. They want to be like you and me, they can't grow the way we can and want to belittle us to make themselves feel bigger. Don't let it bother you. Just think! Why does your mother go around claiming you're only six years old, when everyone knows you're nearly nine? She wants to make you small. Because she senses that she's inferior to you. You're no Klöble, not anymore, just like I'm no longer a pig farmer. I used to use idiotic words like heya, I sounded just like you'd imagine a pig farmer sounds, and I bullied other kids to make myself feel strong. But I've grown! Significantly, all of this started with a root up on Wolf Hill. Pastor Meier told me what someone had carved there: I love you. Those were the first three words I learned. I love you. The ones after that I found in his Bible. And the ones after that in books that an undertaker from out of town gave me in exchange for a pair of juicy porkchops. I read and read and read, until the letters faded on the page and my fingertips grew black. And even then I didn't stop. Every new book honed my mind further. Books became my best friends. Through them I traveled the world, made the acquaintance of places we can only reach with our minds. Thanks to them, I was finally able to see things plainly, as plain as print on paper. I understood that I couldn't, shouldn't, mustn't be the way I'd been any longer. Because almost everything goes by very fast. A love. Our lives. Simply all of it! There's not a lot of time. Anyone who doesn't comprehend that will get lost in hopes and memories and die without ever having lived. The books opened my eyes, I came to understand what I love you really meant: to accept myself. Because that's the first step toward growth. You have to realize who you are. Once you've understood yourself, you can like yourself, and whoever likes himself won't let himself be hurt by others anymore, and when one can't be hurt by others anymore, one is on the path toward setting oneself free. I was my Most Beloved Possession. At that point, it wasn't long before my maturity, ambition, and will became apparent to others. Just the way you noticed me. You're an outstandingly gifted boy, Fred. Not everyone can handle that. Just think about your father, your papa! Where is he? Why is he traveling the world, why isn't he taking care of you? Why didn't he take you with him? Why doesn't he write?

Very simple: he's intimidated by your greatness! But your uncle is even worse. When others have something that he can't have himself, he tries to destroy it. In this case, your talent—where does he get the right to abuse you? The same goes for the honor of this village—why doesn't he marry Mina Reindl? And the same for the faithful love your mother bears for your father—how dare your uncle live in a house with her, alone, for months at a time? Unfortunate as it is, it seems to me that Julius Habom is not a good man. While we grow, he shrivels. And sadly, sadly, he's not the only one. You will have noticed: The racial integrity of the German nation is in grave danger. Like a malignant cancer, lives unworthy of life are proliferating throughout its body. We can't ignore this threat any longer. We have to look it in the eye. Now. Even right here, in our homeland, there are souls, sad, pitiful souls, who are lost forever. I know this won't have escaped someone like you. Like me, you see the truth in things. And in times like these, there's great need for figures like us, with a firm hold on the truth, unswerving, never straying from the right path. We, my good man, must do anything we can to preserve truth whole in the maelstrom of history. We must! Because without the truth, we're nothing."

The End of the Most Beloved Possessions

On January 22, 1940, after night had fallen, Fred rapped at Mina's bedroom window to inform her that I wanted to marry her, right then, that very hour.

Five minutes later, she was rushing down the main street after Fred, dressed in her wedding gown. She assumed she didn't have to worry about Ludwig, that he was with me. And she wasn't wrong about that. Only we weren't waiting for her—we were asleep, tied together with a rope, at the other end of the village.

What with her nephew's long legs, she had to make a considerable effort to match his pace. Her steaming breath vanished in the dark. As they passed the edge of the village, neither of them saw the wooden crate by the side of the road. In it was the new city sign that had just been delivered. It would be erected the following morning, hastening the secularization of the community—most Segendorfers still had no idea that, very soon, they would be Königsdorfers.

"Where's Julius?" asked Mina, gasping for air. "Where are we rushing off to?"

Fred didn't say a thing, and ran faster. Mina tripped and went down on the cobblestones, scraping her hands, and as Fred helped her up again, she saw the moon in the sky, but no stars.

Soon they were crossing one of the bleak fields on the outskirts of the village where stands of winter rye grew. Four dark-green cars were parked in a half circle. Their motors were idling and sounded impatient, and all of their headlights were on, throwing bright light onto a bus in the middle of the field. Shadows flitted between the vehicles.

"Where is Julius Habom!" Mina wanted to know, stopping short. Fred grabbed her arm—she couldn't break loose, and fell to the ground.

"Don't be so rough!" shouted Markus, coming closer and offering her his left hand. In the other, he held his pistol.

Men in surgical masks loomed behind him. The wintry ground crunched beneath their feet. As Mina screamed that she was here for her wedding, and began to thrash around, they gathered her up and carried her onto the bus.

"Are they going to hurt her?" asked Fred.

"No," said Markus, checking his makeup compact to ensure that his toupee was properly situated, and thanked Fred, saying he'd done well.

From within the bus there was a rumbling, followed by a high, mechanical buzzing. Mina's screams were smothered.

Fred covered his ears. "Where is Julius?"

"Probably afraid to get married." Markus grinned. "Looks like we'll have to postpone it."

One of the masked men came back, passing Markus the bridal gown, which he in turn handed to Fred.

"That's all of them," said Markus.

The man in the mask gestured to Fred.

Markus shook his head.

Two more masked men stepped out of the bus, and advanced on Fred. One of them wore white rubber gloves, their fingertips red.

Fred flinched away.

"No," said Markus, and lifted his pistol an inch or two.

Now it was the other men who flinched. The one with the red fingertips spread his arms as if to call for calm.

From the bus there came a dull thud, and the other two men vanished once more. Markus lowered his pistol. A rattling ran through the bus, it shook slightly. From within, a boy hollered—and went silent.

Markus rolled his eyes and nudged Fred: "Typical Klöble!"

Someone turned on the engine, and the bus shook. Then the two masked men stepped out again, opened a hatch in the vehicle's side, pulled a lever, and the door shut. They inspected a hose that ran from the rear of the bus to its roof. One of the two gave a thumbs-up, at which the man with the red fingertips positioned himself at a distance from the bus, walking slowly backward with his eyes fixed on the windows.

Markus noticed that Fred was trembling. "Come," he said, and they climbed into one of the cars. Fred sat in the passenger seat, and Markus tucked the bridal gown around him.

"Better?"

Fred nodded.

Markus put his pistol away, laid his hands on the steering wheel, and stretched out his arms. "A BMW 321." He took a deep breath. "It's a real speedster! Tomorrow I'll give you a driving lesson."

"Where is the bus going?" Fred asked.

"Far, far away." Markus leaned back. In the rearview mirror he inspected his toupee, and nudged it a bit to the left.

They fell silent. The car vibrated.

"I want to go home."

"You know what? I'm going to give you this speedster. It's yours, it belongs to you. What do you think about that?"

"I want my mama!"

"Fred," said Markus, laying his hand on the gearshift, "don't be afraid. Nothing's going to happen to you. I'm here. Just be quiet and close your eyes."

But he didn't do that, he couldn't look away, he didn't even blink. Fred stared and stared.

Hours later, after Markus had driven up and down Reichsstrasse 11 for so long that Fred had finally been able to nod off, the dark-green BMW rolled into Anni's garden and stopped with a soft wheeze. Markus shut off the headlights and glanced over at Fred, sleeping heavily beside him, wrapped in the wedding gown.

Anni knocked at Markus's window. Her greasy hair gleamed, her eyes were bloodshot.

He took his pistol and got out. "Were you over at the Moorsee again? It doesn't agree with you."

She asked him where he'd been and what he'd done with her son and where the car had come from.

Markus bent forward and whispered it in her ear.

Anni exhaled, met his glance for a moment, then looked away again. With a single lunge she grabbed his toupee and tore it from his head.

"I'm exhausted." Markus sighed, scratching his bald spot with the barrel of the Walther. "It was a long day. Really, all I wanted was to bring Fred home. Best to leave him here as he is. I can fetch the car tomorrow."

Anni looked warily at his pistol.

"Oh, I see." He laid it down before her in the grass. "Can I have my hair back now?"

She held the toupee out to him, and as he went to take it, she snatched the pistol and aimed it at him.

Markus arranged his toupee with the help of the mirror. "You have to pull back the hammer."

Anni looked for it.

"It's inside. There," Markus said impassively, pointing it out with his index finger, and Anni cocked it.

"Onto the moor," she ordered, and Markus didn't protest, but tucked the makeup compact away and marched off. She followed at a distance. For a while they went in lockstep, silent. Whenever the pistol grew too heavy for Anni, she switched hands.

"You seem exhausted," said Markus, as they reached the wooden planks that led across the moor. "Fred's worried about you. I worry about you myself. I'm sure it's tough. Your pain must be unimaginable. First your parents, then your husband. But if you pull that trigger, neither of us will be able to take care of your son anymore. They'll come to get him. And don't claim he doesn't mean anything to you. He's all that remains of your Arkadiusz. He's your Most Beloved Possession."

Anni was holding the pistol with both hands now.

"I think that in some strange way I like you because you don't like me. *Your head-shaking is more generous than most people's love. Don't lose the habit. I see so much potential in you. When you consider who Fred's father was, it's amazing how he's turned out. He has you to thank for that. You're a good, a healthy influence. That's why you won't shoot. Because it isn't in you. You're innocent, you dance, you sing, and you could never—"*

Anni shook me awake as dawn was breaking. I was sleeping, tied to Ludwig with a rope, beside the main street. She asked me what she should do. Markus's pistol in her hand, and the splatter of blood on her face, answered my first question. Anni said she'd believed Markus was going to kill them, going to kill them all, but then, when he was lying facedown on the moor, she hadn't been so sure anymore, and she'd gotten scared, scared of herself, because she hadn't thought she'd be able to do it, and now, she said, now that it was over, she was surprised by how easy it had been.

I hugged her without speaking. I held her as tightly as I could, for all the hugs I'd never be able to give her from then on, and when we let go of each other and Anni stood there looking as beautiful to me as only a Most Beloved Possession can, I didn't kiss her little mouth, round as a fish's— even though I sensed that she would have allowed me—because I didn't want to have to miss her kisses, too. Then I took the pistol from her, stuck it in the pocket of my coat, in which the gold was also hidden, and told my sister what had to be done.

Anni ran to the BMW and woke Fred and forbade him to leave the house. Anni stripped off all her clothes and burned them in the oven. Anni washed her body and her face and her hair and got dressed again. Anni locked Fred in the house. Anni found Pastor Meier and told him that during the night she'd secretly seen her own brother shoot Markus, which she couldn't reconcile with her Christian conscience, no matter how much I meant to her, and that was why she was here, to make sure that justice was done. Anni crossed herself and whispered that her brother had fled south. Anni brought the wedding gown to Master Baker Reindl, and didn't need to use many words, because the mother's look showed that she understood immediately. Anni let her know how sorry I was, and that I trusted she would destroy this white scrap of misfortune. Anni raced to the deer stand in the forest, where she and I and Josfer had gone so often together (and from which I'd once been dunked into a bowl of sewage), and asked herself, while she was waiting there for me, exactly where in the North I'd hide myself and when we'd see each other again and if I'd be gone for as long as last time and, not least, how you were supposed to say good-bye to someone who'd never actually returned.

Maybe it's best not to say it at all, thought Anni, once the sun had passed the zenith and there hadn't yet been any sign of me. The fear that they might have captured me left her when she reappeared in the village. Men in uniforms led her away.

She was interrogated for seventy-two hours, given no sustenance, nothing more than a glass of water once in a while, but didn't stray a jot from her story. In the end not even the police were a match for her tenacious head-shaking.

When she returned home, Fred seemed more dead than alive. Whole hanks of hair had fallen from his scalp, his skin was as gray as lead. When she forced him to swallow a gulp of milk, he threw up. His first words were "I own a speedster!"

"As far as I'm concerned, you can do whatever you want with it," she said. "But I'm never going to touch that thing."

"Where were you?" he asked her, and Anni looked him in the eye and asked, "Where were you?"

"Here."

"And before that?"

"There."

"And what did you do there?"

He blinked. "Nothing."

"You have to tell me everything, Fred. It's important. Very important. Otherwise I won't be able to protect us."

He didn't answer.

"Frederick!"

He leapt to his feet, and at first Anni thought he was going to run away, but he snatched up a sheet of paper and a charcoal pencil, an early present from Markus for his ninth birthday, and began to draw. Anni watched him, her eyes following each line. She didn't intervene when she realized what Fred was drawing, she let him go on, because she'd decided that this was going to be Fred's last sketch. If they were going to have a chance at survival, he'd have to give it up, he mustn't ever draw a picture again, especially not of what had happened that night in Segendorf. Anni would do anything to drive it out of him, and she'd manage it, if it was the last thing she did. She'd give him something else, a replacement,

something to fill his mind and time with instead, words from the encyclo-
pedia, maybe, or some simple task, something he'd do every day, some-
thing that would never come to an end, and that's how they'd be able to
live, live safely, and she stroked the top of Fred's head and said, "That's
going to be good."

Paris

Anni sent me Fred's drawing with her first letter because, as she realized, she could neither keep it nor throw it away. Her handwriting was oddly angular, and many of the words she'd set down she'd made incredibly tiny—perhaps in an effort to render them less threatening.

After unfolding the picture, I'd laid my hand against Mina's, so that our fingertips touched, and said good-bye to her. By now I was good at not crying when I felt the need to. Then I placed the gold in the palm of her hand, and wrapped it up in the paper. Mina would look after it for me.

Anni's first letter reached me two weeks after my arrival in a military hospital on the western front. It was addressed to Ludwig Wickenhäuser, the name I'd assumed for my own safety. Julius Habom was wanted in the German Reich for the murder of a local official, and didn't have much of a life expectancy.

Not that my chances on the front were any better. They'd drafted me, but I told myself, now that I'd never be able to see Anni again, it was all the same to me how the rest of my life, from which I had little to hope for, played out—just as long as I didn't have to spend it alone.

I immediately found myself back among old acquaintances. Since I was a former undertaker, a shovel, rather than a rifle, was placed in my hands, and I reported for duty, disposing of the fallen. Once, just after I'd arrived at the hospital, I asked my superior for coffins. He laughed me out of the room, and pointed to the bins where the quicklime was kept. The ragged, scorched, and mutilated corpses disturbed me less than they did my colleagues. I could see what they were thinking as they worked: That's a son. That's a brother. That's a father. That's a child.

They'd soon get used to it, understanding that death comes in many shapes, and that some are simply more unambiguous than others. I'd already passed that stage long, long ago. I didn't see dead men, only ears and feet and shoulder blades. When there were just too many, we had to bury them with backhoes under tons of sand and soil. Sometimes, if I happened to come across a few daisies, I'd lay them on the graves. The only thing that troubled me was the dead soldiers' fear, which didn't drain from their eyes when their hearts finally stopped beating; that fear reminded me of the look in Anni's eyes the last time I'd seen her.

It emerged from her letters that no one suspected her of Markus's murder. She phrased it thus: "No one here in the village believes that I've slaughtered a pig."

She'd succeeded in weaning Fred from his drawing by giving him other tasks to keep him busy. Every day she sent him to the bus stop to count cars the same color as his beloved Speedster; she spurred him on to search the sewers for Arkadiusz; she read to him from the encyclopedia and reported that by now, at least, he could read and write one letter: A.

When Paris was taken and I marched with the army along the Champs-Elysées, impressed by the city, and by how quickly it had fallen, I thought of Wickenhäuser and his dream of having a frock coat cut for himself here. I didn't believe that, as someone as keen on men as on women, and known as he was as the Jew of Schweretsried, he could still be among the living. It was only years later that I learned he'd hidden himself away in Else's log cabin in the forest, and had died there of the cold at the war's end, too terrified of uniformed monsters to venture from the house in search of firewood.

In France, even I had trouble with the women. I couldn't speak to them. And if they understood German, it was worse: for obvious reasons, my mother tongue wasn't particularly attractive to Frenchwomen. Which is why I used hand signals, instead, to convey to them that I was deaf and dumb. My most convincing arguments, however, were little crumbly chips from the gold nugget. Some of them I invested, naturally, in foodstuffs—above all, milk, and whenever I was able to scare some up, bacon—but those hours I spent in the company of lovely women silenced, if only briefly, an entirely different hunger, one not to be underestimated. In bed the

Frenchwomen were much more particular than their German counterparts, they seemed to know exactly what they wanted, and I was always freshly impressed with the intensity of their lovemaking, as if it were the last time.

I didn't tell Anni about any of them. I didn't want her to think there were any other women in my life.

So my letters to her became brief. My daily work was the disposal of the dead. The numberless eyes I couldn't shut—I could hardly write to her about those.

On my final night in Paris—I'd just been assigned to the eastern front— I breathed for the last time the perfume of a pair of French girls and tried to engrave in my memory every detail of their bodies: the color of their nipples, the shapes of their belly buttons, the fluttering of their eyelids, the way their toes curled as they came. I wanted to savor Paris as much as I possibly could. In the Ukraine, so the rumor ran, a soldier who had potato peels to eat could count himself lucky.

That the hands of both girls were cold should have been a warning to me. Their smooth black and brunette hair hid their faces as I lay undressed on the bed and they explored my body with their tongues and lips. I closed my eyes. The weight on the mattress shifted, one of the two rising while the other settled herself on top of me. She bit my neck; first it stung, then grew warm. I brought my hand to my throat, opened my eyes, and saw blood. In her right hand, she held a jackknife. She lunged at me, shouting something in French. I tried to grab her arm, but she was too fast. At the last moment I twisted onto my side, and she struck me in the back. The pain knocked the breath out of me. I managed to grab the hand with the knife, and held it tight with both of my own. She raised herself behind the blade. The bathroom door swung open—the other French girl, the brunette. On the bathroom floor behind her lay my clothing and bag, which she'd been rummaging through. Luckily, I didn't have the gold with me; I kept it at the hospital, never carrying it with me in the city. Instead of helping her accomplice, the brunette scooped up her things and ran from the room. That threw the black-haired girl long enough for me to buck her away, and the knife tumbled from her hand. Immediately she grinned, giggled, wrapped her legs around me, and reached for my cock. As if it had all been merely foreplay. Blood dripped from my throat onto her cheeks. I shook her off, and went to pick up the knife. My legs gave way, and I fell to the ground. The knife lay just in front of me, I reached for it, wrapped my hand around it. The French girl leapt from the bed, pulled on her clothes; all I could see were her slender feet. Within seconds she'd left the room. I concentrated on breathing calmly, pulled the bedsheets to me and pressed them against my throat, crawled to the chair where my own clothes lay, and knocked it over. As I attempted to pull on my pants, I could feel the weakness growing. I was getting cold. I dropped the pants and crawled naked to the open door, the red sheets wrapped around my neck. Blood was flowing from the wound in my back, I was leaving a trail behind me as I went. I felt more and more exhausted. In order to gather strength, I shut my eyes.

I woke, and my hands were numb and stiff. I couldn't say how long I'd been asleep. My legs wouldn't move. The stairs down to the first floor were steep. I let my head sink to the cool floor and thought of Anni.

At least she'd assume I'd fallen in battle.

Two Possibilities

I'd never believed in God. I'd always been convinced that I didn't need him, that I could live my life without having to arrange it around someone for whose existence there was no credible evidence. But after my brush with death in a Paris bedroom, I began to pray. Not out of thankfulness. I didn't fold my hands, take myself to church, or consult a pastor; I simply sent my thoughts Godward—arbitrary thoughts, and not always friendly.

The doctors had told me that, due to the spinal injury, I'd never be able to walk again. What kind of a god was it who, just as I was about to slip into a peaceful sleep, had sent a woman, right on time, into the stairwell, whose hysterical screams had brought the soldiers stationed nearby at a run, only to leave me with half a working body? God could have left me lying there. Instead, he'd sent me (as I learned later from my medical file) on a journey through sick bays and hospitals, of which I have no memory apart from the acid reek of disinfectants and the stink of rotting flesh. At that time many people lost their faith because of the horrible things that had befallen them. For the same reasons, I found my faith. I realized that God must exist. He didn't love and wasn't righteous—rather, he was a sort of malicious scientist. And mankind was his experiment. By means of a sexual act, he'd robbed me of the ability to walk, left me for weeks at a stretch wishing I was dead. Yet he'd also manifested a definite irony, in that he'd unmistakably reanimated—as I found when a ward nurse with azure eyes helped me into a wheelchair for the first time—certain parts of my lower body.

I could have rejoiced, I could have been relieved, but instead I apologized to the ward nurse. To which she replied that I didn't need to be ashamed, that it was a good sign.

She couldn't know that my eternal desire for the proximity of women was what had led me to this wretched pass. I was twenty-seven years old, I was seated in a rolling steel contraption, and I had lost everyone whom I'd ever loved.

Two possibilities remained: I could end my life, or fundamentally alter it, and I chose the second because, as I now believe, I was too craven for the first. I resolved to forswear any romantic attachment to women. As difficult as it would be in the beginning to resist, over time my memories would fade, and with them my longings; I would forget what a kiss felt like, or the touch of a beloved person, or waking up to a warm body snuggling closer to me. And maybe I'd learn to be happy alone, and finally find peace.

In my letters to Anni I didn't mention my misfortune, my now useless legs, so that she wouldn't worry, or attempt to find me. As the German Reich expanded, the possibility that we'd ever see each other again dwindled. I struggled to suppress just how much I missed her, and held fast to the thought that the growing distance between us would at least make my dream of a fulfilling life without women easier to achieve.

My disability abetted it as well. No question about it, women felt less attracted to a man they had to squat in front of in order to look in the eye. Meanwhile I'd reached the final station of my odyssey through the various hospitals of the Reich, the Saint Helena Veterans' Home in Upper Bavaria, which was run by the nuns from an adjacent convent. Their relief that at least one of the soldiers in their charge could contain his libido was palpable. Ludwig Wickenhäuser was one of the most beloved patients at Saint Helena. He believed in God, he shared with them his knowledge regarding burials—knowledge particularly useful at this moment in history—he understood their Bavarian, and understood, too, that they wanted to be perceived as female beings, though not in the single sense in which most female beings were perceived by men.

Presumably this quality was the reason that, once my wounds had healed and I had long since resigned myself to my new existence as a perpetual sitter, barely even needing their help any longer, they didn't demand that I vacate my bed, but rather asked me if I'd stay on with them. I accepted their invitation, and moved into a ground-floor room furnished with a low bed, extra support handles in the bathroom, and a wheelchair ramp in front of a window overlooking the orchard, which I opened first thing every morning. I'd haul myself up onto the sill and lean out and breathe the perfume of the apple trees and think: here I might be able to learn to look for happiness right where I am, rather than in all those places I can't be.

Surrender

On May 7, 1945, the Wehrmacht capitulated; and that night, so did I. It ran counter to my intentions in every sense, but I had to find out if there was any way I might live the life that suddenly, with the war's end, seemed possible again, and that I still wanted more than anything.

I wrote to Anni and begged her to visit me. Without mentioning, of course, that a journey by wheelchair to Königsdorf would have been impossible for me.

She arrived at Saint Helena two weeks later, on a humid May morning. I waited for her in the chapel; it was cooler there, and less oppressive. I was sitting before the altar in my wheelchair when I heard footsteps approaching, pausing, then approaching again. Anni's first word was a question: "Julius?"

It had been five years since anyone had called me that, and the last person who'd used my true name had been my sister. Maybe, I thought, it was a sign that she'd come to fetch me back to my life.

I turned to face her.

When people say that someone they haven't seen for years has barely changed, they're generally lying; they just want to flatter. But Anni hadn't changed at all. Her curls, her full cheeks, her shaking head—they were all exactly as I'd pictured them, night after night.

Still, she didn't move an inch.

"Don't I get a hug?"

She crouched, and laid her hand on mine: "Are you all right? What's happened?"

"A bullet. Right in the spine."

She examined the wheelchair. "How long will you need this?"

I didn't say anything and she understood and flung her arms around my neck.

I slipped my own arms around her, and felt her warmth. "It has its positive side, too. I've gotten a whole new perspective on things, down here."

She pulled away and slapped me. "You should have written me about this!"

"I should have."

And she hugged me again, this time so fiercely that the wheelchair rolled backward and we knocked against a pew, laughing.

"I love you," I said.

"I love you, too," she said.

It sounded different coming from Anni than it did from me.

"Let's get out of here," I said.

"Where?" she asked.

"Who cares. Away, that's all that matters."

"You mean for good? In your state?"

"I can handle it."

"And Fred?"

"Fred's better off in Königsdorf."

"I can't leave him there by himself."

"Fine, then he can come, too."

"But what are we supposed to live on?"

"I have enough gold."

"We can't just disappear like that."

"Why not? I love you," I said.

"I do, too," she said, and kissed me on the brow, and I held her tight and kissed her on the mouth.

"Don't, please," she said.

"Because you don't like it?"

"Because it isn't right."

"It was for our parents."

"Yes, for our parents."

As I went to kiss her again, she flinched away.

"I can't be close to you without being with you," I said finally.

"And I can't be close to you if you want to be with me," she said, and didn't even shake her head.

We fell silent and looked at the altar and the floor and quickly into each other's eyes, then at the altar again; we listened to each other breathing; we waited for one of us to say something.

Anni didn't send me any more letters. I wrote to her every week, and thought about her every day. I pursued the pain, I embraced it. In the evenings, when I lay down to sleep and positioned my legs beside each other with my hands, I imagined Anni, only a few miles away, kissing some man, a handsome, clever, witty, and successful man, whom she loved more than anything, and who, while I strained to wrap the blanket around my body, lifted her with a laugh and threw her over his shoulder and carried her into the bedroom on healthy legs.

After sending hundreds of letters to Anni without getting a single reply, I received two lines from her: "Please don't write anymore. I'm sorry. A." I read these words over and over, searching for clues and ambiguities, for signs that we might be closer to each other again someday. What finally robbed me of all hope was that A. An A was all I was worth to her, just a pointy A.

My last letter to her contained nary a word. I simply returned Fred's drawing of Mina's hand.

Alfonsa

Thirty-six years later, I asked myself how thirty-six years could possibly have passed without my noticing. Saint Helena was the kind of place that let you forget that the outside world existed at all. Especially if, like me, you didn't read the papers, listen to the radio, or watch TV. I'd given them up for good after the news of the '77 bus accident reached us. My son Ludwig had died and taken two people with him. I didn't even try to read

Fred's report in the newspaper. I didn't want to remember that place, those people. That wasn't my life anymore.

In 1981 I was living like an old man. I was an old man! I was facing my sixty-eighth birthday, and my days so resembled each other that only the weather allowed me to tell them apart. I sat at the window and looked out, saw white apple blossoms, saw how the fruit was plucked and fell to the ground, saw the nuns raking leaves and icicles forming on the branches.

At the end of the sixties, after the number of patients at Saint Helena had rapidly diminished and I'd had my last peak season as an undertaker, the Veterans' Home was closed; the remaining dependents had been transferred to a modern institution at Bad Tölz. I remained at Saint Helena. I'd spent the greater part of my life with the nuns. This was my home, here I knew what to expect. At least, that's what I thought.

That same year, Alfonsa arrived at Saint Helena.

Her parents had borne that particular title—which, like most people, they'd simply been given, without having earned it—for a whole ten hours before absconding, leaving her in the care of a Rhineland convent. That's where Alfonsa had been born, and she asserted she was going to die in a convent as well. One word was guiding her from that first event to the last: Sister. The multifariousness of this word had always been the backbone of the religious order. Sister was considered the most stable of currencies, an all-purpose word in any circumstance. Thanks to Sister, you could express what you'd have to keep quiet about, otherwise.

At the age of five she'd appeared at night in the Mother Superior's bedroom, and said, between sobs, "Sister"—meaning that she'd dreamed there were rats beneath her bed, a whole swarm of rats with red eyes, who wanted to gobble her up. At age eleven, she'd whispered, "Sister," actually trying to convey that she thought there was something wrong with her, there was blood all over her bed and her legs. That same year she swallowed the second syllable of "Sister," instead of asking whether the tickling she felt down below when, during Mass, she pressed herself against the pew in front of her, was one of God's blessings. It wasn't long before she said "Sister" through her teeth—withholding from the Mother Superior the fact that Alois from the tenth grade, who owned all of Frank Sinatra's records, had stuck his forefinger into her, though only up to the first knuckle, and that it hadn't been an especially pleasant sensation, she'd expected much better, but regardless, whenever the Body of Christ was laid on her tongue she couldn't help thinking of the Body of Alois, and the way that his thing tasted like Parmesan cheese. A few weeks after her nineteenth birthday, she let a long pause fall between the two syllables of "Sister." She was pregnant, and had scrapped her plan of eloping with Alois, because he—who'd always talked about living with her in a little apartment in a big city, where they could recite the lyrics from Sinatra songs to each other and scream "Fuck you, Jesus!" as often as they wanted—because this Alois had run off without her. In the third month of her pregnancy she lost the child, and said "Sister" soundlessly, wanting to know whether it would have been a girl. From then on, her "Sister" sounded emotionless, and concealed all the thoughts that burrowed within her: she didn't know what she should do with her life, she would have liked to spend all day just lying in bed, reading, even if it was just the Bible, she couldn't bring herself to go outside any longer, she simply couldn't, she hated being forced, she wished someone would ask her how she was doing, nobody ever asked her how she was doing, they all just nodded at each other and scurried around and acted as if they were happy, but they weren't, thought Alfonsa, they couldn't possibly be happy, even she could see that, though she'd been happy only once, once, and it seemed to her that that was already a lot for a lifetime, as far as most people were concerned she should probably be glad, but she wasn't glad, she had a crazy plan, she wanted to be happy twice in her life, the only problem was, to manage it she'd have to go outside, and she couldn't bring herself to do that, it wasn't happening, not yet, anyway, the convent itself was big and rambling and offered so much variety, what were a couple of months without the open sky above her, she could still see the sun, it even shone into her room, Alfonsa felt quite well inside, agora-

phobia or no agoraphobia, she was unable to grasp why the nuns wouldn't leave her alone, at nineteen she knew very well what was good for her, and she definitely preferred the shadows of the convent to the sky, because the sky knew no limits, the sky was immoderate and pretentious, the sky forced itself on everyone, a cheap promise in blue and white and gray, but the walls and ceilings and floors and corners of the convent won you over with their modesty and sincerity, like the ornaments in the library, Alfonsa could grasp them, touch them, they pressed themselves coolly against her skin and proved to her that they were there, dependable pieces of the world.

Even ten months after Alfonsa had lost her child, no one was able to convince her to step out into the open. The growing worry and helplessness among the nuns led to the decision to transfer Alfonsa to Saint Helena. Since the end of the war, the alpine cloister had become famous for its success in treating and curing all sorts of illnesses.

Alfonsa expressed her disappointment that they were sending her away by not saying "Sister" even once. During the drive to Saint Helena she hid herself under a wool blanket on the backseat, took one sleeping pill after another, and ignored every offer by the nuns to pause at a rest stop so she could stretch her legs or use the bathroom.

Two days after her arrival, Alfonsa appeared in my room. I turned my wheelchair away from the window to inspect her: a redheaded twenty-year-old with an expressionless face, stepping silently over to my bed.

"We haven't been introduced," I said, friendly, and extended my hand. "Ludwig Wickenhäuser."

She ignored the hand and said, "Sister Alfonsa," while quickly and efficiently replacing the bedsheets.

I made another attempt: "Alfonsa means 'Ready for battle,' no?"

She paused for a moment, then resumed beating the pillow even harder.

"How do you like Helena so far?"

"A dream."

"You'll settle in soon. Where do you come from?"

"From out there."

"Did you always want to be a nun?"

"Yes. You, too?"

"I guess you've decided not to make any friends, hmm?"

"Not with a cripple, anyway."

I rolled over and planted myself in her path. "I'm not one of your sisters. Get ahold of yourself, and don't make this unnecessarily difficult. I mean to live for a few more years—so let's try to get along. Because as far as I know, Sister Alfonsa, you couldn't leave this place even if you felt like it."

She pressed the dirty sheets to her chest, stepped around the wheelchair, and slammed the door behind her.

Our next encounters passed without a word. She thought I wouldn't be able to tell, but I was familiar with women like her from way back. They didn't spare so much as a look for the people, especially the men, whom they liked, or the women they compared themselves to, and simply turned away from them, thereby making it all the more obvious how much they longed to be spoken to and embraced. After so many quiet years I was excited to see if I could make this lady with her thin lips smile.

One evening after sunset I asked Alfonsa to come with me into the orchard to pick apples.

"It's dark," she said.

"I know," I said, rolling outside and beckoning her to follow.

She remained standing at the door, watching me.

"Come on," I called.

Even back then my eyes were well past their prime, but unless I was very much mistaken she hesitated slightly at the threshold, before disappearing.

From then on I invited her each evening to come into the orchard with me. And each evening she turned me down—but stood there looking after me a little longer every time.

Almost two months passed before, one night when the crescent moon was especially thin, she took a first step outside.

"One more," I encouraged her. "Just a little one."

So we edged our way forward, night after night. The other nuns trusted me, and gave me a free hand. In my thirty-six years there I'd never once tried to approach one of them, and they had no idea what I'd been like before. After so much time, I barely knew myself.

Winter had long since arrived, and there were no more apples to pick, when Alfonsa finally stepped all the way out to my wheelchair.

"Congratulations," I said.

"How did you know I could do it?"

"I didn't know," I said. "But I figured, when the air is black, it swallows up space, the whole sky, and makes the outdoors feel much smaller."

She looked around. "It's as if I were in a room. A very, very big room."

"What you decide to believe is always the truth."

"Thank you, Ludwig." Even now, there was no emotion visible in her face. "I owe you one."

"Nonsense," I said. "You're doing better. That's reward enough."

"I owe you one," she repeated seriously.

"What could a young woman like you do for a sixty-eight-year-old?"

Alfonsa suppressed a comment. "Don't you want anything? Anything at all? There must be something."

I replied: "Uhh-ehh."

I should have simply asked her for a smile. Instead I suggested she accompany me on my nightly rides. Around the convent. Counterclockwise.

We kept our conversations superficial, out of fear of giving too much importance to this relationship of ours. We were bound by our common experience of how dangerous it was to let someone get too close to you. That experience had brought us both to this place. We were outsiders at Saint Helena, we felt we'd been cheated out of a better life, but had come to terms with it. In another world, we would have been happier. In this one, we were learning to treasure the greatest possible happiness available to the unhappy: contentedness.

For my sixty-ninth birthday, in May 1982, Alfonsa gave me a cassette with her favorite songs by Frank Sinatra, and I had to confess to her that I didn't own a tape player, whereupon she brought me her own after our walk that night, and plugged it in beside my bed and pressed "play." And guess who sighs his lullabies through nights that never end, my fickle friend, the summer wind.

We sat facing each other, I on the wheelchair, she on the stool she always used when I gave her chess lessons, and listened to the music. Alfonsa's upper body was leaning a bit to the side, her hands were folded in her lap, her gaze fixed on the turning cogs in the cassette player. Even when she was more or less relaxed, she lived up to her name. I suddenly felt that she felt I was watching her, and I shut my eyes so that our gazes wouldn't meet, and made as if I were concentrating on the music. Now I could feel that she was watching me, and didn't dare open my eyes until the last track on side A ended with a heavy click. Alfonsa stood, flipped the tape to side B, pressed "play," and asked, before Frank Sinatra started in again, if she could lie down next to me on the bed, just lie there next to me. I smiled for the both of us and said that wouldn't work, and she nodded immediately, as if she'd expected that answer, and we went on listening. Take (get a piece of) my (these) arms, I'll never use them.

The next day when she came to make my bed, Alfonsa found my door locked. She knocked and called my name, but I simply stared at the shadow moving in the gap between the door and the floorboards, and said nothing. After a while she gave up and moved away, and I found the Mother Superior and asked her to assign me a different nun. It wasn't Alfonsa's fault, I explained, she simply reminded me of someone I didn't want to be reminded of. I didn't say that that someone was myself. The

Mother Superior seemed to understand, and I left her feeling I'd done the right thing.

But that same evening, after dinner, Alfonsa followed me back to my room. "Why are you doing this?"

I acted surprised. "What have I done?"

"From tomorrow on I'm assigned to the kitchen."

"Well?"

"Did you think I wanted something from you? Because of yesterday?"

"Interesting thought. How did you hit on that?"

"You're old enough to be my grandfather!"

"Exactly."

I'd never seen her so upset. Her lips were a thin, straight line, and so many unspoken emotions were swirling in her eyes that I would have liked to spend longer staring into them, reading them.

Instead, I asked, "Is there anything else?"

She left my room without another word, and I turned back to the window, through which a sudden gust of wind drove a flurry of light-pink petals. Footsteps approached, and even before I could turn again Alfonsa was standing beside me, leaning down, giving me a rough kiss. Then she plucked an apple blossom from my hair, showed me her smirk for the first time, and left.

I didn't lock my door that evening. After midnight, when I was already stretched out in bed, I heard the door open, then close again. In the dark I couldn't distinguish a thing. The sound of bare feet on a stone floor. The covers were lifted and a cool, slender body wrapped in a nightgown snuggled up to me. She laid her hand on my chest. Her breath grazed my throat.

"Sleep well," she said.

"You, too," I said.

The next morning I woke alone. I washed and dressed myself, wondering if I'd imagined it all.

At breakfast in the dining hall Alfonsa sat down across from me. "Sleep well?" she asked.

I looked at her. Her face was as expressionless as ever.

"Yes," I said. "Yes. Very well, actually."

She smirked again. "Me, too."

This smirk was enough to make me ask myself, ask myself seriously, why on earth I hadn't ever wanted this. Soon she visited me every night. Until I couldn't fall asleep without feeling her body next to mine. Like teenagers we hid under the blankets and laughed into the pillows and whispered stories to each other and kissed with half-opened eyes. As aware as we were of the impossibility of our relationship, we were just as aware of the possibility of a bit of happiness. Probably, I thought, it would be the last of my life. Who would have chosen to forgo that?

"Can you feel that?" she asked.

I lay in the bathtub, it was nighttime, the only light came from a solitary candle doubled by my shaving mirror, and Alfonsa, who sat by the tub on the chess stool in her nightgown, rolled up one sleeve, dipped her hand into the water, and touched my ankles.

I shook my head.

Her hand wandered up my leg.

"What about that?"

Again, I shook my head.

"And that?"

This time I nodded.

Whenever we encountered each other by day in the hallways of Saint Helena, we'd make a promise with a nod of the head, one we'd fulfill when we met in secret after dark. It had been so many years; since my accident, I hadn't touched a single woman like that. So I was all the more amazed at how simple and satisfying it was. Alfonsa came to appreciate the advantages *of an experienced man, and I to appreciate her smirk in all its variations. Making love with her was like a gentle dance, not especially spirited, but proceeding in small, even steps, always looking each other in the eye. In me she saw her second happiness, and in her I saw my fourth love. I revealed my real name to her, and she her history to me. And it was only in the mornings, when her hair, so seductively red in the glow of each evening's candles, turned suddenly traitorous by daylight, so that I had to spend hours searching my mattress for strays that might give us away—it was only then that I asked myself where all of this was leading.*

End

It ended as it does so often: with a beginning. During our last evening stroll, in September 1982, Alfonsa told me that she was two months pregnant. As I didn't immediately react to the news, she said, "You don't seem surprised."

I was sixty-nine years old, the son of twins, I came from a town where such terrible things had happened that nobody used its old name anymore, a Frenchwoman had turned me into a cripple, and last but not least, I was the father of innumerable children; I wasn't so easily surprised any longer. But I didn't want to give her the impression that I was going to abandon her now, and so I said, "Of course I am."

Alfonsa looked at me from the corner of her eye, walking silently by my side. I felt sorry for her; she was so young, so inexperienced.

We stopped before the convent's main entrance. I tried to sound as sensitive as possible. "We have to tell the others."

And there, after months of waiting, I saw her smile, not smirk, for the first and only time. A pitying, honest, unlovely smile that I'd rather not have seen. "I already have." She crouched down and took my hands. "We'll definitely find a nice place for you."

"For me?"

"There are a couple of good nursing homes in Bavaria."

I pulled my hands away. "I've lived at Saint Helena for almost forty years!"

"You can't stay here. How could the sisters tolerate a man in their midst who'd gotten one of them pregnant?"

"I don't know," I said, detecting a sulky tone in my voice I didn't like. "But that's my child as well."

"Julius," even considering it was her, she spoke with disturbingly little emotion, "do you want to raise this child? Do you want to change its diapers? Feed it? Do homework with it?"

"No."

"Neither do I," said Alfonsa, sitting down on the step before the door, leaning back, supporting herself with her elbows, and looking at the sky. Suddenly she didn't seem so young and inexperienced anymore. "I might have, once. But if I've learned anything, it's that I'm not really cut out to be a mother."

"Abortion?" I asked.

"Adoption," she replied.

All of a sudden I felt very old and slow. "You're going to give it away, just like that?"

"Him. I'm going to give him away," she said. "We're having a son."

"A son," I said, more to myself than to her.

Alfonsa stood and brushed the dust from her cloak.

"Wait," I said. "Maybe there's another way."

She looked at me in silence.

"Do you know," I asked, "what a Most Beloved Possession is?"

On April 5, 1983—as I lay in my new, distinctly more humble room at the Zwirglstein, staring up at the plasterboard ceiling, and began, for the first time in decades, to scratch my elbow—our son was born. The infirmary at Saint Helena was white like apple blossoms. The little scarlet head of our son formed the only contrast—a drop of blood in the snow. One of the *wrinkles on his forehead was so deep, it was as if he'd been brooding for nine long months over when and how he'd finally be able to give that imprisoning belly the slip. Because of that thoughtful crease, Alfonsa named him Albert. Her cheeks were red, but they were no match for his—flushed as a putto's in a painting. And Albert, our Albert, didn't scream at all, because he had no reason to. After all, he was there with his mother, in the safest place in the world.*

✳

PART IX

On Mothers and Fathers

Alfonsa

Albert walked slowly toward Alfonsa, and as he approached her told himself that he was approaching the woman who'd brought him into the world; he attempted to see that woman in her, to find some evidence of it in her gaze, but as hard as he tried, he couldn't manage it. Before him stood Sister Alfonsa.

He stopped short before stepping on her shadow on the floor; he groped for words; he couldn't find them.

Alfonsa moved to the elevators and pressed the button. "I want you to meet somebody."

Albert didn't move.

"We're almost there," she said.

"How come?" He looked upward. "Who lives here?"

"You'll see."

Now he stepped onto her shadow, and said, "Fred isn't doing well." He ran off, so that she wouldn't notice his tears, toward the exit.

"He isn't your father," Alfonsa called after him, drawing the attention of the old couple at the kiosk, who were watching them now from over their trail map.

Albert stopped and pretended he was scratching his forehead, so as to wipe the tears away unnoticed.

The elevator doors opened with a bright *pling.*

"Come on," said Alfonsa. "I even have a handkerchief for you."

The elevator was small for the two of them. Albert refused Alfonsa's handkerchief and pressed himself into one corner and focused on a pale yellow leaf on the floor, with a tear in its side that resembled a gaping beak. He struggled not to think about the fact that Alfonsa was the woman he'd been searching for all his life.

"Will this," he said, and had to clear his throat, "will this take long?"

"Fred will be able to hold on without you for a few more minutes."

"He needs me."

"Actually, I believe it's the other way around."

Albert stepped on the leaf on the floor and ground it beneath his heel. "I never saw him as my father."

"Just because you never addressed him as *Father* doesn't mean you didn't see him that way."

Albert didn't know how to respond to that.

They left the elevator on the third floor and walked through a rectangular glass tunnel that connected the building's two sections.

Albert said, "Wait a minute," reached into his pocket, took the makeup compact, opened it, and showed her the hair: "Is that yours?"

"I don't know. I never knew."

Albert looked at it for a moment. Then he snapped the compact shut, and tossed it into a trash bin.

An Old Man

They stepped into a common room painted in warm colors, where a few patients lingered, reading newspapers, playing Scrabble, and following a TV program about the fall of the Berlin Wall. The place smelled like vanilla tea.

Alfonsa knocked at the door of room 341, and without waiting for a response, walked in, gesturing for Albert to follow.

Hardly any light penetrated the drawn curtains, and it took a moment before Albert's eyes adjusted. The first thing he saw was a framed picture hanging on an otherwise empty wall. It was a black-and-white aerial photograph of Königsdorf, showing the farmhouses huddling close to the church.

On the opposite side of the room there stood a hospital bed, in which a man lay whom Albert had never seen before. A tube connected his left arm to an IV bag. In the dimness it was hard to tell his age, but it was clear that the bulk of this man's life was now behind him. His body seemed as delicate as a child's, and sank into the pillow and mattress; shimmering silver hair grew from his scalp, his skin was the light-gray color of dirty snow. His deep-set milk-white eyes scanned the room: "Who's there?"

"It's me." Alfonsa opened a window slightly, settled herself on a stool beside the man, and took his hand. "It helps if you touch him while you're talking," she said to Albert.

"How well can he see?"

She shook her head. "Detached retinas."

"I'm blind, not deaf!" said the man. "Who's there?"

"Julius," explained Alfonsa, "I've brought along a friend."

"What kind of friend? Since when do you bring friends with you?"

Albert noticed that one of Julius's elbows was bandaged.

"We're in a good mood today, aren't we?" said Alfonsa.

"Don't talk to me like I'm an old man."

"You are an old man."

"So what if I am?" Julius pointed to his cheek. "Give me a kiss."

Alfonsa exchanged a look with Albert. "Later."

"What," said Julius, "you're embarrassed in front of your friend?" He smiled. "Have you told him that we were lovers, once upon a time?"

"That was long ago."

"Only nineteen years," said Julius. "I haven't forgotten."

"Do you have children?" asked Albert.

Julius made a smacking noise, as if he were trying to taste something. "Sounds young, this friend of yours," he said to Alfonsa. "Have you seduced him?" And without waiting for her answer, he said in Albert's direction, "I know all about that."

"Do you have children?" Albert repeated, and saw how Julius held Alfonsa's hand somewhat tighter.

"He isn't especially polite, though, your friend. He still hasn't introduced himself."

"My name isn't important," said Albert, before Alfonsa could say anything.

Julius smacked his lips. "Afraid I won't be able to keep your affair to myself?"

Alfonsa sighed.

Albert moved a step closer to the bed. "How long have you been here now?"

"My turn first, my nameless friend: how do you know our pretty little nun?"

"I was brought up at Saint Helena."

"An orphan! So we have something in common." Musingly, Julius brought his free hand across to the bandaged elbow, and immediately Alfonsa grabbed it and laid it back in its place; it looked habitual, as though she'd been doing it for years. "Though I didn't have the luxury of growing up in an orphanage like Saint Helena. Did you know that Alfonsa was one of its founders?"

"No." Albert glanced at Alfonsa, who dodged his look. "I didn't know that."

"Before that, war veterans were housed at Saint Helena. Alfonsa had the idea of turning the facility into an orphanage. She claims it had nothing to do with the fact that we'd given our son away. But I don't believe her."

"Julius." Alfonsa let go of his hand.

"I believe," Julius continued, "that she founded that orphanage to salve her conscience. That's just how she works, our Sister Alfonsa. On the outside, a statue—on the inside, an emotional hurricane." He turned his head to her. "What did you call the boy, again?" He ran his hand over his face.

"Albert," said Albert.

"Albert, right. I would have remembered it on my own." Julius pressed a switch, and raised the bed's backrest. The conversation was clearly giving him strength. "Do you know him?"

"A little," said Albert.

"How's he doing?"

"He lives in Königsdorf. Have you ever met him?"

"Who, Albert? Never! But that doesn't mean much. He was only one of many," said Julius, smacking. "Children, I mean."

"How many did you have?"

"Five? Eight? Twelve? Who can say for sure."

"Are you still in contact with any of them?"

He didn't answer that.

"Albert sent you here?" said Julius finally; it was less a question than a statement.

Before Albert could answer, the door opened and Fred stepped into the room.

Alfonsa rose.

Albert said, "What are you doing here? How did you find us?"

"A woman woke me up. She asked why I was here. I told her that me and you and Sister Alfonsa—" He fell silent. The smile slipped from his face.

"Fred?" Julius croaked. "Fred, is that you?"

But Fred didn't seem to hear him. He pushed Albert aside, stretched out his arm, and touched the framed photograph; he whispered, "Segendorf."

Julius sat up in his bed. Alfonsa went to lay a hand on his shoulder—he slapped her away. "What's he doing here?" he went on. "I've told you, I don't want that!"

Fred turned to him and said, casually, as if he came to visit daily, "Hello, Julius."

Julius froze. "Fred."

"I have less than two fingers left, Julius."

"So I've heard."

Fred looked at Julius. "How about you? You also don't have many fingers left, do you?"

"Possibly." Again, he grabbed for his elbow, but this time didn't let Alfonsa stop him from scratching at it. "You should go now."

"Not yet," said Albert.

And Fred said, "I'm hungry, Albert!"

For a few seconds, long seconds, nobody said anything.

Alfonsa was the first to stir. "Let's go have a look at the cafeteria," she suggested to Fred, and pushed him out of the room.

Albert watched them go.

The door shut behind them, and the room went dark again.

"Well, what now?" asked Julius.

"You know."

"Ask Alfonsa."

"I'm asking you."

"You don't want to hear it."

"You don't know me," said Albert, who was losing his patience. "You have no idea who I am and what I want."

Julius sighed.

Then he nodded. "Let's get it over with." He pointed to the place beside the bed where the stool stood.

Albert came closer, but didn't sit down.

Julius extended his hand, mottled with age spots. It didn't tremble. "It helps if you touch him while you're talking," Julius said.

Albert couldn't bring himself to do it. That's when Julius grabbed his arm. Albert tried to free himself, but Julius's grip only grew firmer. "I was against her bringing you here. I always wanted this to be a place that had nothing to do with things from before. A place in the present where I wouldn't have to remember things, especially Anni. A place where I could forget." Julius let go. "But I can't forget." He shut his eyes and smacked his lips a few more times and pointed his index finger straight at the photograph. "I haven't forgotten a thing."

Albert took a closer look at his face. This man is my father, he thought, wishing he could feel something other than irritation and repugnance.

"When was the last time you saw Anni?" Albert asked, and immediately wished he could rephrase the sentence.

"I'm not sure anymore."

"I thought you hadn't forgotten a thing."

"A long time before she died," Julius said quickly.

"You didn't go to her funeral? Weren't you close to her?"

"No. No, no."

"Not even earlier?"

Julius ignored his question. "Alfonsa and I agreed that it would be better if you were raised by her."

Anni had always wanted a healthy son, a Most Beloved Possession, he explained, and she would have raised him like her own child. If only her heart hadn't stopped. After Anni's death, Alfonsa had decided to bring him to Saint Helena. "She loves you," said Julius. "It's just that she isn't especially good at it."

"And Fred?"

"What about him?"

"Why him?"

"As a father?"

Albert nodded, and Julius reacted as if he'd seen it. "It was the obvious choice." He tugged at the bandage on his elbow until at last it unraveled, and Julius was able to scratch at the scabbed skin beneath. "That's all."

Albert let himself fall onto the stool.

"I've warned you," said Julius. "There are a lot of things one doesn't want to know."

Albert was forced to think of the many nights Fred had crawled into his bed after having a nightmare, and Albert, a child, had to comfort a man more than forty years older, and what a painfully lonely feeling that had been. And yet, on those same nights, cuddled up with Fred, he'd always felt safer, less lonely, than in his bunk bed at Saint Helena.

Julius smacked his lips. "At least you'll be free of him soon. Are you making plans already? Hopefully you won't stay in Königsdorf. I can only advise you—"

Albert grabbed Julius's hand. "He wasn't such a bad father."

"Only natural that you defend him. Who wouldn't? After nineteen years with him!"

The knuckles on Albert's hands stood white beneath the skin. "He risked his life for me!"

"Ah." Julius smacked. "It's almost touching. But we both know what a relief it'll be for you when he isn't around anymore. No reason to be sad! I'm telling you: Fred won't be missed."

Albert let go of him and stood and wanted to reply that he wasn't afraid of anything as much as losing Fred; that he couldn't imagine life without him; that he still secretly hoped that Fred's heart would keep on beating much, much longer than that doctor had predicted.

But Albert was exhausted, and he didn't see any point in arguing with this man who had nothing left but a barren room and a black-and-white photograph, and who would have to be alone with himself for the rest of his life. He pitied Julius, who would never be able to understand him. It was only in the last week that Albert himself had learned to understand how lucky he could count himself for having grown up with Fred. Nobody loved as unconditionally as his father.

"Why don't you leave?" said Julius. "It's about time." He pulled the bandage back over the wound on his elbow. There were traces of blood beneath his fingernails.

"One more thing," said Albert.

Julius's bloodshot eyes searched for him.

"Fred discovered a piece of gold . . . do you know anything about that?"

Julius blinked. "Gold? Never had any."

Fog

Fred and Alfonsa were waiting for Albert outside the building. They stood on a promontory that served as an observation deck, staring out at the fog. Alfonsa carried a pair of plastic containers, one of which held a sandwich with a bite taken out of it.

Albert stood beside them, and for a while all three stared down, trying to make out something, anything, through the white.

"I visit him once a month," said Alfonsa. "We talk a bit about the quality of the food and about the weather, and then I leave again. He's never asked about you. I thought he wanted to leave all of that behind. Until he gave me the gold." She straightened her black veil. "I should have brought you here long, long ago."

Albert agreed by saying nothing.

Alfonsa turned to go. "Sister Simone is picking us up."

"I have to go back," said Albert. "Forgot something."

Alfonsa handed him the makeup compact.

Albert took it from her, astonished. "How did you know . . . ?"

Alfonsa shrugged her shoulders, and showed him a genuine smile, which Albert returned.

"Where are we going now?" asked Fred.

Albert took off Fred's backpack, picked a couple of crumbs out of his beard, and hugged him. "We're going home."

Epilogue

Tickling. It comes from inside and gets bigger and bigger. It's a warm feeling—a little like stepping out of a shadow into the sun. That's what he tells Albert, he tells him that it's starting now, and Albert drops his bowl with its vanilla ice cream and rushes over and kneels in the grass by the deck chair. He asks Albert if everything's okay, because Albert looks exhausted. Albert isn't listening to him. Albert wants to grab the telephone and call a doctor. But he tells Albert that he doesn't need a doctor, tells him that he's very sorry that he has to leave Albert all alone, and with so many fingers left. But he also says that almost everything goes by very fast. Albert certainly won't have to live for as long as he thinks. He should eat some more vanilla ice cream. And visit Sister Alfonsa. And get away from Königsdorf, too, since he has the gold now. And then, before he knows it, he'll go dead much faster. Albert looks at him for a long time. He doesn't close his eyes at all. No cars are driving down the main street. It's as quiet as if nobody else were living in Königsdorf. Albert cries a little, says that it doesn't have to happen, not yet. But that's not true, he responds, it does have to happen! Albert says that he certainly has at least a few more fingers left. He answers that he doesn't know about that, because he's already had many more—seven fingers more—than the doctor had showed him. That's precisely twelve fingers, in all. More fingers than a normal person has! But if he does, in fact, have any extra fingers, he explains to Albert, then he'd like to eat pancakes with raspberry jam. And Albert takes his hands and holds them, holds them rather tight, and promises he'll make him as many pancakes as he wants. And then Albert starts crying again! The tickling now comes into his arms and legs and head. It's strong, it hurts a little. But he lets it grow. He doesn't want to have to wait any longer for his swan-white tombstone, so close to the red tree. Because he's very much looking forward to that. From there, he'll be able to see the church tower, and the moor, and the sky. And he'll be able to see Albert and Klondi, and maybe Violet, too, and Sister Alfonsa, and Julius. They'll come to visit him, and tell him how they're pushing the world, or how it's pushing them. And *that,* he knows, he knows for sure, will be ambrosial.

ACKNOWLEDGMENTS

It is no secret that a book, though written in solitude, is never composed by one person alone. I want to thank everyone who helped me turn this story into a Most Beloved Possession. Special thanks are due to:

Saskya, wielder of superpowers, with whom I fell in love thanks to this book.

Anna, Antje, and Til, who taught me the meaning of Most Beloved Possessions.

Günther Opitz, without whose trust and opening of doors "Alfred" would never have reached their goal.

Julia Eichhorn, because she believed in the story from the beginning.

Carolina Franzen, for leading Fred by the hand.

Krishna Winston and Riky Stock, for taking Fred and Albert across the Atlantic.

Kathleen Anderson, for making their passage safe.

Aaron Kerner, for providing them with a new and beautiful language.

Fiona McCrae and Katie Dublinski, for giving them this wonderful home in the United States.

When I was living in Königsdorf in the 1990s and attending the high school in Bad Tölz, I had to take the bus every morning. During that time I first noticed this tall, bearded man greeting the cars. It seems so long ago now and yet I remember exactly the touching conviction with which he raised his arm in the air, spread his fingers, fixed his gaze on an approaching vehicle, and gave a quick shake of the hand. In retrospect it seems as if he had waved to me, as if he were saying, "I'm here! I have a story to tell! Talk to me!"

You, Fred, deserve my biggest thanks.

CHRISTOPHER KLOEBLE is an award-winning German novelist and scriptwriter. *Almost Everything Very Fast* is his third book, and his first to be published in English. He lives in Berlin and New Delhi.

AARON KERNER is a translator, editor, and teacher. He lives in Boston.

The Lannan Translation Series

Funding the translation and publication
of exceptional literary works

The Scattered Papers of Penelope by Katerina Anghelaki-Rooke, edited and translated from the Greek by Karen Van Dyck

The Last Brother by Nathacha Appanah, translated from the French by Geoffrey Strachan

The Accordionist's Son by Bernardo Atxaga, translated from the Spanish by Margaret Jull Costa

The Lovers of Algeria by Anouar Benmalek, translated from the French by Joanna Kilmartin

The Star of Algiers by Aziz Chouaki, translated from the French by Ros Schwartz and Lulu Norman

Before I Burn by Gaute Heivoll, translated from the Norwegian by Don Bartlett

Child Wonder by Roy Jacobsen, translated from the Norwegian by Don Bartlett with Don Shaw

A House at the Edge of Tears by Vénus Khoury-Ghata, translated from the French by Marilyn Hacker

Nettles by Vénus Khoury-Ghata, translated from the French by Marilyn Hacker

She Says by Vénus Khoury-Ghata, translated from the French by Marilyn Hacker

A Wake for the Living by Radmila Lazic, translated from the Serbian by Charles Simic

Empty Chairs by Liu Xia, translated from the Chinese by Ming Di and Jennifer Stern

June Fourth Elegies by Liu Xiaobo, translated from the Chinese by Jeffrey Yang

No Shelter by Pura López-Colomé, translated from the Spanish by Forrest Gander

The Life of an Unknown Man by Andreï Makine, translated from the French by Geoffrey Strachan

New European Poets, edited by Wayne Miller and Kevin Prufer

Look There by Agi Mishol, translated from the Hebrew by Lisa Katz

Karate Chop by Dorthe Nors, translated from the Danish by Martin Aitken

Ashes in My Mouth, Sand in My Shoes by Per Petterson, translated from the Norwegian by Don Bartlett

I Curse the River of Time by Per Petterson, translated from the Norwegian by Charlotte Barslund with Per Petterson

I Refuse by Per Petterson, translated from the Norwegian by Don Bartlett

Out Stealing Horses by Per Petterson, translated from the Norwegian by Anne Born

To Siberia by Per Petterson, translated from the Norwegian by Anne Born

Tesla: A Portrait with Masks by Vladimir Pištalo, translated from the Serbian by Bogdan Rakić and John Jeffries

In Times of Fading Light by Eugen Ruge, translated from the German by Anthea Bell

Shyness and Dignity by Dag Solstad, translated from the Norwegian by Sverre Lyngstad

Meanwhile Take My Hand by Kirmen Uribe, translated from the Basque by Elizabeth Macklin

Without an Alphabet, Without a Face by Saadi Youssef, translated from the Arabic by Khaled Mattawa

The text of *Almost Everything Very Fast* is set in Arno Pro. Book design by Ann Sudmeier. Composition by Bookmobile Design & Digital Publisher Services, Minneapolis, Minnesota. Manufactured by Versa Press on acid-free, 30 percent postconsumer wastepaper.